Bugs Bunny

WHAT'S UP, DOC?

Written by:
Craig Boldman
Terry Collins
Michael Eury
Terry LaBan
Barry Liebmann
Bill Matheny
David Cody Weiss

Illustrated by:
David Alvarez
Jim Amash
Omar Aranda
Leo Batic
Terry Beatty
Walter Carzon
Mike DeCarlo
Nelson Luty
Scott McRae
Horacio Ottolini
Ruben Torreiro
Pablo Zamboni

Colored by:
Digital Chameleon
Prismacolor
Dave Tanguay
Jahrome Youngker

Lettered by:
John Costanza
Daniel Griffo
Peter Tumminello

BUGS BUNNY VOL. 1: WHAT'S UP, DOC?
Published by DC Comics. Cover and compilation copyright © 2005 DC Comics. All Rights Reserved. Originally published
in single magazine form in LOONEY TUNES 37, 41, 43-45, 48, 52, 55, 57-59, 63. Copyright © 1998, 1999, 2000 Warner Bros.
Entertainment Inc. All Rights Reserved. LOONEY TUNES and all related characters and elements are trademarks of and
© Warner Bros. Entertainment Inc. The stories, characters and incidents featured in this publication are entirely fictional.
DC Comics does not read or accept unsolicited submissions of ideas, stories or artwork.

CARTOON NETWORK and logo are trademarks of and © Cartoon Network.

DC Comics, 1700 Broadway, New York, NY 10019
A Warner Bros. Entertainment Company.
Printed in Canada. First Printing.
ISBN: 1-4012-0516-X
Cover illustration by Walter Carzon and Ruben Torreiro.
Publication design by John J. Hill.

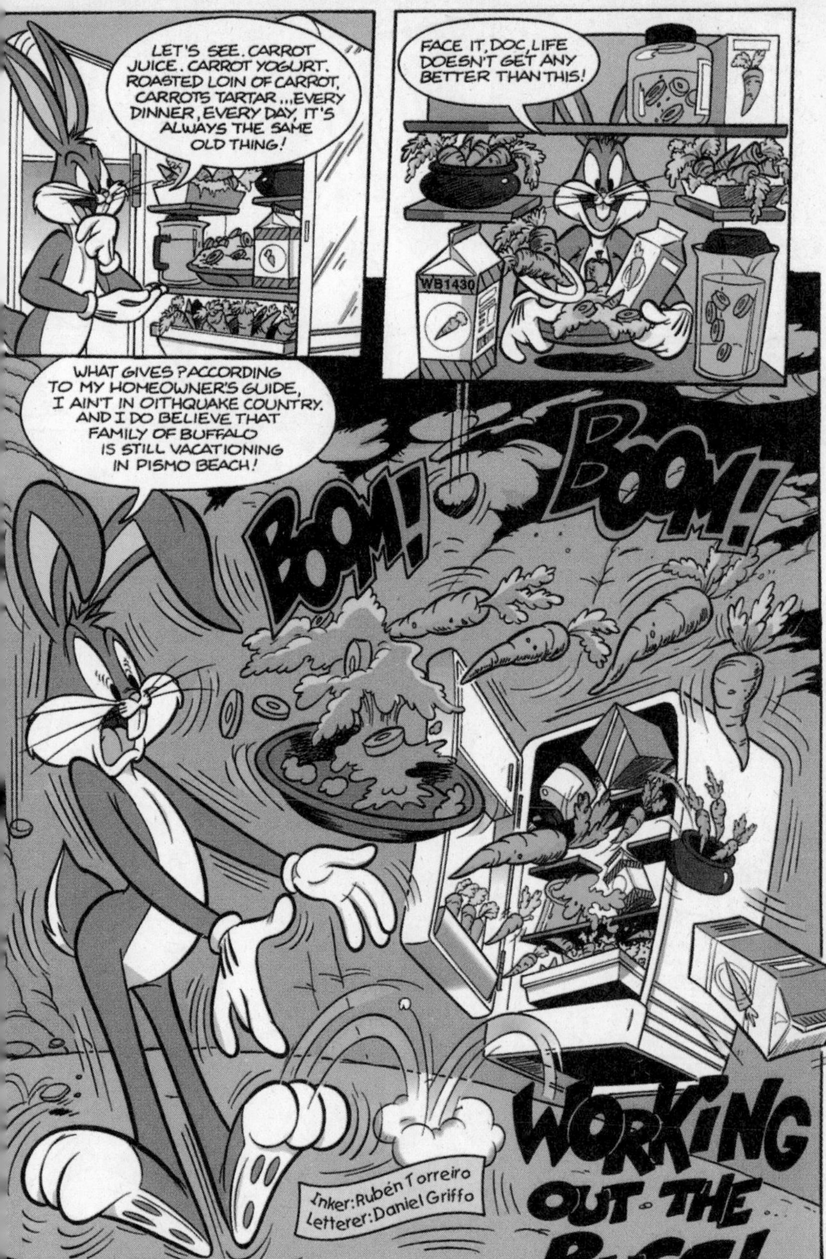
LET'S SEE. CARROT JUICE. CARROT YOGURT. ROASTED LOIN OF CARROT, CARROTS TARTAR ... EVERY DINNER, EVERY DAY, IT'S ALWAYS THE SAME OLD THING!
FACE IT, DOC, LIFE DOESN'T GET ANY BETTER THAN THIS!
WB1430
WHAT GIVES? ACCORDING TO MY HOMEOWNER'S GUIDE, I AIN'T IN OITHQUAKE COUNTRY. AND I DO BELIEVE THAT FAMILY OF BUFFALO IS STILL VACATIONING IN PISMO BEACH!
BOOM! BOOM!
WORKING OUT THE BUGS!
Inker: Rubén Torreiro
Letterer: Daniel Griffo
Writter: Bill Matheny
Penciller: Pablo Zamboni
Colorist: Jahrome Youngker

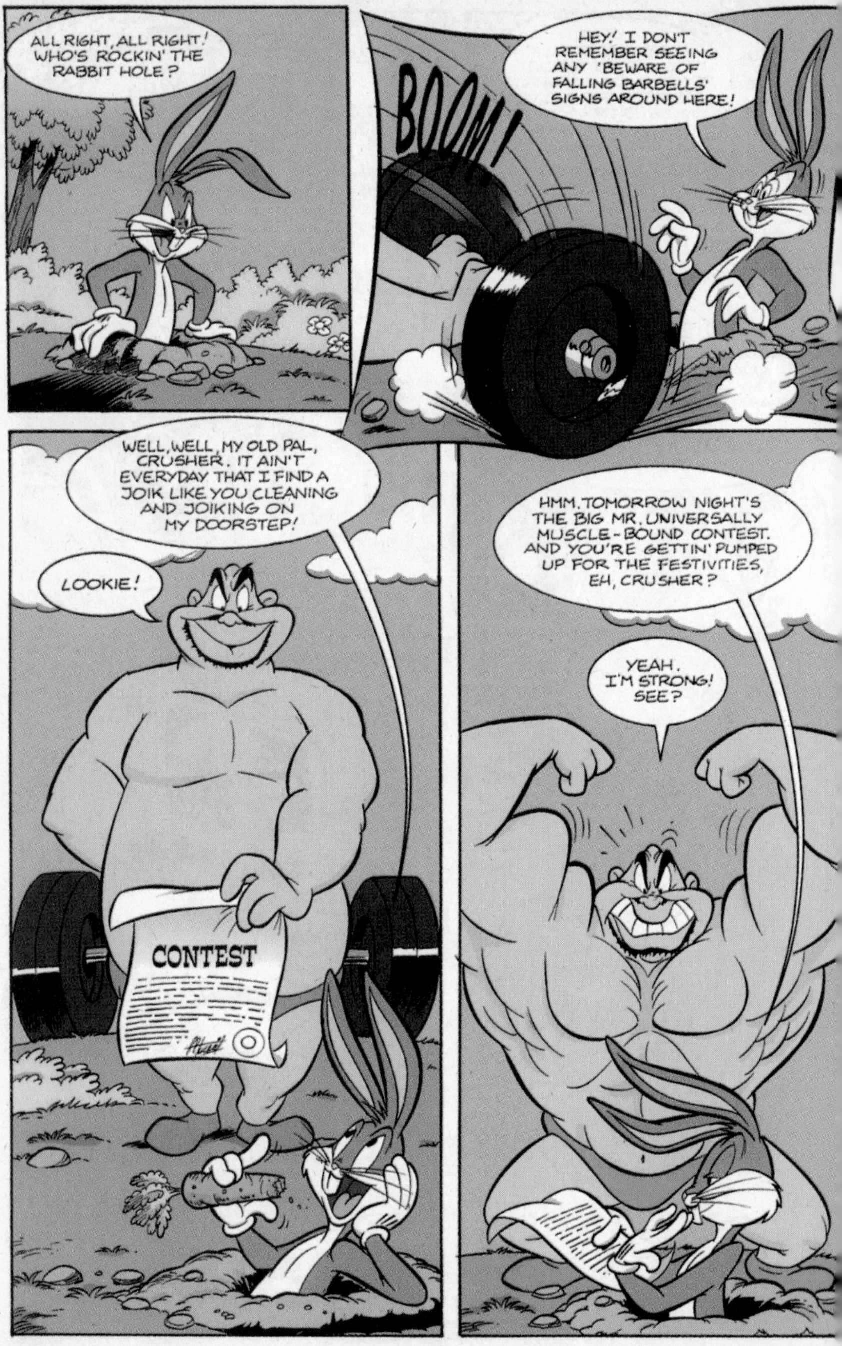
ALL RIGHT, ALL RIGHT! WHO'S ROCKIN' THE RABBIT HOLE?
BOOM!
HEY! I DON'T REMEMBER SEEING ANY 'BEWARE OF FALLING BARBELLS' SIGNS AROUND HERE!
WELL, WELL, MY OLD PAL, CRUSHER. IT AIN'T EVERYDAY THAT I FIND A JOIK LIKE YOU CLEANING AND JOIKING ON MY DOORSTEP!
LOOKIE!
CONTEST
HMM. TOMORROW NIGHT'S THE BIG MR. UNIVERSALLY MUSCLE-BOUND CONTEST. AND YOU'RE GETTIN' PUMPED UP FOR THE FESTIVITIES, EH, CRUSHER?
YEAH. I'M STRONG! SEE?

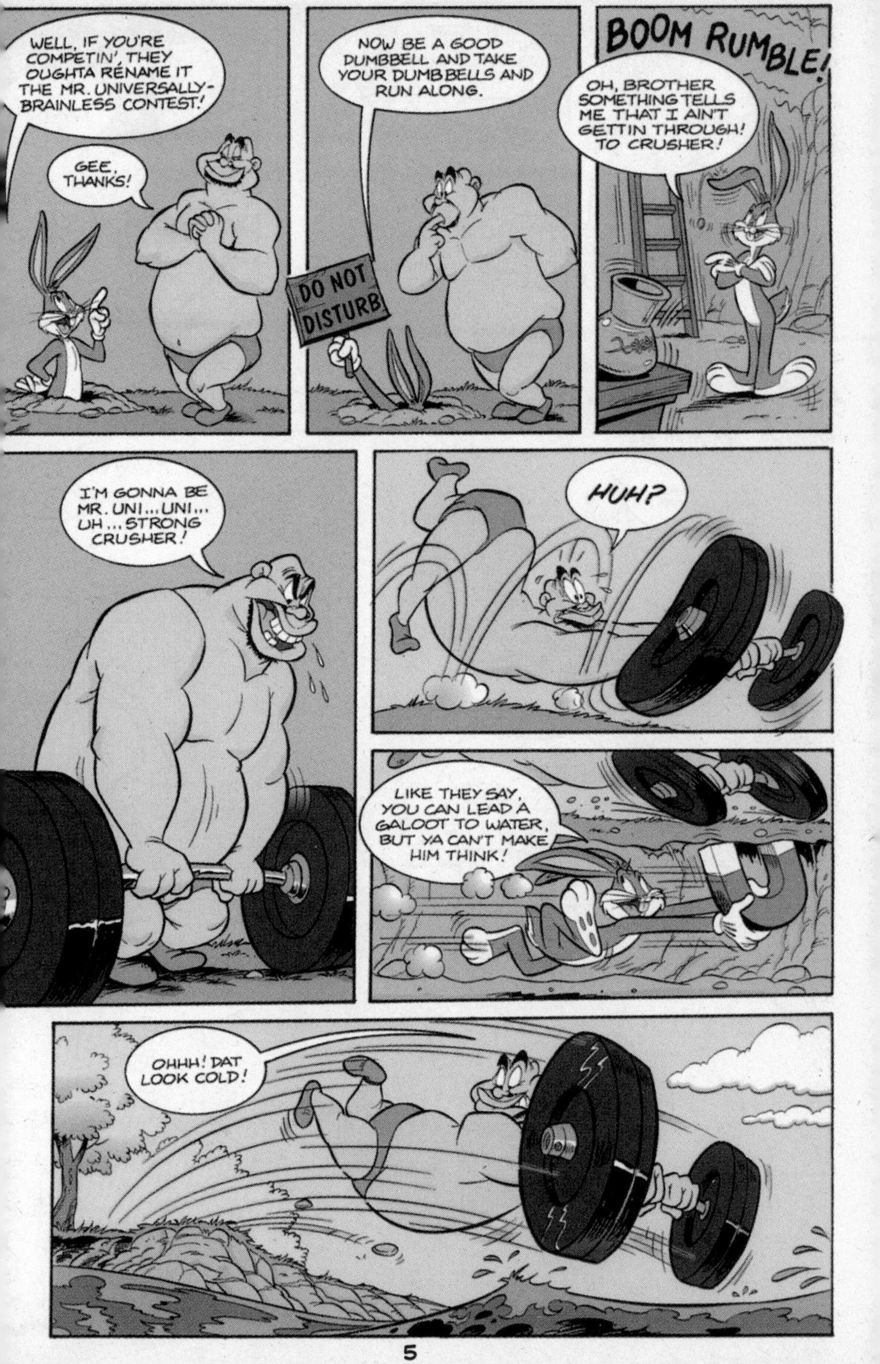
WELL, IF YOU'RE COMPETIN', THEY OUGHTA RENAME IT THE MR. UNIVERSALLY-BRAINLESS CONTEST!
GEE, THANKS!
NOW BE A GOOD DUMBBELL AND TAKE YOUR DUMBBELLS AND RUN ALONG.
DO NOT DISTURB
BOOM RUMBLE!
OH, BROTHER SOMETHING TELLS ME THAT I AIN'T GETTIN THROUGH! TO CRUSHER!
I'M GONNA BE MR. UNI...UNI... UH...STRONG CRUSHER!
HUH?
LIKE THEY SAY, YOU CAN LEAD A GALOOT TO WATER, BUT YA CAN'T MAKE HIM THINK!
OHHH! DAT LOOK COLD!

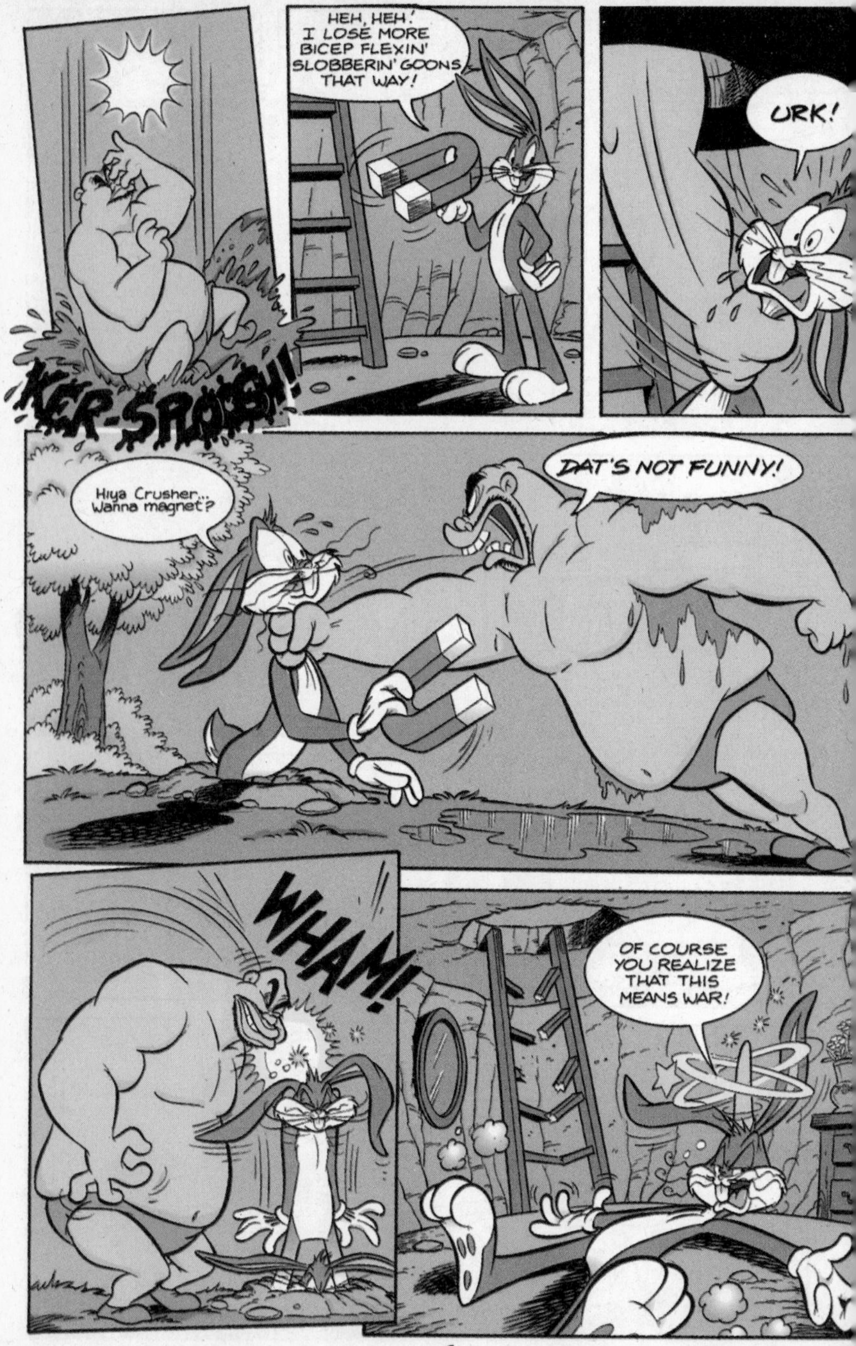
KER-SPLOOSH!
HEH, HEH! I LOSE MORE BICEP FLEXIN' SLOBBERIN' GOONS THAT WAY!
URK!
Hiya Crusher... Wanna magnet?
DAT'S NOT FUNNY!
WHAM!
OF COURSE YOU REALIZE THAT THIS MEANS WAR!

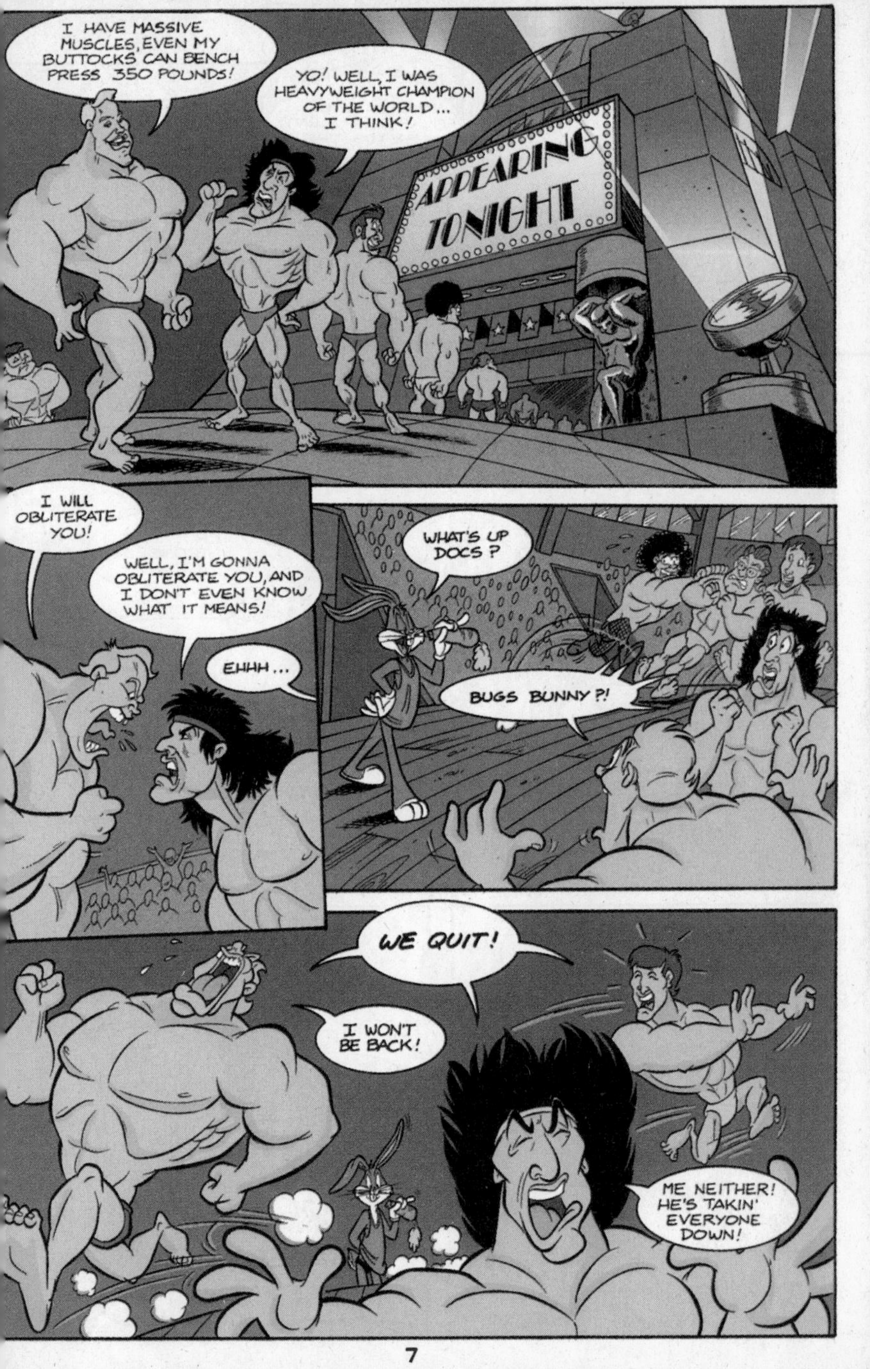
I HAVE MASSIVE MUSCLES, EVEN MY BUTTOCKS CAN BENCH PRESS 350 POUNDS!
YO! WELL, I WAS HEAVYWEIGHT CHAMPION OF THE WORLD... I THINK!
APPEARING TONIGHT
I WILL OBLITERATE YOU!
WELL, I'M GONNA OBLITERATE YOU, AND I DON'T EVEN KNOW WHAT IT MEANS!
EHHH...
WHAT'S UP DOCS?
BUGS BUNNY?!
WE QUIT!
I WON'T BE BACK!
ME NEITHER! HE'S 'TAKIN' EVERYONE DOWN!

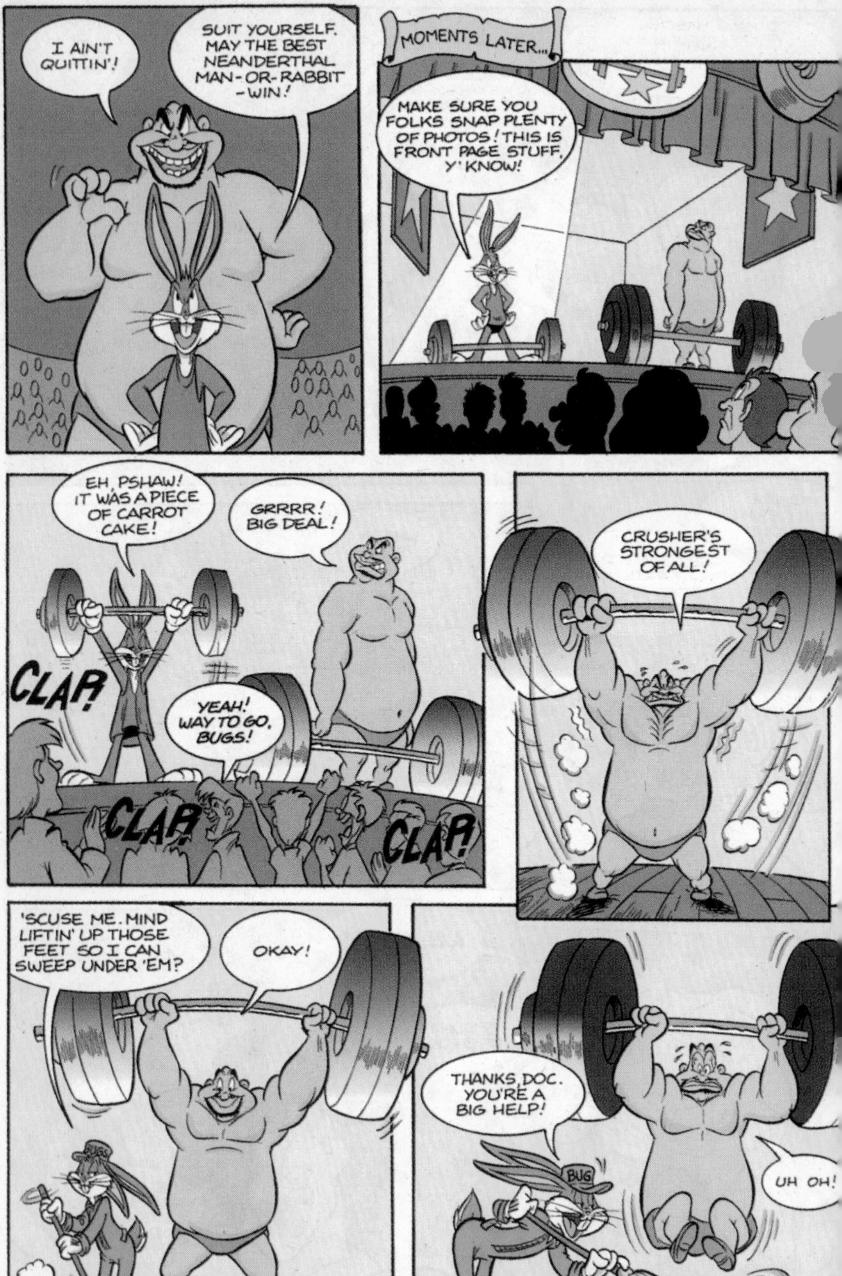
I AIN'T QUITTIN'!
SUIT YOURSELF. MAY THE BEST NEANDERTHAL MAN-OR-RABBIT -WIN!
MOMENTS LATER...
MAKE SURE YOU FOLKS SNAP PLENTY OF PHOTOS! THIS IS FRONT PAGE STUFF, Y' KNOW!
EH, PSHAW! IT WAS A PIECE OF CARROT CAKE!
GRRRR! BIG DEAL!
CLAP!
YEAH! WAY TO GO, BUGS!
CLAP!
CLAP!
CRUSHER'S STRONGEST OF ALL!
'SCUSE ME. MIND LIFTIN' UP THOSE FEET SO I CAN SWEEP UNDER 'EM?
OKAY!
BUGS
THANKS, DOC. YOU'RE A BIG HELP!
BUG
UH OH!

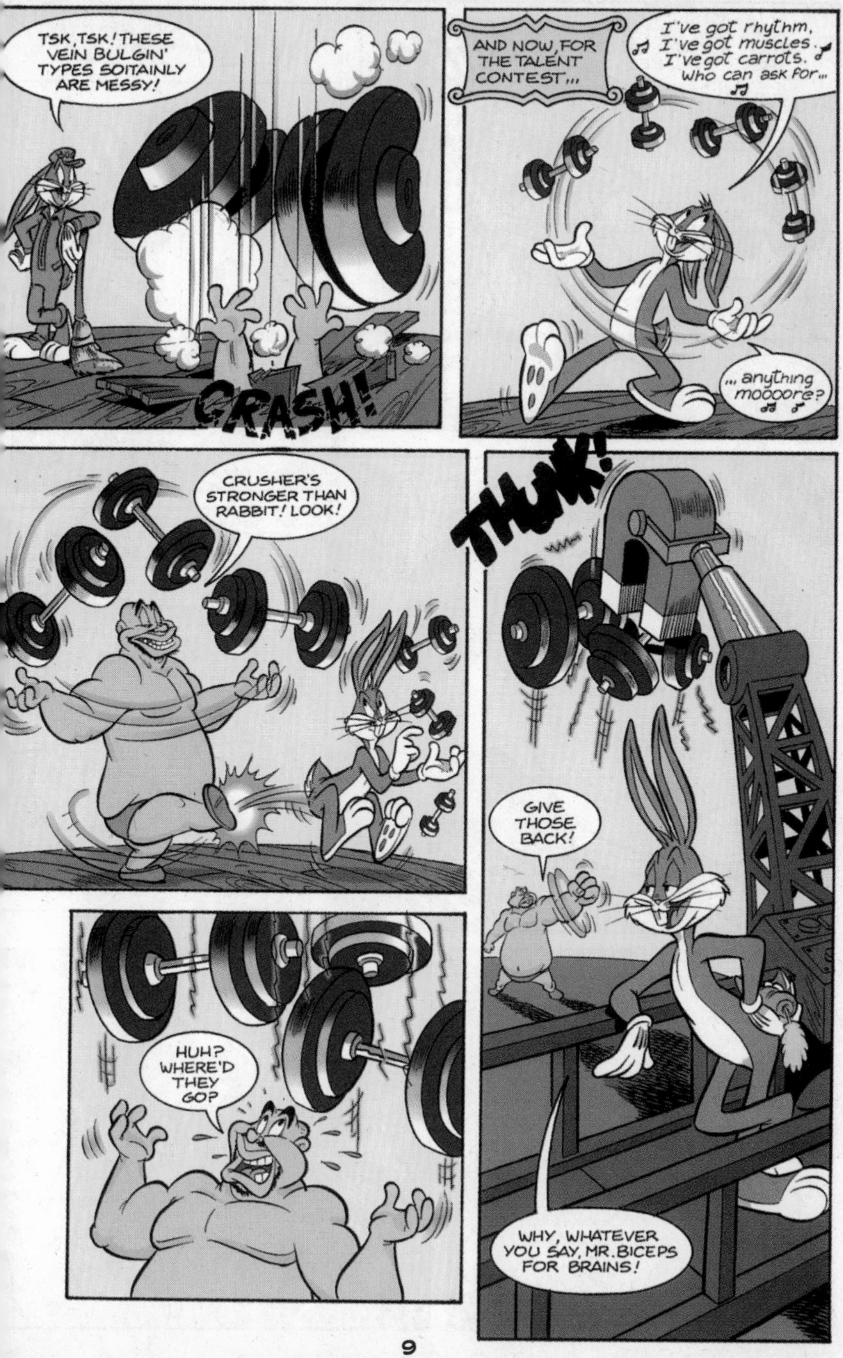
TSK, TSK! THESE VEIN BULGIN' TYPES SOITAINLY ARE MESSY!
CRASH!
AND NOW, FOR THE TALENT CONTEST...
I've got rhythm, I've got muscles. I've got carrots. Who can ask for...
... anything moooore?
CRUSHER'S STRONGER THAN RABBIT! LOOK!
THUNK!
GIVE THOSE BACK!
WHY, WHATEVER YOU SAY, MR. BICEPS FOR BRAINS!
HUH? WHERE'D THEY GO?

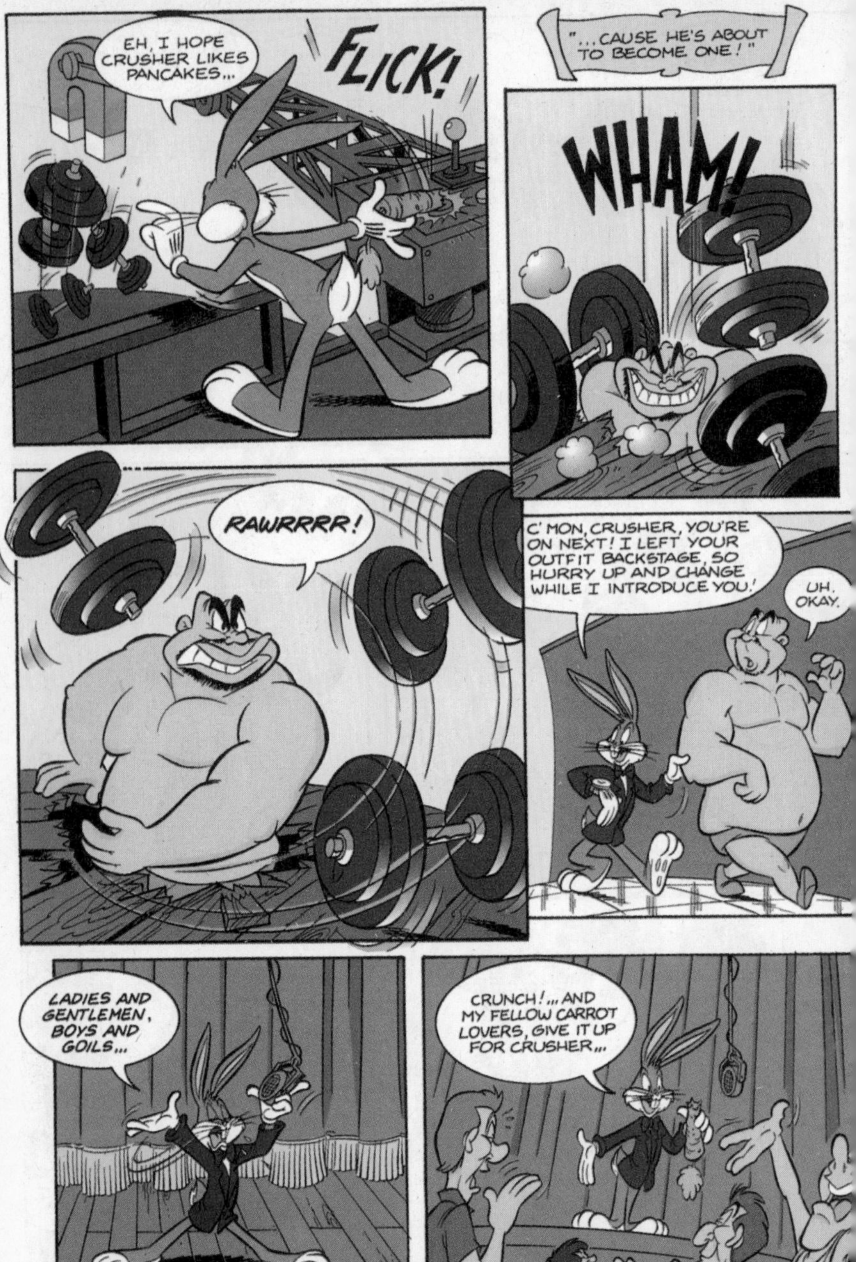
EH, I HOPE CRUSHER LIKES PANCAKES...
FLICK!
"...CAUSE HE'S ABOUT TO BECOME ONE!"
WHAM!
RAWRRRR!
C'MON, CRUSHER, YOU'RE ON NEXT! I LEFT YOUR OUTFIT BACKSTAGE, SO HURRY UP AND CHANGE WHILE I INTRODUCE YOU!
UH, OKAY.
LADIES AND GENTLEMEN, BOYS AND GOILS...
CRUNCH!... AND MY FELLOW CARROT LOVERS, GIVE IT UP FOR CRUSHER...

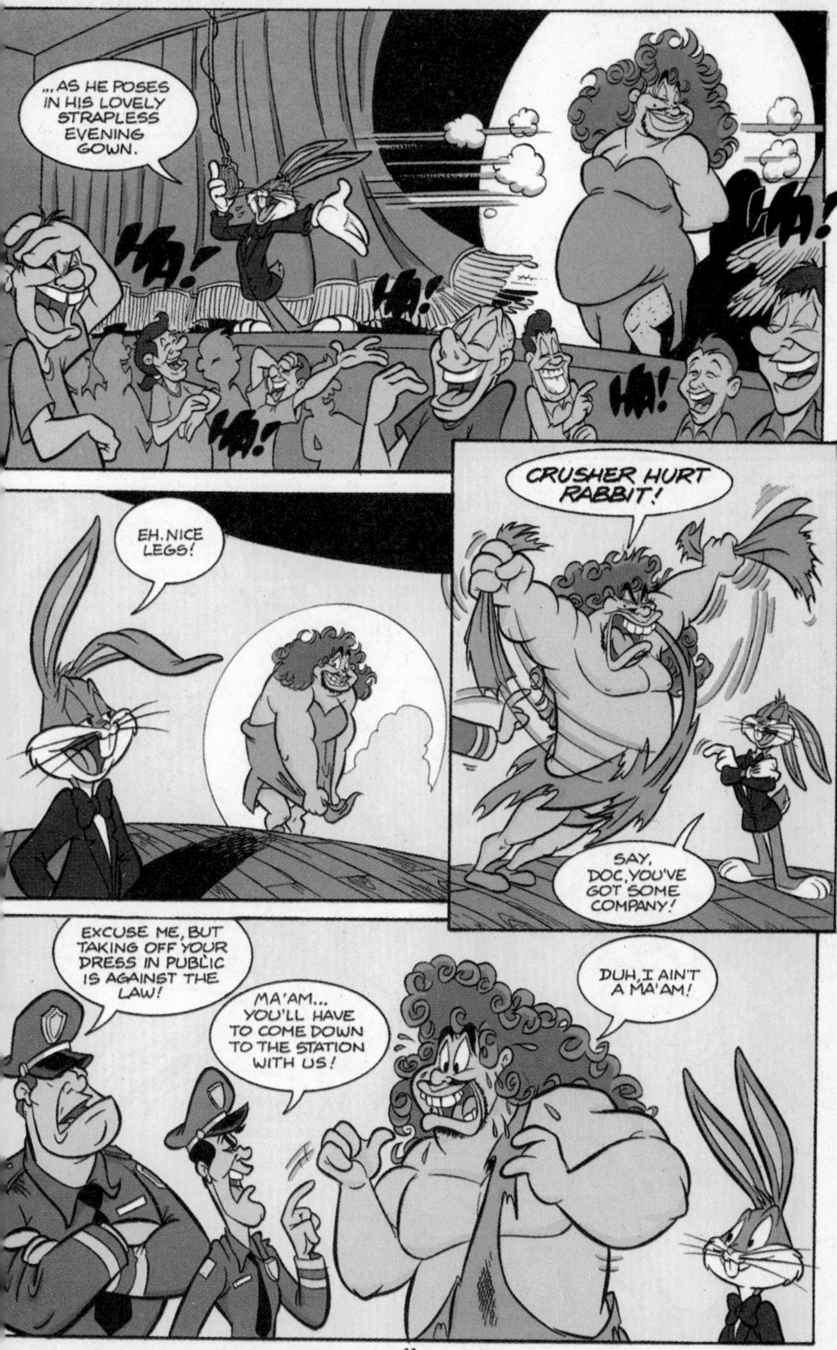
...AS HE POSES IN HIS LOVELY STRAPLESS EVENING GOWN.
HA!
HA!
HA!
HA!
HA!
EH. NICE LEGS!
CRUSHER HURT RABBIT!
SAY, DOC, YOU'VE GOT SOME COMPANY!
EXCUSE ME, BUT TAKING OFF YOUR DRESS IN PUBLIC IS AGAINST THE LAW!
MA'AM... YOU'LL HAVE TO COME DOWN TO THE STATION WITH US!
DUH, I AIN'T A MA'AM!

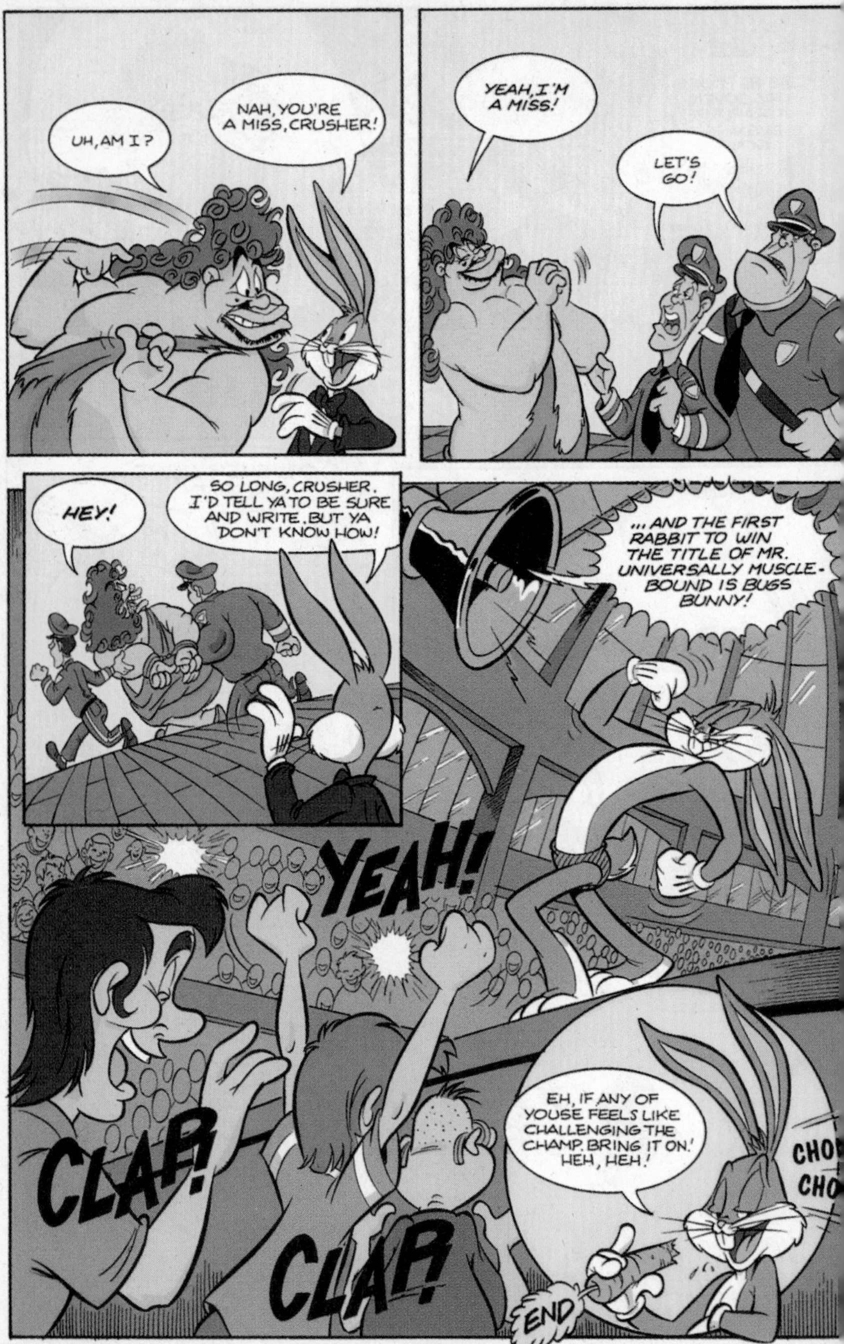
UH, AM I?
NAH, YOU'RE A MISS, CRUSHER!
YEAH, I'M A MISS!
LET'S GO!
HEY!
SO LONG, CRUSHER. I'D TELL YA TO BE SURE AND WRITE, BUT YA DON'T KNOW HOW!
...AND THE FIRST RABBIT TO WIN THE TITLE OF MR. UNIVERSALLY MUSCLE-BOUND IS BUGS BUNNY!
YEAH!
CLAP!
CLAP!
EH, IF ANY OF YOUSE FEELS LIKE CHALLENGING THE CHAMP, BRING IT ON! HEH, HEH!
END

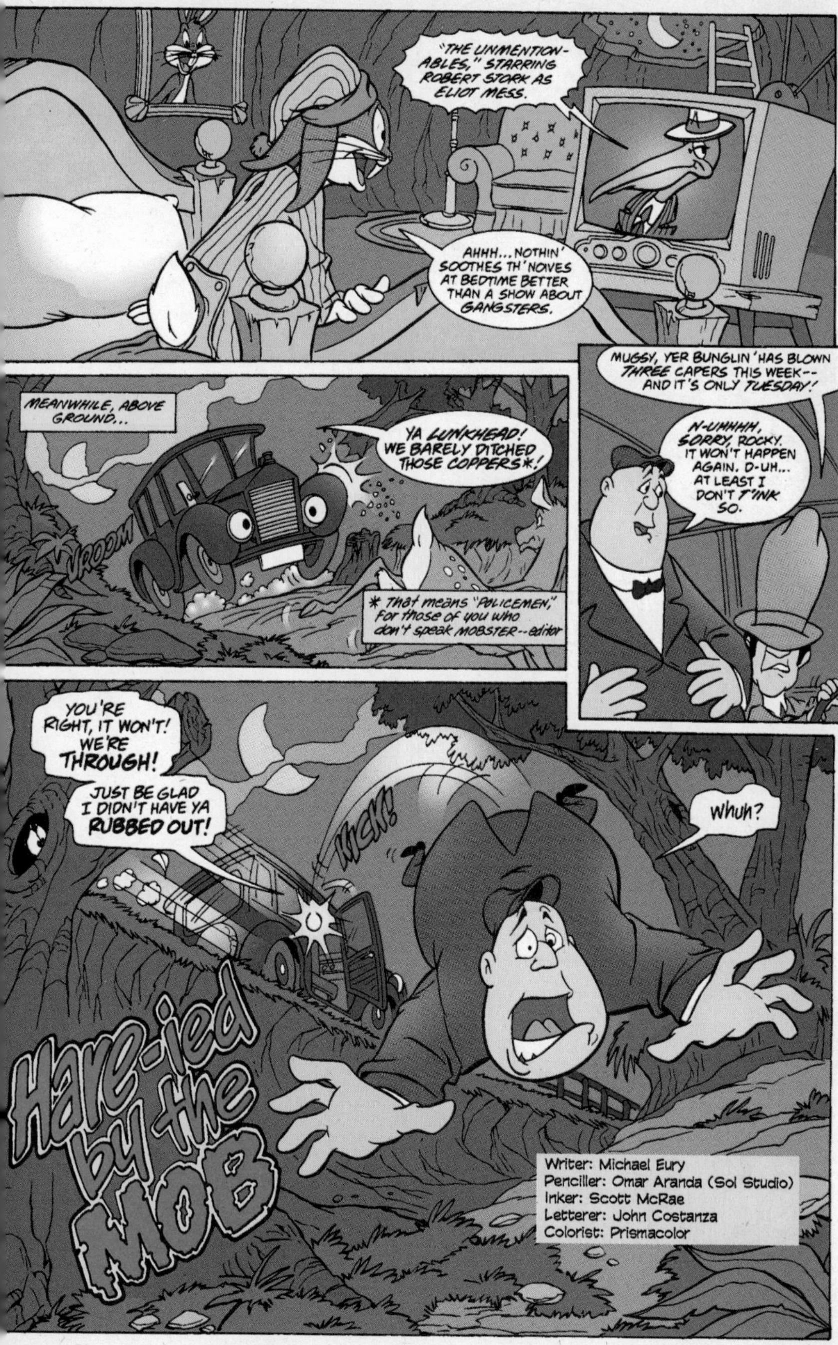
"THE UNMENTION-ABLES," STARRING ROBERT STORK AS ELIOT MESS.
AHHH... NOTHIN' SOOTHES TH' NOIVES AT BEDTIME BETTER THAN A SHOW ABOUT GANGSTERS.
MEANWHILE, ABOVE GROUND...
VROOM
YA LUNKHEAD! WE BARELY DITCHED THOSE COPPERS*!
* That means "POLICEMEN," for those of you who don't speak MOBSTER--editor
MUGGY, YER BUNGLIN' HAS BLOWN THREE CAPERS THIS WEEK-- AND IT'S ONLY TUESDAY!
N-UHHHH, SORRY, ROCKY. IT WON'T HAPPEN AGAIN. D-UH... AT LEAST I DON'T T'INK SO.
YOU'RE RIGHT, IT WON'T! WE'RE THROUGH!
JUST BE GLAD I DIDN'T HAVE YA RUBBED OUT!
KICK!
Whuh?
Hare-ied by the MOB
Writer: Michael Eury
Penciller: Omar Aranda (Sol Studio)
Inker: Scott McRae
Letterer: John Costanza
Colorist: Prismacolor

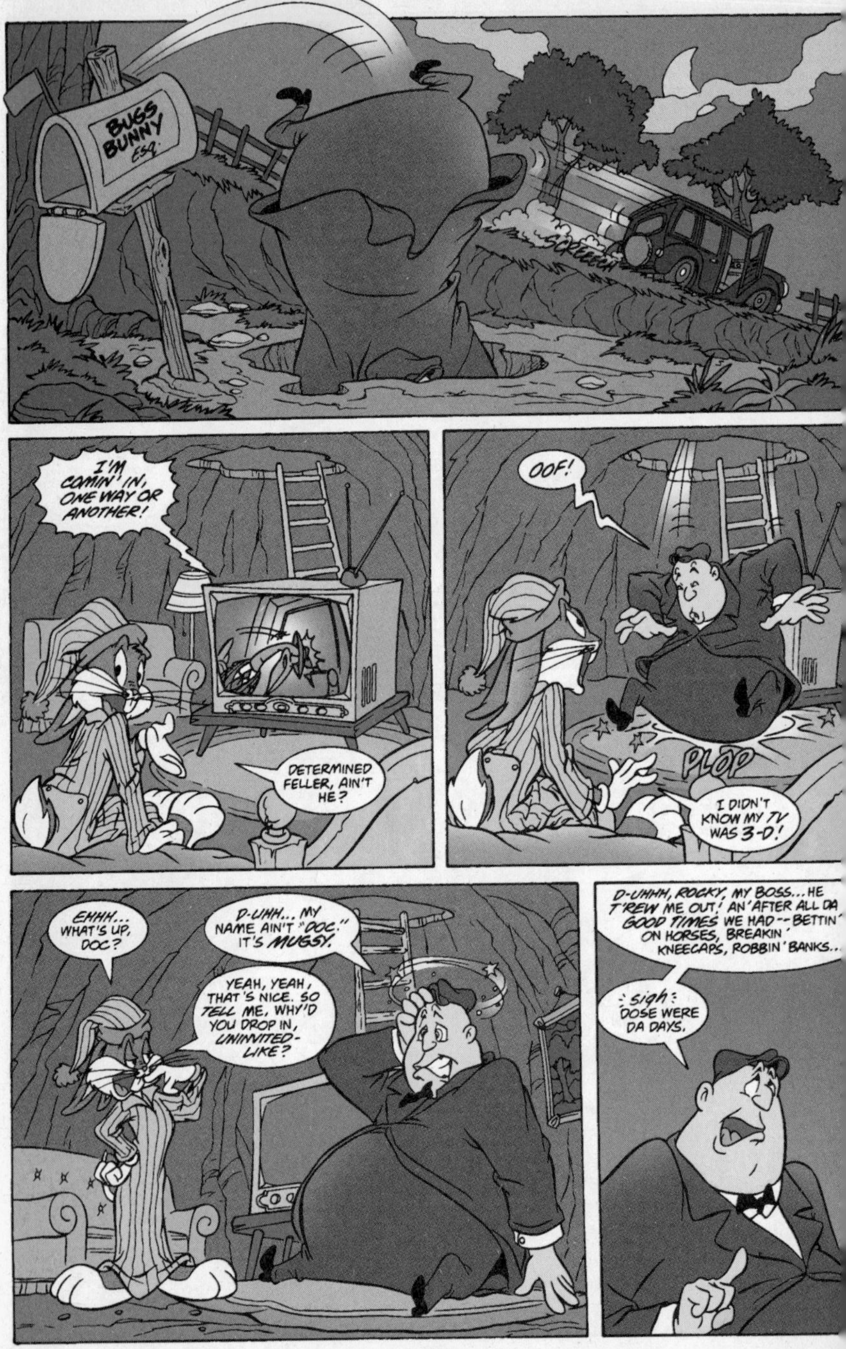
BUGS BUNNY ESQ.
SCREEECH
I'M COMIN' IN, ONE WAY OR ANOTHER!
DETERMINED FELLER, AIN'T HE?
OOF!
PLOP
I DIDN'T KNOW MY TV WAS 3-D!
EHHH... WHAT'S UP, DOC?
D-UHH... MY NAME AIN'T "DOC." IT'S MUGSY.
YEAH, YEAH, THAT'S NICE. SO TELL ME, WHY'D YOU DROP IN, UNINVITED-LIKE?
D-UHHH, ROCKY, MY BOSS... HE T'REW ME OUT! AN' AFTER ALL DA GOOD TIMES WE HAD--BETTIN' ON HORSES, BREAKIN' KNEECAPS, ROBBIN' BANKS...
:sigh: DOSE WERE DA DAYS.

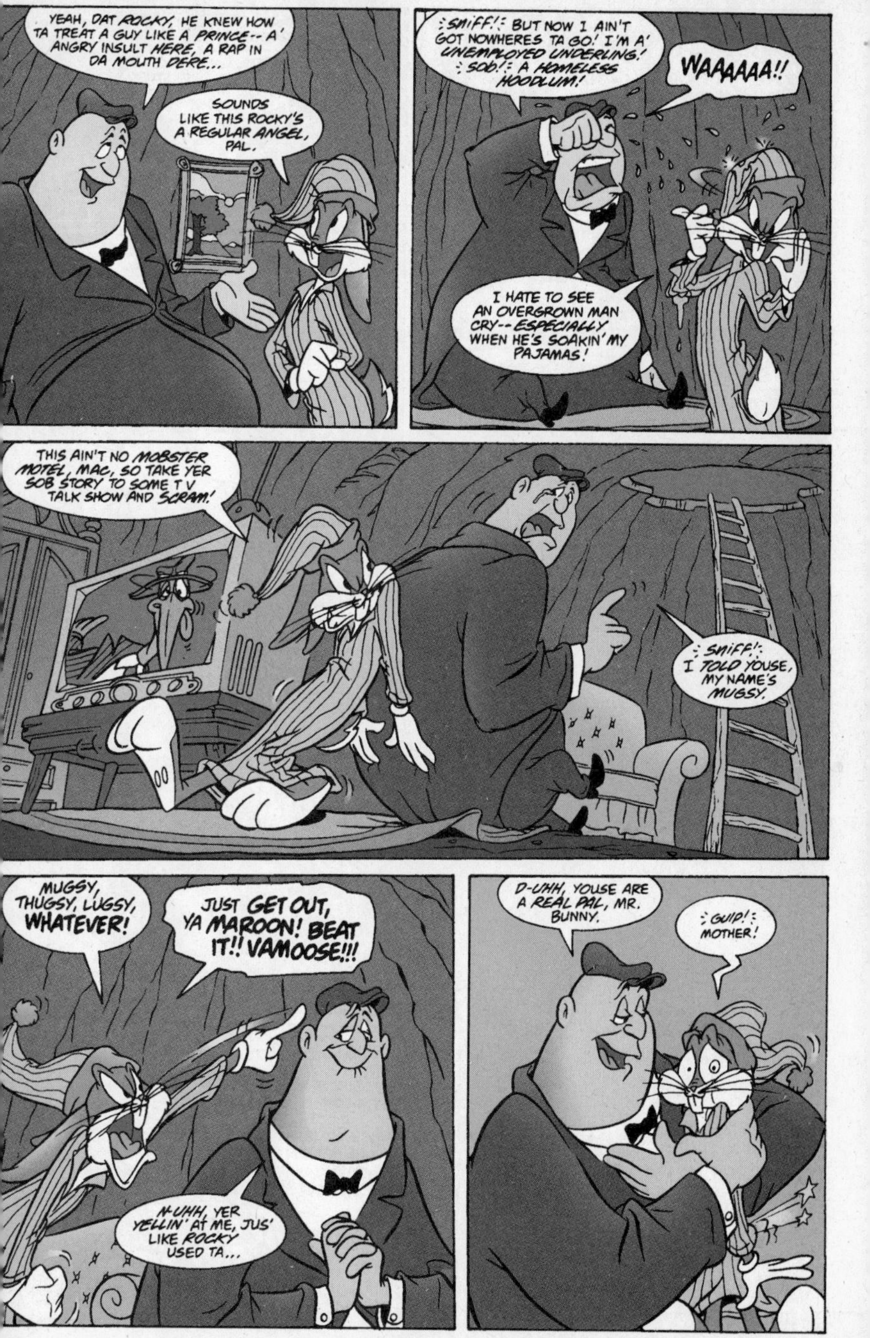
YEAH, DAT ROCKY, HE KNEW HOW TA TREAT A GUY LIKE A PRINCE-- A' ANGRY INSULT HERE, A RAP IN DA MOUTH DERE...
SOUNDS LIKE THIS ROCKY'S A REGULAR ANGEL, PAL.
:SNIFF!: BUT NOW I AIN'T GOT NOWHERES TA GO! I'M A' UNEMPLOYED UNDERLING! :SOB!: A HOMELESS HOODLUM!
WAAAAAA!!
I HATE TO SEE AN OVERGROWN MAN CRY-- ESPECIALLY WHEN HE'S SOAKIN' MY PAJAMAS!
THIS AIN'T NO MOBSTER MOTEL, MAC, SO TAKE YER SOB STORY TO SOME T V TALK SHOW AND SCRAM!
:SNIFF!: I TOLD YOUSE, MY NAME'S MUGSY.
MUGSY, THUGSY, LUGSY, WHATEVER!
JUST GET OUT, YA MAROON! BEAT IT!! VAMOOSE!!!
N-UHH, YER YELLIN' AT ME, JUS' LIKE ROCKY USED TA...
D-UHH, YOUSE ARE A REAL PAL, MR. BUNNY.
:GULP!: MOTHER!

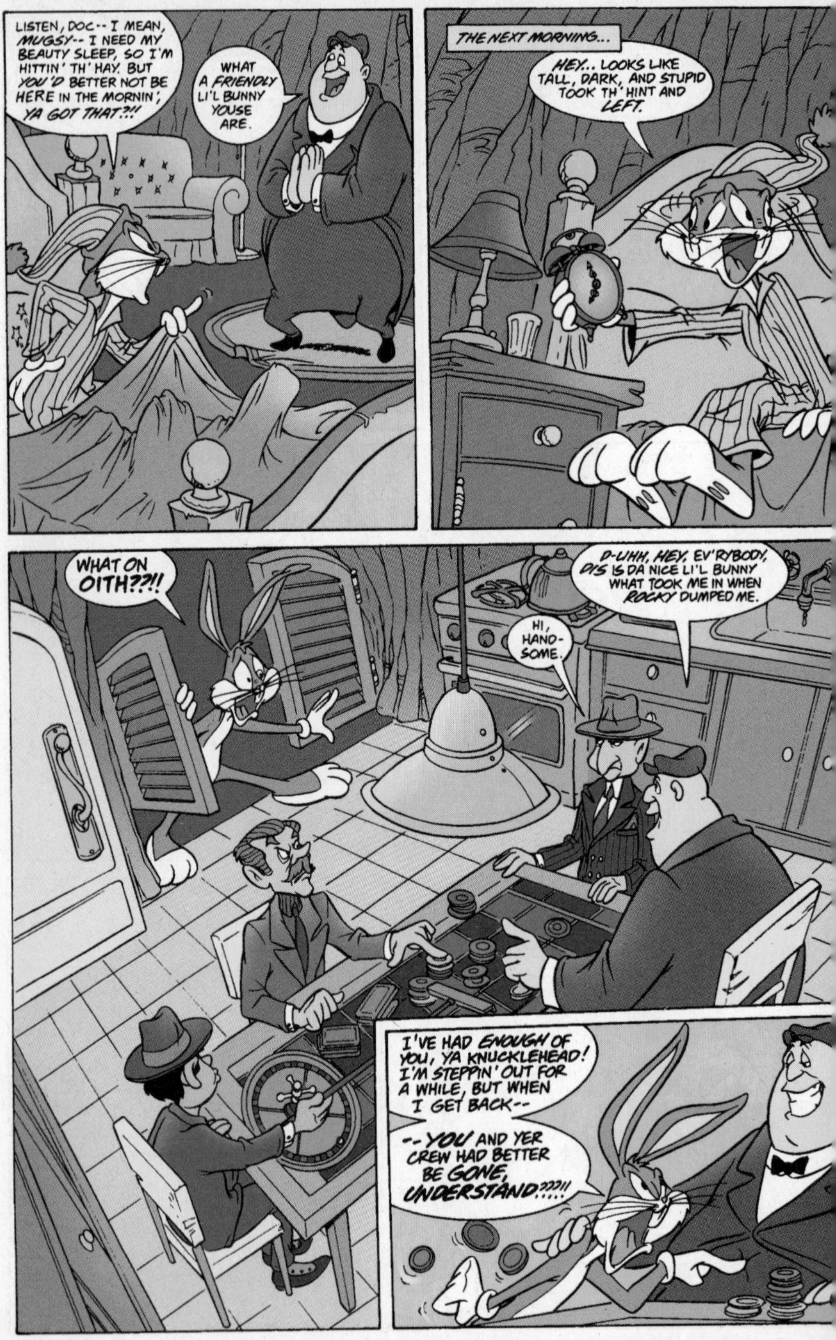
LISTEN, DOC-- I MEAN, MUGSY-- I NEED MY BEAUTY SLEEP, SO I'M HITTIN' TH' HAY. BUT YOU'D BETTER NOT BE HERE IN THE MORNIN'; YA GOT THAT?!!
WHAT A FRIENDLY LI'L BUNNY YOUSE ARE.
THE NEXT MORNING...
HEY... LOOKS LIKE TALL, DARK, AND STUPID TOOK TH' HINT AND LEFT.
WHAT ON OITH??!!
D-UHH, HEY, EV'RYBODY, DIS IS DA NICE LI'L BUNNY WHAT TOOK ME IN WHEN ROCKY DUMPED ME.
HI, HAND-SOME.
I'VE HAD ENOUGH OF YOU, YA KNUCKLEHEAD! I'M STEPPIN' OUT FOR A WHILE, BUT WHEN I GET BACK--
--YOU AND YER CREW HAD BETTER BE GONE, UNDERSTAND???!!

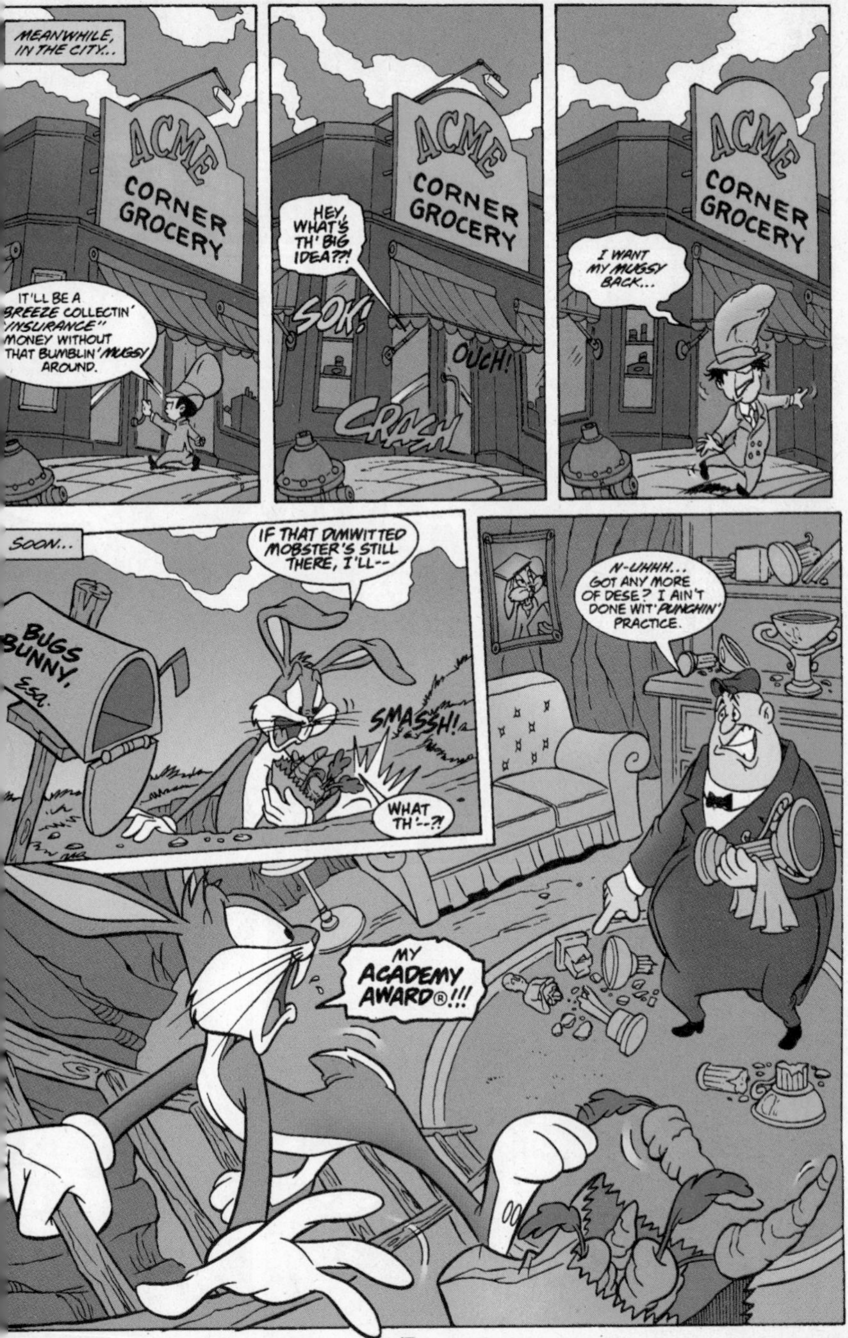
MEANWHILE, IN THE CITY...
ACME CORNER GROCERY
IT'LL BE A BREEZE COLLECTIN' "INSURANCE" MONEY WITHOUT THAT BUMBLIN' MUGSY AROUND.
HEY, WHAT'S TH' BIG IDEA??!
SOK!
OUCH!
CRASH
I WANT MY MUGSY BACK...
SOON...
IF THAT DIMWITTED MOBSTER'S STILL THERE, I'LL--
BUGS BUNNY, ESQ.
SMASSH!
WHAT TH'--?!
N-UHHH... GOT ANY MORE OF DESE? I AIN'T DONE WIT' PUNCHIN' PRACTICE.
MY ACADEMY AWARD®!!!

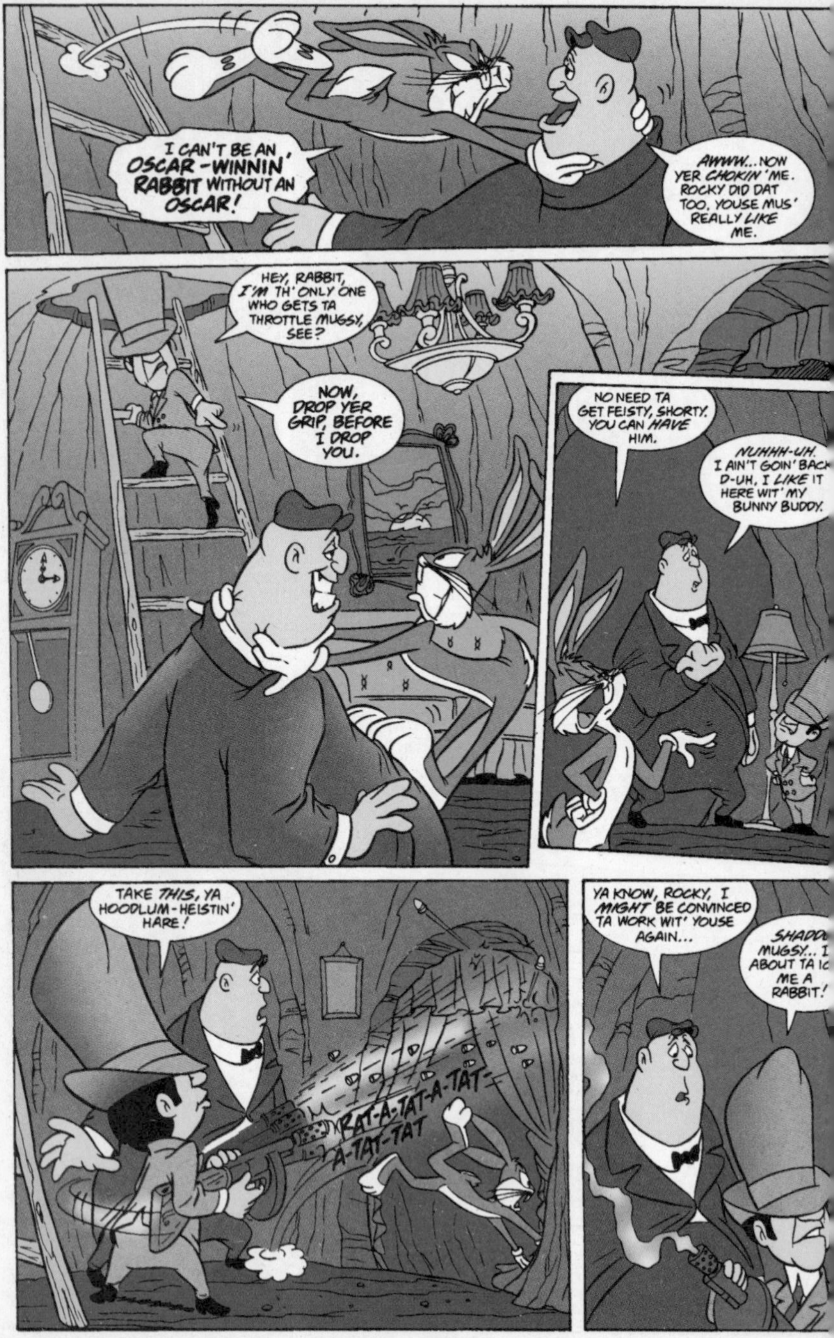
I CAN'T BE AN OSCAR-WINNIN' RABBIT WITHOUT AN OSCAR!
AWWW...NOW YER CHOKIN' ME. ROCKY DID DAT TOO. YOUSE MUS' REALLY LIKE ME.
HEY, RABBIT, I'M TH' ONLY ONE WHO GETS TA THROTTLE MUGSY, SEE?
NOW, DROP YER GRIP, BEFORE I DROP YOU.
NO NEED TA GET FEISTY, SHORTY. YOU CAN HAVE HIM.
NUHHH-UH. I AIN'T GOIN' BAC D-UH, I LIKE IT HERE WIT' MY BUNNY BUDDY.
TAKE THIS, YA HOODLUM-HEISTIN' HARE!
RAT-A-TAT-A-TAT A-TAT-TAT
YA KNOW, ROCKY, I MIGHT BE CONVINCED TA WORK WIT' YOUSE AGAIN...
SHADD MUGSY... I ABOUT TA I ME A RABBIT!

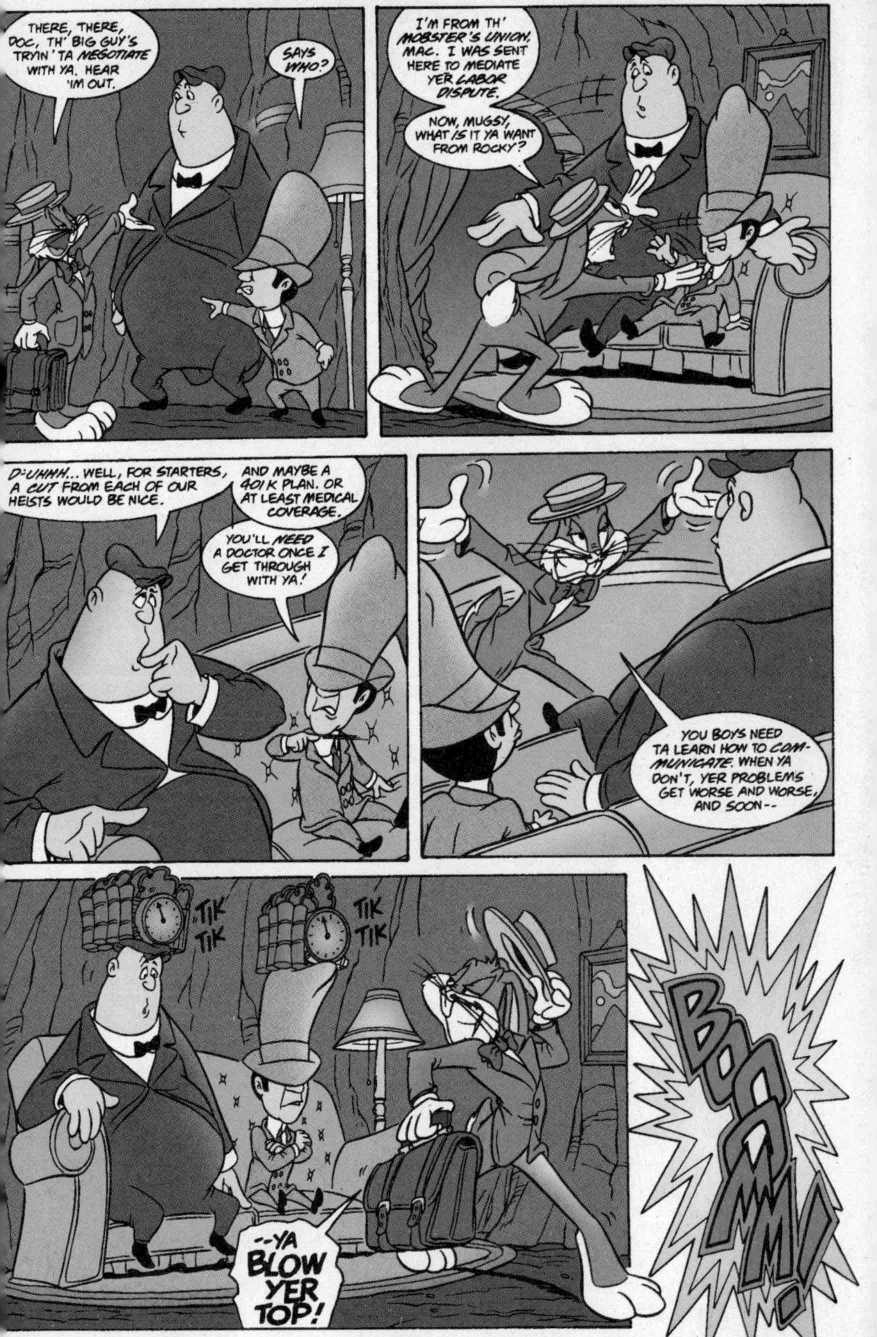

THERE, THERE, DOC, TH' BIG GUY'S TRYIN' TA NEGOTIATE WITH YA. HEAR 'IM OUT.
SAYS WHO?
I'M FROM TH' MOBSTER'S UNION, MAC. I WAS SENT HERE TO MEDIATE YER LABOR DISPUTE.
NOW, MUGSY, WHAT IS IT YA WANT FROM ROCKY?
D-UHHH... WELL, FOR STARTERS, A CUT FROM EACH OF OUR HEISTS WOULD BE NICE.
AND MAYBE A 401 K PLAN. OR AT LEAST MEDICAL COVERAGE.
YOU'LL NEED A DOCTOR ONCE I GET THROUGH WITH YA!
YOU BOYS NEED TA LEARN HOW TO COMMUNICATE. WHEN YA DON'T, YER PROBLEMS GET WORSE AND WORSE, AND SOON--
TIK TIK
TIK TIK
--YA BLOW YER TOP!
BOOOMM!

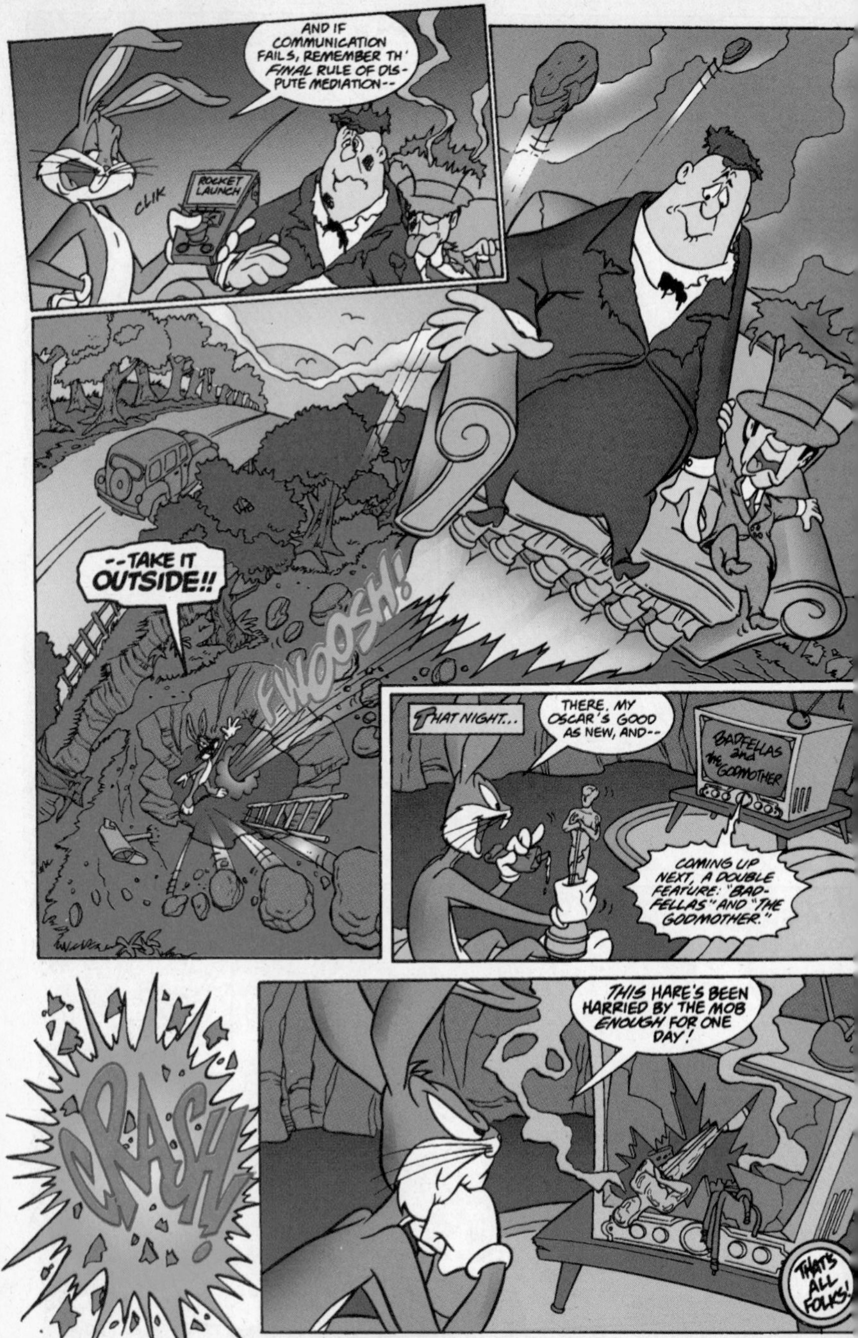
AND IF COMMUNICATION FAILS, REMEMBER TH' FINAL RULE OF DISPUTE MEDIATION--
ROCKET LAUNCH
CLIK
--TAKE IT OUTSIDE!!
FWOOSH!
THAT NIGHT...
THERE, MY OSCAR'S GOOD AS NEW, AND--
BADFELLAS and the GODMOTHER
COMING UP NEXT, A DOUBLE FEATURE: "BADFELLAS" AND "THE GODMOTHER."
CRASH
THIS HARE'S BEEN HARRIED BY THE MOB ENOUGH FOR ONE DAY!
THAT'S ALL FOLKS!

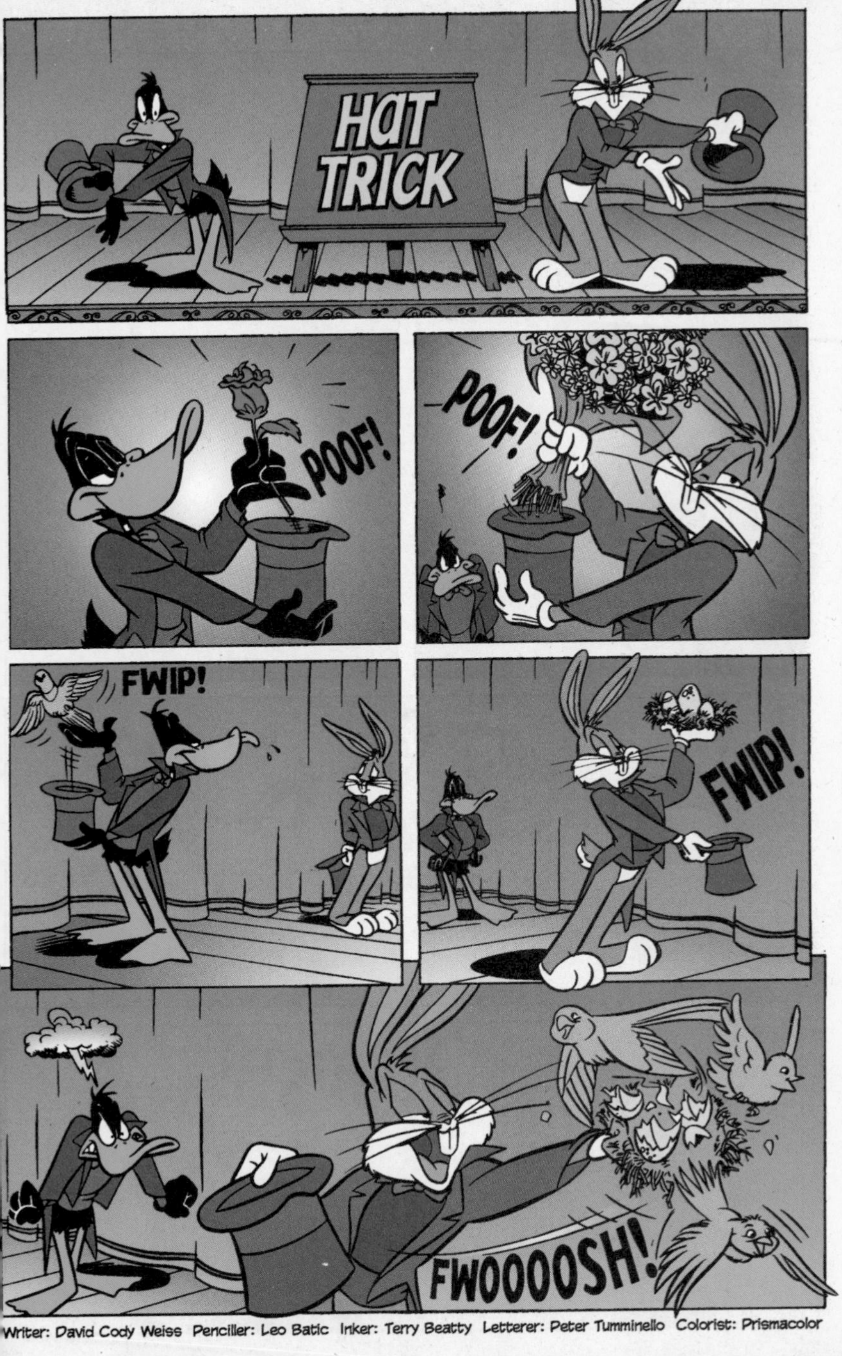
HAT TRICK
POOF!
POOF!
FWIP!
FWIP!
FWOOOOSH!

Writer: David Cody Weiss Penciller: Leo Batic Inker: Terry Beatty Letterer: Peter Tumminello Colorist: Prismacolor

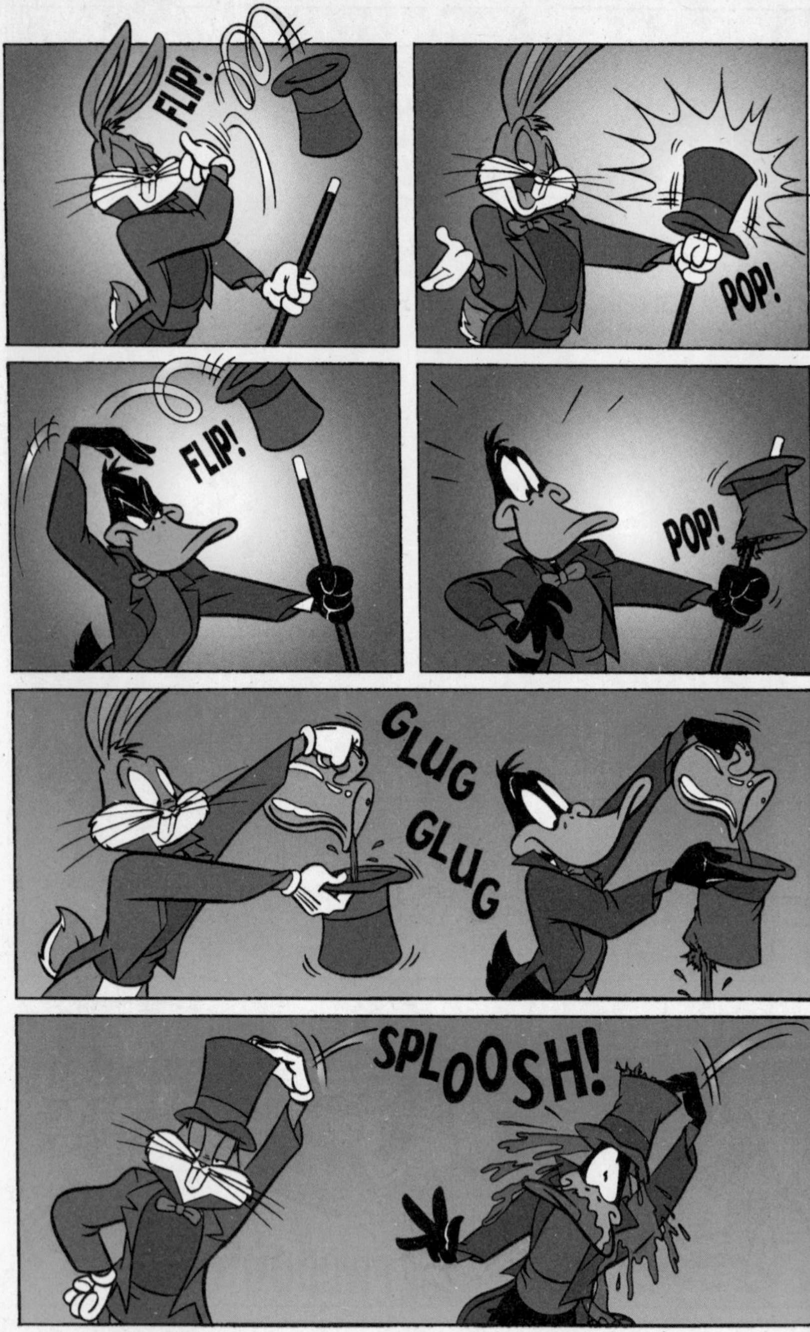
FLIP!
POP!
FLIP!
POP!
GLUG GLUG
SPLOOSH!

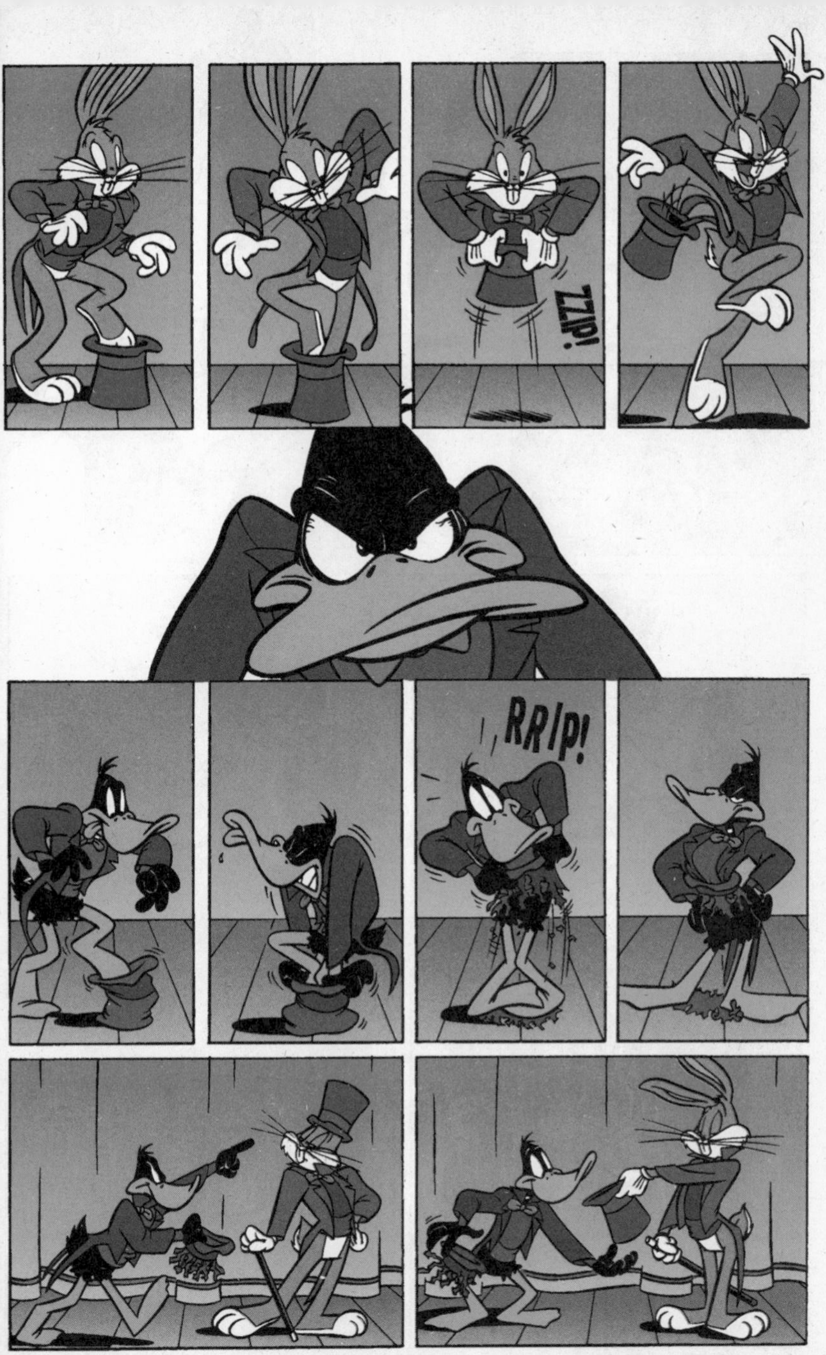
ZZIP!
RRIP!

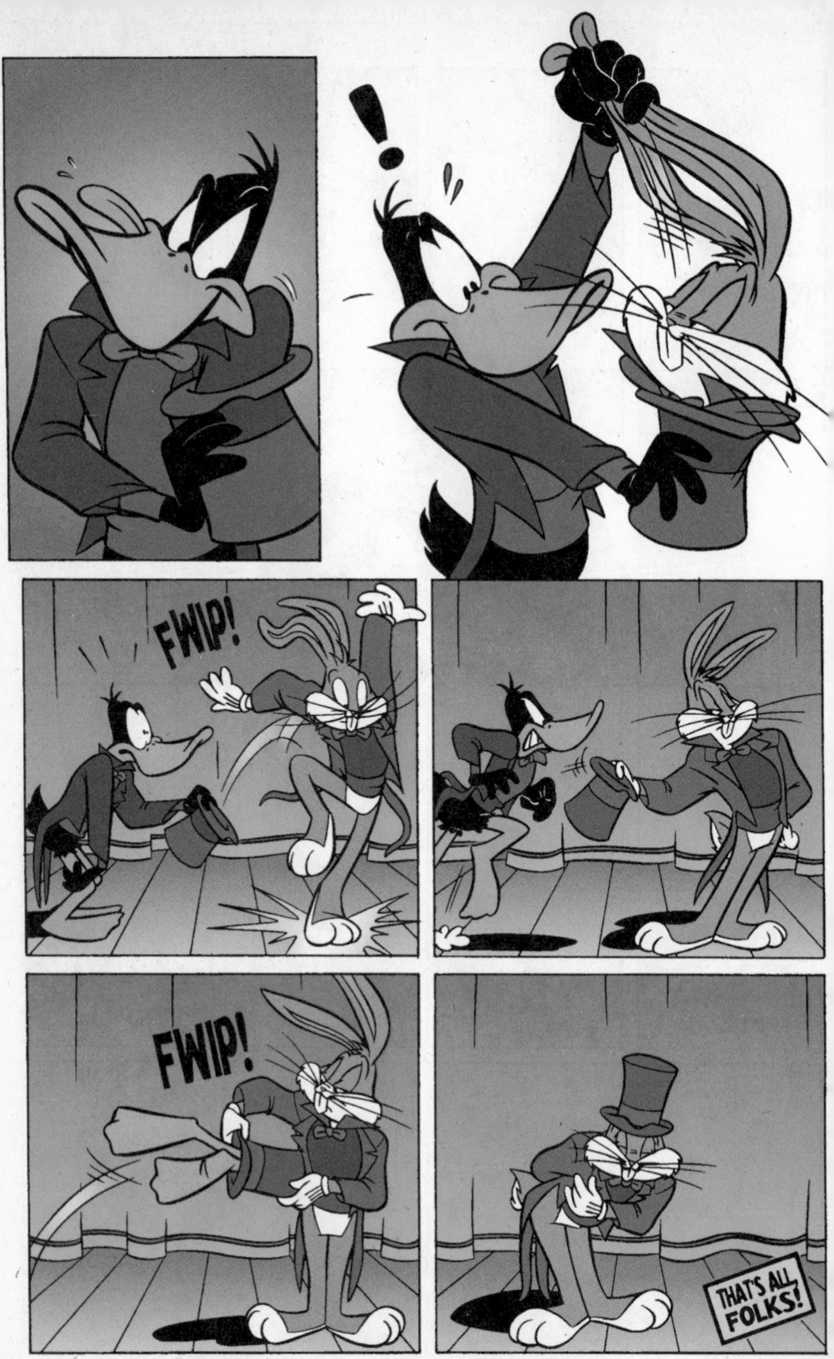
!
FWIP!
FWIP!
THAT'S ALL FOLKS!

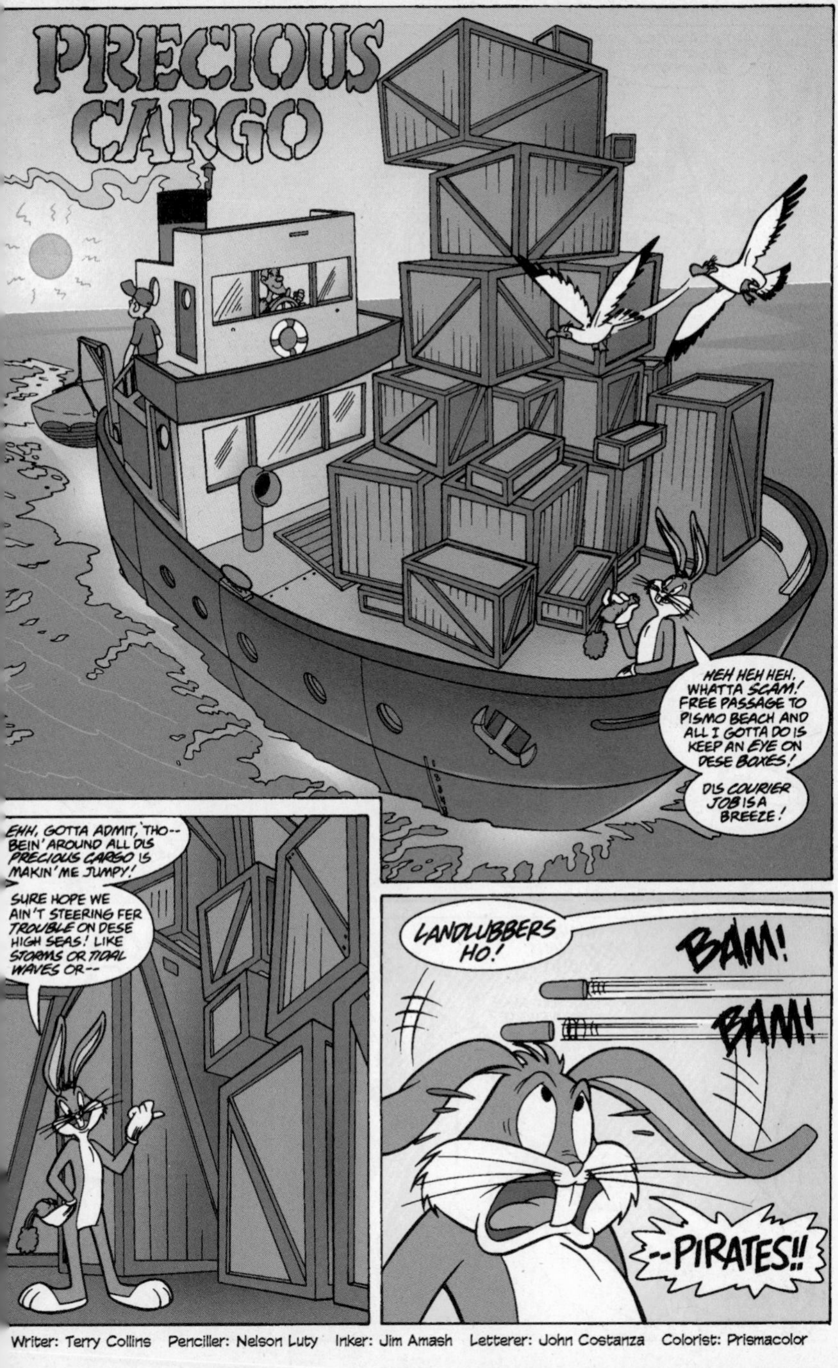
PRECIOUS CARGO
HEH HEH HEH. WHATTA SCAM! FREE PASSAGE TO PISMO BEACH AND ALL I GOTTA DO IS KEEP AN EYE ON DESE BOXES!
DIS COURIER JOB IS A BREEZE!
EHH, GOTTA ADMIT, 'THO-- BEIN' AROUND ALL DIS PRECIOUS CARGO IS MAKIN' ME JUMPY!
SURE HOPE WE AIN'T STEERING FER TROUBLE ON DESE HIGH SEAS! LIKE STORMS OR TIDAL WAVES OR--
LANDLUBBERS HO!
BAM!
BAM!
--PIRATES!!

Writer: Terry Collins Penciller: Nelson Luty Inker: Jim Amash Letterer: John Costanza Colorist: Prismacolor

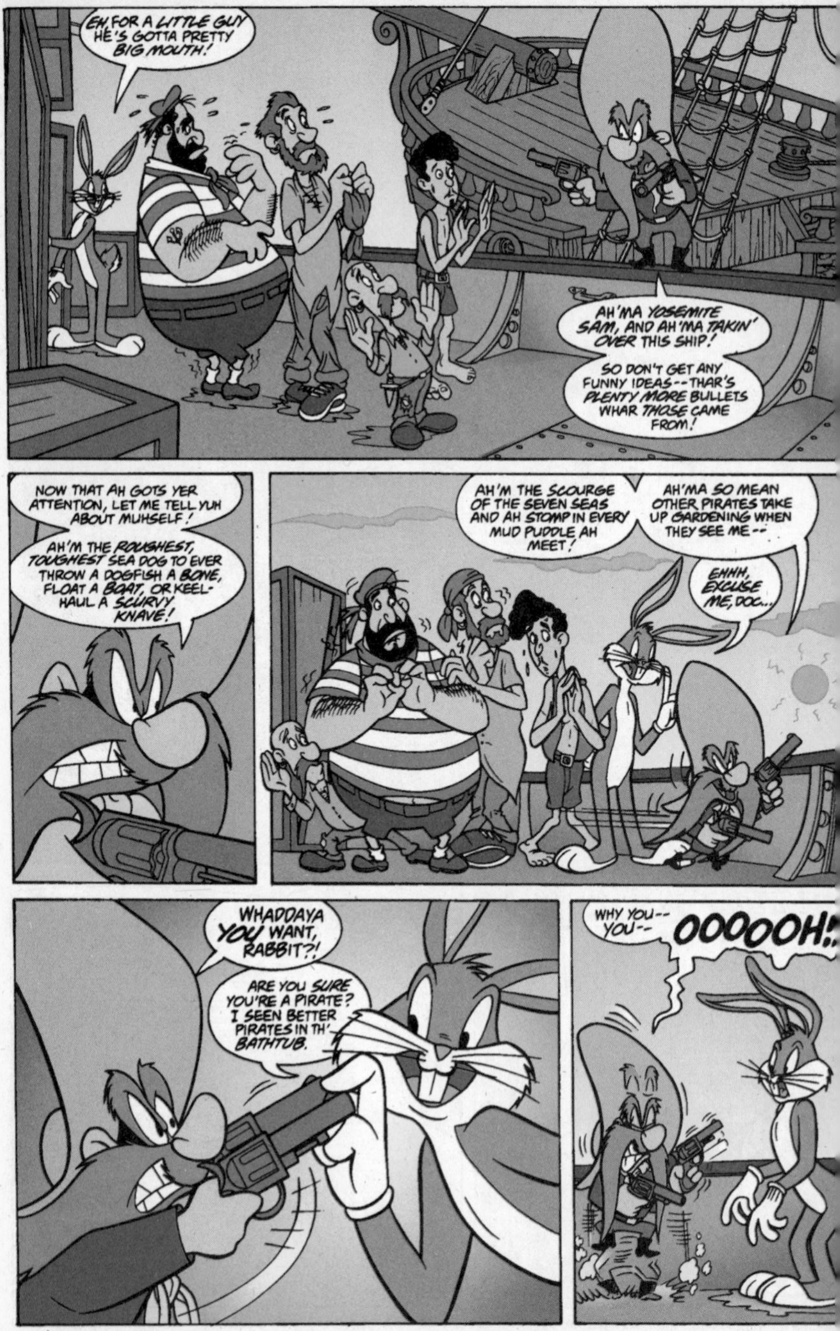
EH, FOR A LITTLE GUY HE'S GOTTA PRETTY BIG MOUTH!
AH'MA YOSEMITE SAM, AND AH'MA TAKIN' OVER THIS SHIP!
SO DON'T GET ANY FUNNY IDEAS--THAR'S PLENTY MORE BULLETS WHAR THOSE CAME FROM!
NOW THAT AH GOTS YER ATTENTION, LET ME TELL YUH ABOUT MUHSELF!
AH'M THE ROUGHEST, TOUGHEST SEA DOG TO EVER THROW A DOGFISH A BONE, FLOAT A BOAT, OR KEEL-HAUL A SCURVY KNAVE!
AH'M THE SCOURGE OF THE SEVEN SEAS AND AH STOMP IN EVERY MUD PUDDLE AH MEET!
AH'MA SO MEAN OTHER PIRATES TAKE UP GARDENING WHEN THEY SEE ME--
EHHH, EXCUSE ME, DOC...
WHADDAYA YOU WANT, RABBIT?!
ARE YOU SURE YOU'RE A PIRATE? I SEEN BETTER PIRATES IN TH' BATHTUB.
WHY YOU-- YOU--
OOOOOH!!

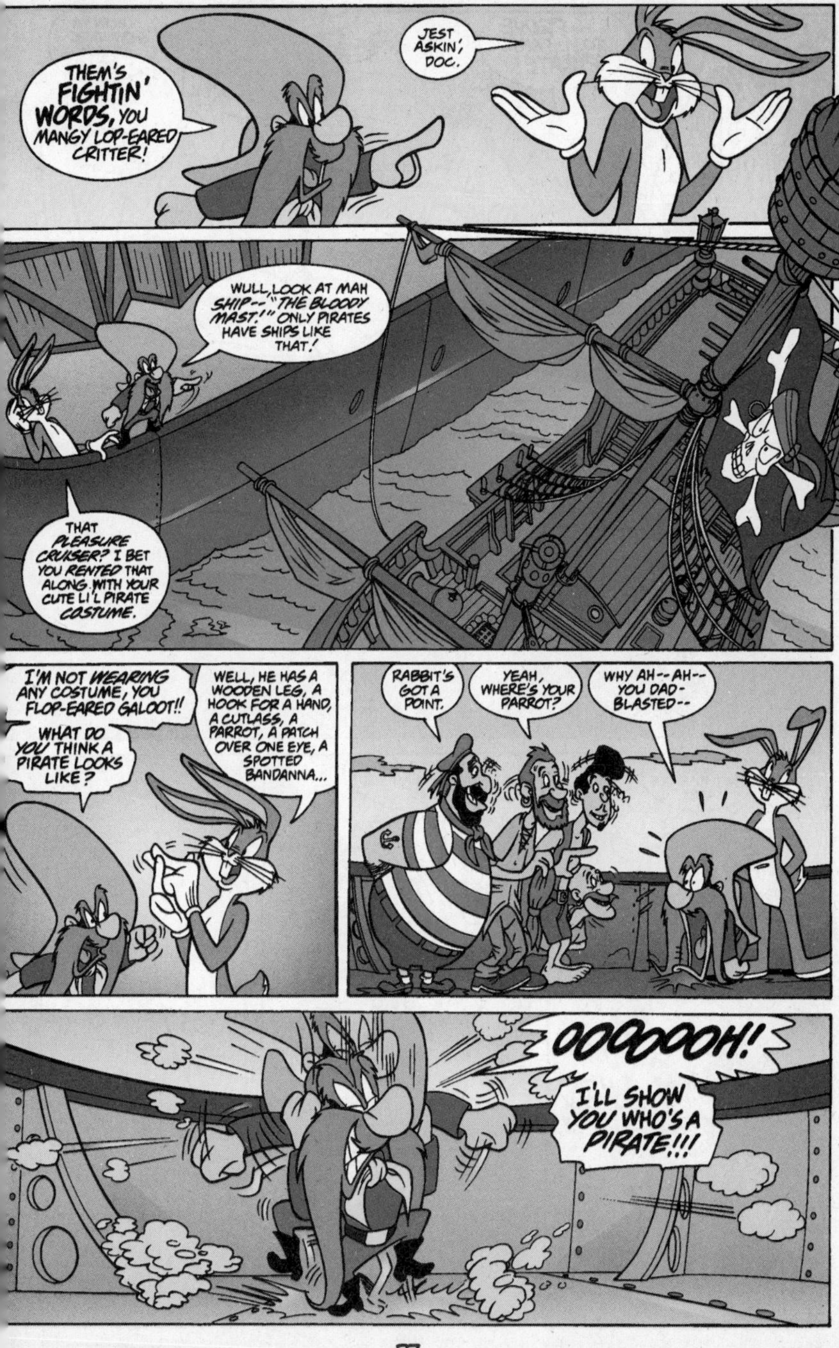
THEM'S FIGHTIN' WORDS, YOU MANGY LOP-EARED CRITTER!
JEST ASKIN', DOC.
WULL, LOOK AT MAH SHIP-- "THE BLOODY MAST!" ONLY PIRATES HAVE SHIPS LIKE THAT!
THAT PLEASURE CRUISER? I BET YOU RENTED THAT ALONG WITH YOUR CUTE LI'L PIRATE COSTUME.
I'M NOT WEARING ANY COSTUME, YOU FLOP-EARED GALOOT!!
WHAT DO YOU THINK A PIRATE LOOKS LIKE?
WELL, HE HAS A WOODEN LEG, A HOOK FOR A HAND, A CUTLASS, A PARROT, A PATCH OVER ONE EYE, A SPOTTED BANDANNA...
RABBIT'S GOT A POINT.
YEAH, WHERE'S YOUR PARROT?
WHY AH--AH-- YOU DAD-BLASTED--
OOOOOOOH!
I'LL SHOW YOU WHO'S A PIRATE!!!

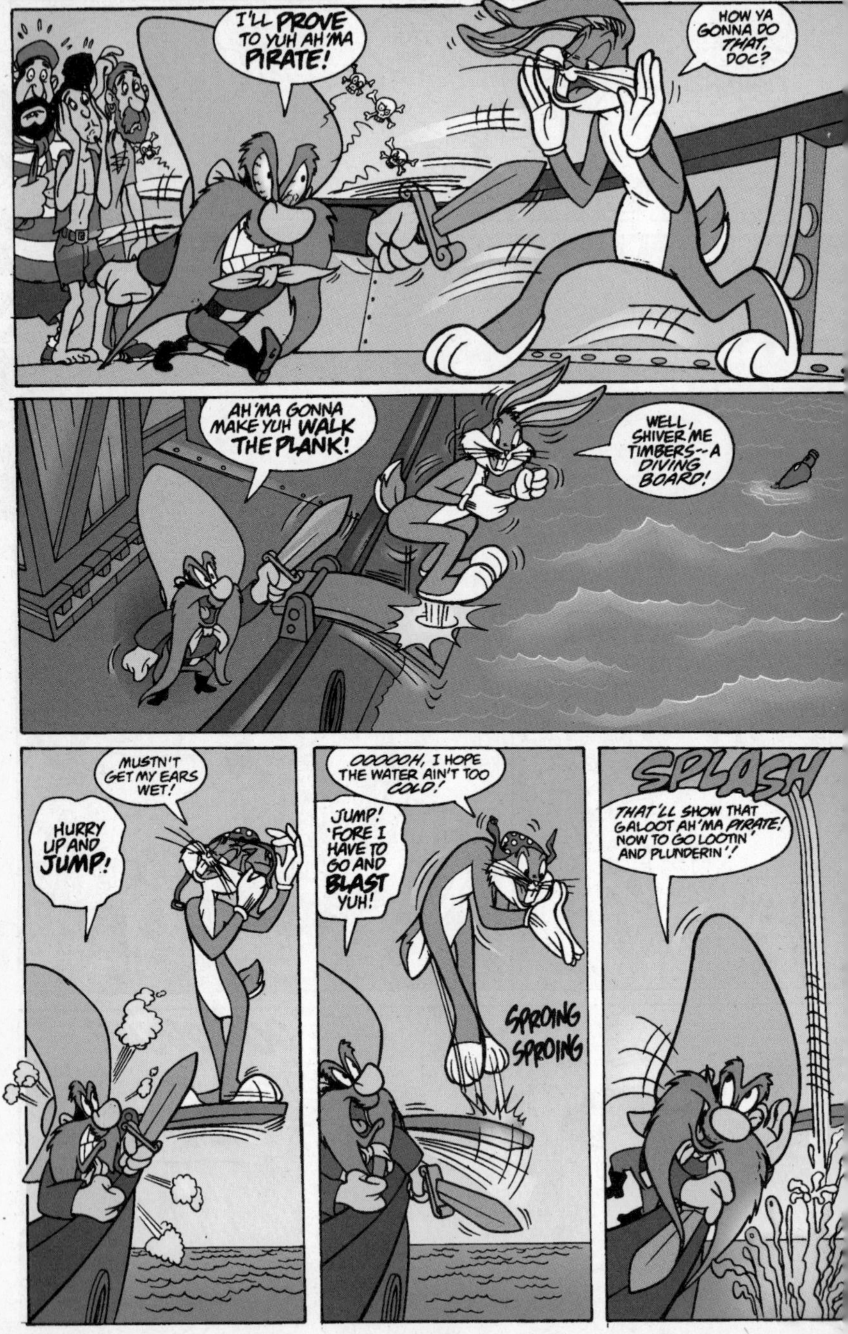
I'LL PROVE TO YUH AH'MA PIRATE!
HOW YA GONNA DO THAT, DOC?
AH'MA GONNA MAKE YUH WALK THE PLANK!
WELL, SHIVER ME TIMBERS--A DIVING BOARD!
MUSTN'T GET MY EARS WET!
HURRY UP AND JUMP!
OOOOOH, I HOPE THE WATER AIN'T TOO COLD!
JUMP! 'FORE I HAVE TO GO AND BLAST YUH!
SPROING SPROING
SPLASH
THAT'LL SHOW THAT GALOOT AH'MA PIRATE! NOW TO GO LOOTIN' AND PLUNDERIN'!

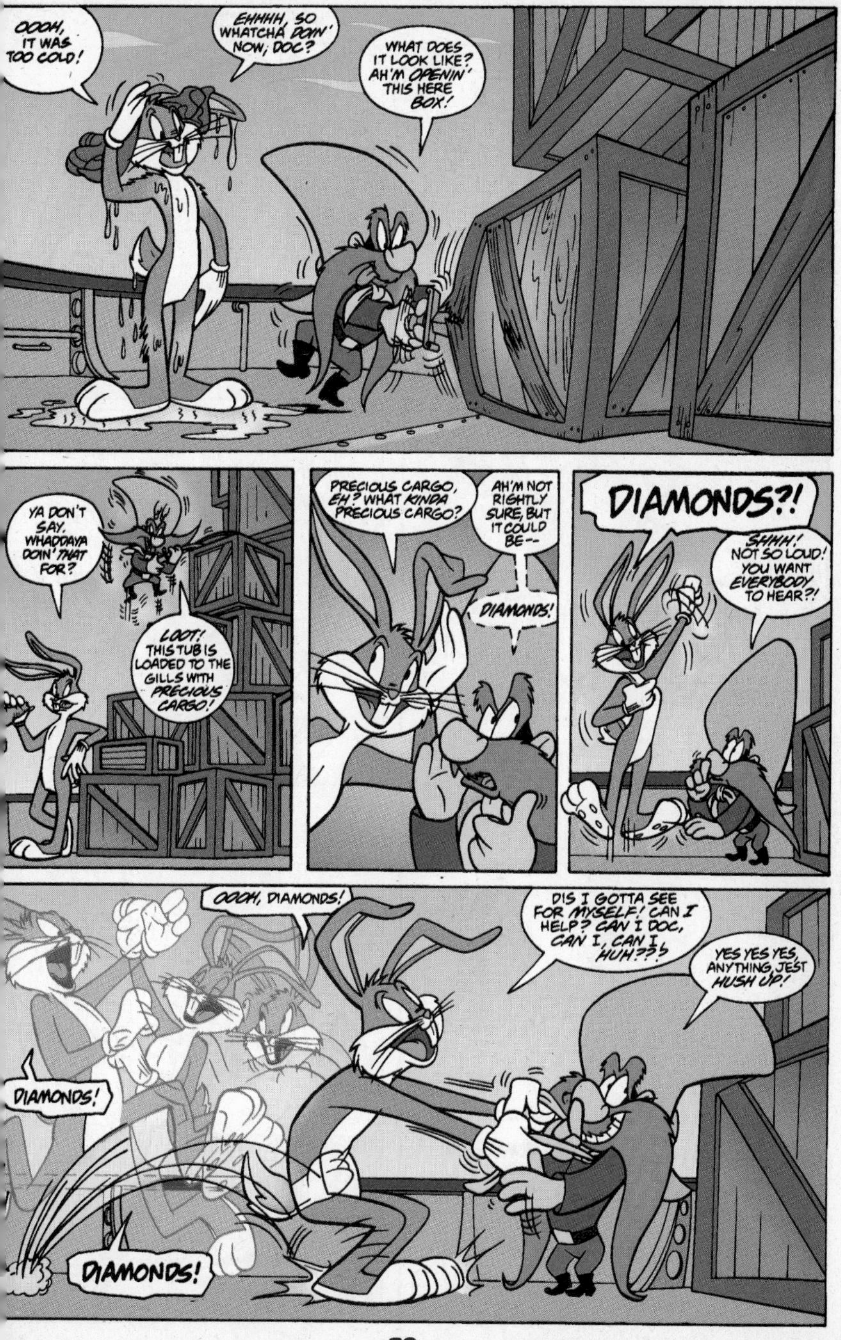
OOOH, IT WAS TOO COLD!
EHHHH, SO WHATCHA DOIN' NOW, DOC?
WHAT DOES IT LOOK LIKE? AH'M OPENIN' THIS HERE BOX!
YA DON'T SAY. WHADDAYA DOIN' THAT FOR?
LOOT! THIS TUB IS LOADED TO THE GILLS WITH PRECIOUS CARGO!
PRECIOUS CARGO, EH? WHAT KINDA PRECIOUS CARGO?
AH'M NOT RIGHTLY SURE, BUT IT COULD BE--
DIAMONDS!
DIAMONDS?!
SHHH! NOT SO LOUD! YOU WANT EVERYBODY TO HEAR?!
OOOH, DIAMONDS!
DIAMONDS!
DIAMONDS!
DIS I GOTTA SEE FOR MYSELF! CAN I HELP? CAN I DOC, CAN I, CAN I HUH???
YES YES YES, ANYTHING, JEST HUSH UP!

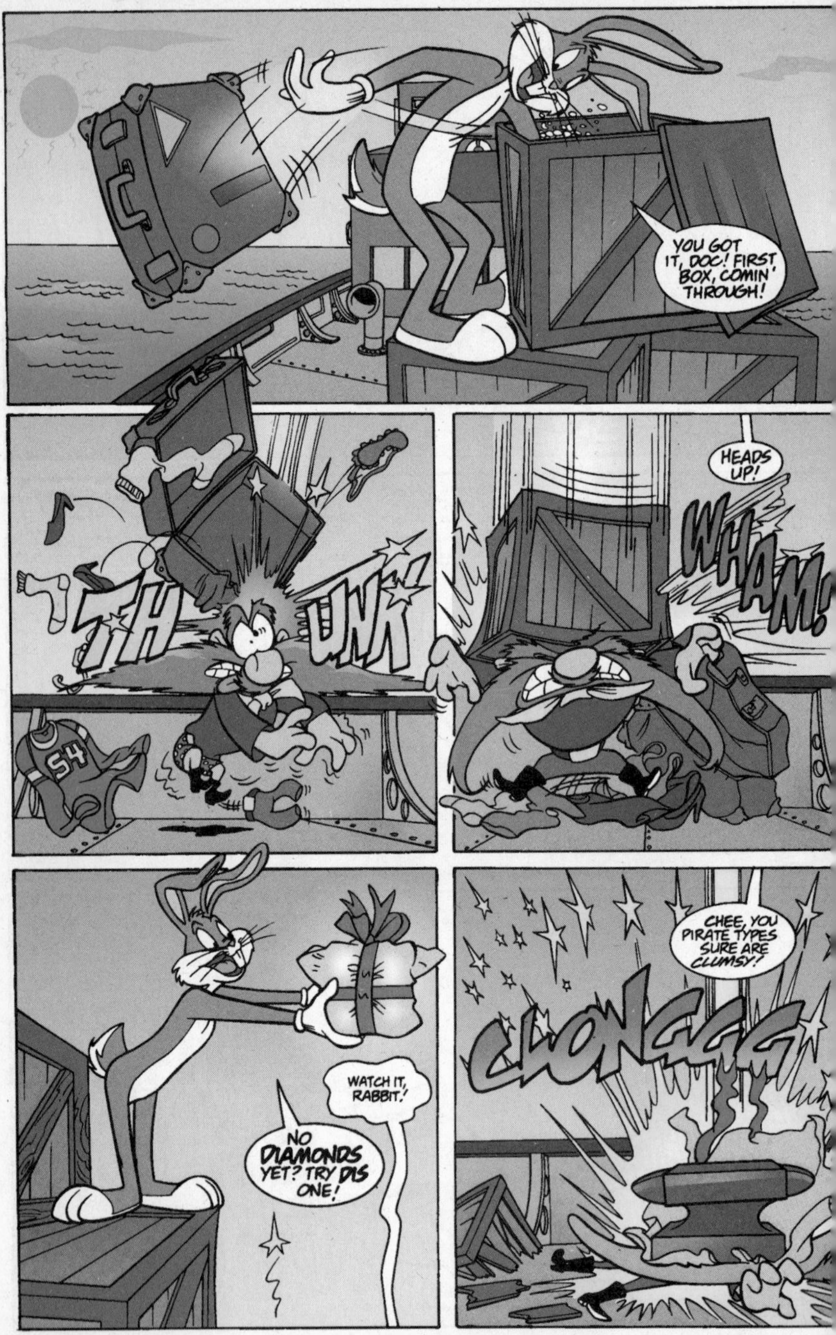
YOU GOT IT, DOC! FIRST BOX, COMIN' THROUGH!
THUNK!
HEADS UP!
WHAM!
NO DIAMONDS YET? TRY DIS ONE!
WATCH IT, RABBIT!
CHEE, YOU PIRATE TYPES SURE ARE CLUMSY!
CLONGGG

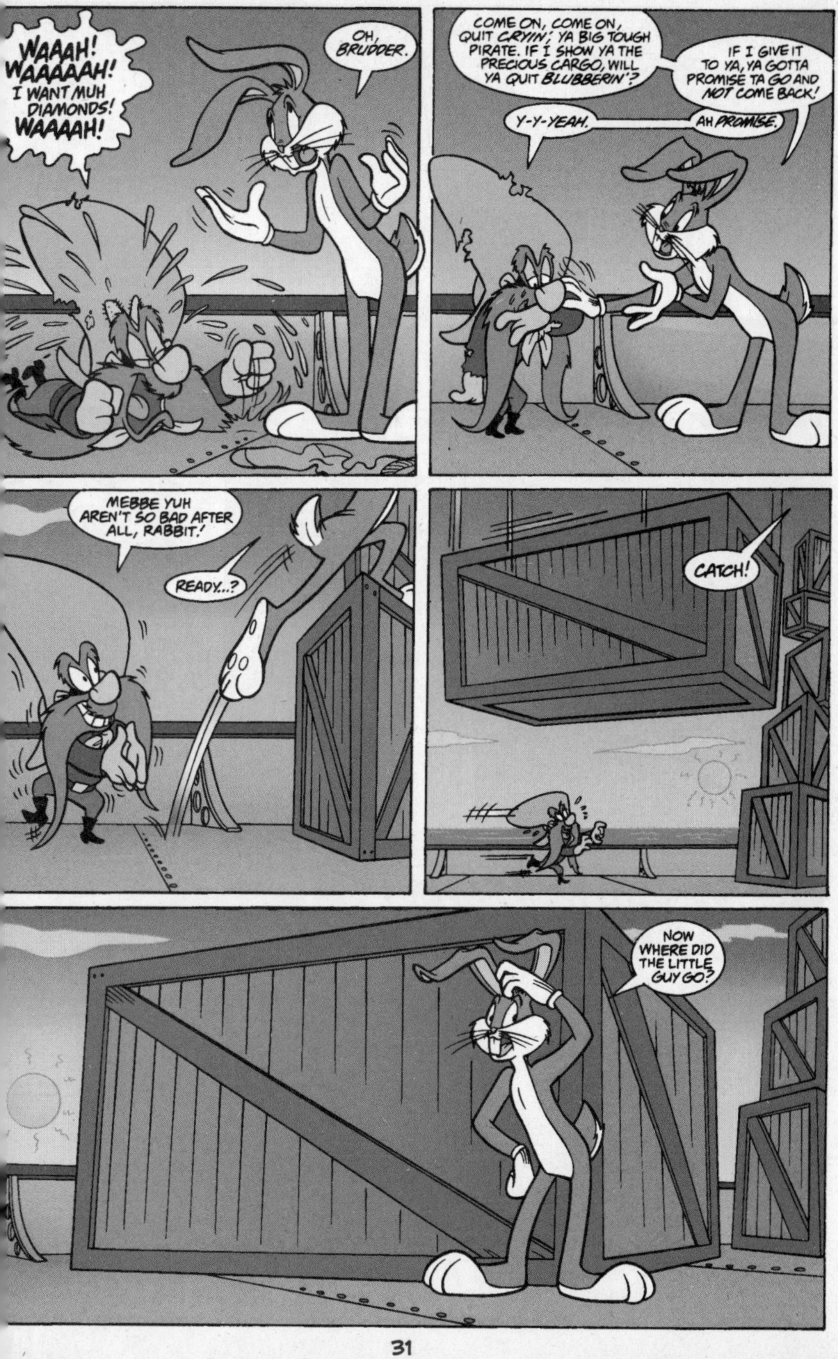
WAAAH! WAAAAAAH! I WANT MUH DIAMONDS! WAAAAH!
OH, BRUDDER.
COME ON, COME ON, QUIT CRYIN', YA BIG TOUGH PIRATE. IF I SHOW YA THE PRECIOUS CARGO, WILL YA QUIT BLUBBERIN'?
IF I GIVE IT TO YA, YA GOTTA PROMISE TA GO AND NOT COME BACK!
Y-Y-YEAH.
AH PROMISE.
MEBBE YUH AREN'T SO BAD AFTER ALL, RABBIT!
READY...?
CATCH!
NOW WHERE DID THE LITTLE GUY GO?

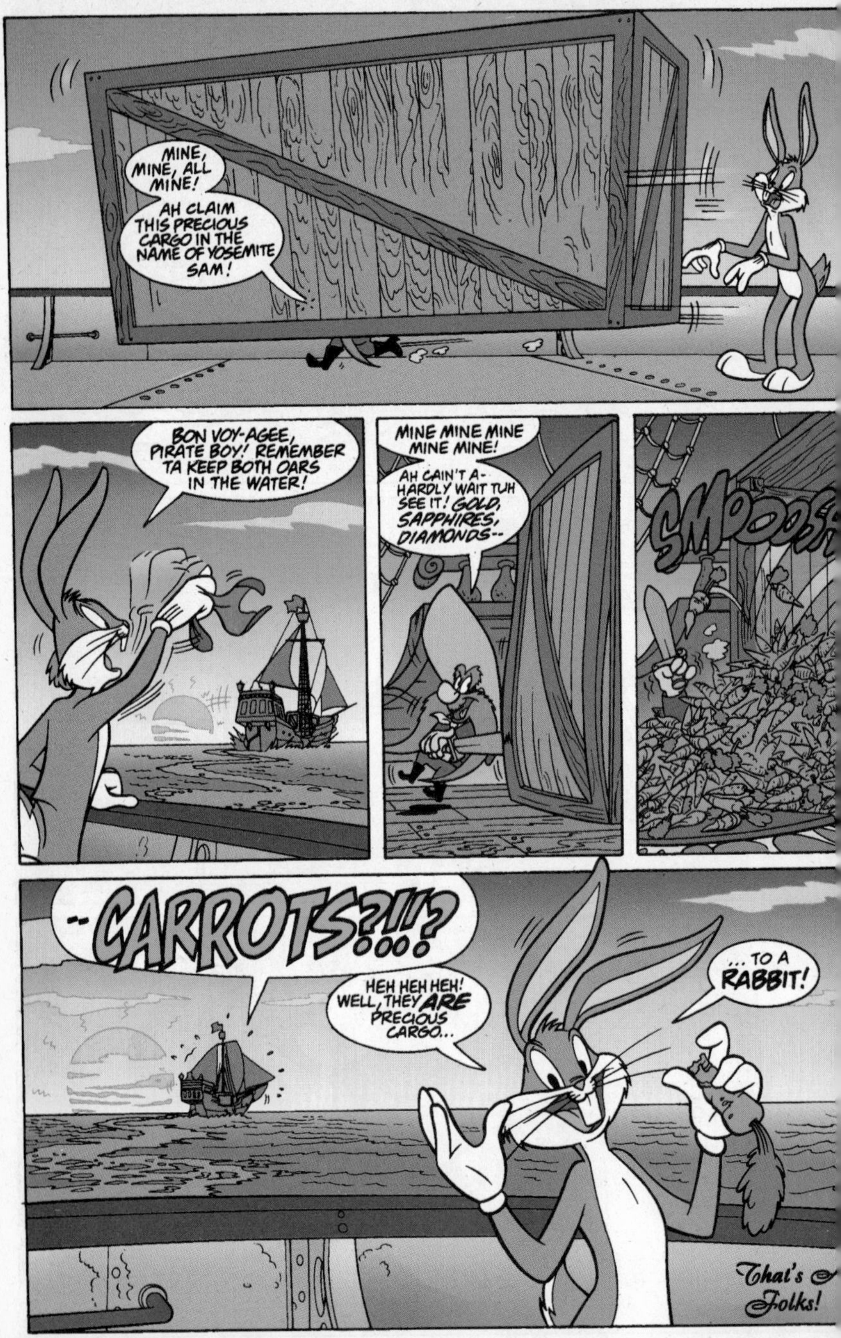

MINE, MINE, ALL MINE!
AH CLAIM THIS PRECIOUS CARGO IN THE NAME OF YOSEMITE SAM!
BON VOY-AGEE, PIRATE BOY! REMEMBER TA KEEP BOTH OARS IN THE WATER!
MINE MINE MINE MINE MINE!
AH CAIN'T A-HARDLY WAIT TUH SEE IT! GOLD, SAPPHIRES, DIAMONDS--
SMOOOSH
--CARROTS?!!?
HEH HEH HEH! WELL, THEY ARE PRECIOUS CARGO...
...TO A RABBIT!
That's All Folks!

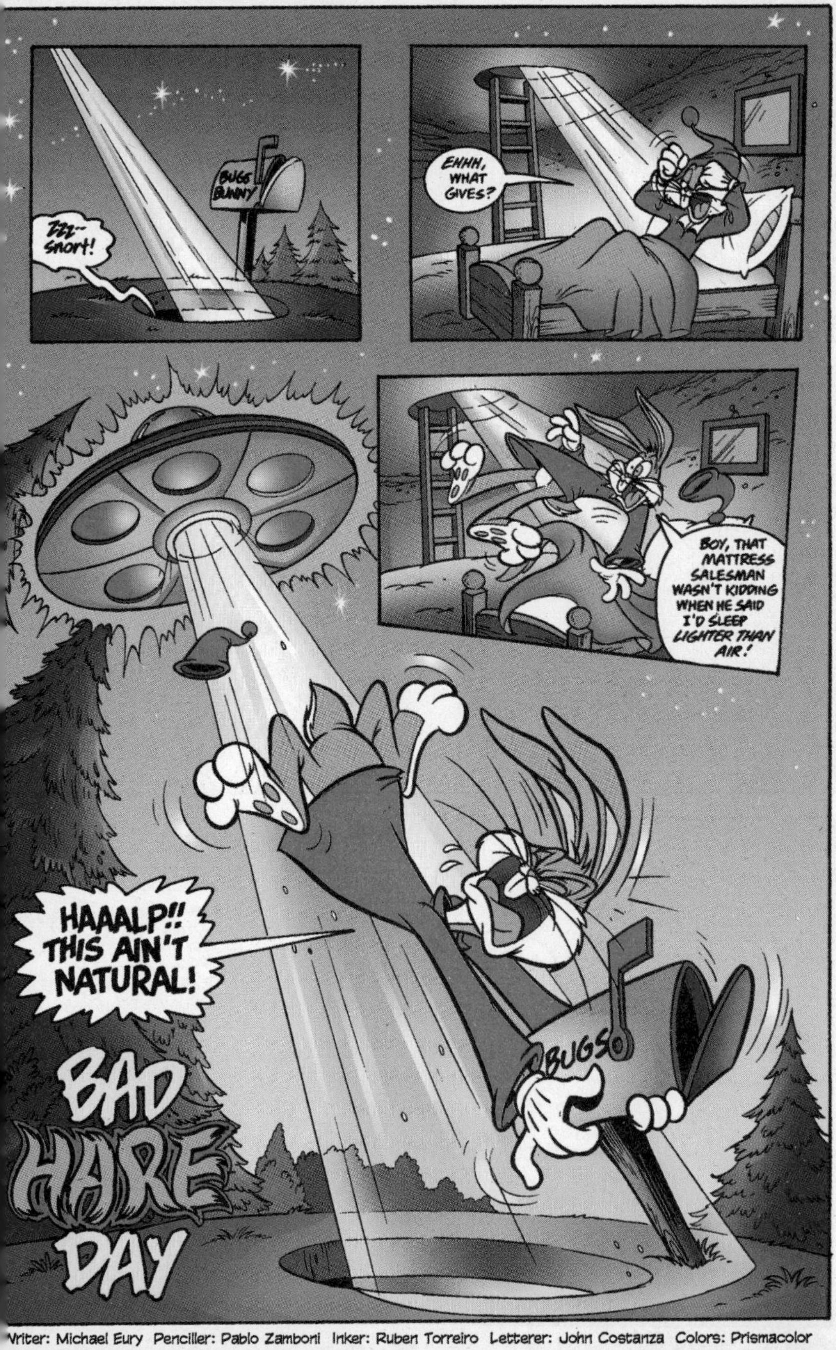
BUGS BUNNY
Zzz-- snort!
EHHH, WHAT GIVES?
BOY, THAT MATTRESS SALESMAN WASN'T KIDDING WHEN HE SAID I'D SLEEP LIGHTER THAN AIR!
HAAALP!! THIS AIN'T NATURAL!
BAD HARE DAY
BUGS

Writer: Michael Eury Penciller: Pablo Zamboni Inker: Ruben Torreiro Letterer: John Costanza Colors: Prismacolor

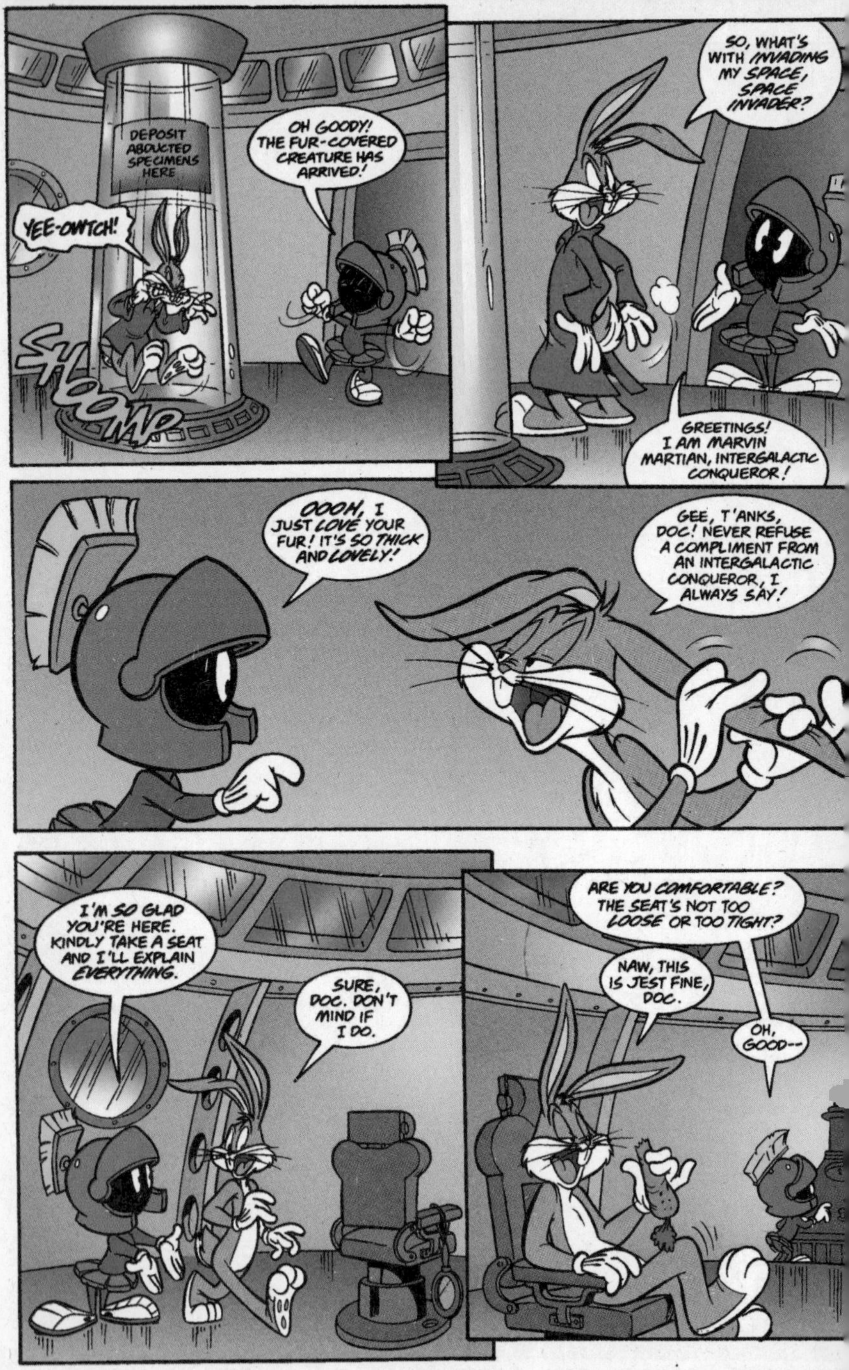
DEPOSIT ABDUCTED SPECIMENS HERE
YEE-OWTCH!
SHOOMP
OH GOODY! THE FUR-COVERED CREATURE HAS ARRIVED!
SO, WHAT'S WITH INVADING MY SPACE, SPACE INVADER?
GREETINGS! I AM MARVIN MARTIAN, INTERGALACTIC CONQUEROR!
OOOH, I JUST LOVE YOUR FUR! IT'S SO THICK AND LOVELY!
GEE, T'ANKS, DOC! NEVER REFUSE A COMPLIMENT FROM AN INTERGALACTIC CONQUEROR, I ALWAYS SAY!
I'M SO GLAD YOU'RE HERE. KINDLY TAKE A SEAT AND I'LL EXPLAIN EVERYTHING.
SURE, DOC. DON'T MIND IF I DO.
ARE YOU COMFORTABLE? THE SEAT'S NOT TOO LOOSE OR TOO TIGHT?
NAW, THIS IS JEST FINE, DOC.
OH, GOOD--

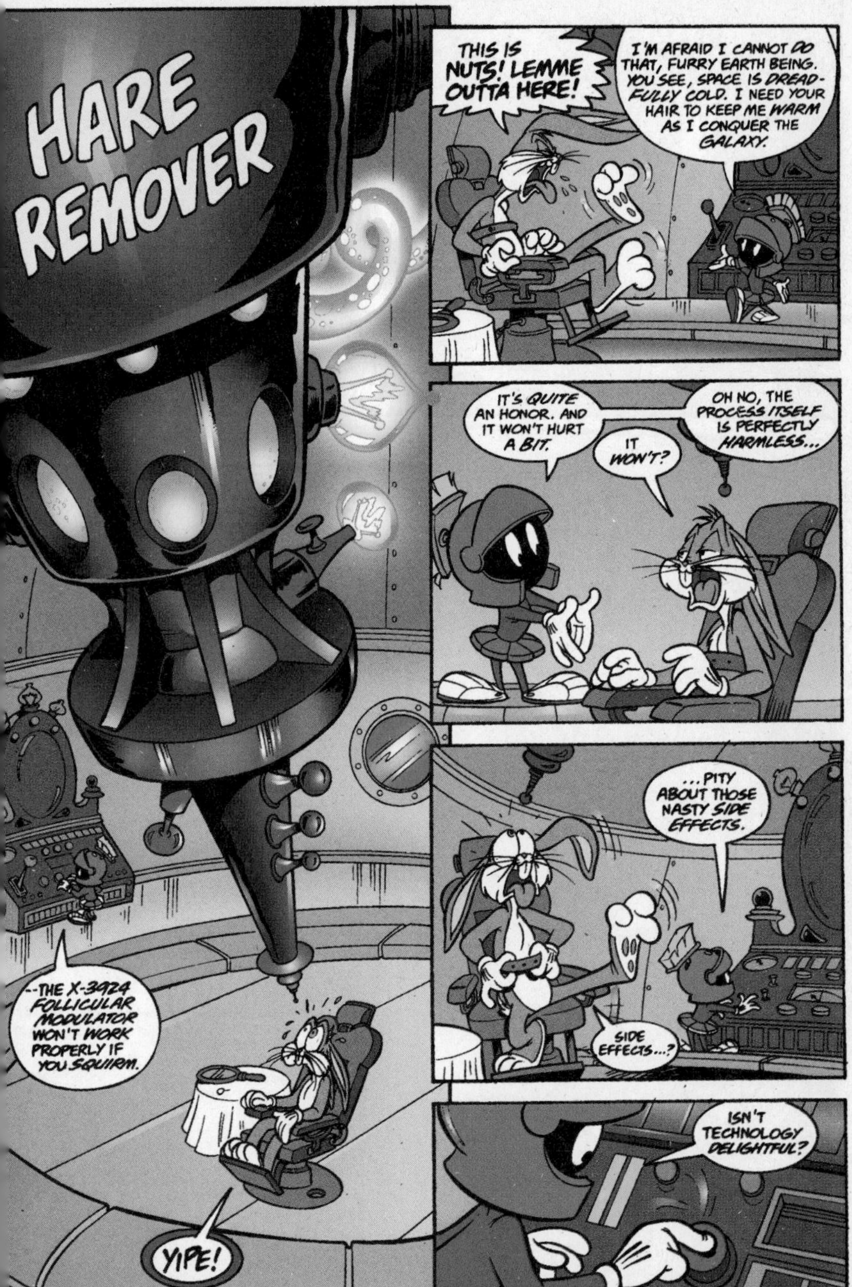
HARE REMOVER
THIS IS NUTS! LEMME OUTTA HERE!
I'M AFRAID I CANNOT DO THAT, FURRY EARTH BEING. YOU SEE, SPACE IS DREAD-FULLY COLD. I NEED YOUR HAIR TO KEEP ME WARM AS I CONQUER THE GALAXY.
IT'S QUITE AN HONOR. AND IT WON'T HURT A BIT.
IT WON'T?
OH NO, THE PROCESS ITSELF IS PERFECTLY HARMLESS...
...PITY ABOUT THOSE NASTY SIDE EFFECTS.
SIDE EFFECTS...?
ISN'T TECHNOLOGY DELIGHTFUL?
--THE X-3924 FOLLICULAR MODULATOR WON'T WORK PROPERLY IF YOU SQUIRM.
YIPE!

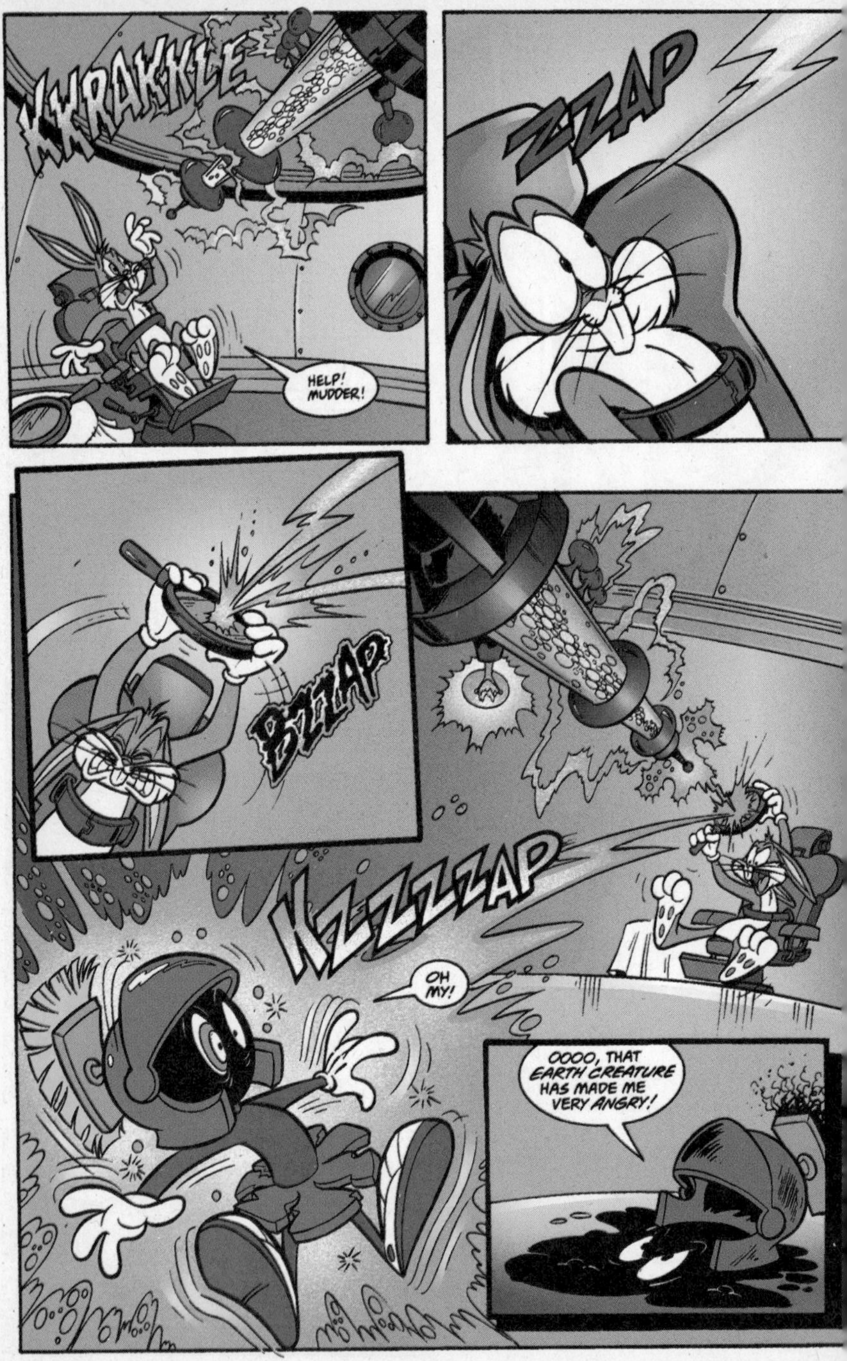
KKRAKKLE
HELP! MUDDER!
ZZAP
BZZAP
KZZZZZAP
OH MY!
OOOO, THAT EARTH CREATURE HAS MADE ME VERY ANGRY!

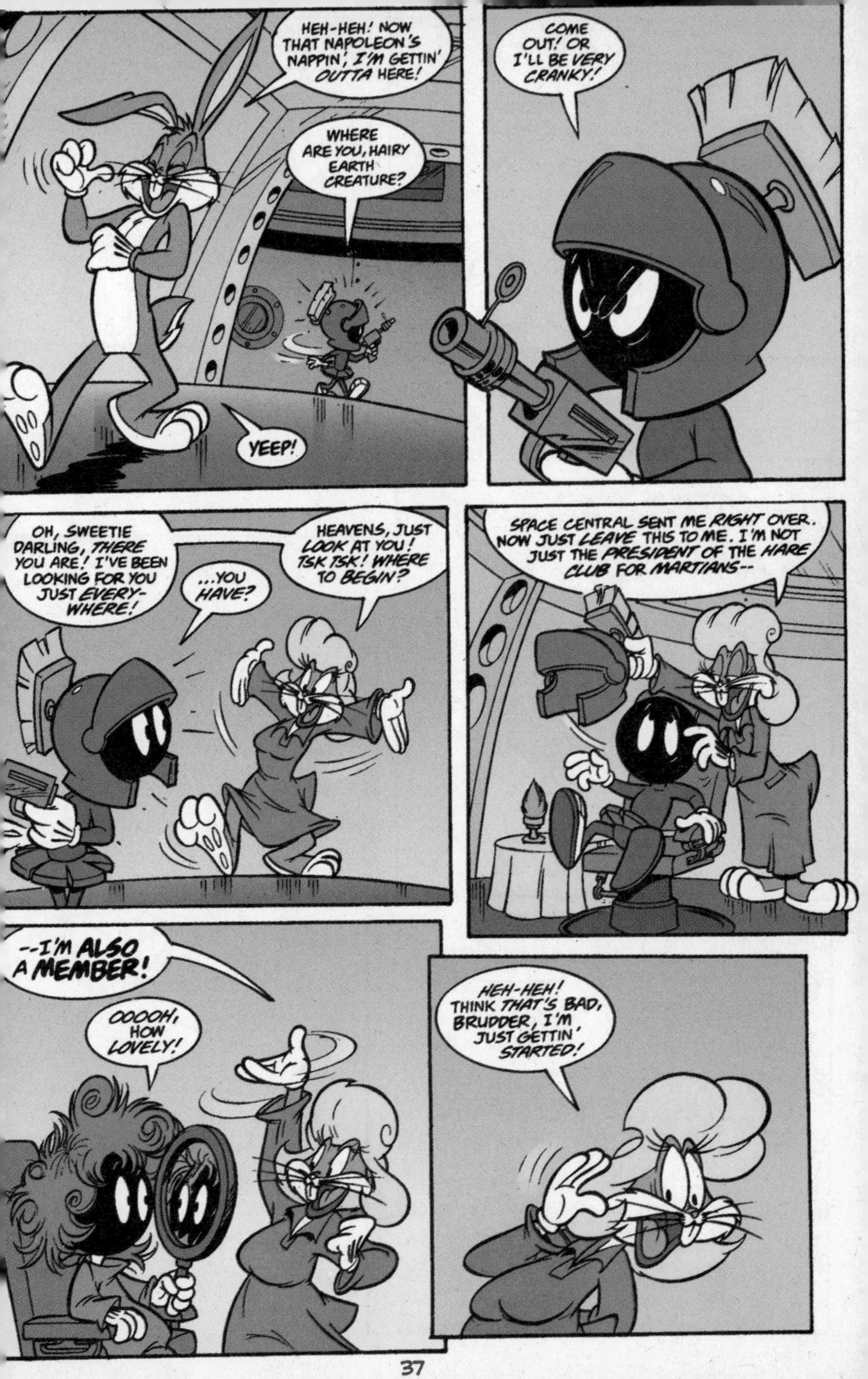
HEH-HEH! NOW THAT NAPOLEON'S NAPPIN', I'M GETTIN' OUTTA HERE!
WHERE ARE YOU, HAIRY EARTH CREATURE?
YEEP!
COME OUT! OR I'LL BE VERY CRANKY!
OH, SWEETIE DARLING, THERE YOU ARE! I'VE BEEN LOOKING FOR YOU JUST EVERY-WHERE!
...YOU HAVE?
HEAVENS, JUST LOOK AT YOU! TSK TSK! WHERE TO BEGIN?
SPACE CENTRAL SENT ME RIGHT OVER. NOW JUST LEAVE THIS TO ME. I'M NOT JUST THE PRESIDENT OF THE HARE CLUB FOR MARTIANS--
--I'M ALSO A MEMBER!
OOOOH, HOW LOVELY!
HEH-HEH! THINK THAT'S BAD, BRUDDER, I'M JUST GETTIN' STARTED!

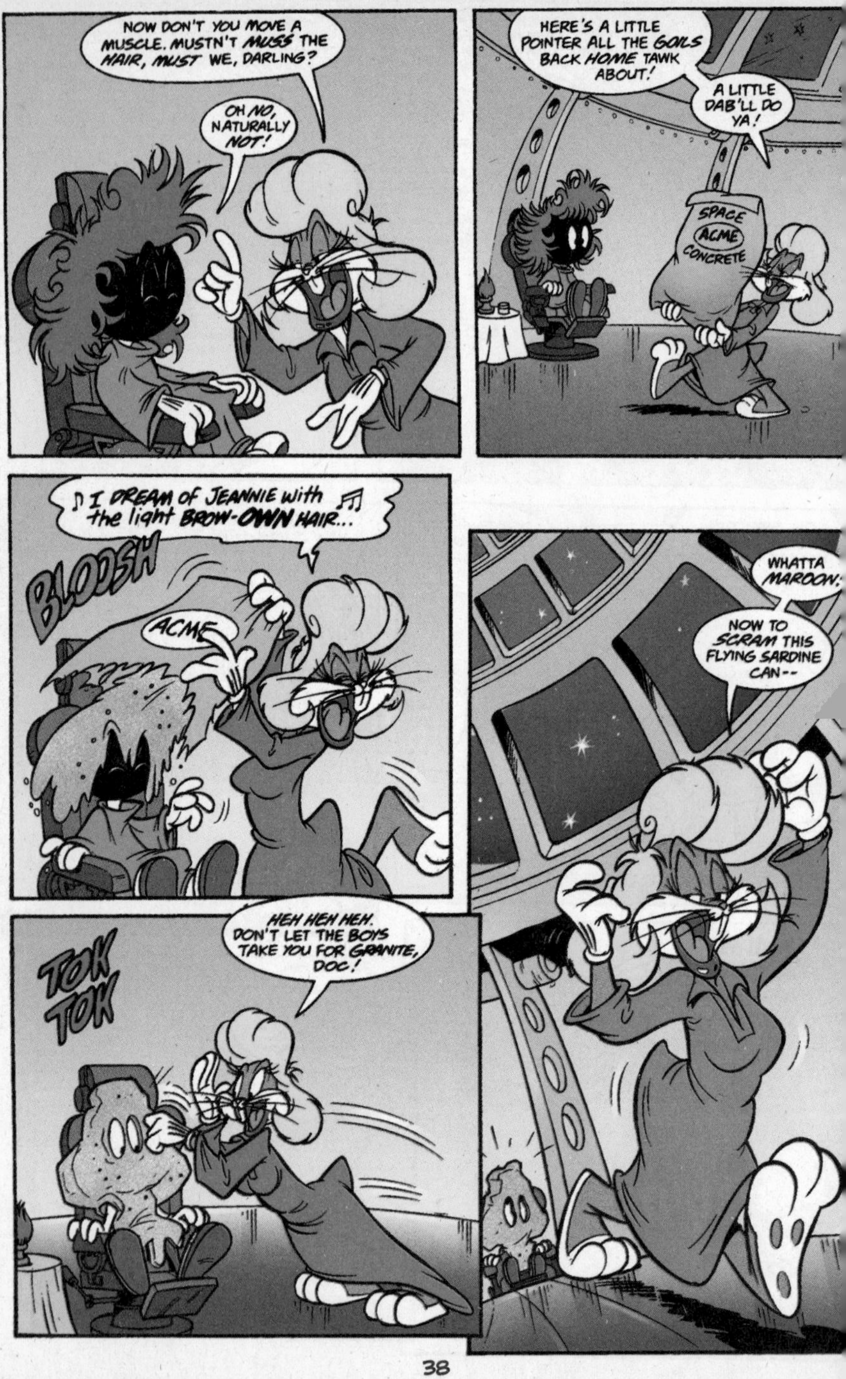

NOW DON'T YOU MOVE A MUSCLE. MUSTN'T MUSS THE HAIR, MUST WE, DARLING?
OH NO, NATURALLY NOT!
HERE'S A LITTLE POINTER ALL THE GOILS BACK HOME TAWK ABOUT!
A LITTLE DAB'LL DO YA!
SPACE ACME CONCRETE
♪ I DREAM of JEANNIE with the light BROW-OWN HAIR... ♫
BLOOSH
ACME
WHATTA MAROON!
NOW TO SCRAM THIS FLYING SARDINE CAN--
HEH HEH HEH. DON'T LET THE BOYS TAKE YOU FOR GRANITE, DOC!
TOK TOK

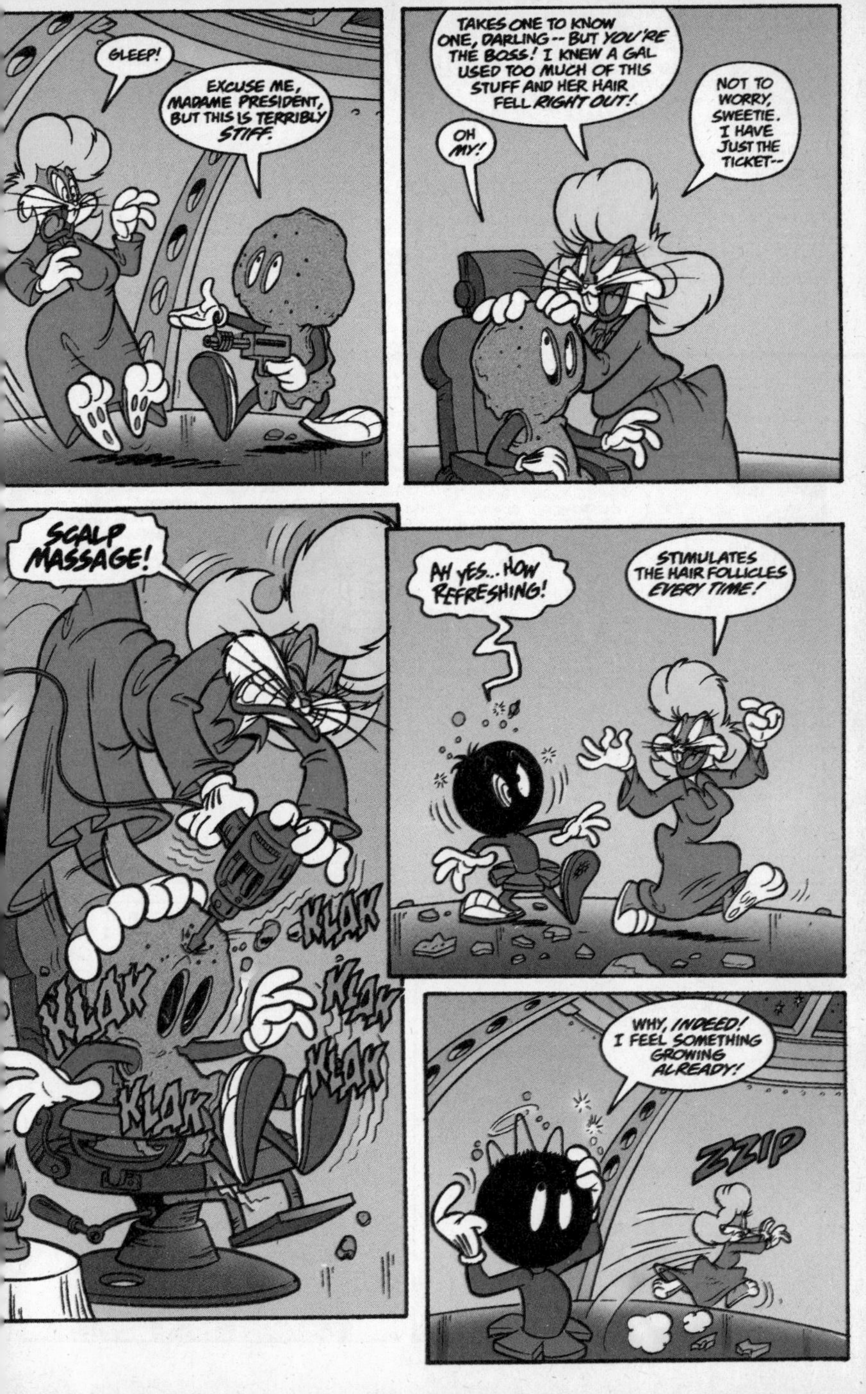
GLEEP!
EXCUSE ME, MADAME PRESIDENT, BUT THIS IS TERRIBLY STIFF.
TAKES ONE TO KNOW ONE, DARLING -- BUT YOU'RE THE BOSS! I KNEW A GAL USED TOO MUCH OF THIS STUFF AND HER HAIR FELL RIGHT OUT!
OH MY!
NOT TO WORRY, SWEETIE. I HAVE JUST THE TICKET--
SCALP MASSAGE!
KLAK
KLAK
KLAK
KLAK
KLAK
AH YES... HOW REFRESHING!
STIMULATES THE HAIR FOLLICLES EVERY TIME!
WHY, INDEED! I FEEL SOMETHING GROWING ALREADY!
ZZIP

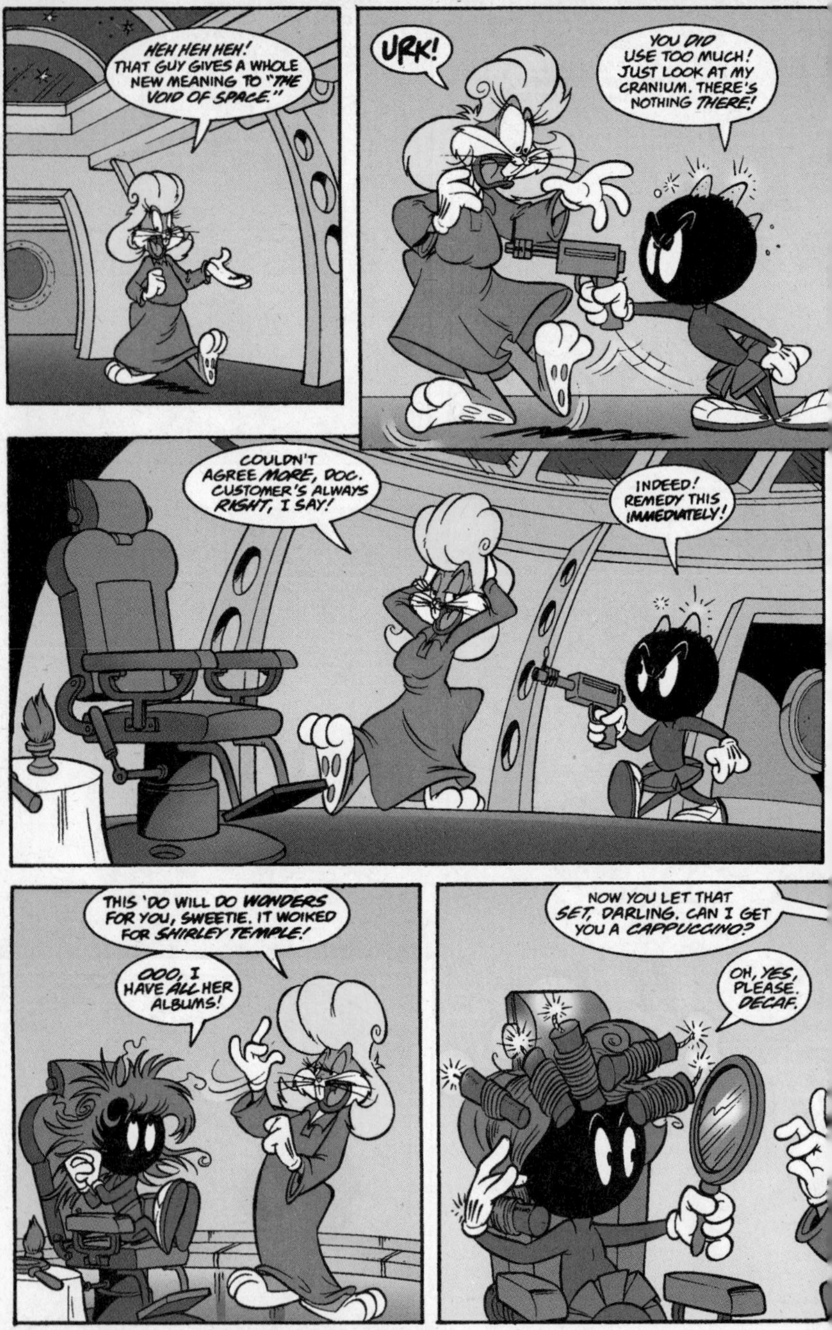
HEH HEH HEH! THAT GUY GIVES A WHOLE NEW MEANING TO "THE VOID OF SPACE."
URK!
YOU DID USE TOO MUCH! JUST LOOK AT MY CRANIUM. THERE'S NOTHING THERE!
COULDN'T AGREE MORE, DOC. CUSTOMER'S ALWAYS RIGHT, I SAY!
INDEED! REMEDY THIS IMMEDIATELY!
THIS 'DO WILL DO WONDERS FOR YOU, SWEETIE. IT WOIKED FOR SHIRLEY TEMPLE!
OOO, I HAVE ALL HER ALBUMS!
NOW YOU LET THAT SET, DARLING. CAN I GET YOU A CAPPUCCINO?
OH, YES, PLEASE. DECAF.

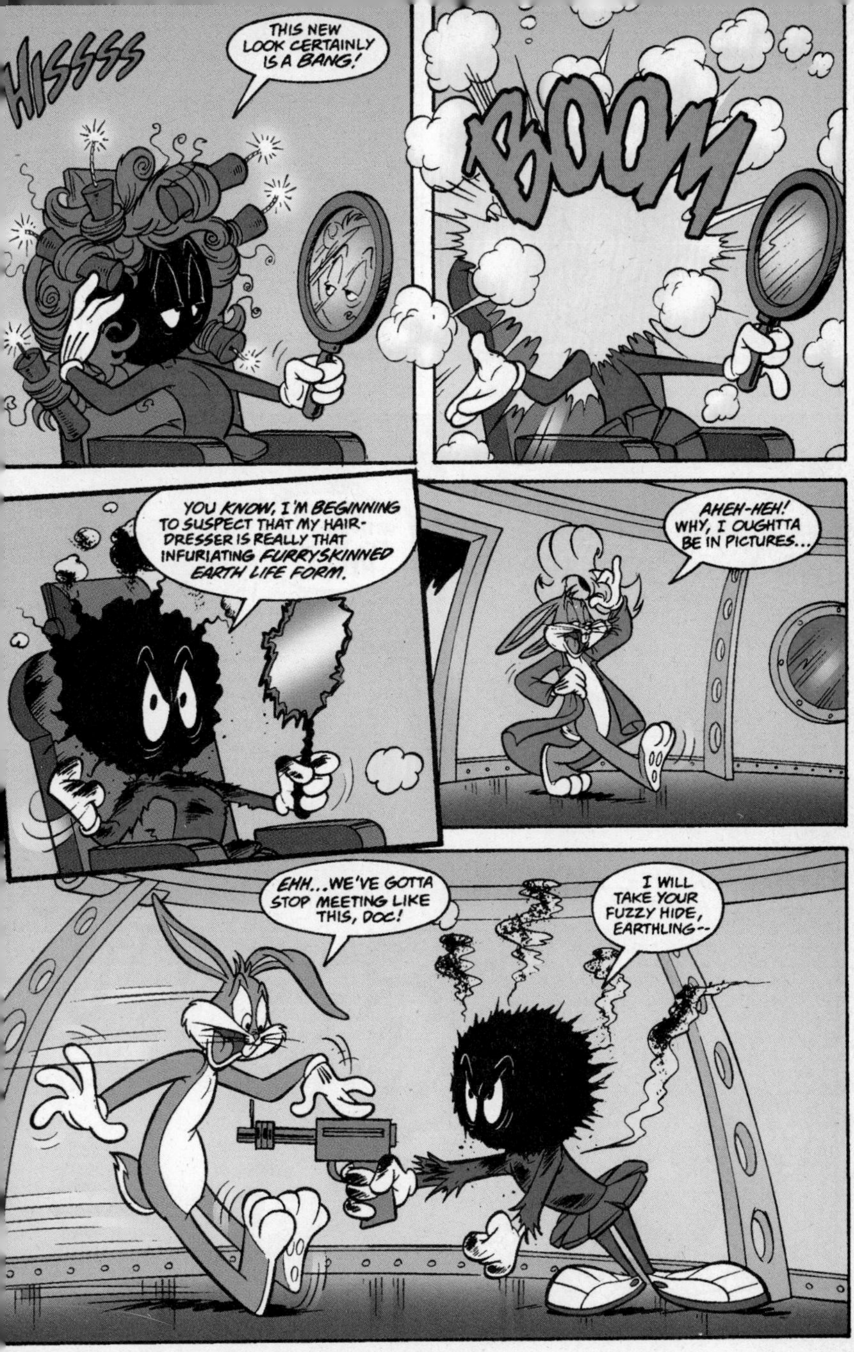
HISSSSS
THIS NEW LOOK CERTAINLY IS A BANG!
BOOM
YOU KNOW, I'M BEGINNING TO SUSPECT THAT MY HAIR-DRESSER IS REALLY THAT INFURIATING FURRYSKINNED EARTH LIFE FORM.
AHEH-HEH! WHY, I OUGHTTA BE IN PICTURES...
EHH...WE'VE GOTTA STOP MEETING LIKE THIS, DOC!
I WILL TAKE YOUR FUZZY HIDE, EARTHLING--

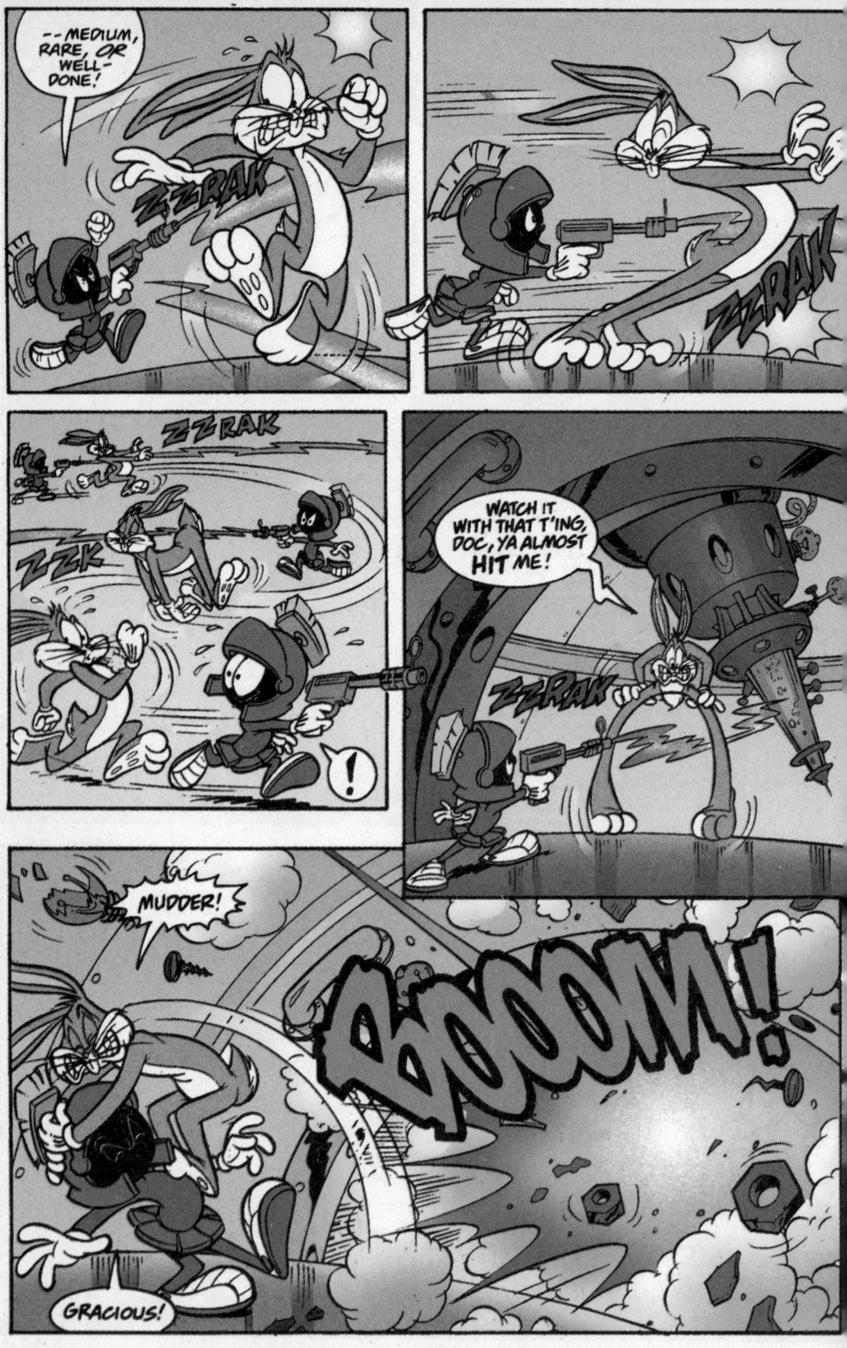
--MEDIUM, RARE, OR WELL-DONE!
ZZRAK
ZZRAK
ZZRAK
ZZK
!
WATCH IT WITH THAT T'ING, DOC, YA ALMOST HIT ME!
ZZRAK
MUDDER!
BOOOOM!
GRACIOUS!

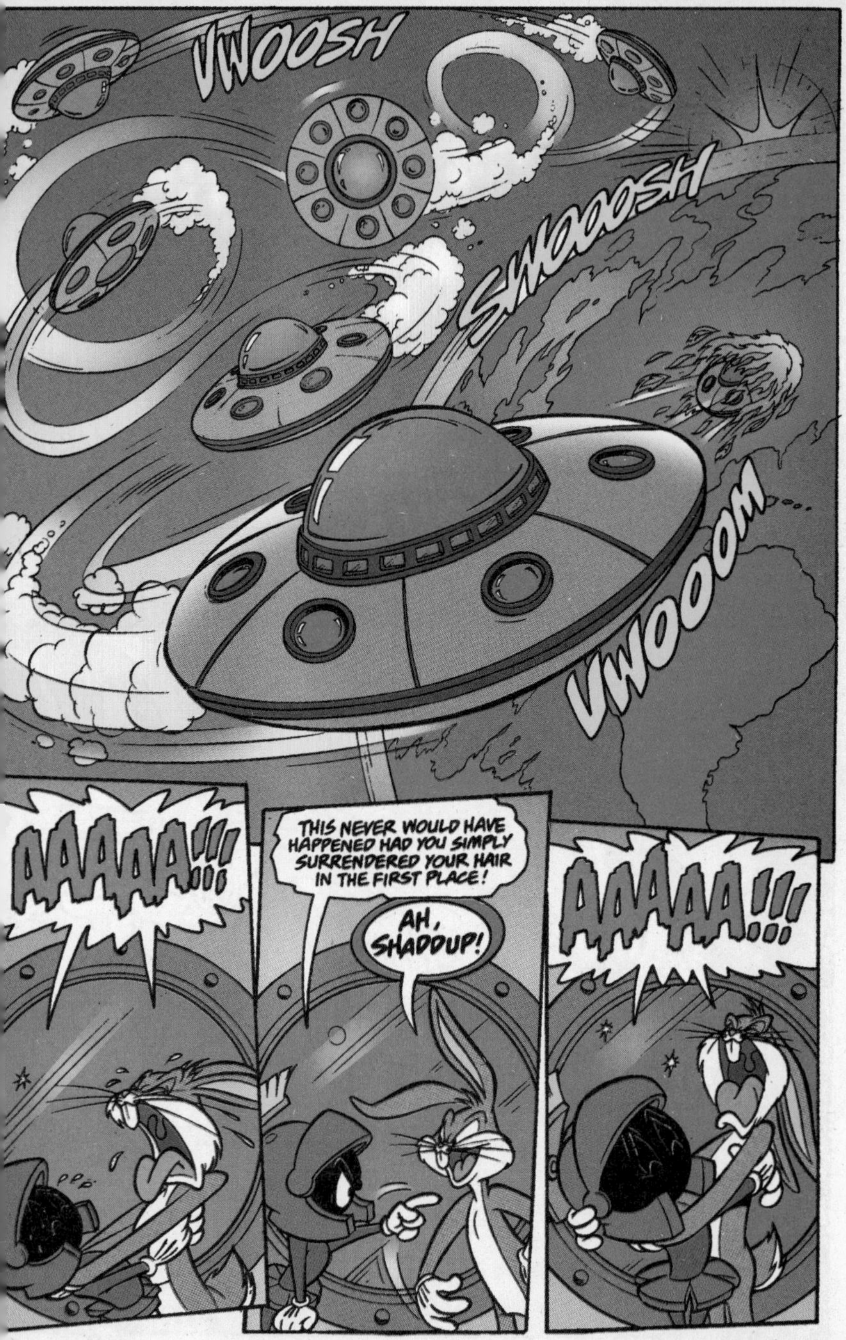
VWOOSH
SHOOOSH
VWOOOM
AAAAA!!!
THIS NEVER WOULD HAVE HAPPENED HAD YOU SIMPLY SURRENDERED YOUR HAIR IN THE FIRST PLACE!
AH, SHADDUP!
AAAAA!!!

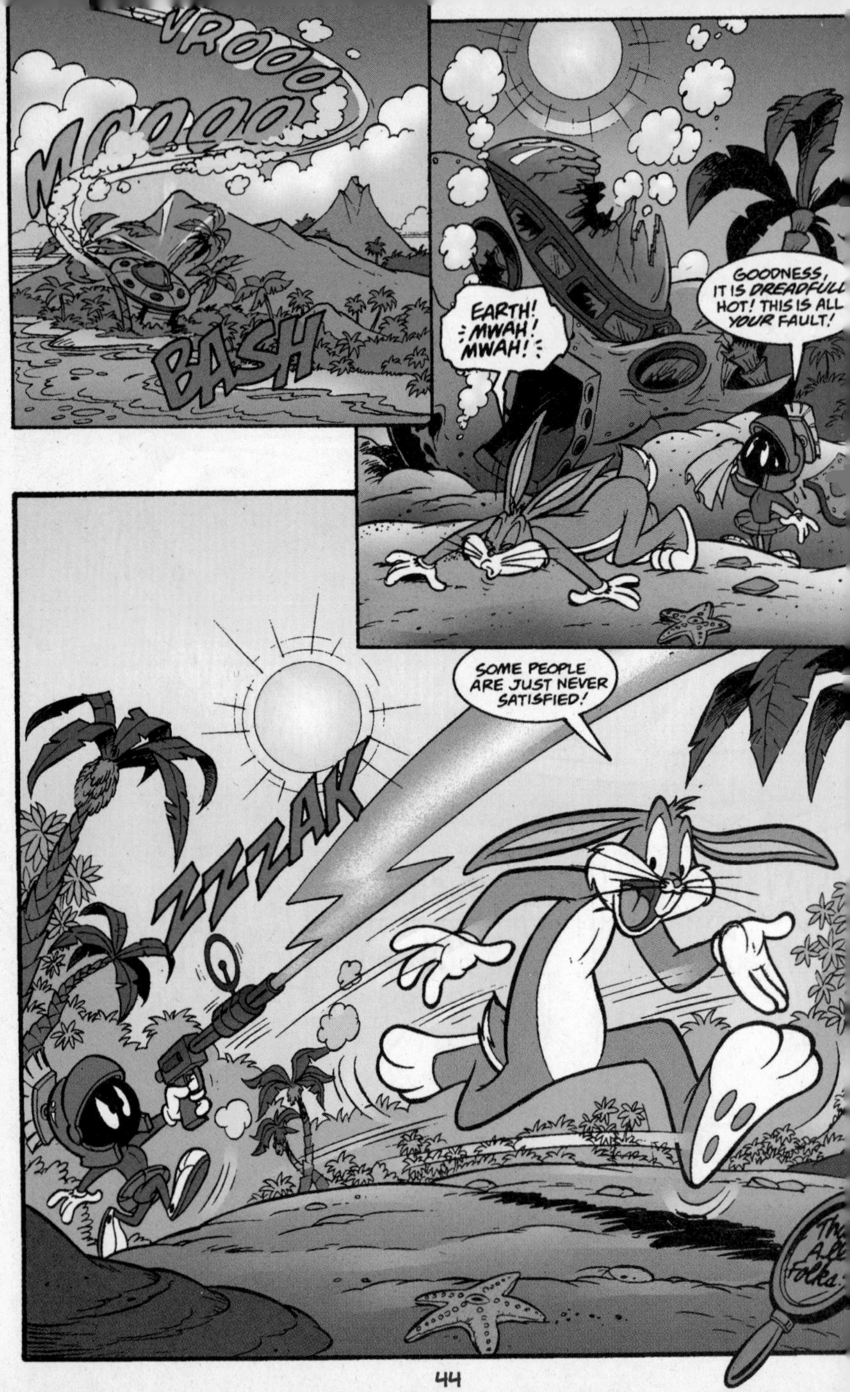
VROOOO
MOOOOO
BASH
EARTH! MWAH! MWAH!
GOODNESS, IT IS DREADFULL HOT! THIS IS ALL YOUR FAULT!
SOME PEOPLE ARE JUST NEVER SATISFIED!
ZZZZAK

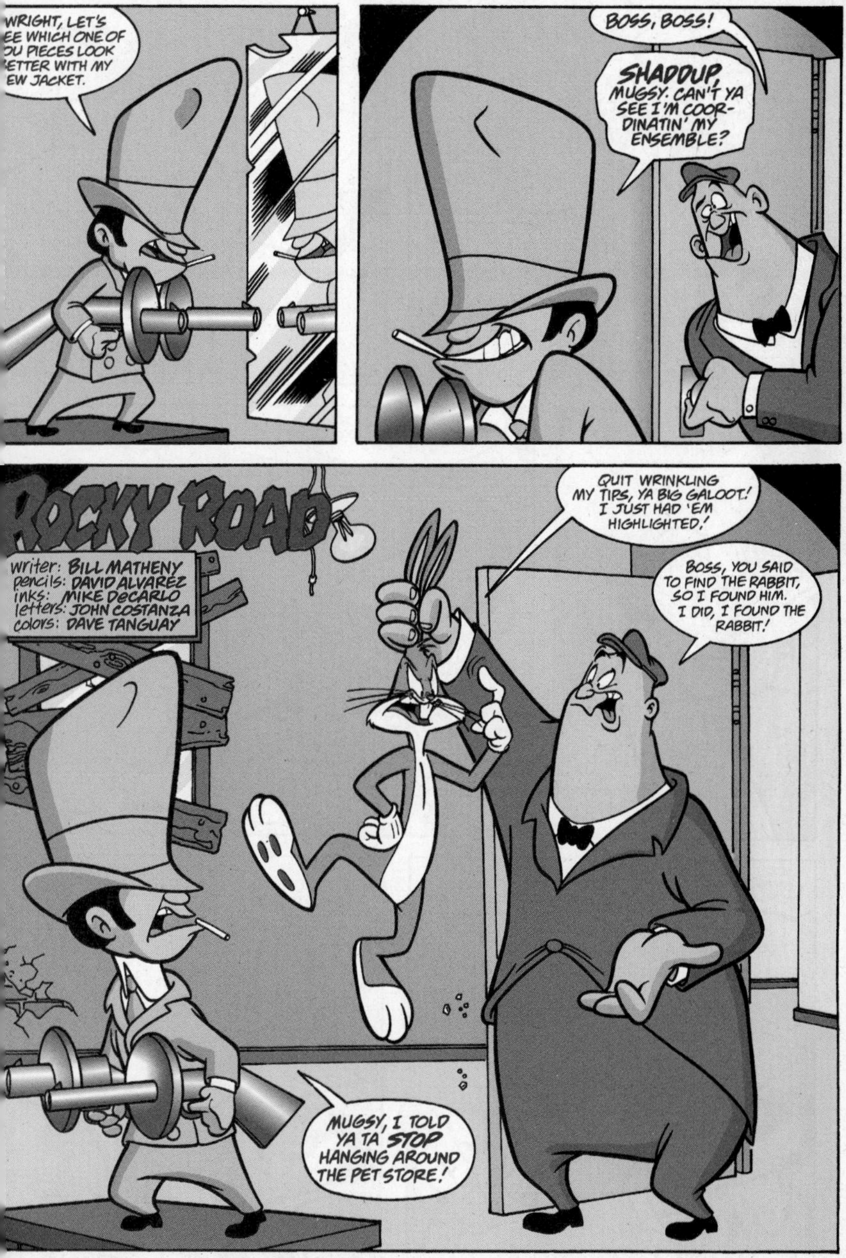
WRIGHT, LET'S
EE WHICH ONE OF
OU PIECES LOOK
ETTER WITH MY
EW JACKET.
BOSS, BOSS!
SHADDUP, MUGSY. CAN'T YA SEE I'M COOR-DINATIN' MY ENSEMBLE?
ROCKY ROAD
writer: BILL MATHENY
pencils: DAVID ALVAREZ
inks: MIKE DeCARLO
letters: JOHN COSTANZA
colors: DAVE TANGUAY
QUIT WRINKLING MY TIPS, YA BIG GALOOT! I JUST HAD 'EM HIGHLIGHTED!
BOSS, YOU SAID TO FIND THE RABBIT, SO I FOUND HIM. I DID, I FOUND THE RABBIT!
MUGSY, I TOLD YA TA' STOP HANGING AROUND THE PET STORE!

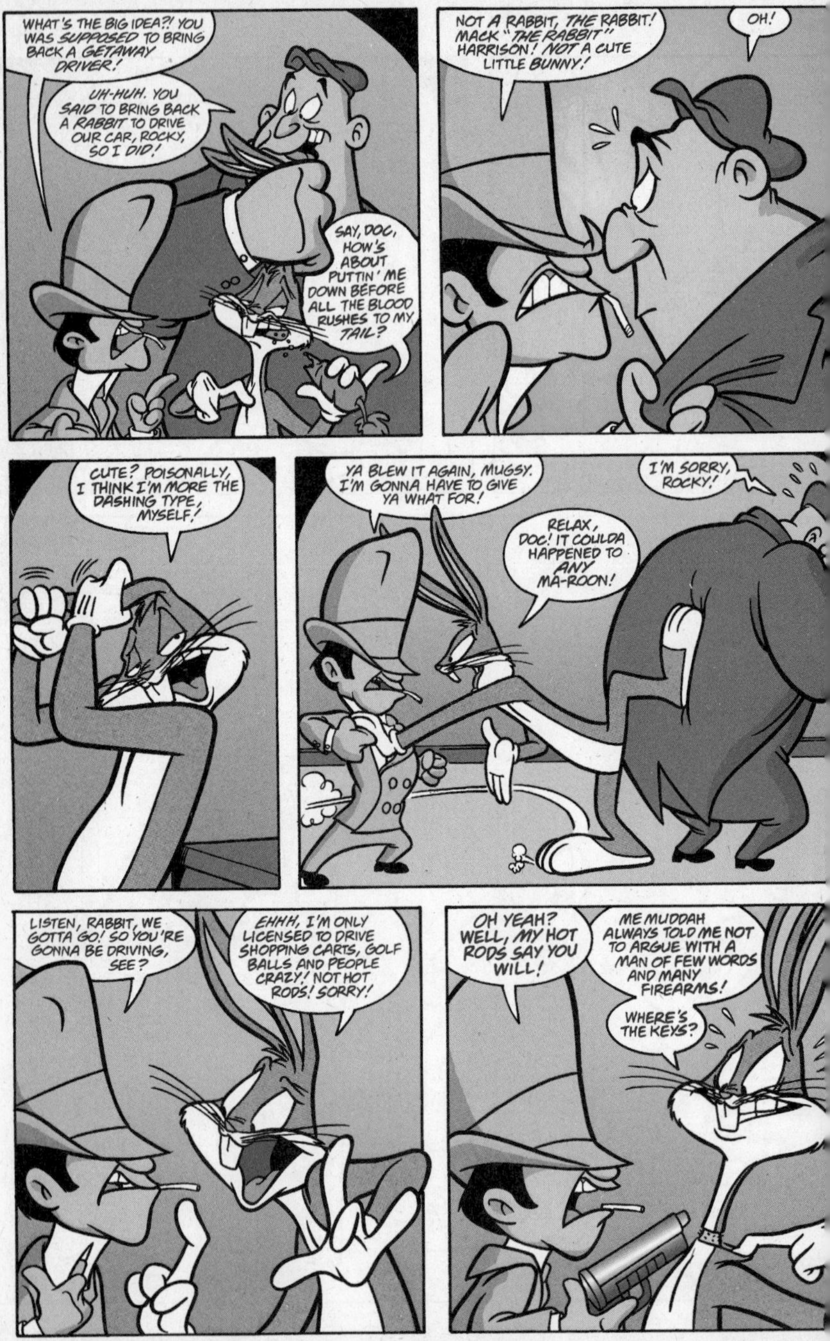
WHAT'S THE BIG IDEA?! YOU WAS SUPPOSED TO BRING BACK A GETAWAY DRIVER!
UH-HUH. YOU SAID TO BRING BACK A RABBIT TO DRIVE OUR CAR, ROCKY, SO I DID!
SAY, DOC, HOW'S ABOUT PUTTIN' ME DOWN BEFORE ALL THE BLOOD RUSHES TO MY TAIL?
NOT A RABBIT, THE RABBIT! MACK "THE RABBIT" HARRISON! NOT A CUTE LITTLE BUNNY!
OH!
CUTE? POISONALLY, I THINK I'M MORE THE DASHING TYPE, MYSELF!
YA BLEW IT AGAIN, MUGSY. I'M GONNA HAVE TO GIVE YA WHAT FOR!
I'M SORRY, ROCKY!
RELAX, DOC! IT COULDA HAPPENED TO ANY MA-ROON!
LISTEN, RABBIT, WE GOTTA GO! SO YOU'RE GONNA BE DRIVING, SEE?
EHHH, I'M ONLY LICENSED TO DRIVE SHOPPING CARTS, GOLF BALLS AND PEOPLE CRAZY! NOT HOT RODS! SORRY!
OH YEAH? WELL, MY HOT RODS SAY YOU WILL!
ME MUDDAH ALWAYS TOLD ME NOT TO ARGUE WITH A MAN OF FEW WORDS AND MANY FIREARMS!
WHERE'S THE KEYS?

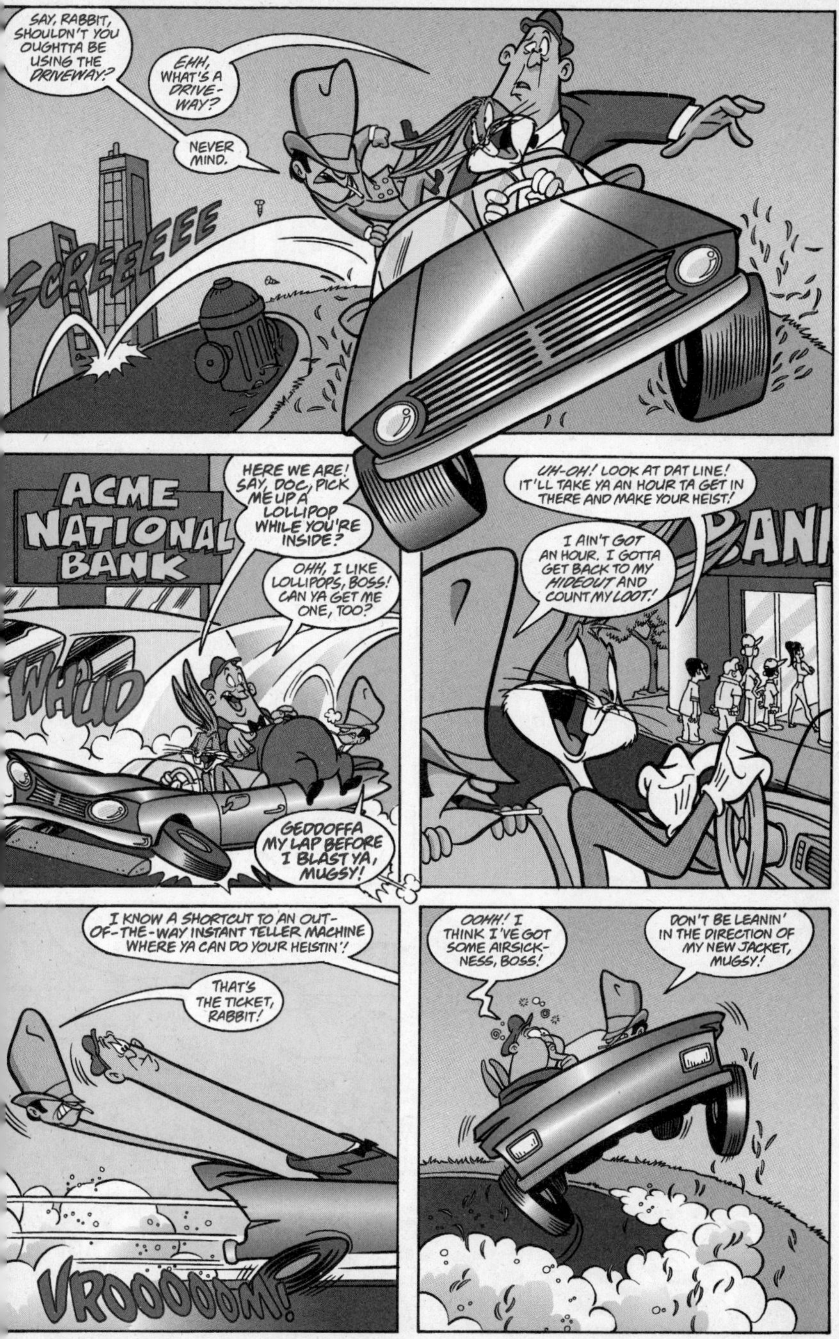
SAY, RABBIT, SHOULDN'T YOU OUGHTTA BE USING THE DRIVEWAY?
EHH, WHAT'S A DRIVE-WAY?
NEVER MIND.
SCREEEEE
HERE WE ARE! SAY, DOC, PICK ME UP A LOLLIPOP WHILE YOU'RE INSIDE?
ACME NATIONAL BANK
OHH, I LIKE LOLLIPOPS, BOSS! CAN YA GET ME ONE, TOO?
WHUD
GEDDOFFA MY LAP BEFORE I BLAST YA, MUGSY!
UH-OH! LOOK AT DAT LINE! IT'LL TAKE YA AN HOUR TA GET IN THERE AND MAKE YOUR HEIST!
I AIN'T GOT AN HOUR. I GOTTA GET BACK TO MY HIDEOUT AND COUNT MY LOOT!
BANK
I KNOW A SHORTCUT TO AN OUT-OF-THE-WAY INSTANT TELLER MACHINE WHERE YA CAN DO YOUR HEISTIN'!
THAT'S THE TICKET, RABBIT!
VROOOOOM!
OOHH! I THINK I'VE GOT SOME AIRSICK-NESS, BOSS!
DON'T BE LEANIN' IN THE DIRECTION OF MY NEW JACKET, MUGSY!

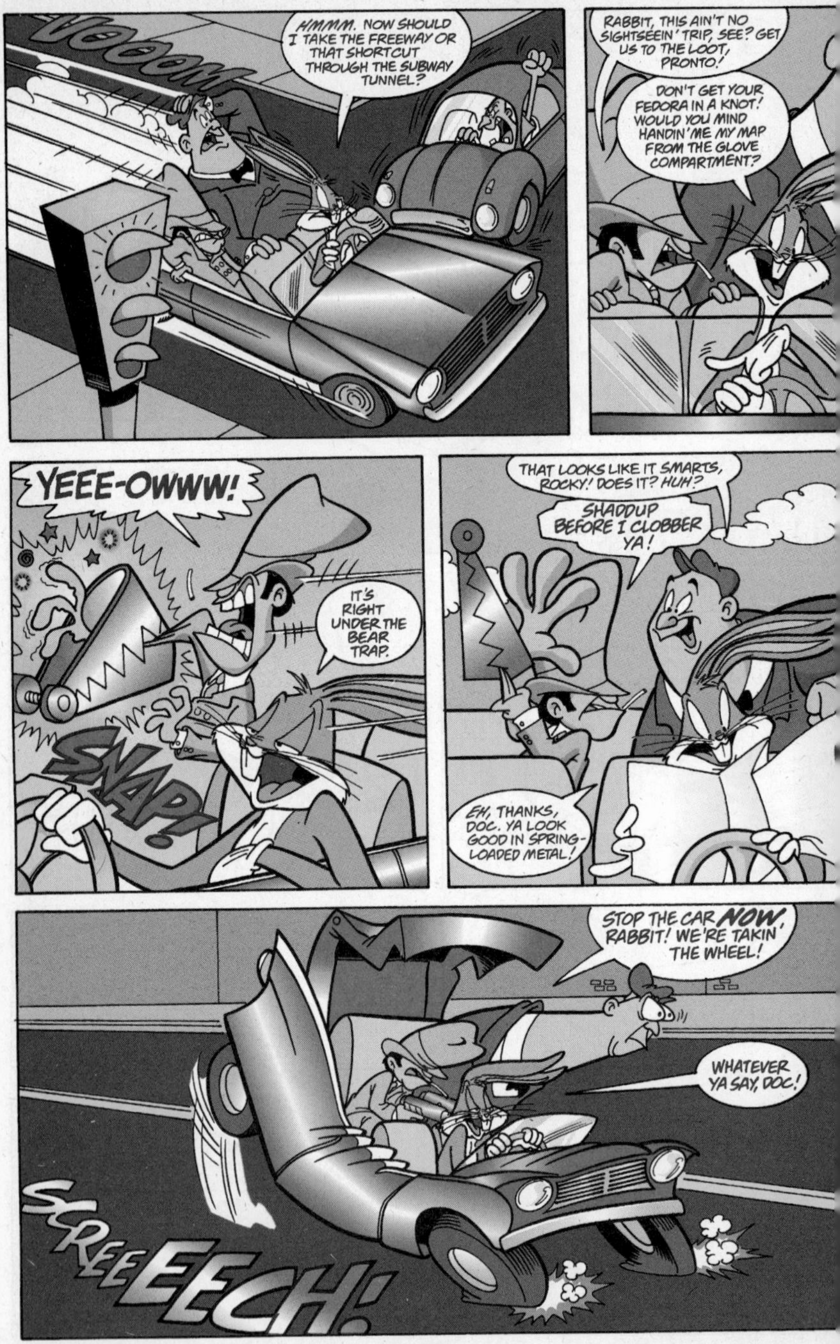
VOOOOM!
HMMM. NOW SHOULD I TAKE THE FREEWAY OR THAT SHORTCUT THROUGH THE SUBWAY TUNNEL?
RABBIT, THIS AIN'T NO SIGHTSEEIN' TRIP, SEE? GET US TO THE LOOT, PRONTO!
DON'T GET YOUR FEDORA IN A KNOT! WOULD YOU MIND HANDIN' ME MY MAP FROM THE GLOVE COMPARTMENT?
YEEE-OWWW!
IT'S RIGHT UNDER THE BEAR TRAP.
SNAP!
THAT LOOKS LIKE IT SMARTS, ROCKY! DOES IT? HUH?
SHADDUP BEFORE I CLOBBER YA!
EH, THANKS, DOC. YA LOOK GOOD IN SPRING-LOADED METAL!
STOP THE CAR NOW, RABBIT! WE'RE TAKIN' THE WHEEL!
WHATEVER YA SAY, DOC!
SCREEEECH!

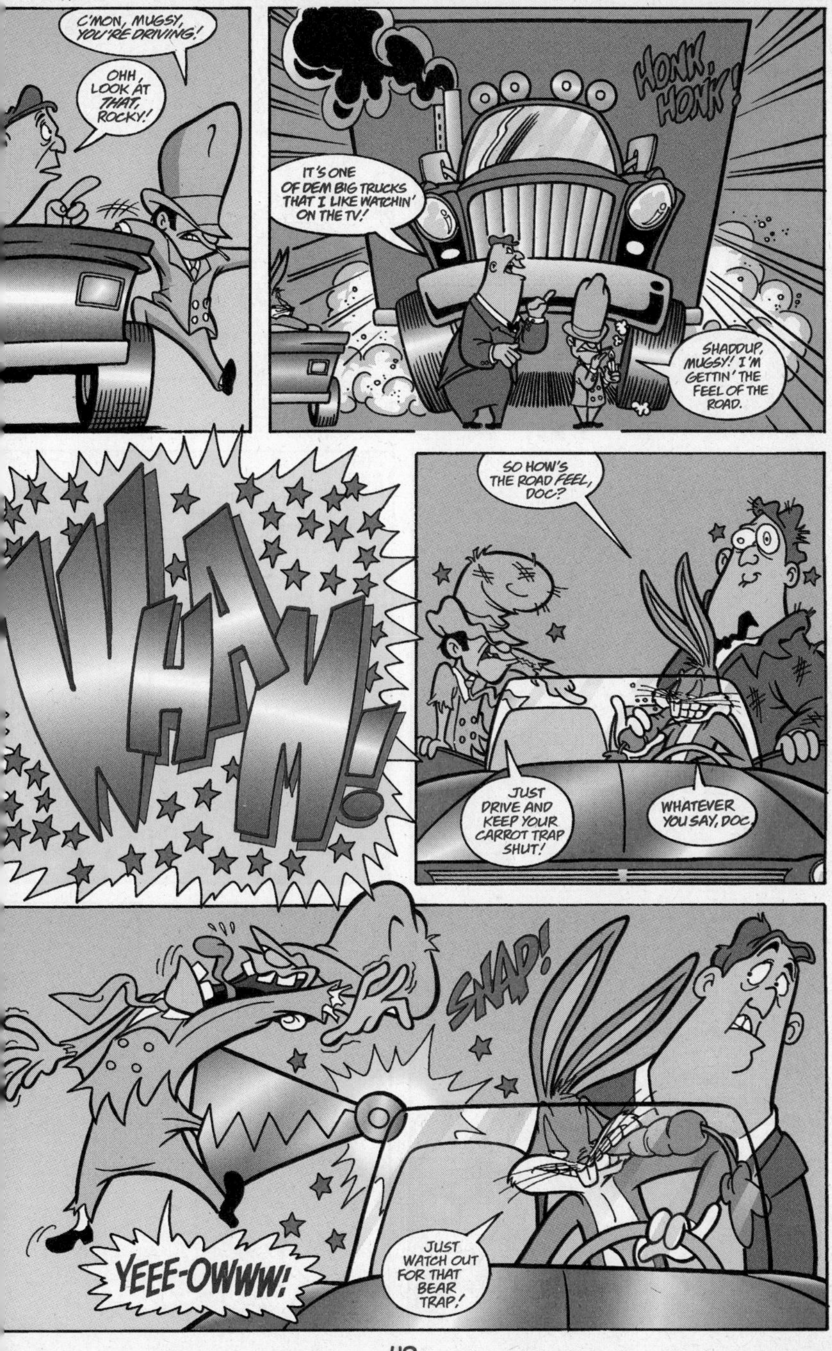
C'MON, MUGSY, YOU'RE DRIVING!
OHH, LOOK AT THAT, ROCKY!
HONK, HONK!
IT'S ONE OF DEM BIG TRUCKS THAT I LIKE WATCHIN' ON THE TV!
SHADDUP, MUGSY! I'M GETTIN' THE FEEL OF THE ROAD.
WHAM!
SO HOW'S THE ROAD FEEL, DOC?
JUST DRIVE AND KEEP YOUR CARROT TRAP SHUT!
WHATEVER YOU SAY, DOC.
SNAP!
YEEE-OWWW!
JUST WATCH OUT FOR THAT BEAR TRAP!

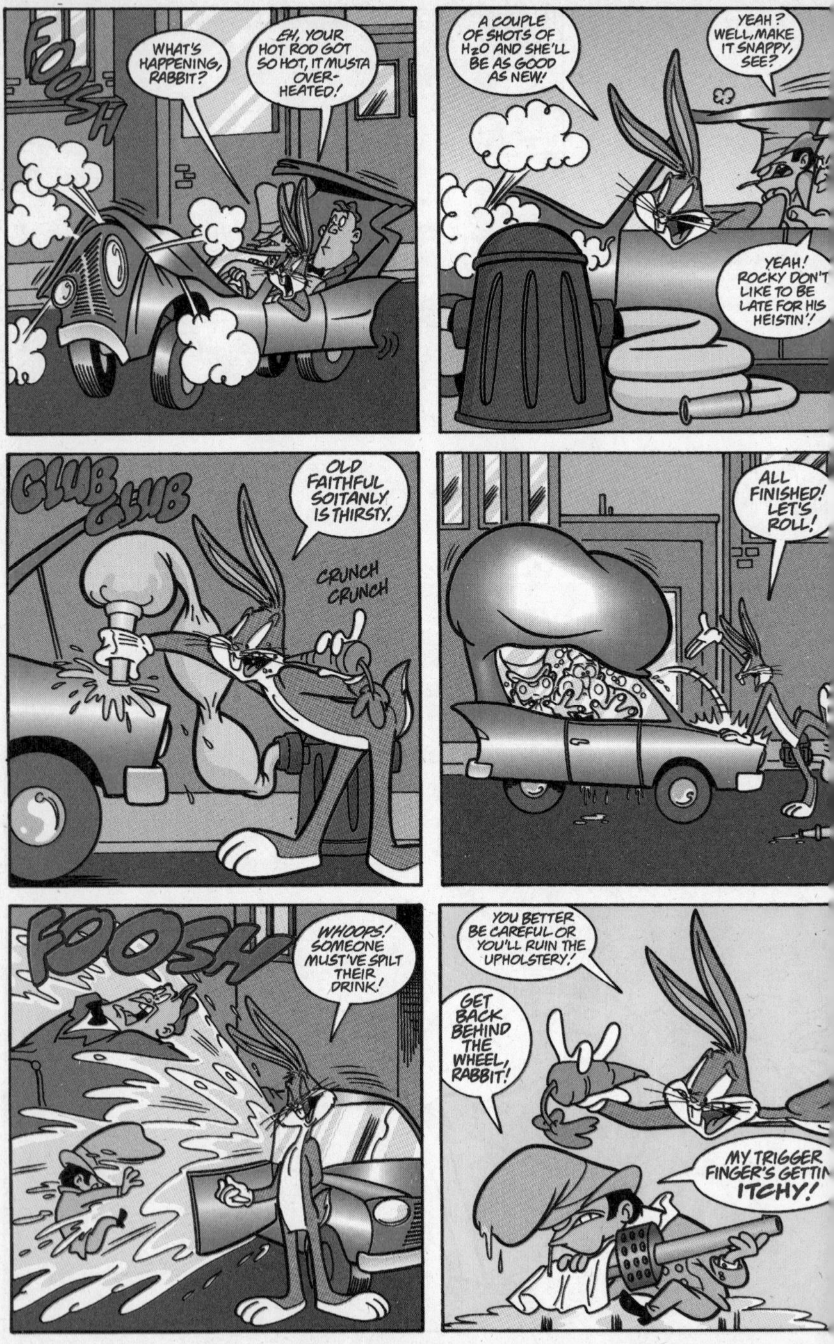
FOOOSH
WHAT'S HAPPENING, RABBIT?
EH, YOUR HOT ROD GOT SO HOT, IT MUSTA OVER-HEATED!
A COUPLE OF SHOTS OF H_2O AND SHE'LL BE AS GOOD AS NEW!
YEAH? WELL, MAKE IT SNAPPY, SEE?
YEAH! ROCKY DON'T LIKE TO BE LATE FOR HIS HEISTIN'!
GLUB GLUB
OLD FAITHFUL SOITANLY IS THIRSTY.
CRUNCH CRUNCH
ALL FINISHED! LET'S ROLL!
FOOSH
WHOOPS! SOMEONE MUST'VE SPILT THEIR DRINK!
YOU BETTER BE CAREFUL OR YOU'LL RUIN THE UPHOLSTERY!
GET BACK BEHIND THE WHEEL, RABBIT!
MY TRIGGER FINGER'S GETTIN ITCHY!

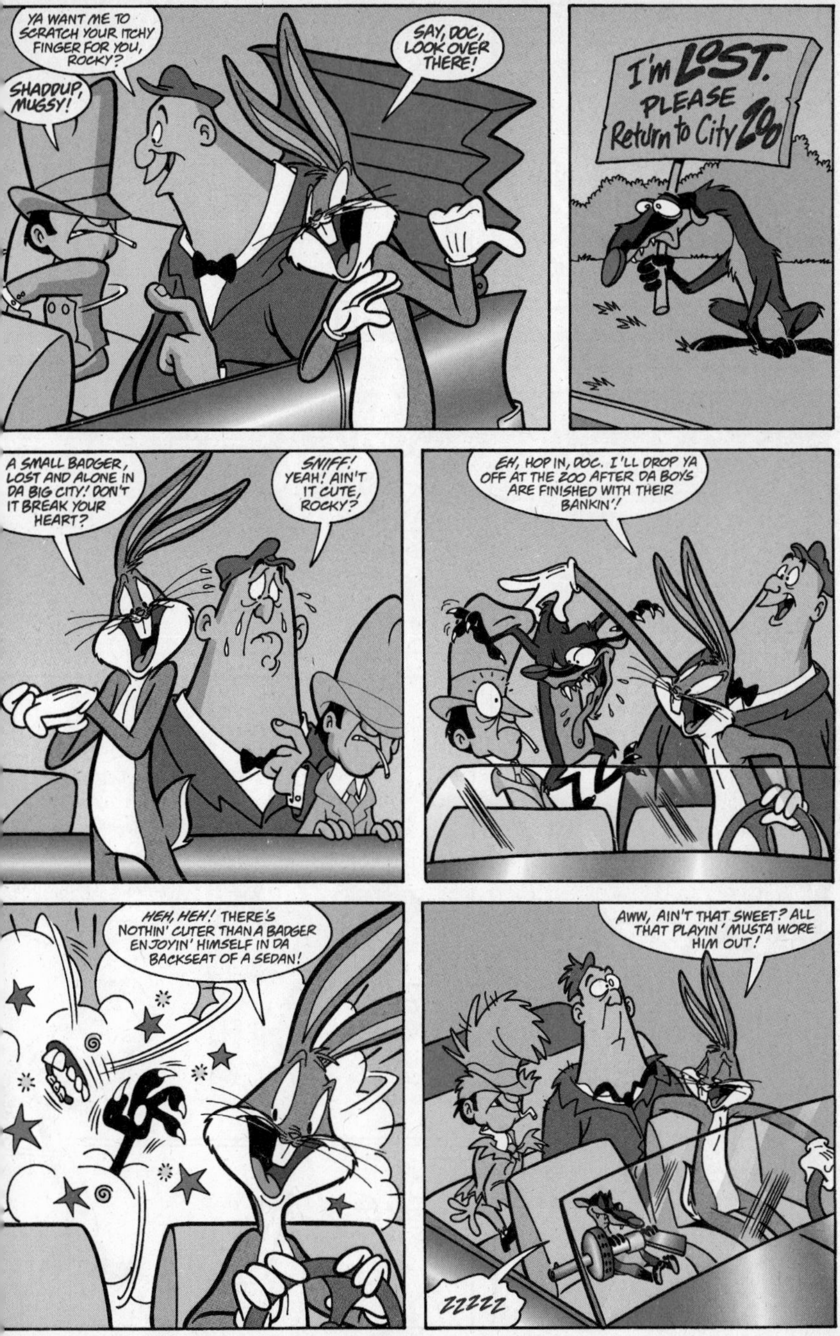
YA WANT ME TO SCRATCH YOUR ITCHY FINGER FOR YOU, ROCKY?
SHADDUP, MUGSY!
SAY, DOC, LOOK OVER THERE!
I'm LOST. PLEASE Return to City ZOO
A SMALL BADGER, LOST AND ALONE IN DA BIG CITY! DON'T IT BREAK YOUR HEART?
SNIFF! YEAH! AIN'T IT CUTE, ROCKY?
EH, HOP IN, DOC. I'LL DROP YA OFF AT THE ZOO AFTER DA BOYS ARE FINISHED WITH THEIR BANKIN'!
HEH, HEH! THERE'S NOTHIN' CUTER THAN A BADGER ENJOYIN' HIMSELF IN DA BACKSEAT OF A SEDAN!
AWW, AIN'T THAT SWEET? ALL THAT PLAYIN' MUSTA WORE HIM OUT!
ZZZZZ

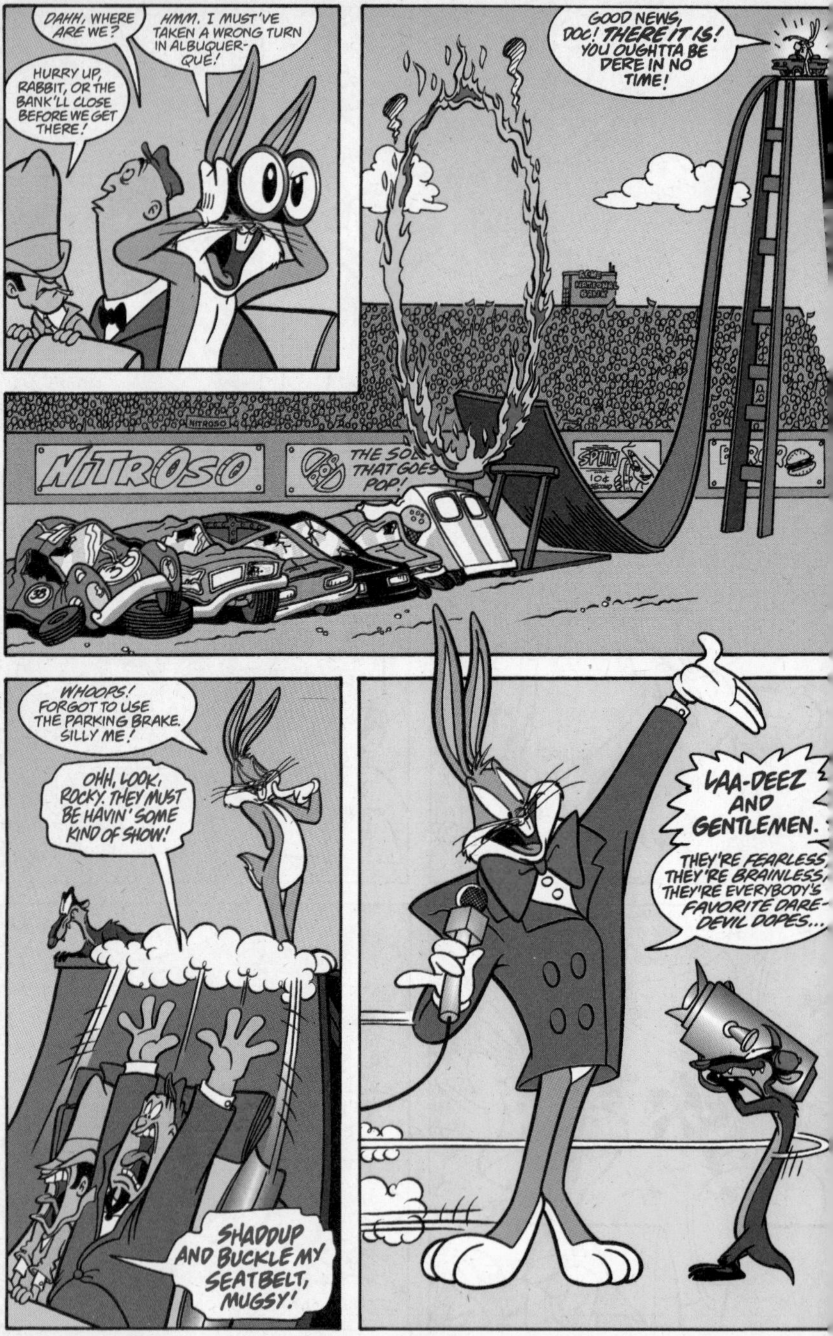
DAHH, WHERE ARE WE?
HMM. I MUST'VE TAKEN A WRONG TURN IN ALBUQUERQUE!
HURRY UP, RABBIT, OR THE BANK'LL CLOSE BEFORE WE GET THERE!
GOOD NEWS, DOC! THERE IT IS! YOU OUGHTTA BE DERE IN NO TIME!
ACME NATIONAL BANK
NITROSO
NITROSO
THE SO... THAT GOES POP!
SPLUN
WHOOPS! FORGOT TO USE THE PARKING BRAKE. SILLY ME!
OHH, LOOK, ROCKY. THEY MUST BE HAVIN' SOME KIND OF SHOW!
SHADDUP AND BUCKLE MY SEATBELT, MUGSY!
LAA-DEEZ AND GENTLEMEN.
THEY'RE FEARLESS, THEY'RE BRAINLESS, THEY'RE EVERYBODY'S FAVORITE DARE-DEVIL DOPES...

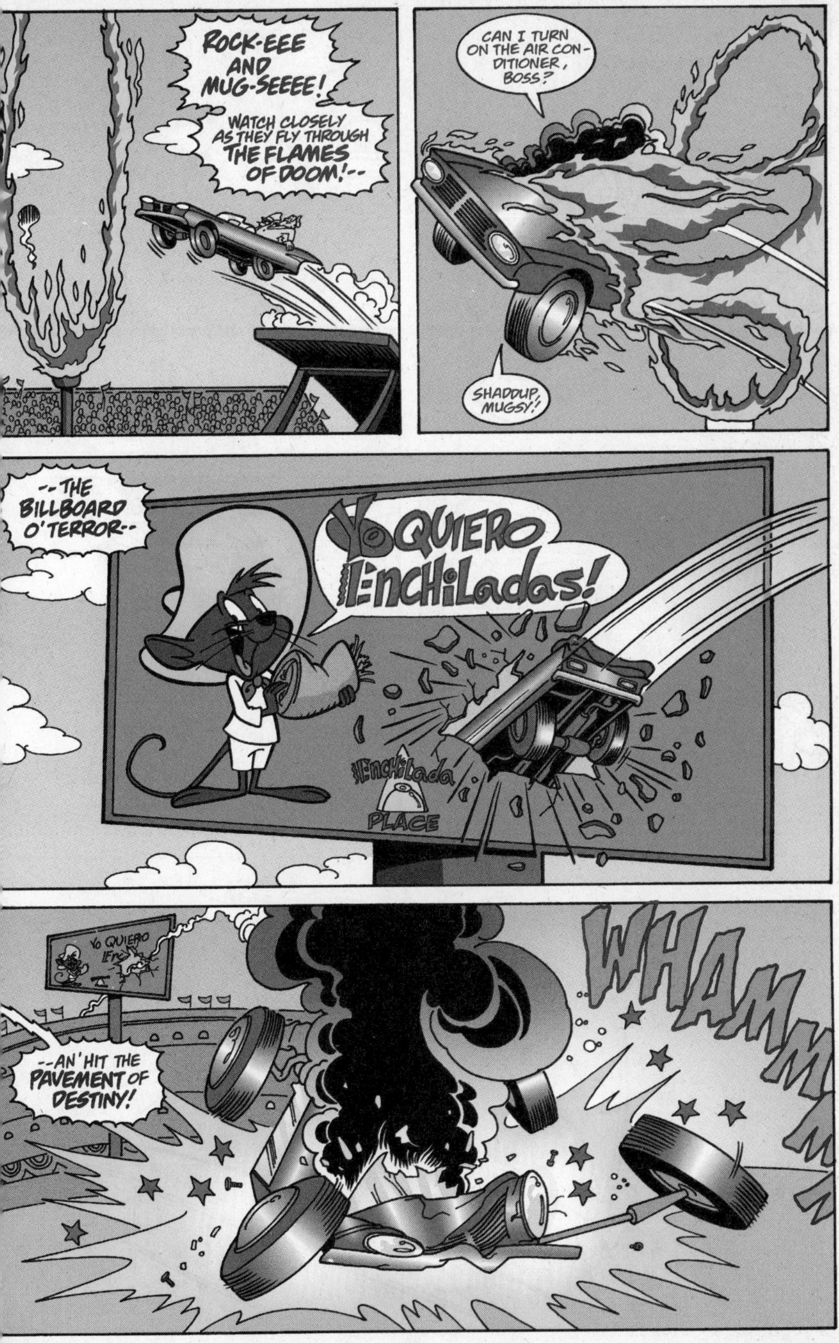
ROCK-EEE AND MUG-SEEEE!
WATCH CLOSELY AS THEY FLY THROUGH THE FLAMES OF DOOM!--
CAN I TURN ON THE AIR CON-DITIONER, BOSS?
SHADDUP, MUGSY!
--THE BILLBOARD O'TERROR--
YO QUIERO ENCHILADAS!
ENCHILADA PLACE
--AN' HIT THE PAVEMENT OF DESTINY!
WHAMM

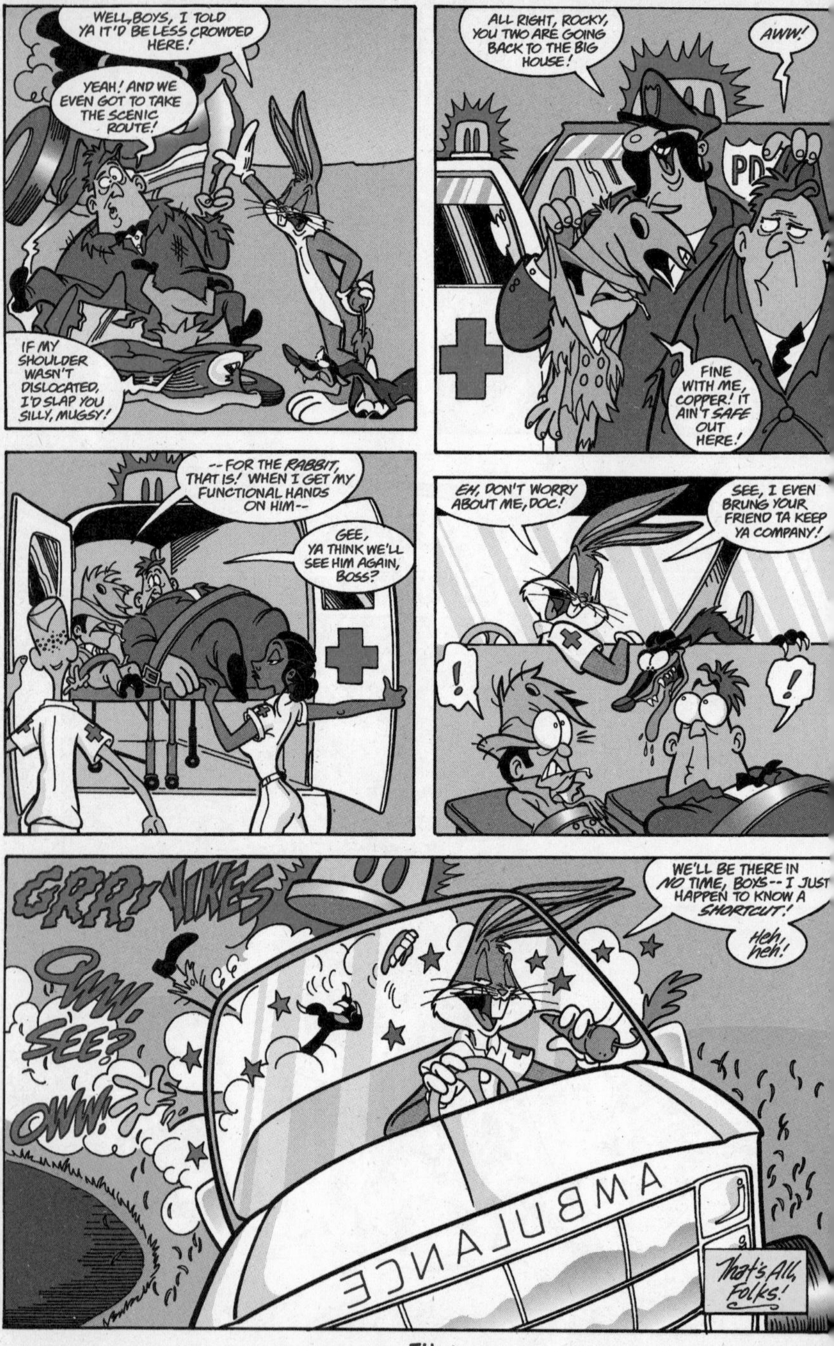
WELL, BOYS, I TOLD YA IT'D BE LESS CROWDED HERE!
YEAH! AND WE EVEN GOT TO TAKE THE SCENIC ROUTE!
IF MY SHOULDER WASN'T DISLOCATED, I'D SLAP YOU SILLY, MUGSY!
ALL RIGHT, ROCKY, YOU TWO ARE GOING BACK TO THE BIG HOUSE!
AWW!
PD
FINE WITH ME, COPPER! IT AIN'T SAFE OUT HERE!
--FOR THE RABBIT, THAT IS! WHEN I GET MY FUNCTIONAL HANDS ON HIM--
GEE, YA THINK WE'LL SEE HIM AGAIN, BOSS?
EH, DON'T WORRY ABOUT ME, DOC!
SEE, I EVEN BRUNG YOUR FRIEND TA KEEP YA COMPANY!
!
!
GRR!
YIKES
WE'LL BE THERE IN NO TIME, BOYS-- I JUST HAPPEN TO KNOW A SHORTCUT!
Heh, heh!
OWW.
SEE?
OWW!
AMBULANCE
That's All, Folks!

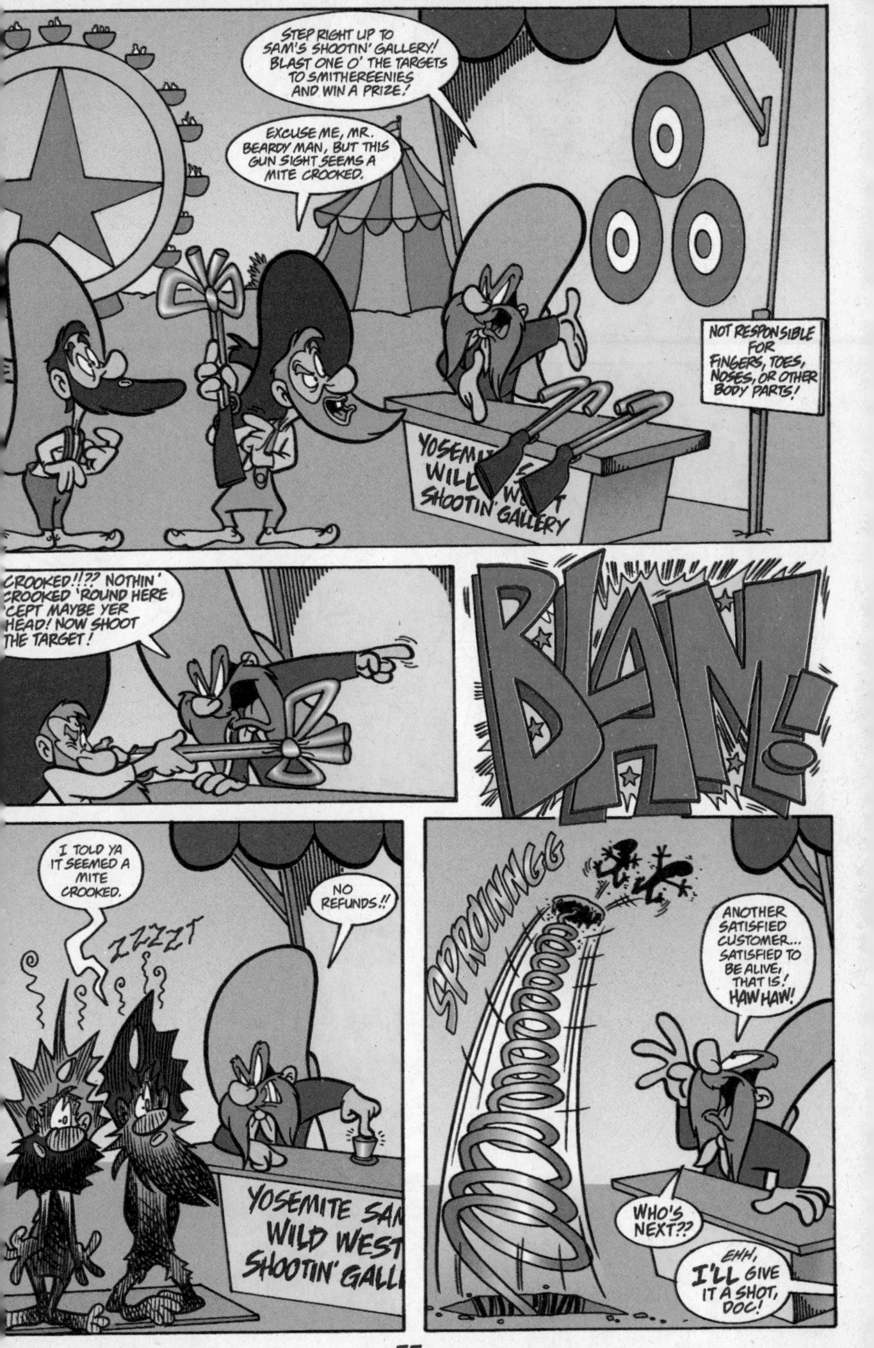

STEP RIGHT UP TO SAM'S SHOOTIN' GALLERY! BLAST ONE O' THE TARGETS TO SMITHEREENIES AND WIN A PRIZE!
EXCUSE ME, MR. BEARDY MAN, BUT THIS GUN SIGHT SEEMS A MITE CROOKED.
NOT RESPONSIBLE FOR FINGERS, TOES, NOSES, OR OTHER BODY PARTS!
CROOKED!!?? NOTHIN' CROOKED 'ROUND HERE 'CEPT MAYBE YER HEAD! NOW SHOOT THE TARGET!
BLAM!
I TOLD YA IT SEEMED A MITE CROOKED.
ZZZZT
NO REFUNDS!!
YOSEMITE SAM WILD WEST SHOOTIN' GALL
SPROINNGG
ANOTHER SATISFIED CUSTOMER... SATISFIED TO BE ALIVE, THAT IS! HAW HAW!
WHO'S NEXT??
EHH, I'LL GIVE IT A SHOT, DOC!

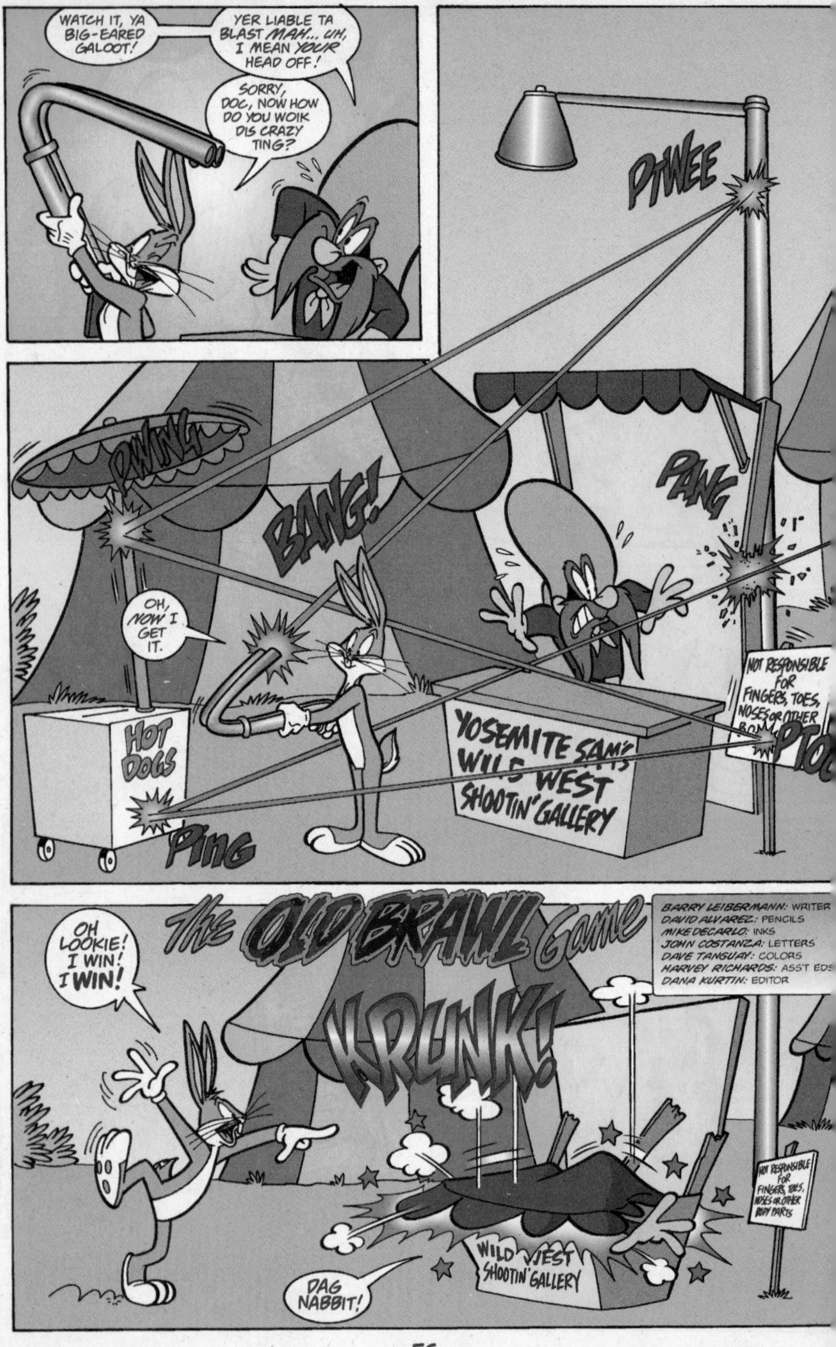
WATCH IT, YA BIG-EARED GALOOT!
YER LIABLE TA BLAST MAH... UH, I MEAN YOUR HEAD OFF!
SORRY, DOC, NOW HOW DO YOU WOIK DIS CRAZY TING?
PTWEE
PWING
BANG!
PANG
OH, NOW I GET IT.
NOT RESPONSIBLE FOR FINGERS, TOES, NOSES OR OTHER
HOT DOGS
YOSEMITE SAM'S WILS WEST SHOOTIN' GALLERY
PING
The OLD BRAWL Game
BARRY LEIBERMANN: WRITER
DAVID ALVAREZ: PENCILS
MIKE DECARLO: INKS
JOHN COSTANZA: LETTERS
DAVE TANGUAY: COLORS
MARVEY RICHARDS: ASS'T EDS
DANA KURTIN: EDITOR
OH LOOKIE! I WIN! I WIN!
KRUNK!
NOT RESPONSIBLE FOR FINGERS, TOES, NOSES OR OTHER BODY PARTS
WILD WEST SHOOTIN' GALLERY
DAG NABBIT!

SO, EH, WHERE'S MY PRIZE, DOC?

PRIZE!?!? AH'LL GIVE YA A PRIZE--

YOSEMITE SAM'S WILD WEST SHOOTIN' GALLERY

-- A NICE STUFFED TEDDY BEAR!

GRR!

EH, THIS BEAR DON'T LOOKED STUFFED TO ME, DOC.

YOSEMITE WILD WEST SHOOTIN' GALLER

GRRROWWWLLLLL!!!

SURE HE IS--

HE ATE FIVE CUSTOMERS JUST THIS MORNING! HYAR-HAR-HAR!

WHAKP!

YOU KNOW, OF COURSE, THIS MEANS WAR!!!

PUNT!

STEP RIGHT UP!

STEP RIGHT UP AND TEST YOUR SKILL!

YOSEMITE SAM'S WILD WEST 'GALLERY

WHA'? WHO'S TRYIN' TO CUT INTA MAH BUSINESS?

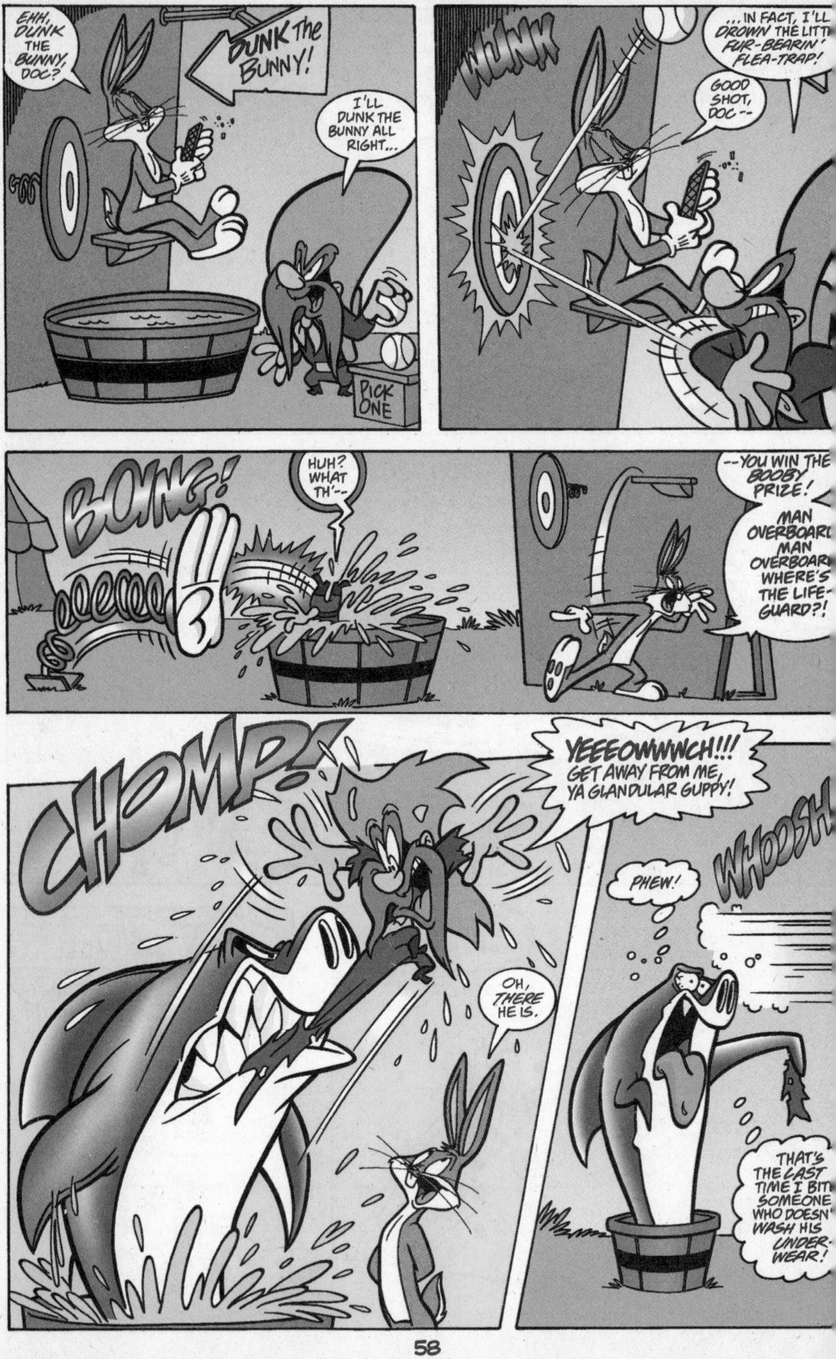
EHH, DUNK THE BUNNY, DOC?
DUNK THE BUNNY!
I'LL DUNK THE BUNNY ALL RIGHT...
PICK ONE
WHUNK
...IN FACT, I'LL DROWN THE LITT FUR-BEARIN' FLEA-TRAP!
GOOD SHOT, DOC--
BOING!
HUH? WHAT TH'--
--YOU WIN THE BOOBY PRIZE!
MAN OVERBOAR MAN OVERBOAR WHERE'S THE LIFE-GUARD?!
CHOMP!
YEEEOWWWCH!!! GET AWAY FROM ME, YA GLANDULAR GUPPY!
OH, THERE HE IS.
PHEW!
WHOOSH
THAT'S THE LAST TIME I BIT SOMEONE WHO DOESN' WASH HIS UNDER-WEAR!

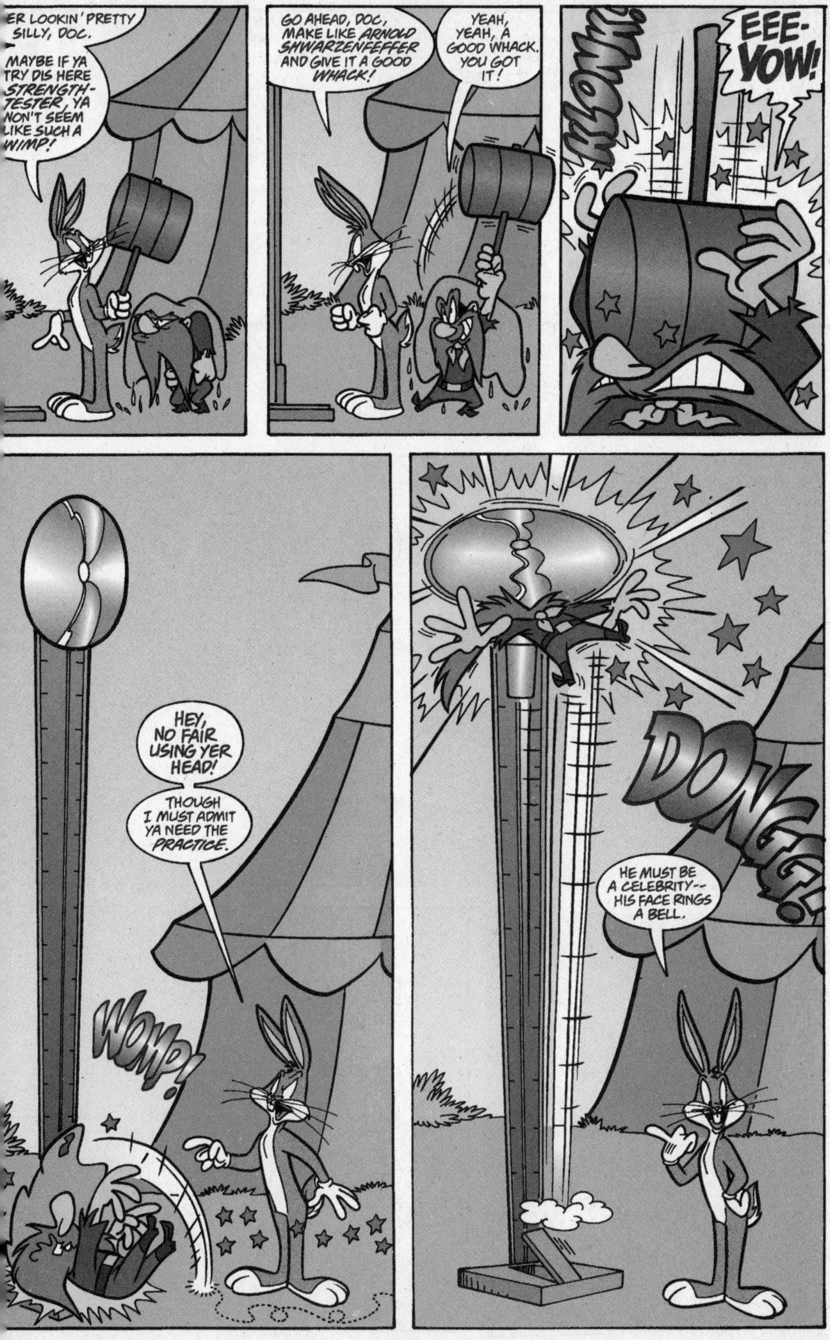

ER LOOKIN' PRETTY SILLY, DOC.
MAYBE IF YA TRY DIS HERE STRENGTH-TESTER, YA WON'T SEEM LIKE SUCH A WIMP!
GO AHEAD, DOC, MAKE LIKE ARNOLD SHWARZENFEFFER AND GIVE IT A GOOD WHACK!
YEAH, YEAH, A GOOD WHACK. YOU GOT IT!
WHOMM!
EEE-YOW!
HEY, NO FAIR USING YER HEAD!
THOUGH I MUST ADMIT YA NEED THE PRACTICE.
WOMP!
DONGG!
HE MUST BE A CELEBRITY-- HIS FACE RINGS A BELL.

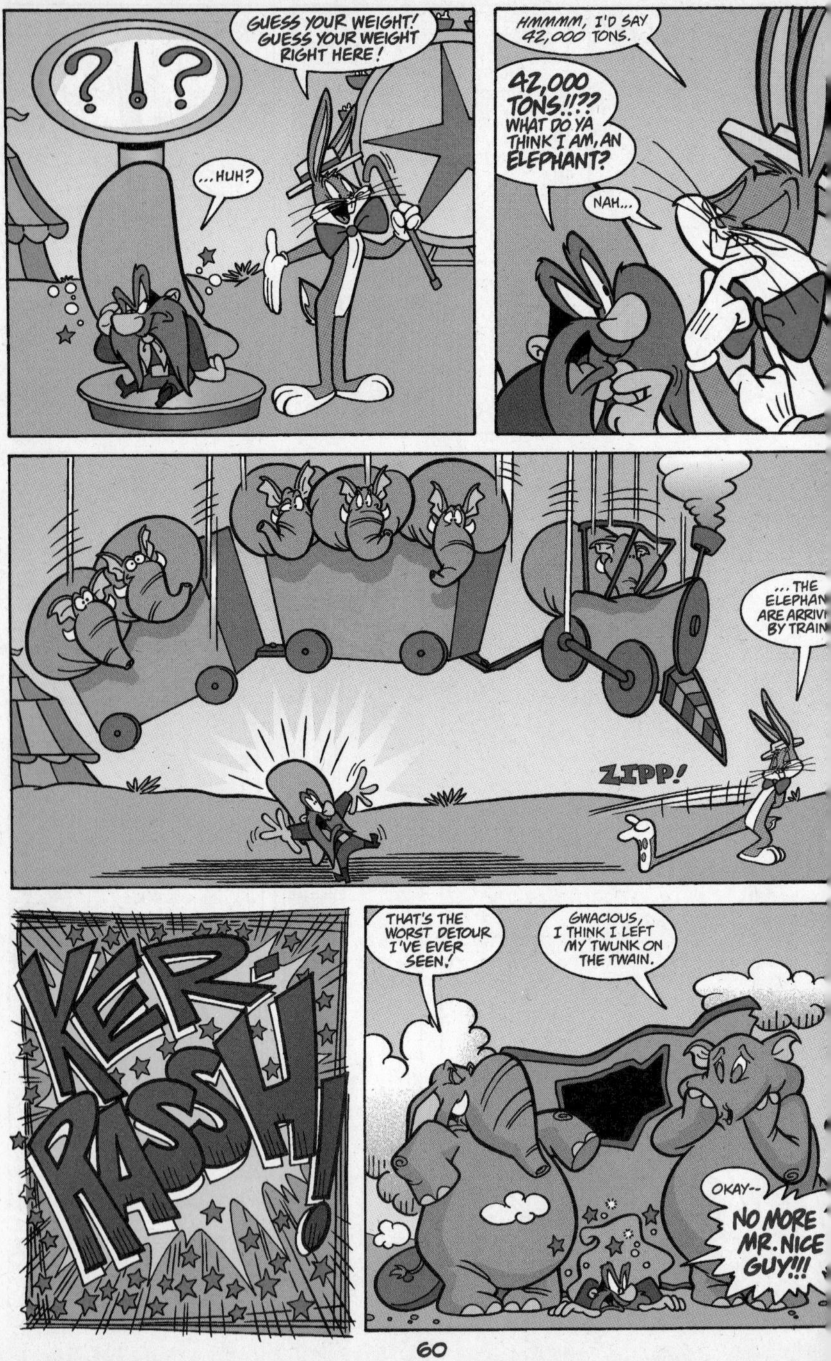
GUESS YOUR WEIGHT! GUESS YOUR WEIGHT RIGHT HERE!
...HUH?
HMMMM, I'D SAY 42,000 TONS.
42,000 TONS!!?? WHAT DO YA THINK I AM, AN ELEPHANT?
NAH...
...THE ELEPHAN ARE ARRIVI BY TRAIN
ZIPP!
KER-RASH!
THAT'S THE WORST DETOUR I'VE EVER SEEN!
GWACIOUS, I THINK I LEFT MY TWUNK ON THE TWAIN.
OKAY-- NO MORE MR. NICE GUY!!!

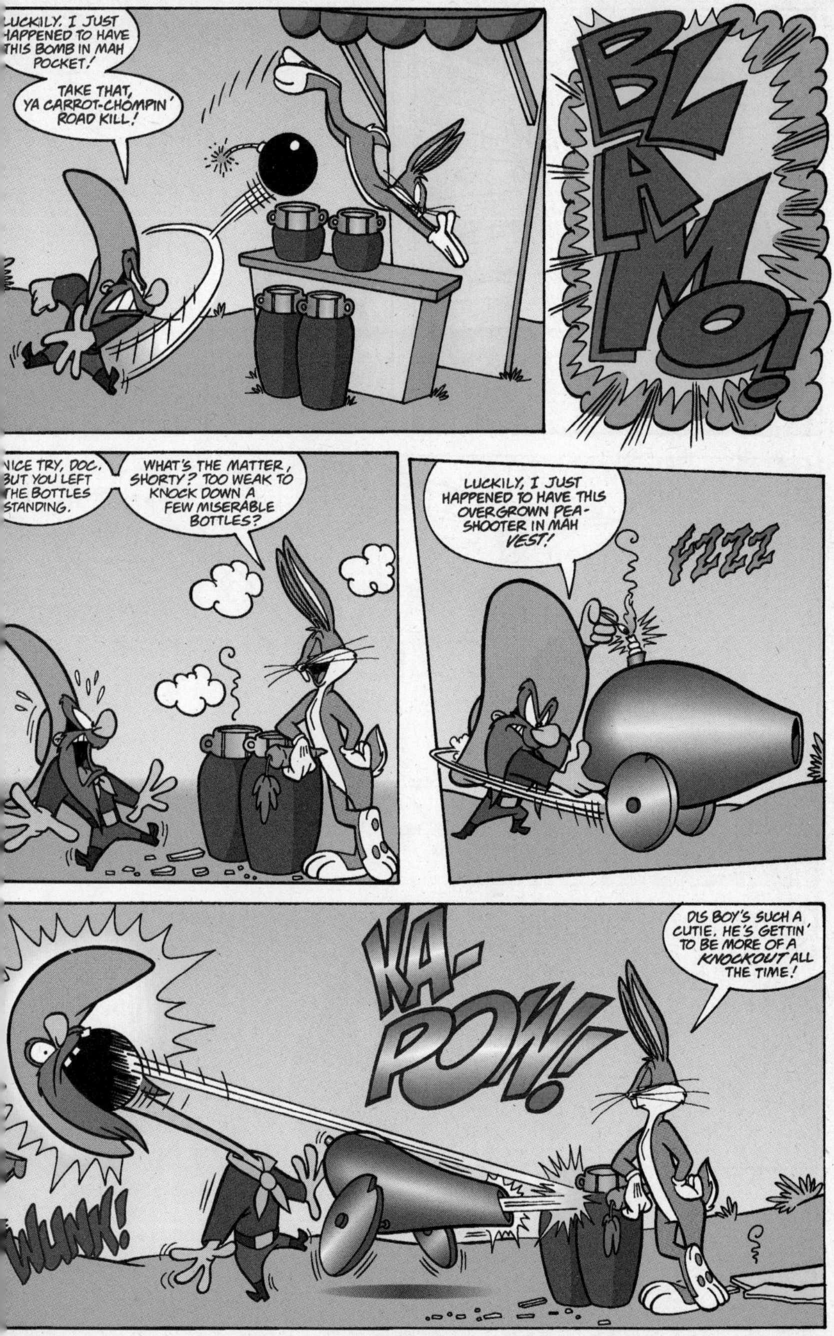
LUCKILY, I JUST HAPPENED TO HAVE THIS BOMB IN MAH POCKET!
TAKE THAT, YA CARROT-CHOMPIN' ROAD KILL!
BLAMO!
NICE TRY, DOC. BUT YOU LEFT THE BOTTLES STANDING.
WHAT'S THE MATTER, SHORTY? TOO WEAK TO KNOCK DOWN A FEW MISERABLE BOTTLES?
LUCKILY, I JUST HAPPENED TO HAVE THIS OVERGROWN PEA-SHOOTER IN MAH VEST!
FZZZ
KA-POW!
WUNK!
DIS BOY'S SUCH A CUTIE. HE'S GETTIN' TO BE MORE OF A KNOCKOUT ALL THE TIME!

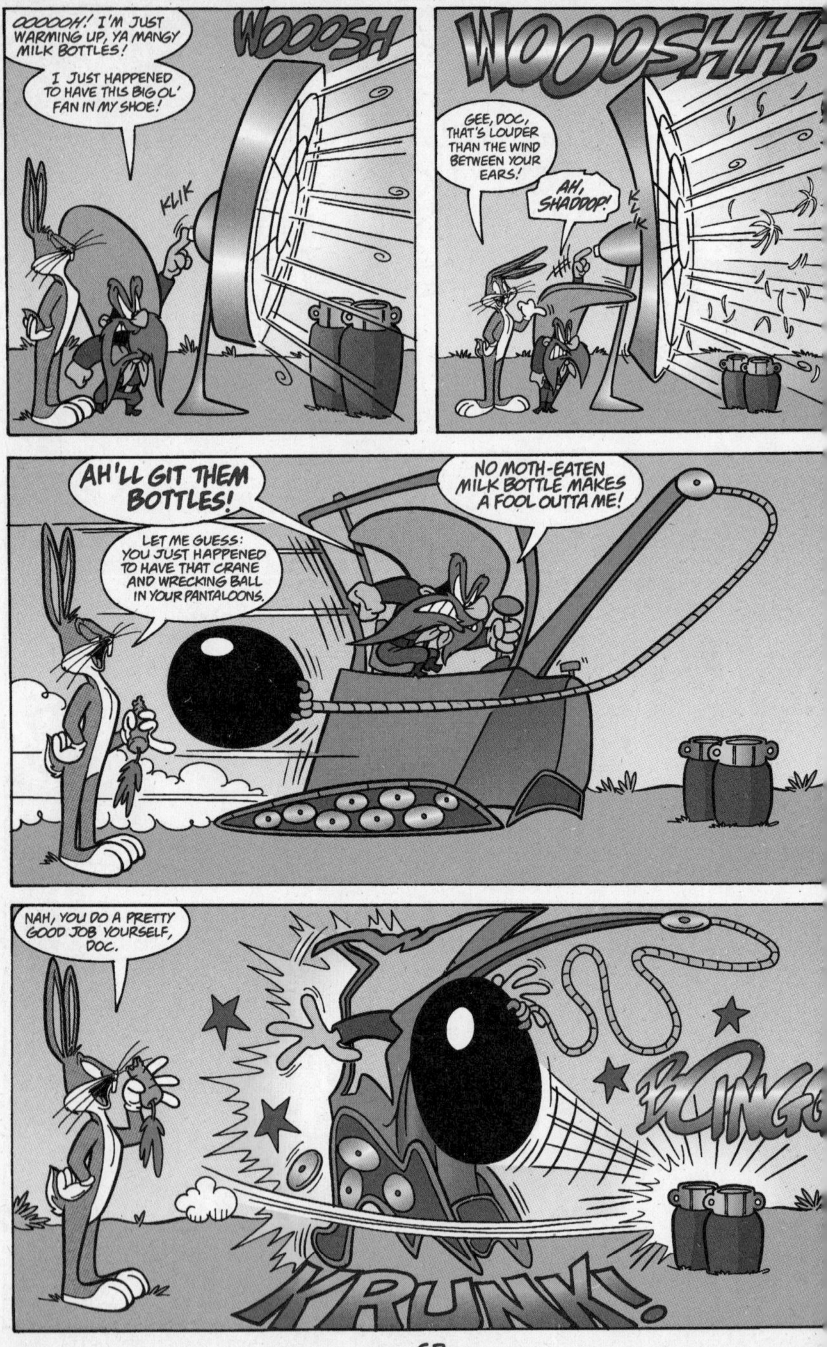

OOOOOH! I'M JUST WARMING UP, YA MANGY MILK BOTTLES!
I JUST HAPPENED TO HAVE THIS BIG OL' FAN IN MY SHOE!
WOOOSH
KLIK
WOOOSHH!
GEE, DOC, THAT'S LOUDER THAN THE WIND BETWEEN YOUR EARS!
AH, SHADDUP!
AH'LL GIT THEM BOTTLES!
NO MOTH-EATEN MILK BOTTLE MAKES A FOOL OUTTA ME!
LET ME GUESS: YOU JUST HAPPENED TO HAVE THAT CRANE AND WRECKING BALL IN YOUR PANTALOONS.
NAH, YOU DO A PRETTY GOOD JOB YOURSELF, DOC.
KRUNK!

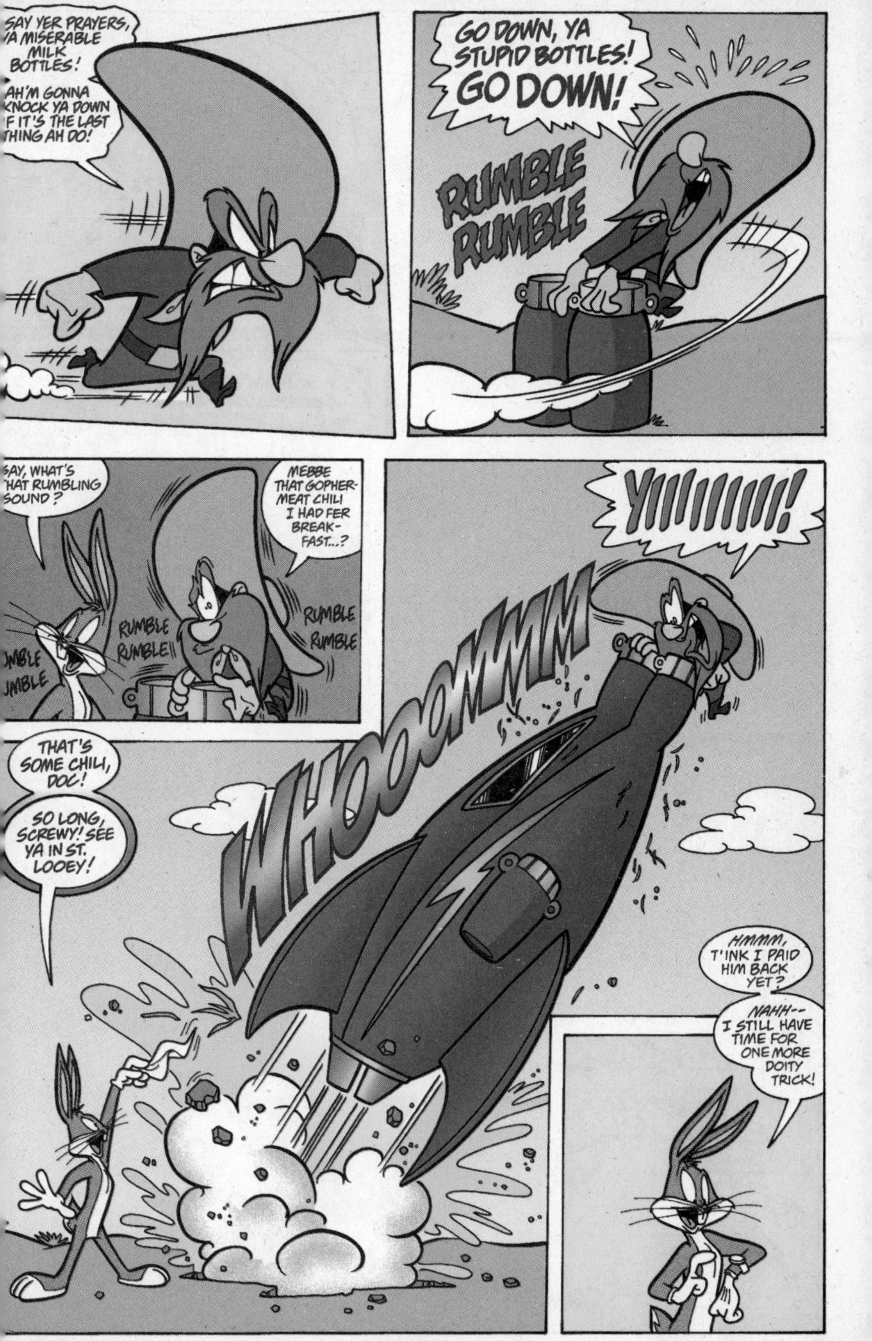
SAY YER PRAYERS, YA MISERABLE MILK BOTTLES!
AH'M GONNA KNOCK YA DOWN IF IT'S THE LAST THING AH DO!
GO DOWN, YA STUPID BOTTLES! GO DOWN!
RUMBLE RUMBLE
SAY, WHAT'S THAT RUMBLING SOUND?
MEBBE THAT GOPHER-MEAT CHILI I HAD FER BREAK-FAST...?
RUMBLE RUMBLE
RUMBLE RUMBLE
YIIIIIIII!
WHOOOMMM
THAT'S SOME CHILI, DOC!
SO LONG, SCREWY! SEE YA IN ST. LOOEY!
HMMM, T'INK I PAID HIM BACK YET?
NAHH-- I STILL HAVE TIME FOR ONE MORE DOITY TRICK!

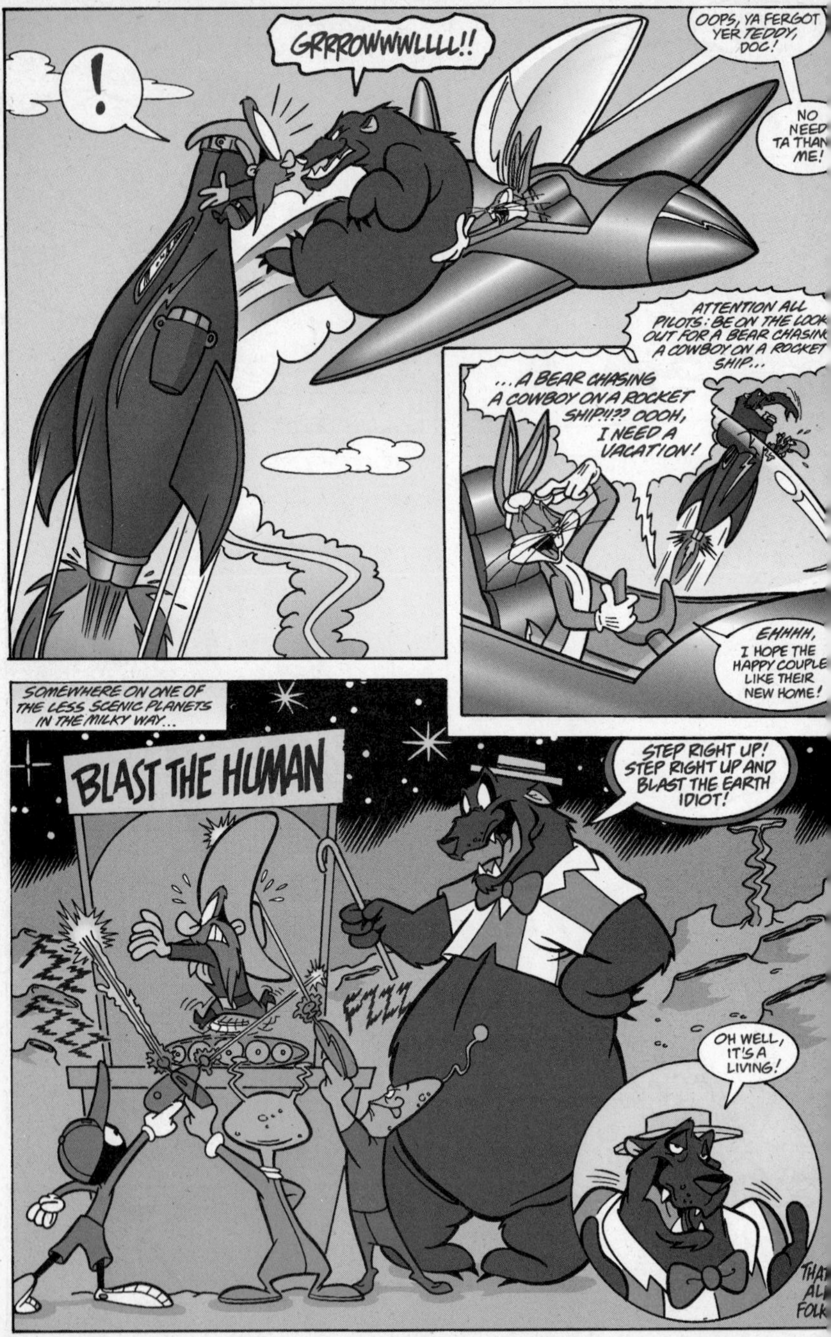
!
GRRROWWWLLLLL!!
OOPS, YA FERGOT YER TEDDY, DOC!
NO NEED TA THAN ME!
ATTENTION ALL PILOTS: BE ON THE LOOK OUT FOR A BEAR CHASING A COWBOY ON A ROCKET SHIP...
...A BEAR CHASING A COWBOY ON A ROCKET SHIP!!?? OOOH, I NEED A VACATION!
EHHHH, I HOPE THE HAPPY COUPLE LIKE THEIR NEW HOME!
SOMEWHERE ON ONE OF THE LESS SCENIC PLANETS IN THE MILKY WAY...
BLAST THE HUMAN
STEP RIGHT UP! STEP RIGHT UP AND BLAST THE EARTH IDIOT!
FZZZ
FZZZ
FZZZ
OH WELL, IT'S A LIVING!

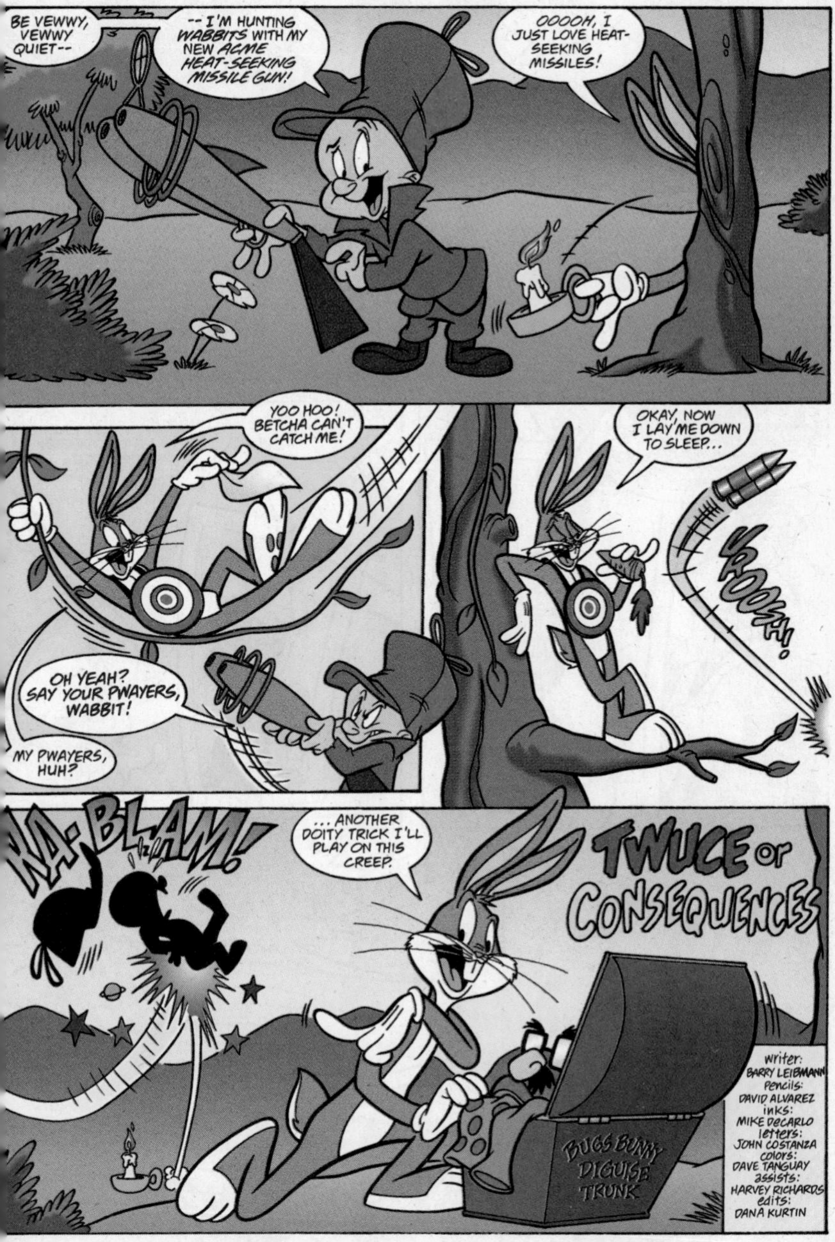
BE VEWWY, VEWWY QUIET--
-- I'M HUNTING WABBITS WITH MY NEW ACME HEAT-SEEKING MISSILE GUN!
OOOOH, I JUST LOVE HEAT-SEEKING MISSILES!
YOO HOO! BETCHA CAN'T CATCH ME!
OH YEAH? SAY YOUR PWAYERS, WABBIT!
MY PWAYERS, HUH?
OKAY, NOW I LAY ME DOWN TO SLEEP...
VROOSH!
KA-BLAM!
... ANOTHER DOITY TRICK I'LL PLAY ON THIS CREEP.
TWUCE or CONSEQUENCES
BUGS BUNNY DIGUISE TRUNK
writer: BARRY LEIBMANN
pencils: DAVID ALVAREZ
inks: MIKE DECARLO
letters: JOHN COSTANZA
colors: DAVE TANGUAY
assists: HARVEY RICHARDS
edits: DANA KURTIN

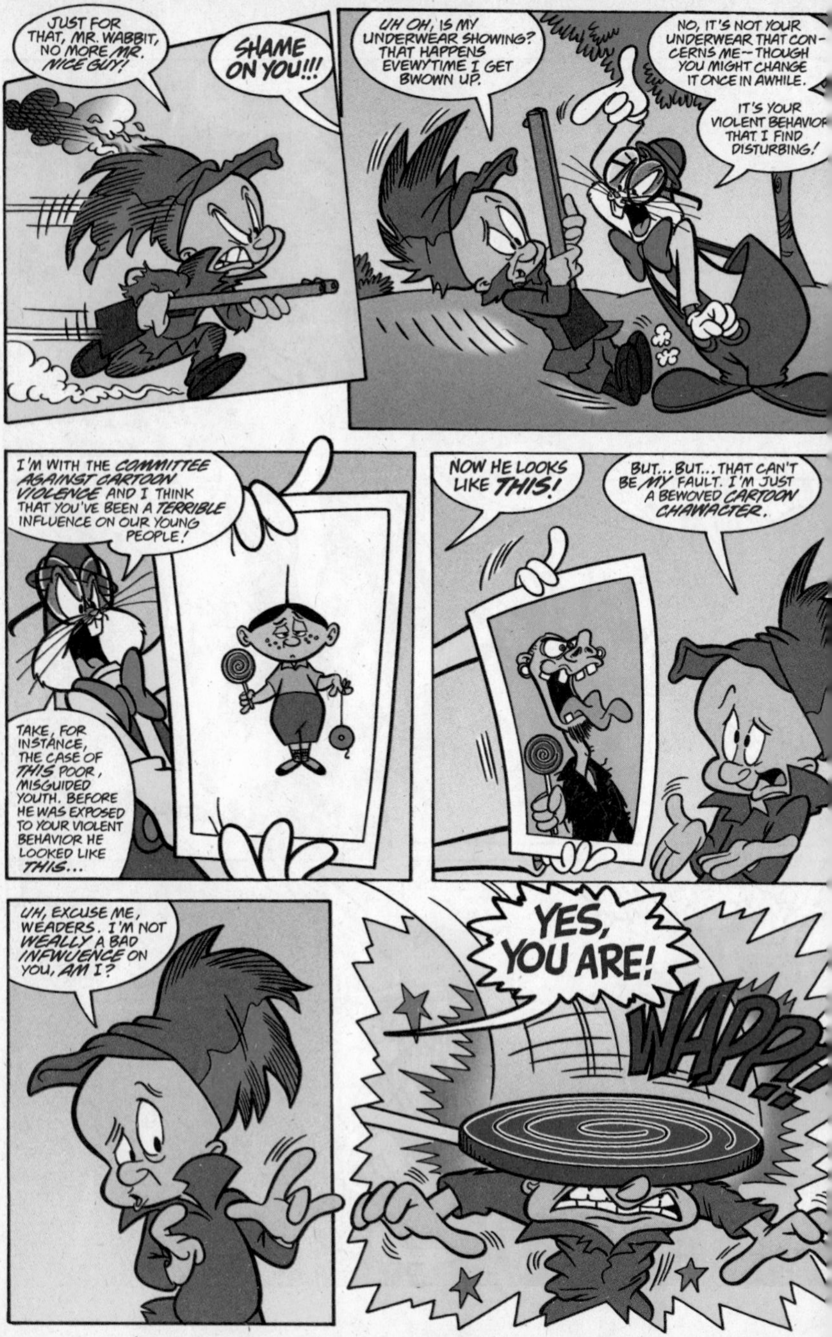

JUST FOR THAT, MR. WABBIT, NO MORE MR. NICE GUY!
SHAME ON YOU!!!
UH OH, IS MY UNDERWEAR SHOWING? THAT HAPPENS EVEWYTIME I GET BWOWN UP.
NO, IT'S NOT YOUR UNDERWEAR THAT CONCERNS ME-- THOUGH YOU MIGHT CHANGE IT ONCE IN AWHILE.
IT'S YOUR VIOLENT BEHAVIOR THAT I FIND DISTURBING!
I'M WITH THE COMMITTEE AGAINST CARTOON VIOLENCE AND I THINK THAT YOU'VE BEEN A TERRIBLE INFLUENCE ON OUR YOUNG PEOPLE!
TAKE, FOR INSTANCE, THE CASE OF THIS POOR, MISGUIDED YOUTH. BEFORE HE WAS EXPOSED TO YOUR VIOLENT BEHAVIOR HE LOOKED LIKE THIS...
NOW HE LOOKS LIKE THIS!
BUT... BUT... THAT CAN'T BE MY FAULT. I'M JUST A BEWOVED CARTOON CHAWACTER.
UH, EXCUSE ME, WEADERS. I'M NOT WEALLY A BAD INFWUENCE ON YOU, AM I?
YES, YOU ARE!
WAPP!!

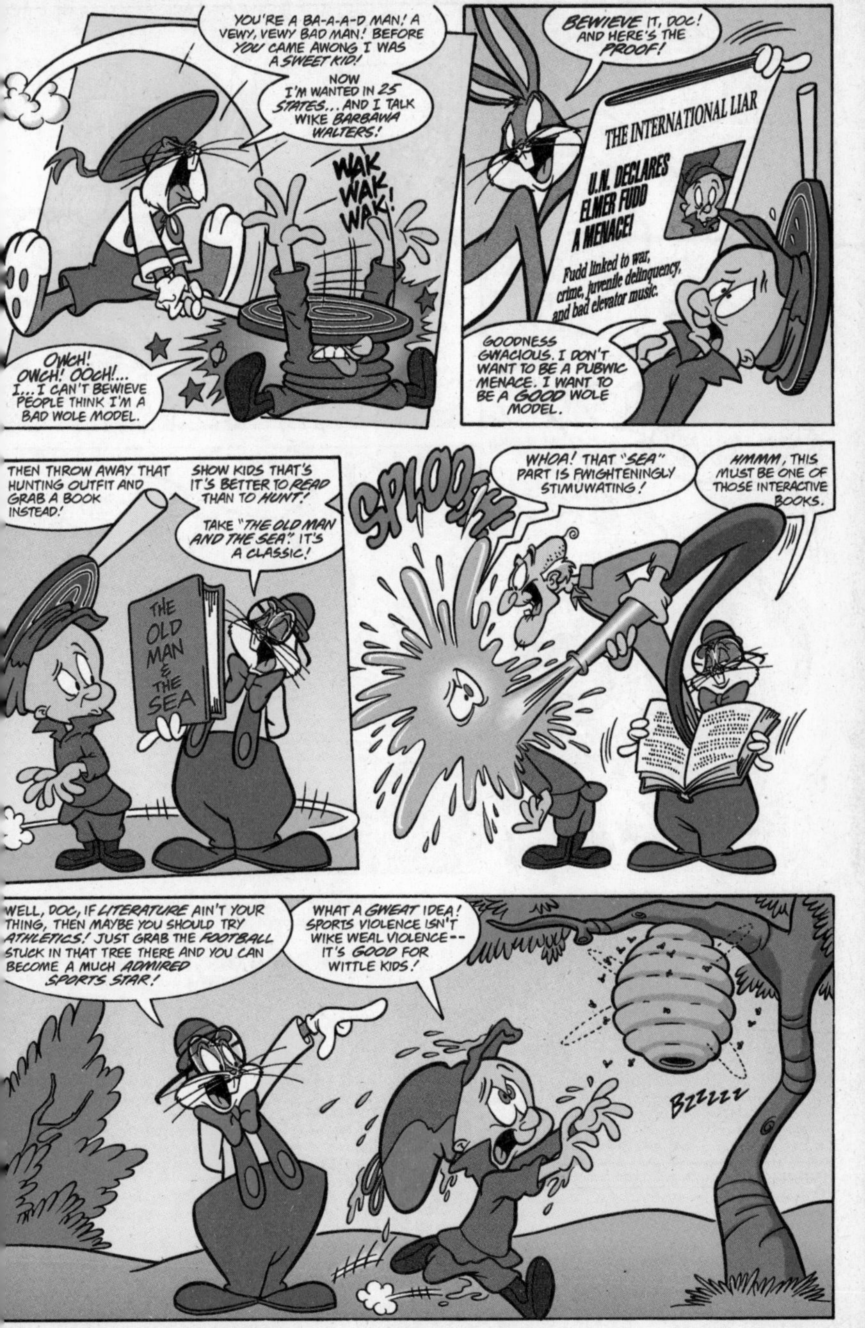
YOU'RE A BA-A-A-D MAN! A VEWY, VEWY BAD MAN! BEFORE YOU CAME AWONG I WAS A SWEET KID!
NOW I'M WANTED IN 25 STATES... AND I TALK WIKE BARBAWA WALTERS!
WAK WAK WAK!
OWCH! OWCH! OOCH!... I... I CAN'T BEWIEVE PEOPLE THINK I'M A BAD WOLE MODEL.
BEWIEVE IT, DOC! AND HERE'S THE PROOF!
THE INTERNATIONAL LIAR
U.N. DECLARES ELMER FUDD A MENACE!
Fudd linked to war, crime, juvenile delinquency, and bad elevator music.
GOODNESS GWACIOUS. I DON'T WANT TO BE A PUBWIC MENACE. I WANT TO BE A GOOD WOLE MODEL.
THEN THROW AWAY THAT HUNTING OUTFIT AND GRAB A BOOK INSTEAD!
SHOW KIDS THAT'S IT'S BETTER TO READ THAN TO HUNT!
TAKE "THE OLD MAN AND THE SEA." IT'S A CLASSIC!
THE OLD MAN & THE SEA
SPLOOSH
WHOA! THAT "SEA" PART IS FWIGHTENINGLY STIMUWATING!
HMMM, THIS MUST BE ONE OF THOSE INTERACTIVE BOOKS.
WELL, DOC, IF LITERATURE AIN'T YOUR THING, THEN MAYBE YOU SHOULD TRY ATHLETICS! JUST GRAB THE FOOTBALL STUCK IN THAT TREE THERE AND YOU CAN BECOME A MUCH ADMIRED SPORTS STAR!
WHAT A GWEAT IDEA! SPORTS VIOLENCE ISN'T WIKE WEAL VIOLENCE-- IT'S GOOD FOR WITTLE KIDS!
BZZZZZ

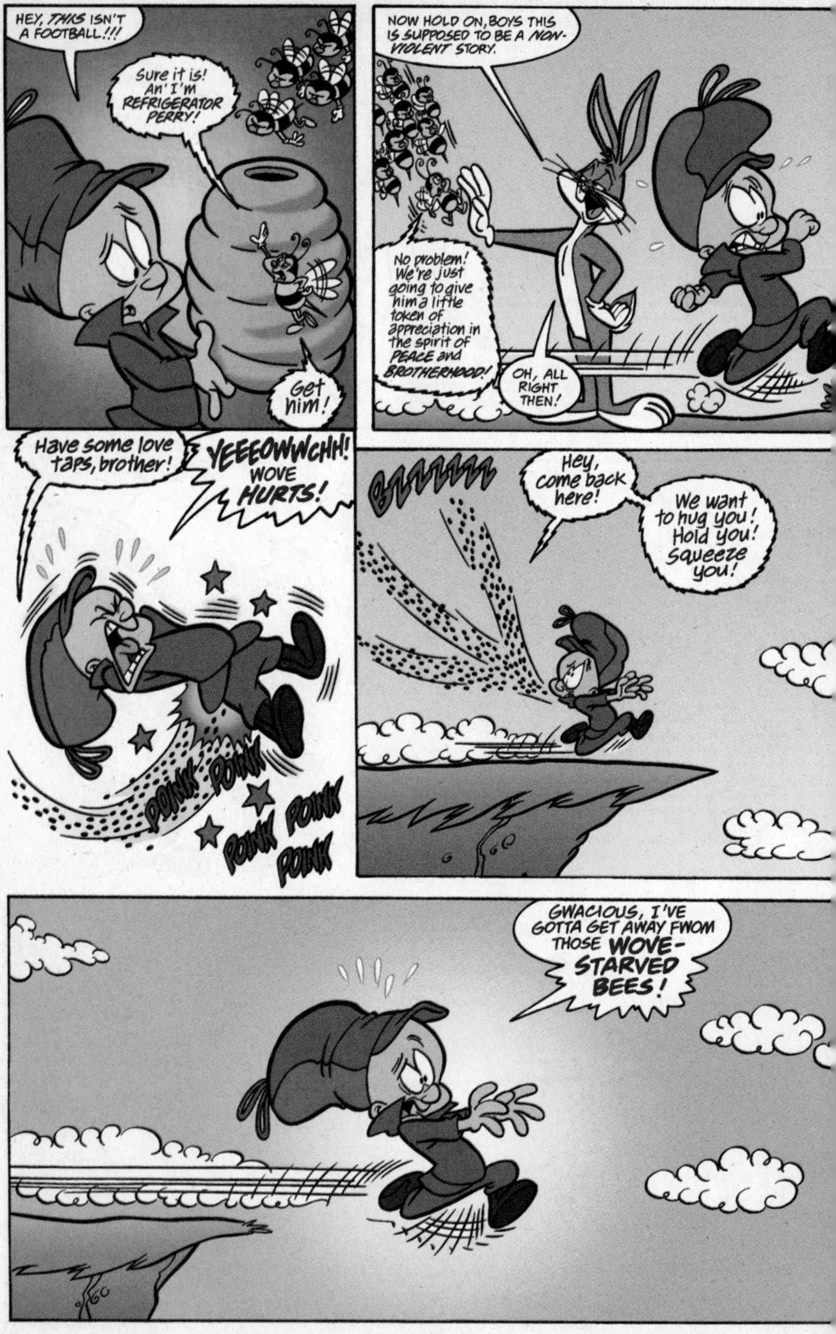
HEY, THIS ISN'T A FOOTBALL!!!
Sure it is! An' I'm REFRIGERATOR PERRY!
Get him!
NOW HOLD ON, BOYS THIS IS SUPPOSED TO BE A NON-VIOLENT STORY.
No problem! We're just going to give him a little token of appreciation in the spirit of PEACE and BROTHERHOOD!
OH, ALL RIGHT THEN!
Have some love taps, brother!
YEEEOWWCHH! WOVE HURTS!
POINK POINK POINK POINK POINK
BZZZZZZ
Hey, come back here!
We want to hug you! Hold you! Squeeze you!
GWACIOUS, I'VE GOTTA GET AWAY FWOM THOSE WOVE-STARVED BEES!

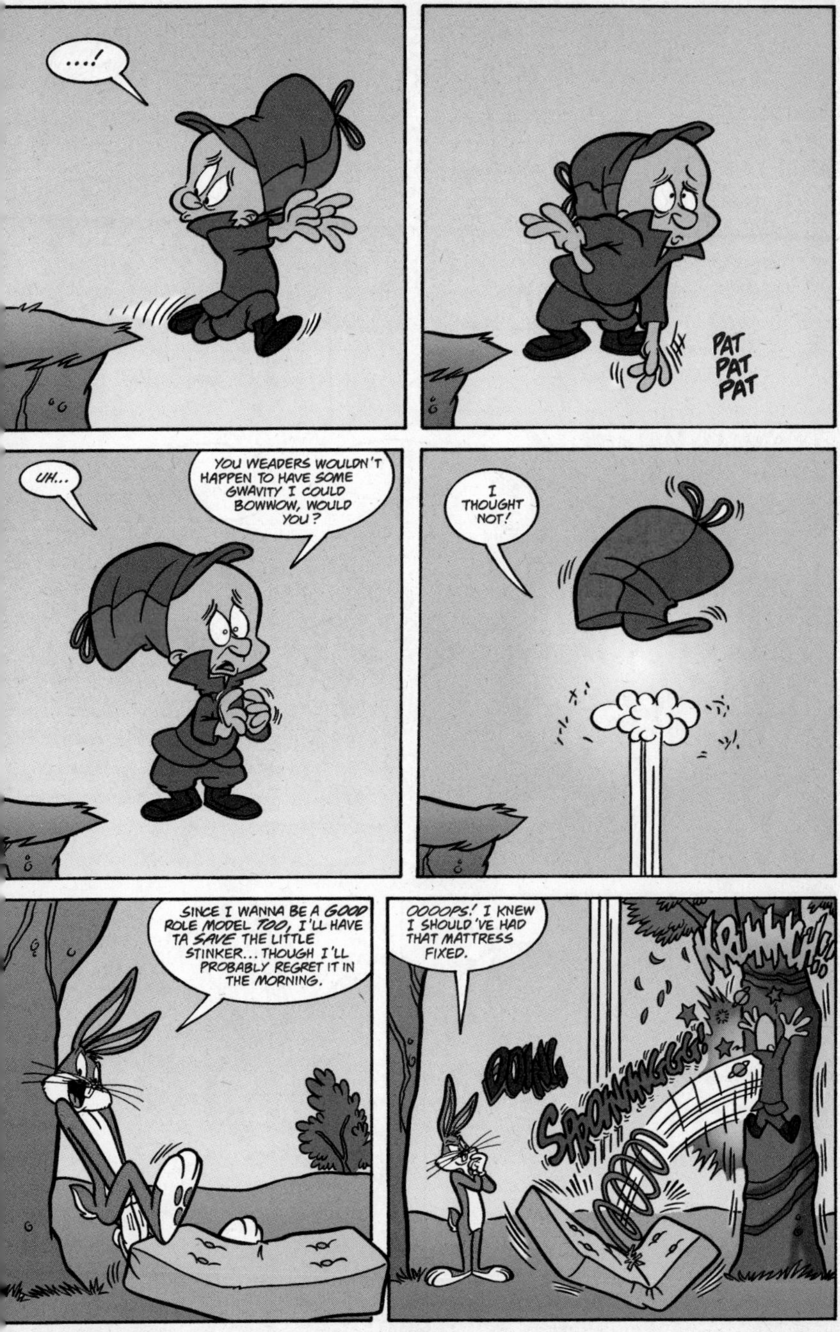
....!
PAT
PAT
PAT
UH...
YOU WEADERS WOULDN'T HAPPEN TO HAVE SOME GWAVITY I COULD BOWWOW, WOULD YOU?
I THOUGHT NOT!
SINCE I WANNA BE A GOOD ROLE MODEL TOO, I'LL HAVE TA SAVE THE LITTLE STINKER... THOUGH I'LL PROBABLY REGRET IT IN THE MORNING.
OOOOPS! I KNEW I SHOULD'VE HAD THAT MATTRESS FIXED.

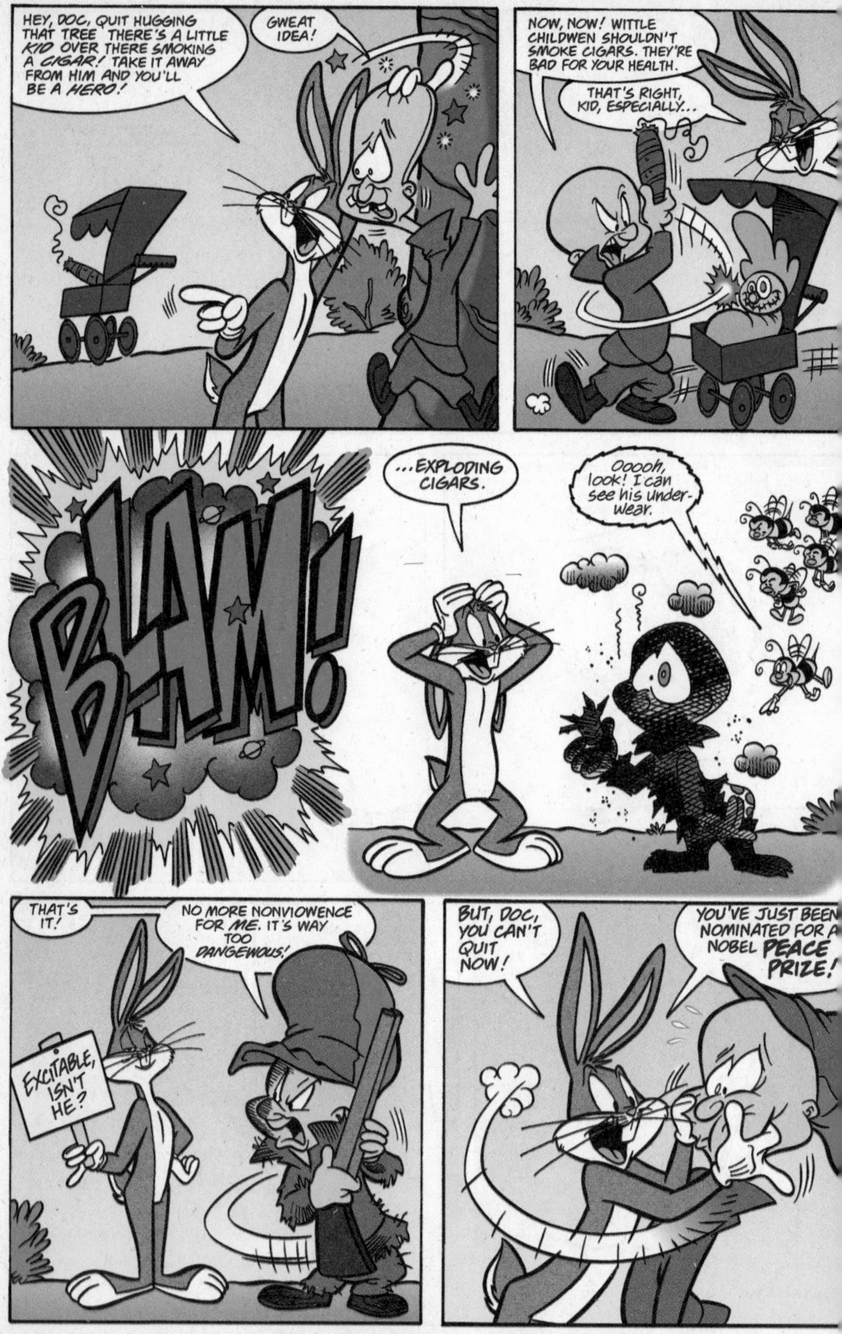
HEY, DOC, QUIT HUGGING THAT TREE THERE'S A LITTLE KID OVER THERE SMOKING A CIGAR! TAKE IT AWAY FROM HIM AND YOU'LL BE A HERO!
GWEAT IDEA!
NOW, NOW! WITTLE CHILDWEN SHOULDN'T SMOKE CIGARS. THEY'RE BAD FOR YOUR HEALTH.
THAT'S RIGHT, KID, ESPECIALLY...
BLAM!
...EXPLODING CIGARS.
Oooooh, look! I can see his under-wear.
THAT'S IT!
NO MORE NONVIOWENCE FOR ME. IT'S WAY TOO DANGEWOUS!
EXCITABLE, ISN'T HE?
BUT, DOC, YOU CAN'T QUIT NOW!
YOU'VE JUST BEEN NOMINATED FOR A NOBEL PEACE PRIZE!

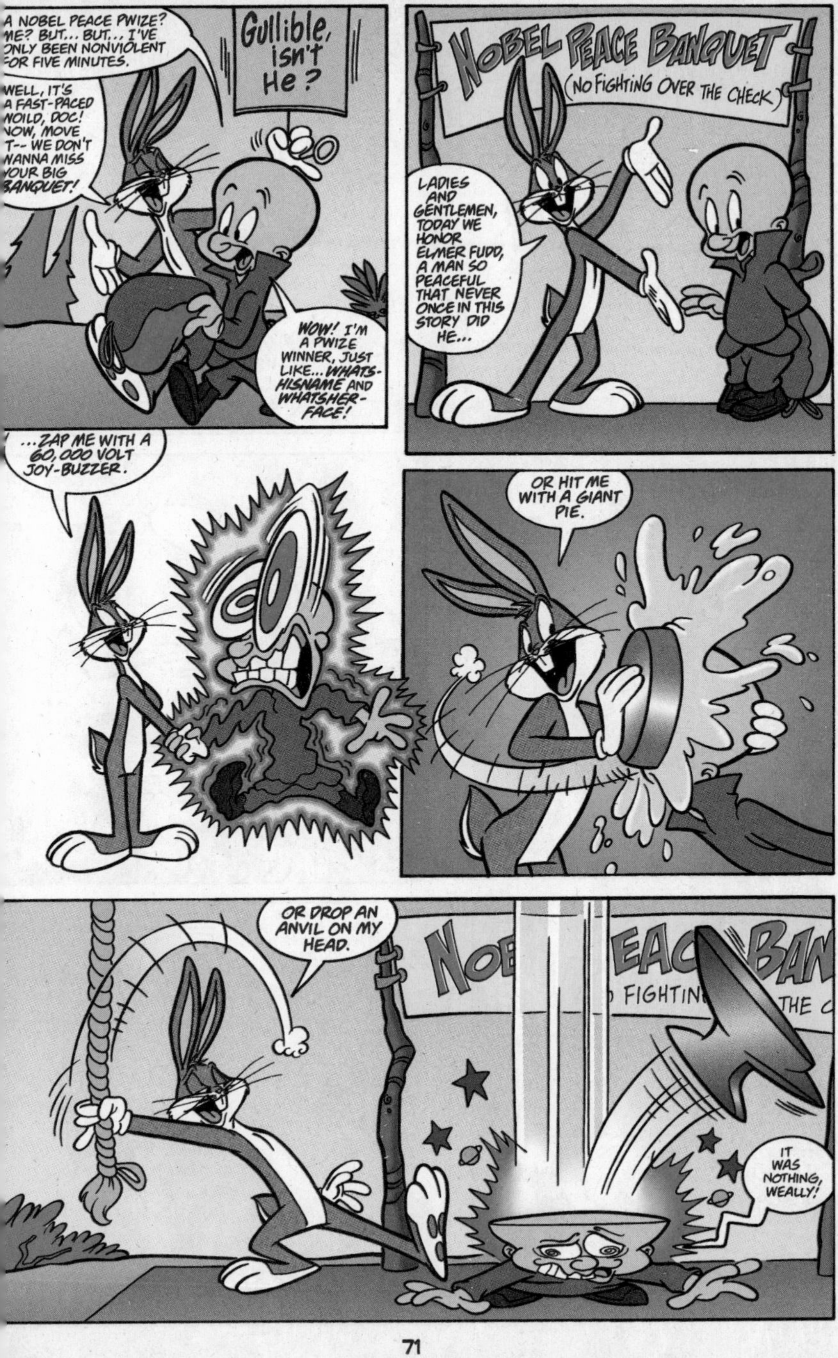

A NOBEL PEACE PWIZE? ME? BUT... BUT... I'VE ONLY BEEN NONVIOLENT FOR FIVE MINUTES.
Gullible, isn't He?
WELL, IT'S A FAST-PACED WOILD, DOC! NOW, MOVE IT-- WE DON'T WANNA MISS YOUR BIG BANQUET!
WOW! I'M A PWIZE WINNER, JUST LIKE... WHATS-HISNAME AND WHATSHER-FACE!
NOBEL PEACE BANQUET
(NO FIGHTING OVER THE CHECK)
LADIES AND GENTLEMEN, TODAY WE HONOR ELMER FUDD, A MAN SO PEACEFUL THAT NEVER ONCE IN THIS STORY DID HE...
...ZAP ME WITH A 60,000 VOLT JOY-BUZZER.
OR HIT ME WITH A GIANT PIE.
OR DROP AN ANVIL ON MY HEAD.
IT WAS NOTHING, WEALLY!

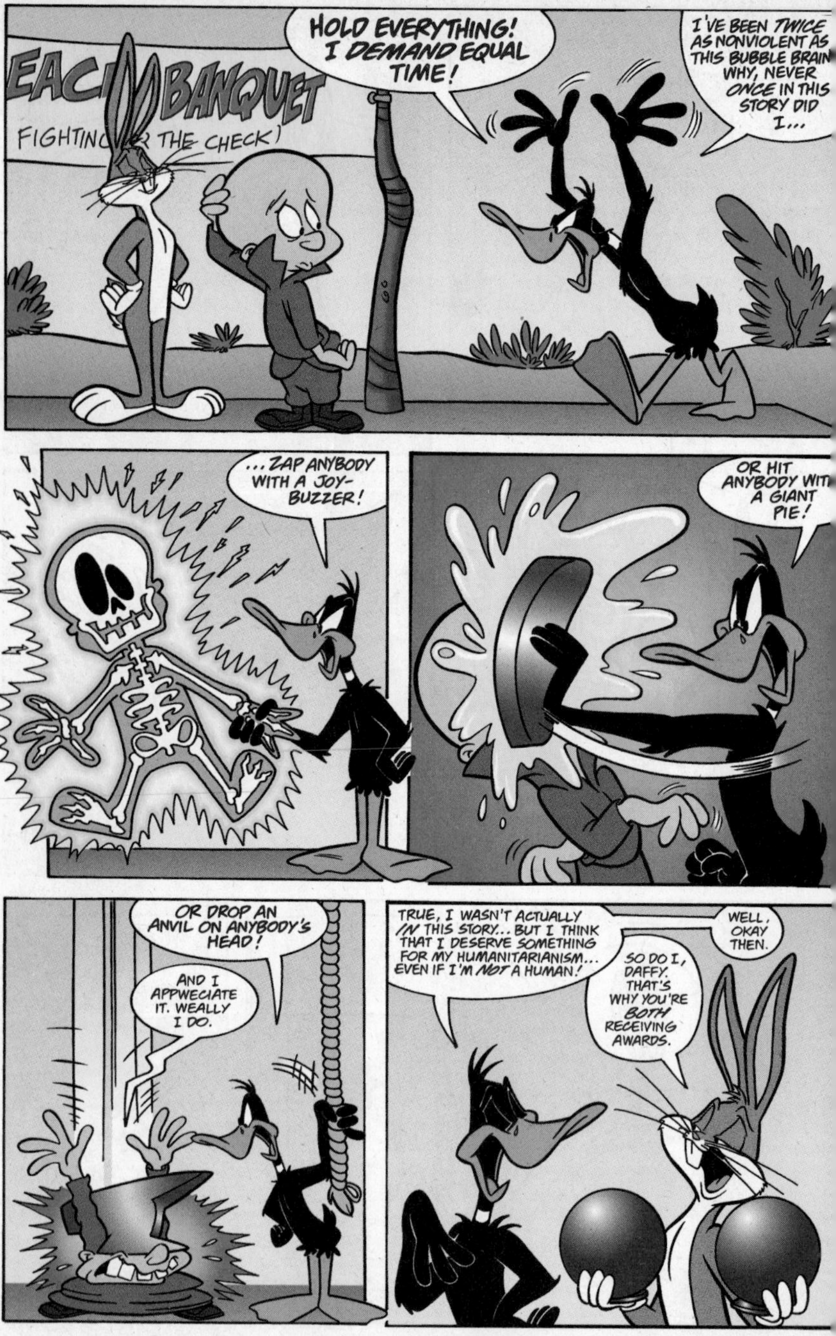
EAC BANQUET
FIGHTIN THE CHECK)
HOLD EVERYTHING! I DEMAND EQUAL TIME!
I'VE BEEN TWICE AS NONVIOLENT AS THIS BUBBLE BRAIN WHY, NEVER ONCE IN THIS STORY DID I...
...ZAP ANYBODY WITH A JOY-BUZZER!
OR HIT ANYBODY WIT A GIANT PIE!
OR DROP AN ANVIL ON ANYBODY'S HEAD!
AND I APPWECIATE IT. WEALLY I DO.
TRUE, I WASN'T ACTUALLY IN THIS STORY... BUT I THINK THAT I DESERVE SOMETHING FOR MY HUMANITARIANISM... EVEN IF I'M NOT A HUMAN!
SO DO I, DAFFY. THAT'S WHY YOU'RE BOTH RECEIVING AWARDS.
WELL, OKAY THEN.

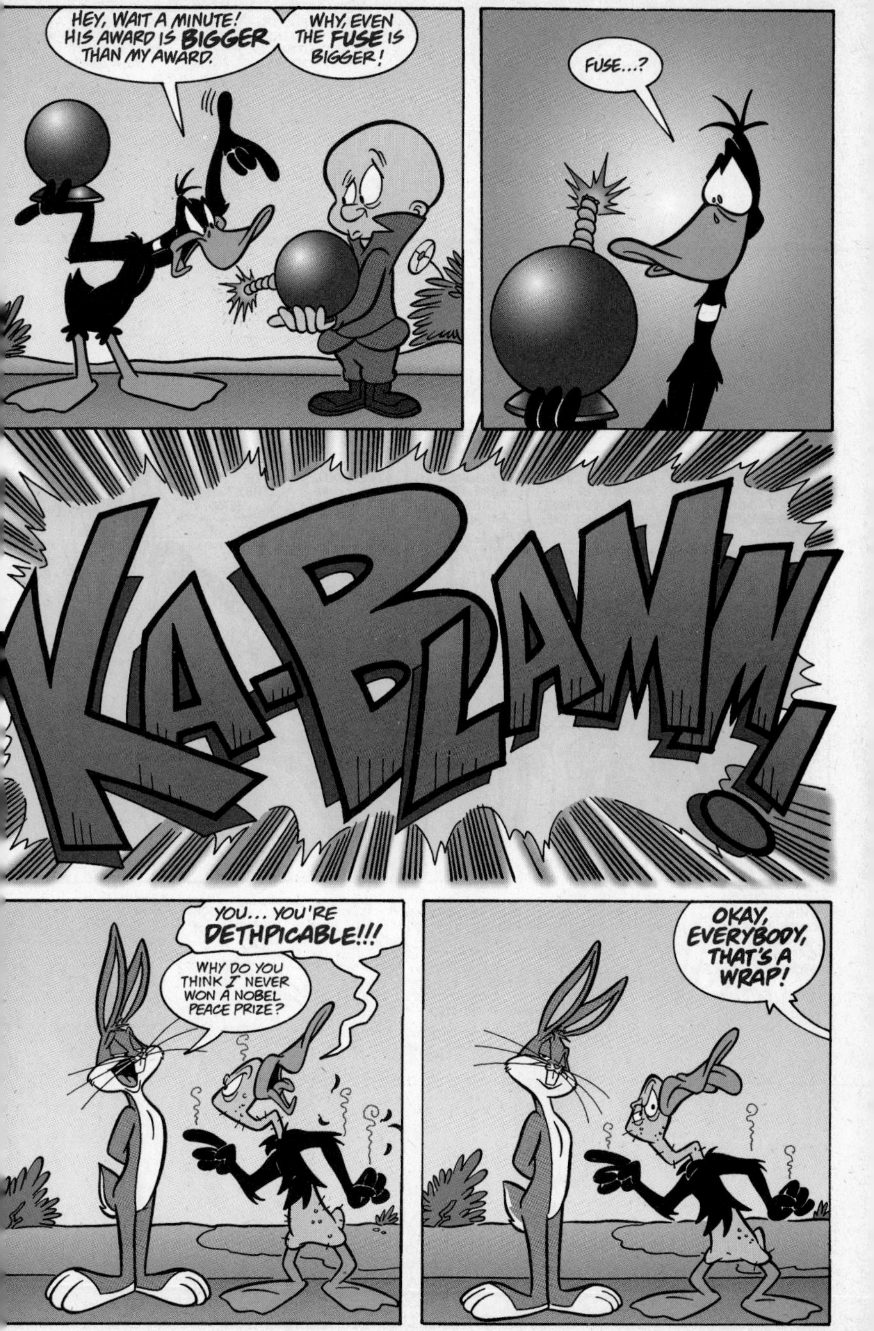
HEY, WAIT A MINUTE! HIS AWARD IS BIGGER THAN MY AWARD.
WHY, EVEN THE FUSE IS BIGGER!
FUSE...?
KA-BLAMM!
YOU... YOU'RE DETHPICABLE!!!
WHY DO YOU THINK I NEVER WON A NOBEL PEACE PRIZE?
OKAY, EVERYBODY, THAT'S A WRAP!

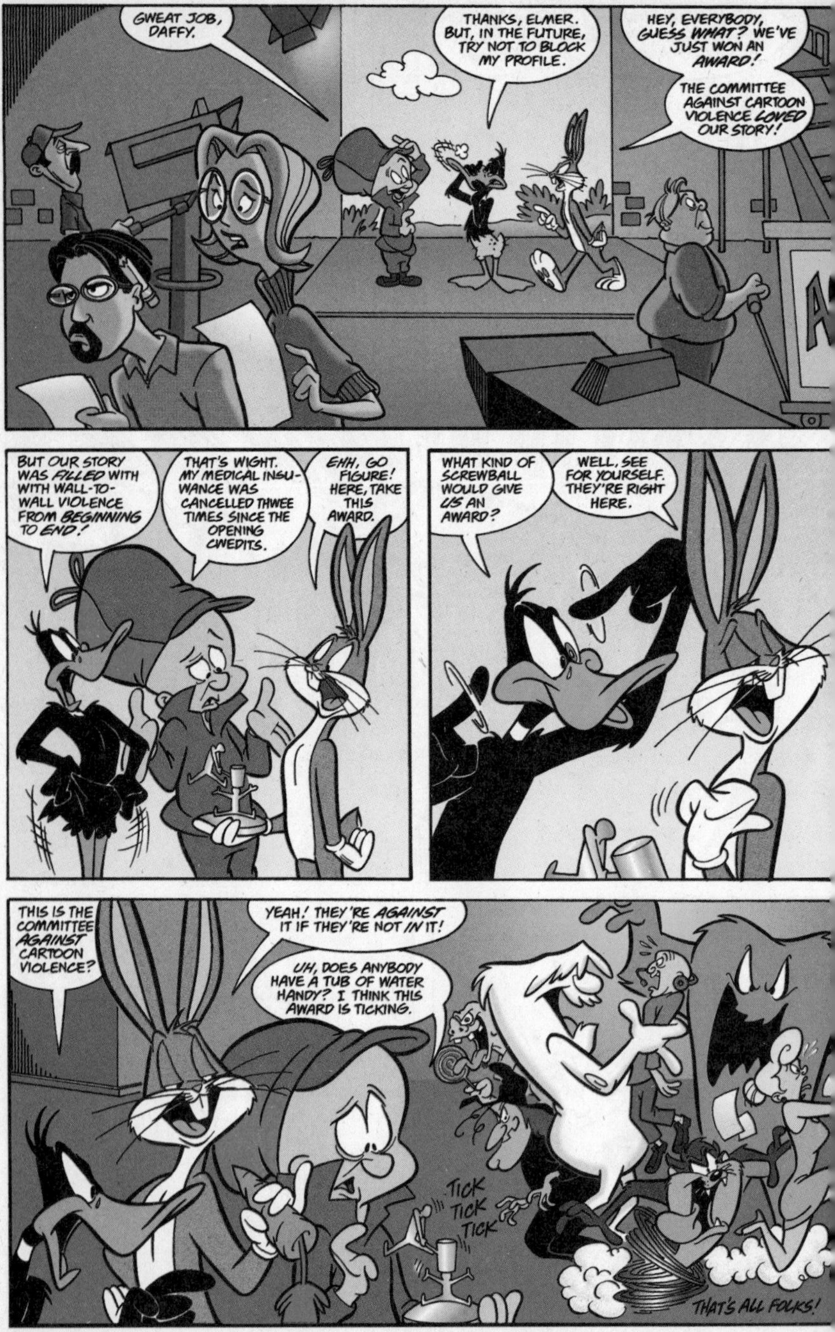
GWEAT JOB, DAFFY.
THANKS, ELMER. BUT, IN THE FUTURE, TRY NOT TO BLOCK MY PROFILE.
HEY, EVERYBODY, GUESS WHAT? WE'VE JUST WON AN AWARD!
THE COMMITTEE AGAINST CARTOON VIOLENCE LOVED OUR STORY!
BUT OUR STORY WAS FILLED WITH WITH WALL-TO-WALL VIOLENCE FROM BEGINNING TO END!
THAT'S WIGHT. MY MEDICAL INSU-WANCE WAS CANCELLED THWEE TIMES SINCE THE OPENING CWEDITS.
EHH, GO FIGURE! HERE, TAKE THIS AWARD.
WHAT KIND OF SCREWBALL WOULD GIVE US AN AWARD?
WELL, SEE FOR YOURSELF. THEY'RE RIGHT HERE.
THIS IS THE COMMITTEE AGAINST CARTOON VIOLENCE?
YEAH! THEY'RE AGAINST IT IF THEY'RE NOT IN IT!
UH, DOES ANYBODY HAVE A TUB OF WATER HANDY? I THINK THIS AWARD IS TICKING.
TICK TICK TICK
THAT'S ALL FOLKS!

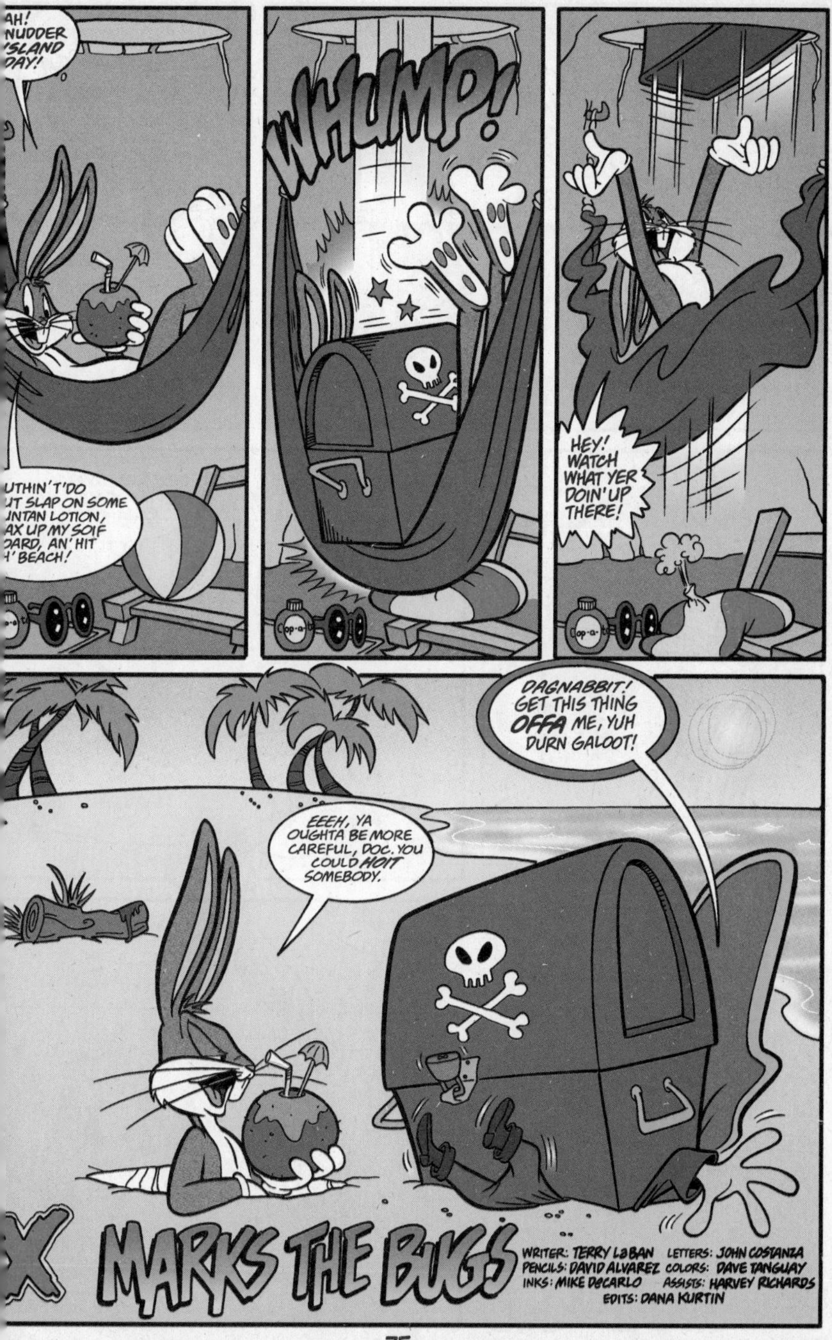
AH! NUDDER YSLAND DAY!
UTHIN' T'DO UT SLAP ON SOME UNTAN LOTION, AX UP MY SOIF OARD, AN' HIT H' BEACH!
WHUMP!
HEY! WATCH WHAT YER DOIN' UP THERE!
DAGNABBIT! GET THIS THING OFFA ME, YUH DURN GALOOT!
EEEH, YA OUGHTA BE MORE CAREFUL, DOC. YOU COULD HOIT SOMEBODY.
X MARKS THE BUGS
WRITER: TERRY LaBAN LETTERS: JOHN COSTANZA
PENCILS: DAVID ALVAREZ COLORS: DAVE TANGUAY
INKS: MIKE DeCARLO ASSISTS: HARVEY RICHARDS
EDITS: DANA KURTIN

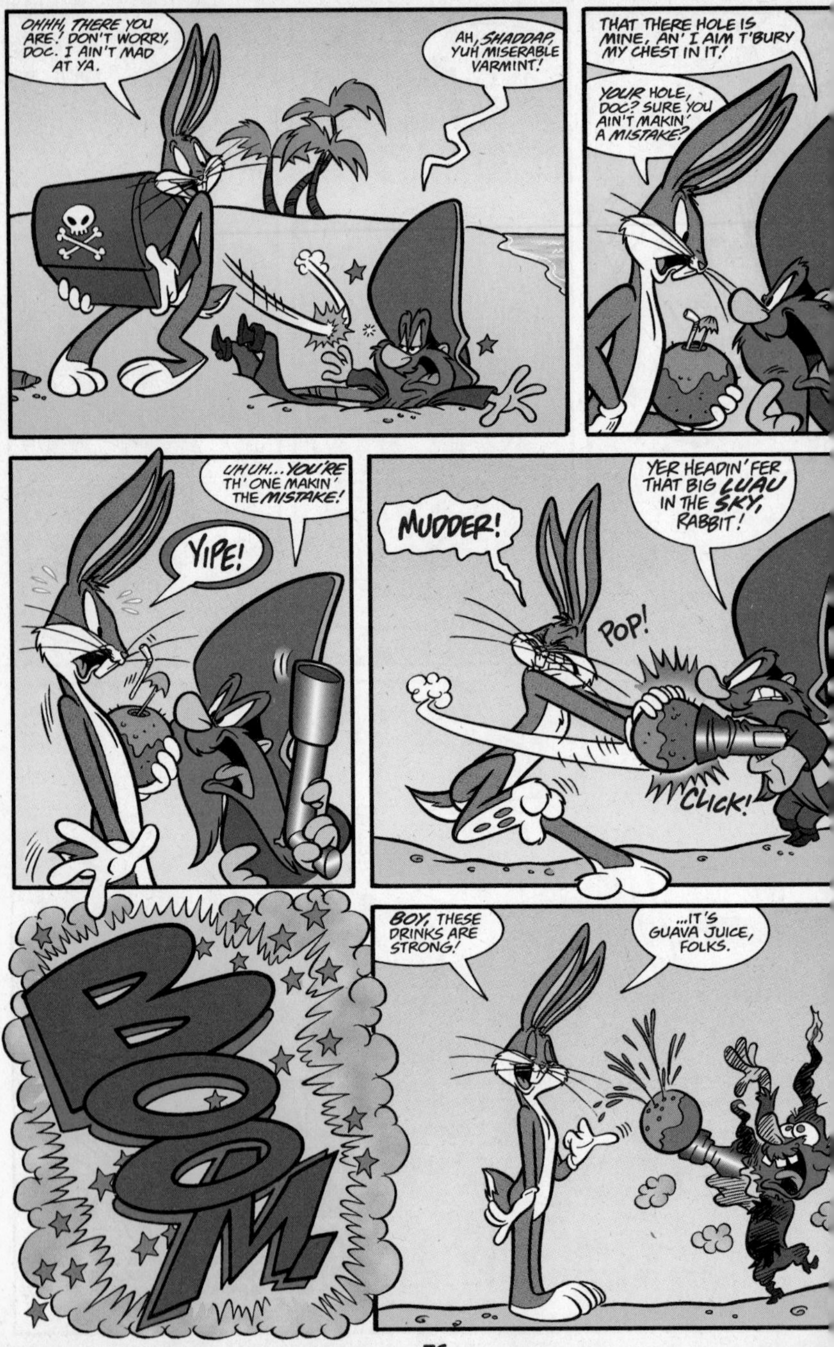

OHHH, THERE YOU ARE! DON'T WORRY, DOC. I AIN'T MAD AT YA.
AH, SHADDAP, YUH MISERABLE VARMINT!
THAT THERE HOLE IS MINE, AN' I AIM T'BURY MY CHEST IN IT!
YOUR HOLE, DOC? SURE YOU AIN'T MAKIN' A MISTAKE?
UH UH... YOU'RE TH' ONE MAKIN' THE MISTAKE!
YIPE!
MUDDER!
YER HEADIN' FER THAT BIG LUAU IN THE SKY, RABBIT!
POP!
CLICK!
BOOM!
BOY, THESE DRINKS ARE STRONG!
...IT'S GUAVA JUICE, FOLKS.

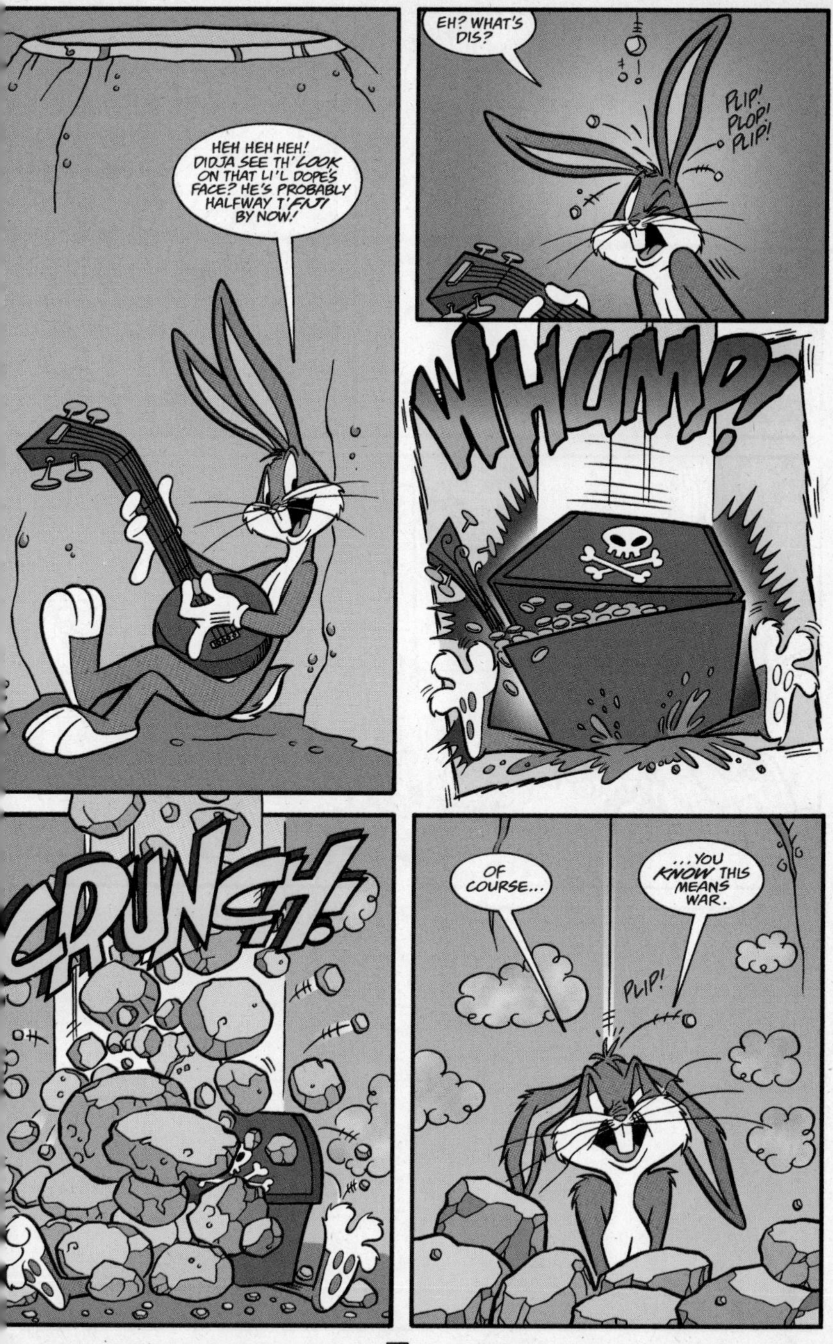
HEH HEH HEH! DIDJA SEE TH' LOOK ON THAT LI'L DOPE'S FACE? HE'S PROBABLY HALFWAY T' FIJI BY NOW!
EH? WHAT'S DIS?
PLIP! PLOP! PLIP!
WHUMP!
CRUNCH!
OF COURSE...
...YOU KNOW THIS MEANS WAR.
PLIP!

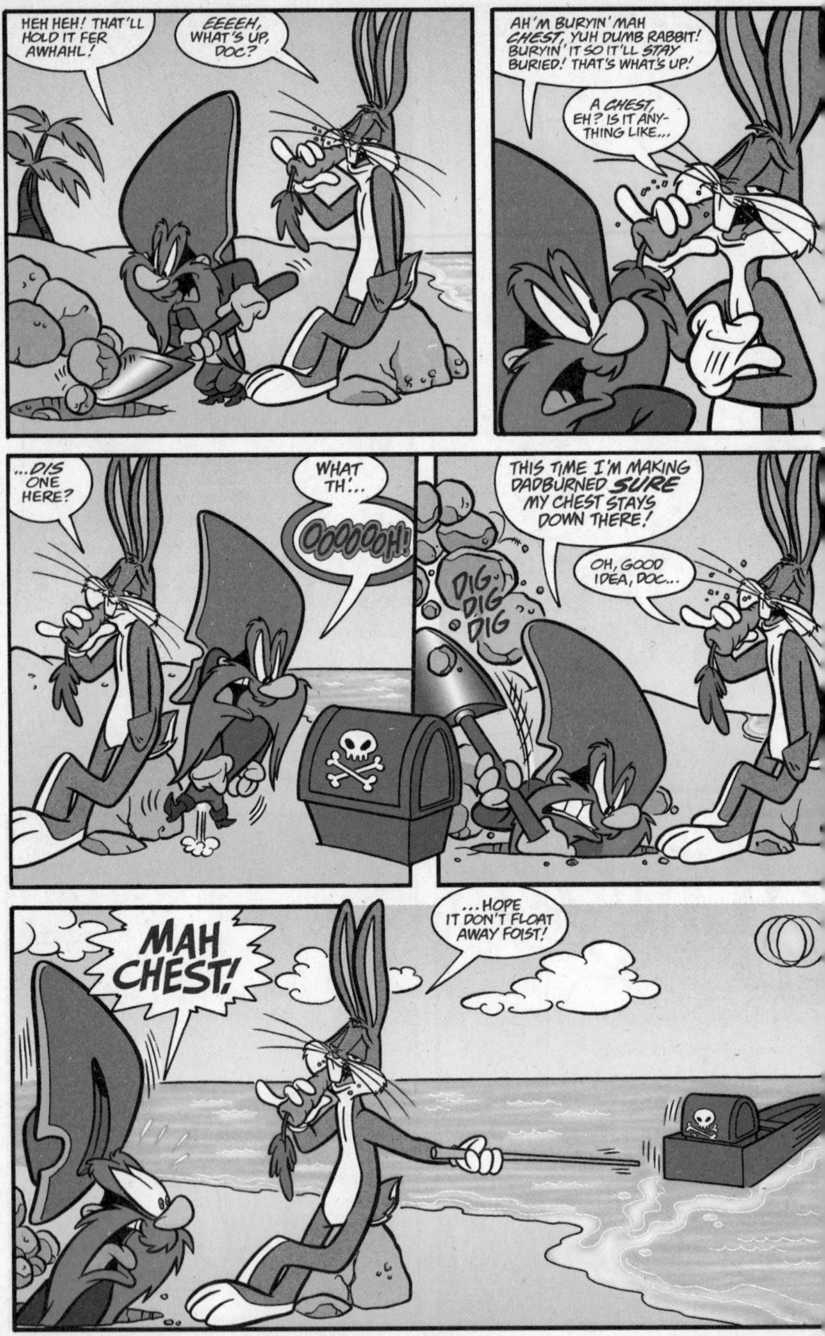
HEH HEH! THAT'LL HOLD IT FER AWHAHL!
EEEEH, WHAT'S UP, DOC?
AH'M BURYIN' MAH CHEST, YUH DUMB RABBIT! BURYIN' IT SO IT'LL STAY BURIED! THAT'S WHAT'S UP!
A CHEST, EH? IS IT ANY-THING LIKE...
...DIS ONE HERE?
WHAT TH'...
OOOOOOH!
THIS TIME I'M MAKING DADBURNED SURE MY CHEST STAYS DOWN THERE!
DIG DIG DIG
OH, GOOD IDEA, DOC...
MAH CHEST!
...HOPE IT DON'T FLOAT AWAY FOIST!

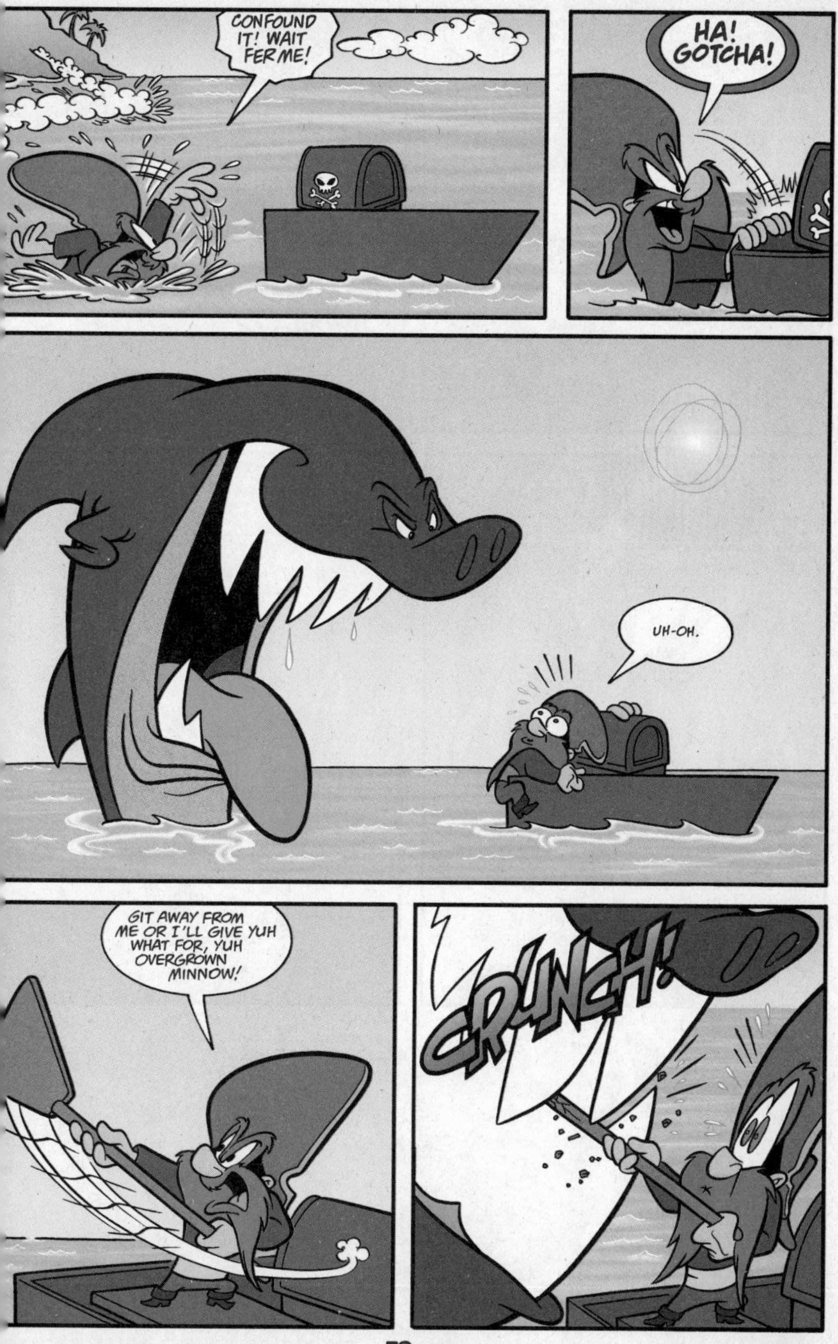
CONFOUND IT! WAIT FER ME!
HA! GOTCHA!
UH-OH.
GIT AWAY FROM ME OR I'LL GIVE YUH WHAT FOR, YUH OVERGROWN MINNOW!
CRUNCH!

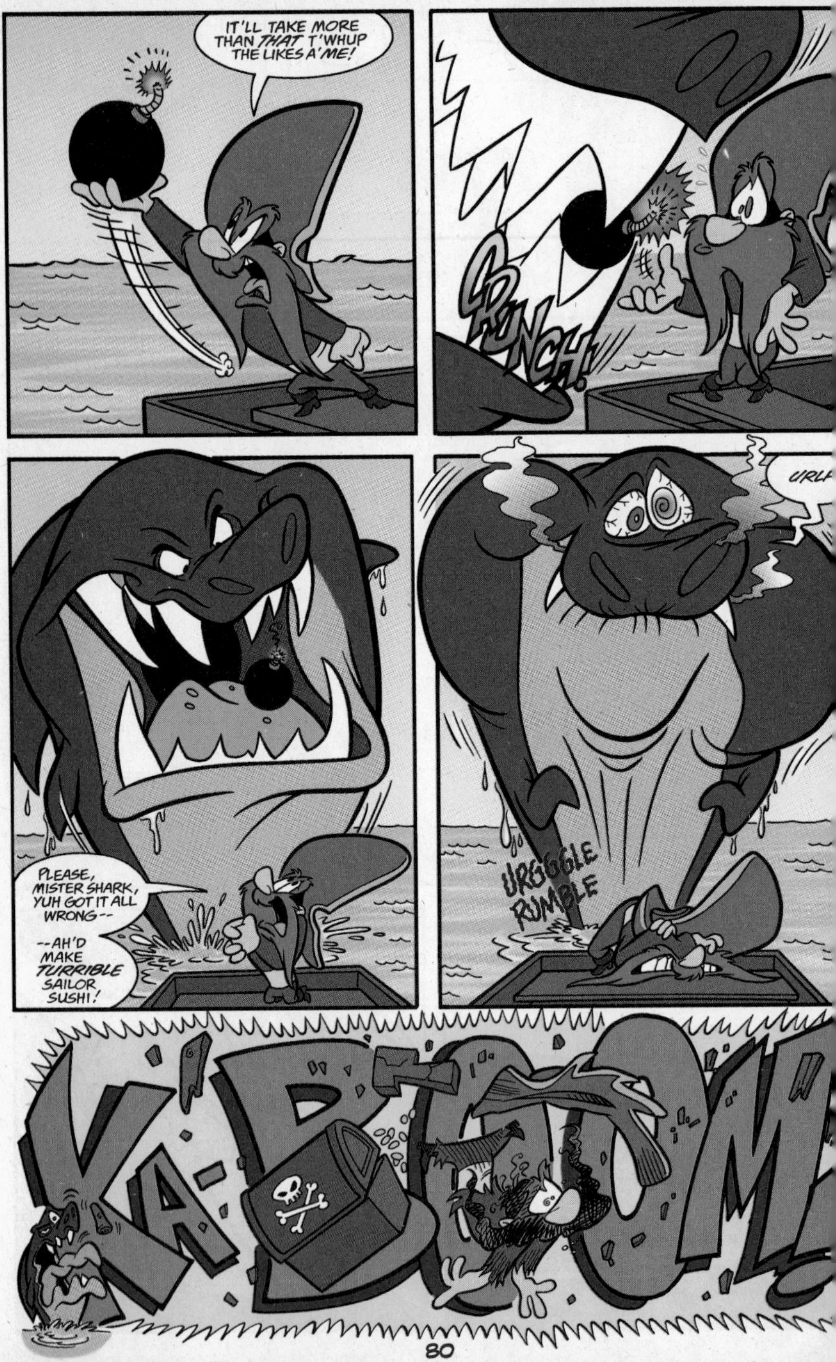
IT'LL TAKE MORE THAN THAT T'WHUP THE LIKES A'ME!
CRUNCH!
URLP
PLEASE, MISTER SHARK, YUH GOT IT ALL WRONG--
--AH'D MAKE TURRIBLE SAILOR SUSHI!
URGGLE RUMBLE
KA-BOOM!

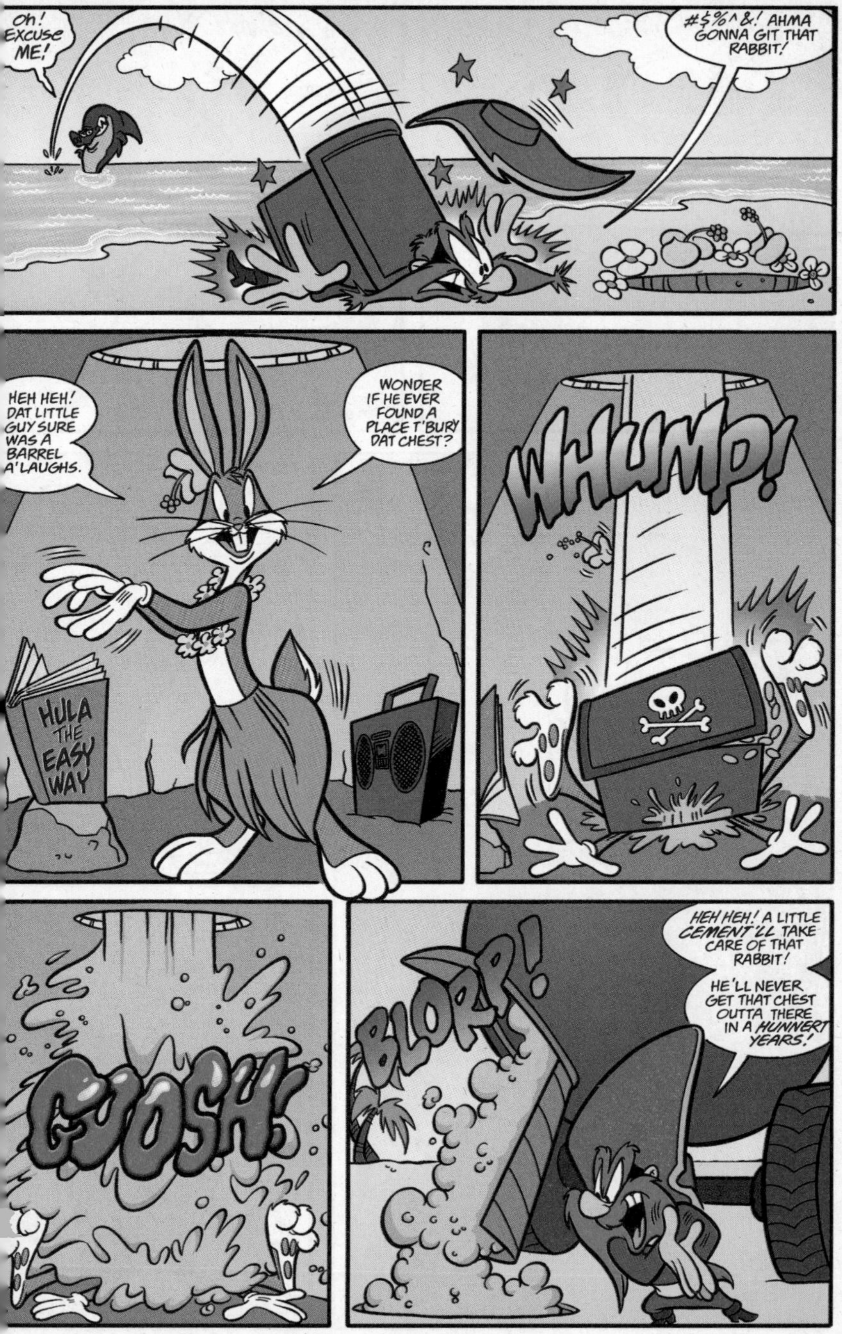
Oh! EXCUSE ME!
#$%^&! AHMA GONNA GIT THAT RABBIT!
HEH HEH! DAT LITTLE GUY SURE WAS A BARREL A'LAUGHS.
WONDER IF HE EVER FOUND A PLACE T'BURY DAT CHEST?
HULA THE EASY WAY
WHUMP!
GLOSH!
BLORP!
HEH HEH! A LITTLE CEMENT'LL TAKE CARE OF THAT RABBIT!
HE'LL NEVER GET THAT CHEST OUTTA THERE IN A HUNNERT YEARS!

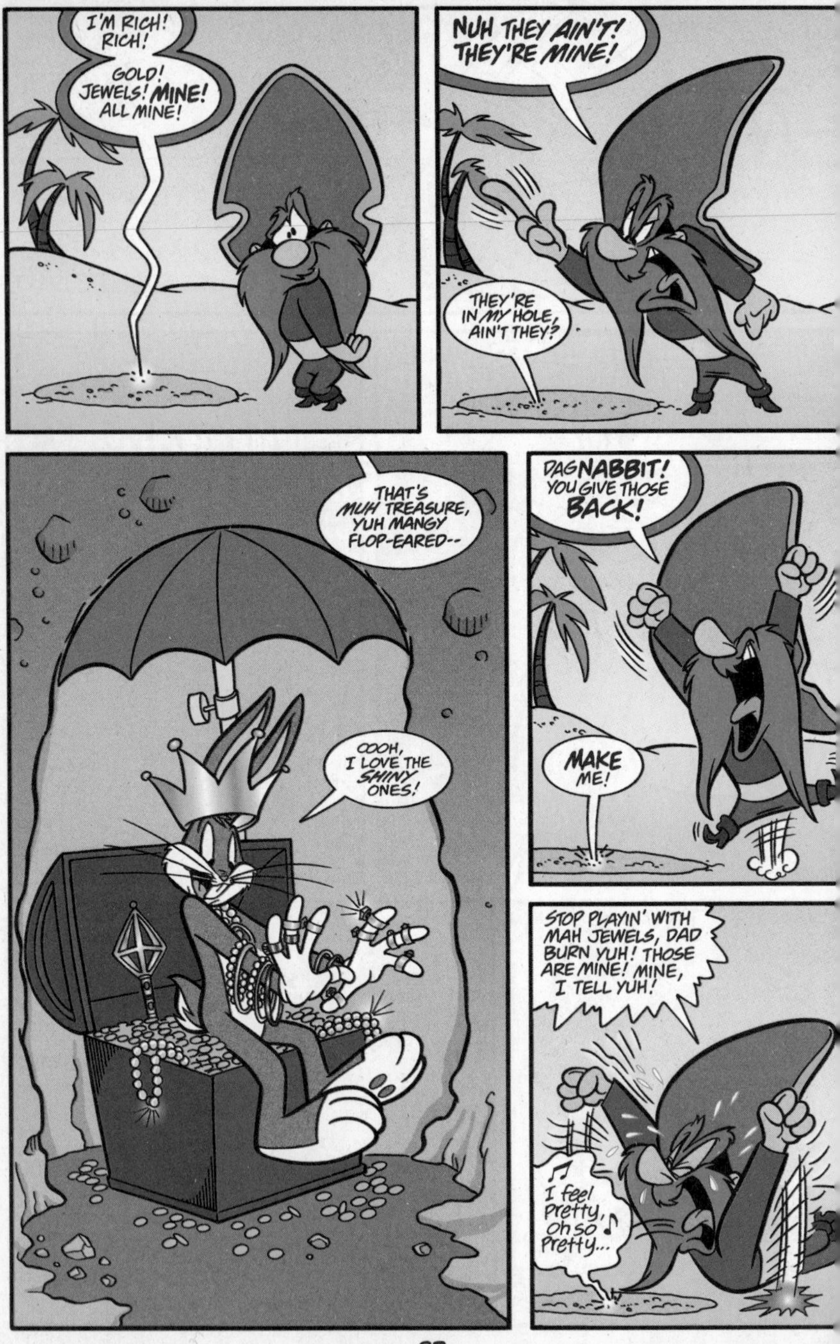
I'M RICH! RICH!
GOLD! JEWELS! MINE! ALL MINE!
NUH THEY AIN'T! THEY'RE MINE!
THEY'RE IN MY HOLE, AIN'T THEY?
THAT'S MUH TREASURE, YUH MANGY FLOP-EARED--
OOOH, I LOVE THE SHINY ONES!
DAGNABBIT! YOU GIVE THOSE BACK!
MAKE ME!
STOP PLAYIN' WITH MAH JEWELS, DAD BURN YUH! THOSE ARE MINE! MINE, I TELL YUH!
I feel Pretty, oh so Pretty...

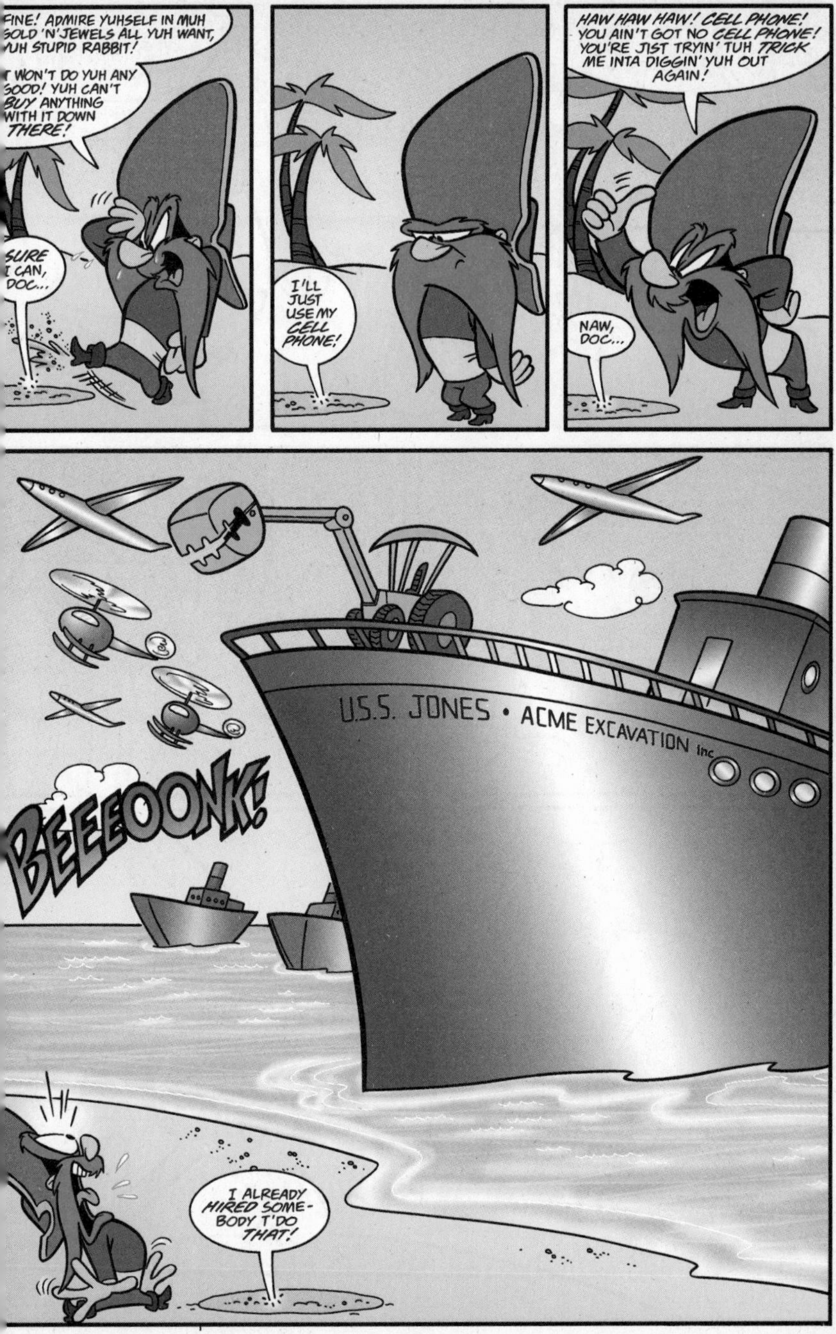
FINE! ADMIRE YUHSELF IN MUH GOLD 'N' JEWELS ALL YUH WANT, YUH STUPID RABBIT!
IT WON'T DO YUH ANY GOOD! YUH CAN'T BUY ANYTHING WITH IT DOWN THERE!
SURE I CAN, DOC...
I'LL JUST USE MY CELL PHONE!
HAW HAW HAW! CELL PHONE! YOU AIN'T GOT NO CELL PHONE! YOU'RE JIST TRYIN' TUH TRICK ME INTA DIGGIN' YUH OUT AGAIN!
NAW, DOC...
U.S.S. JONES • ACME EXCAVATION inc
BEEEOONK!
I ALREADY HIRED SOME-BODY T'DO THAT!

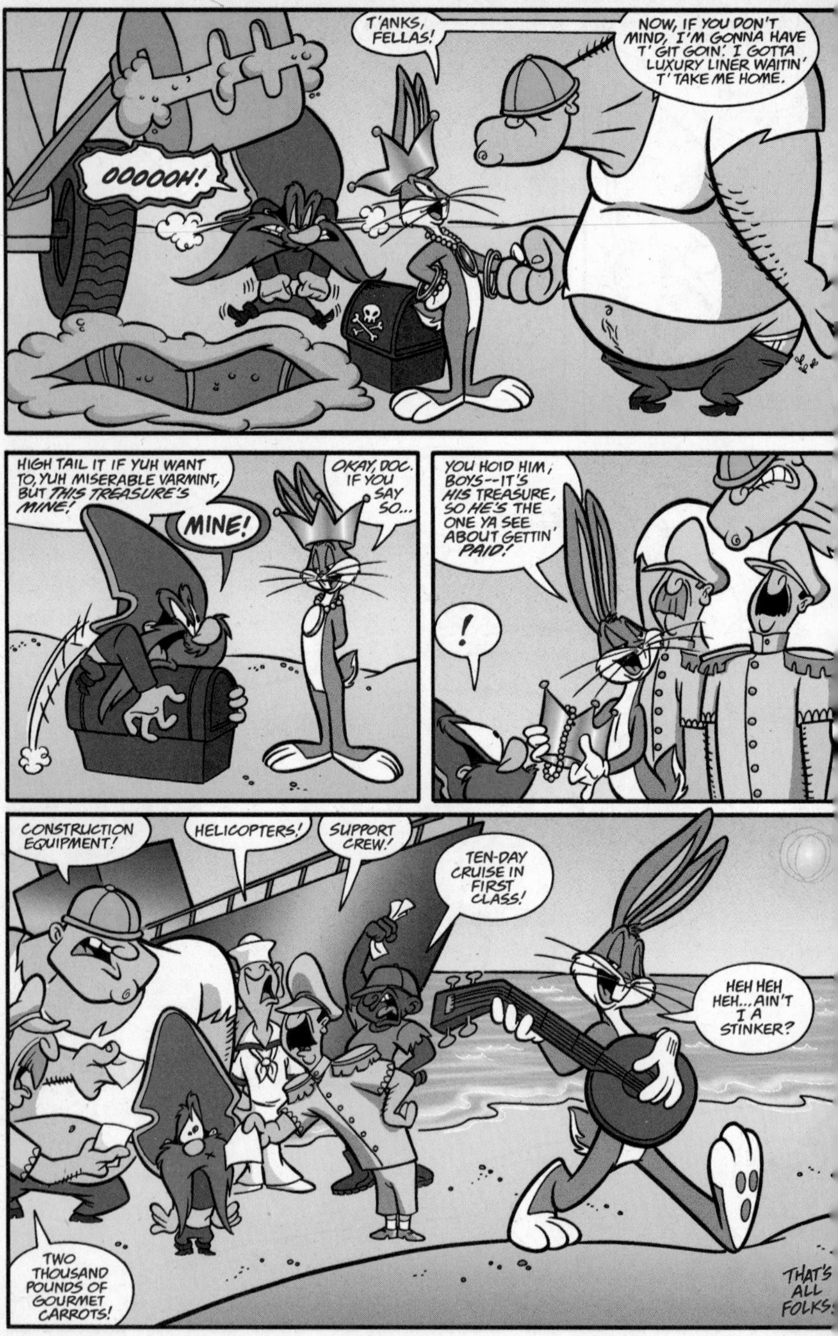
T'ANKS, FELLAS!
NOW, IF YOU DON'T MIND, I'M GONNA HAVE T' GIT GOIN'. I GOTTA LUXURY LINER WAITIN' T' TAKE ME HOME.
OOOOOH!
HIGH TAIL IT IF YUH WANT TO, YUH MISERABLE VARMINT, BUT THIS TREASURE'S MINE!
MINE!
OKAY, DOC. IF YOU SAY SO...
YOU HOID HIM, BOYS--IT'S HIS TREASURE, SO HE'S THE ONE YA SEE ABOUT GETTIN' PAID!
!
CONSTRUCTION EQUIPMENT!
HELICOPTERS!
SUPPORT CREW!
TEN-DAY CRUISE IN FIRST CLASS!
TWO THOUSAND POUNDS OF GOURMET CARROTS!
HEH HEH HEH...AIN'T I A STINKER?
THAT'S ALL FOLKS!

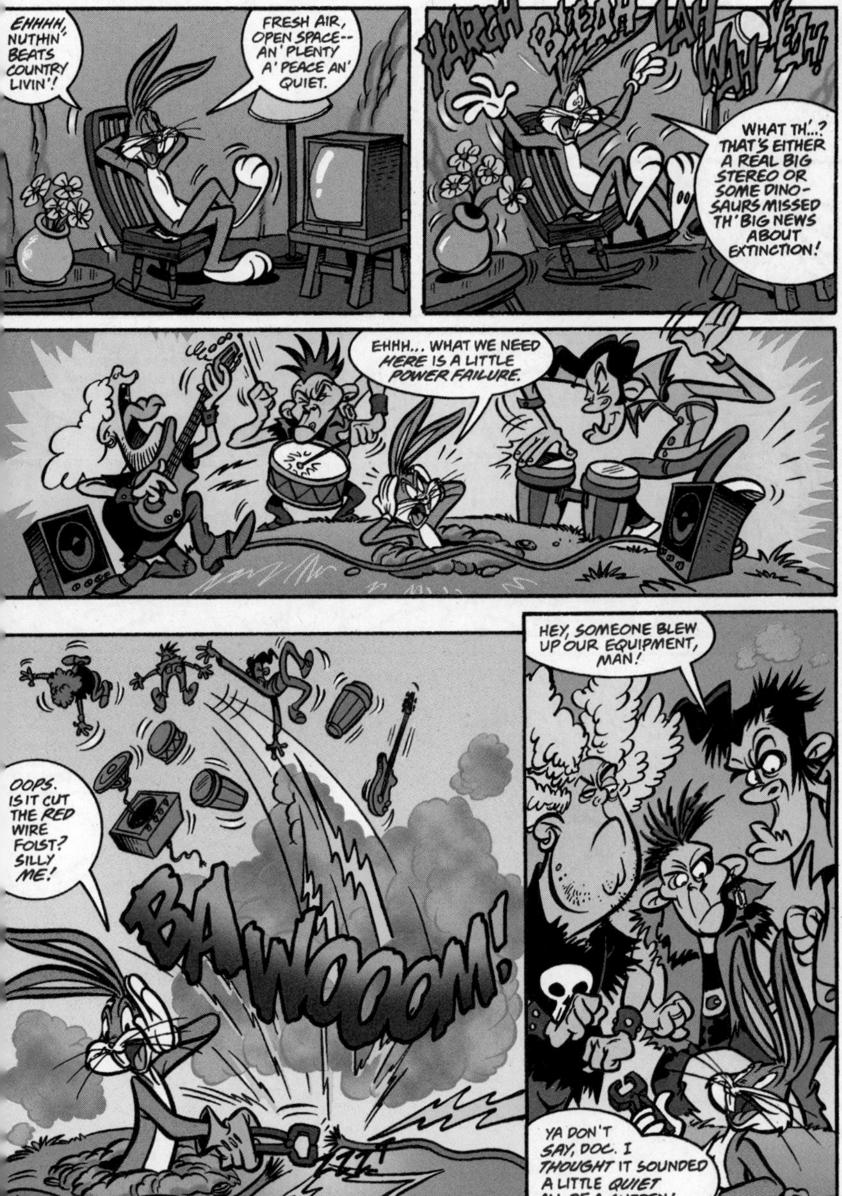
EHHHH, NUTHIN' BEATS COUNTRY LIVIN'!
FRESH AIR, OPEN SPACE-- AN' PLENTY A' PEACE AN' QUIET.
YARGH BLEAH LAH WAH YEAH!
WHAT TH'...? THAT'S EITHER A REAL BIG STEREO OR SOME DINOSAURS MISSED TH' BIG NEWS ABOUT EXTINCTION!
EHHH... WHAT WE NEED *HERE* IS A LITTLE *POWER FAILURE.*
OOPS. IS IT CUT THE *RED* WIRE FOIST? SILLY *ME!*
BAWOOOM!
HEY, SOMEONE BLEW UP OUR EQUIPMENT, MAN!
YA DON'T *SAY*, DOC. I *THOUGHT* IT SOUNDED A LITTLE *QUIET* ALL OF A SUDDEN!

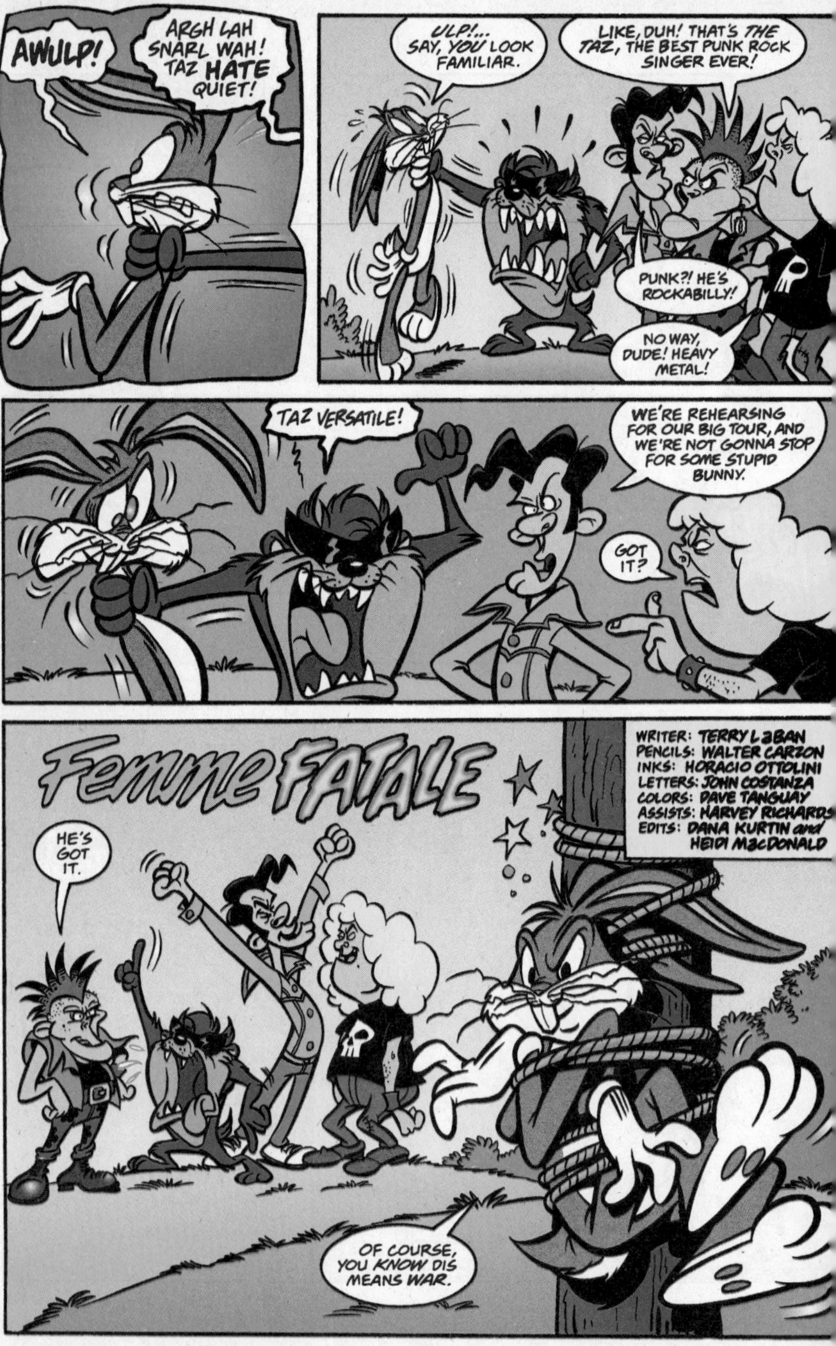
AWULP!
ARGH LAH SNARL WAH! TAZ HATE QUIET!
ULP!... SAY, YOU LOOK FAMILIAR.
LIKE, DUH! THAT'S THE TAZ, THE BEST PUNK ROCK SINGER EVER!
PUNK?! HE'S ROCKABILLY!
NO WAY, DUDE! HEAVY METAL!
TAZ VERSATILE!
WE'RE REHEARSING FOR OUR BIG TOUR, AND WE'RE NOT GONNA STOP FOR SOME STUPID BUNNY.
GOT IT?
Femme FATALE
WRITER: TERRY LABAN
PENCILS: WALTER CARZON
INKS: HORACIO OTTOLINI
LETTERS: JOHN COSTANZA
COLORS: DAVE TANGUAY
ASSISTS: HARVEY RICHARDS
EDITS: DANA KURTIN and HEIDI MacDONALD
HE'S GOT IT.
OF COURSE, YOU KNOW DIS MEANS WAR.

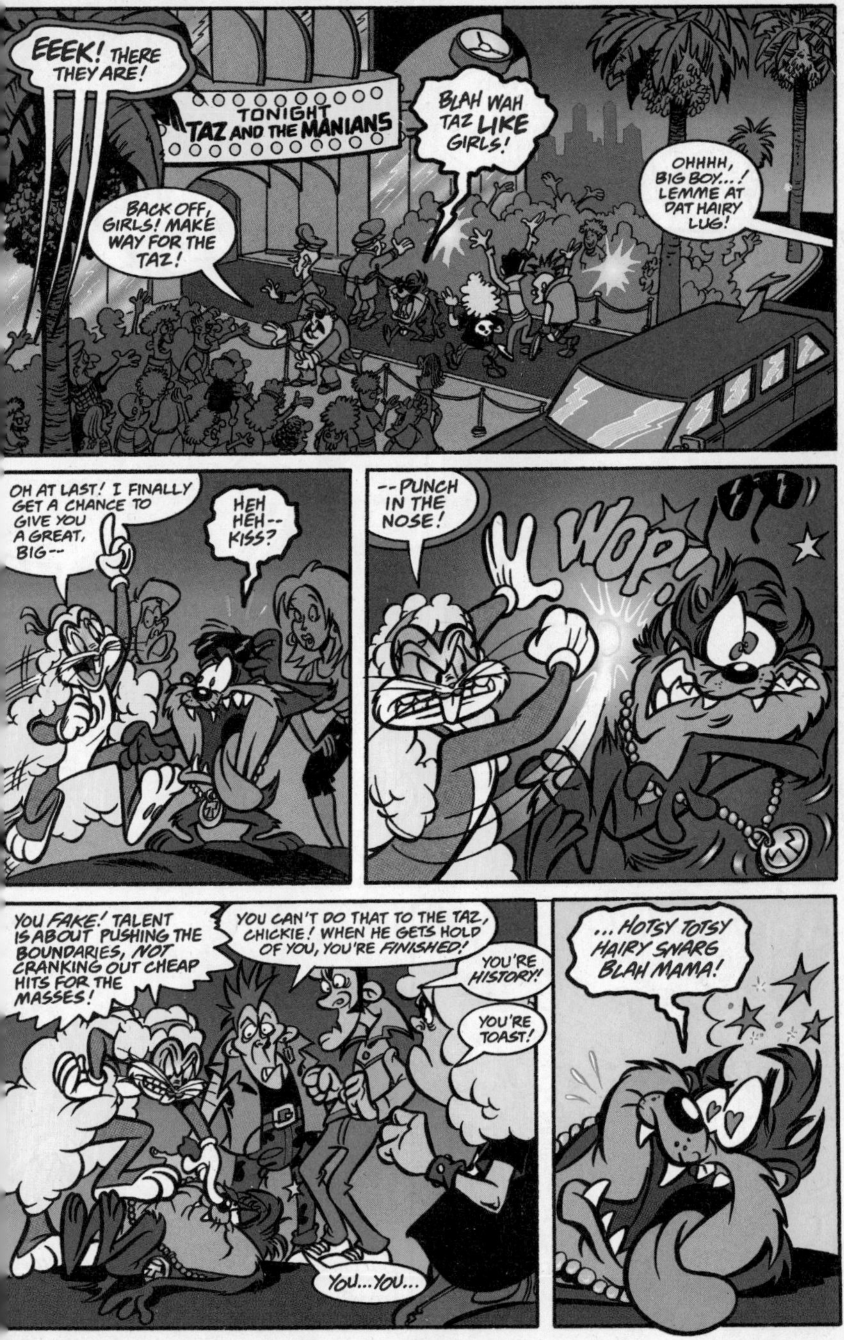
EEEK! THERE THEY ARE!
TONIGHT TAZ AND THE MANIANS
BLAH WAH TAZ LIKE GIRLS!
OHHHH, BIG BOY...! LEMME AT DAT HAIRY LUG!
BACK OFF, GIRLS! MAKE WAY FOR THE TAZ!
OH AT LAST! I FINALLY GET A CHANCE TO GIVE YOU A GREAT, BIG--
HEH HEH-- KISS?
--PUNCH IN THE NOSE!
WOP!
YOU FAKE! TALENT IS ABOUT PUSHING THE BOUNDARIES, NOT CRANKING OUT CHEAP HITS FOR THE MASSES!
YOU CAN'T DO THAT TO THE TAZ, CHICKIE! WHEN HE GETS HOLD OF YOU, YOU'RE FINISHED!
YOU'RE HISTORY!
YOU'RE TOAST!
YOU...YOU...
...HOTSY TOTSY HAIRY SNARG BLAH MAMA!

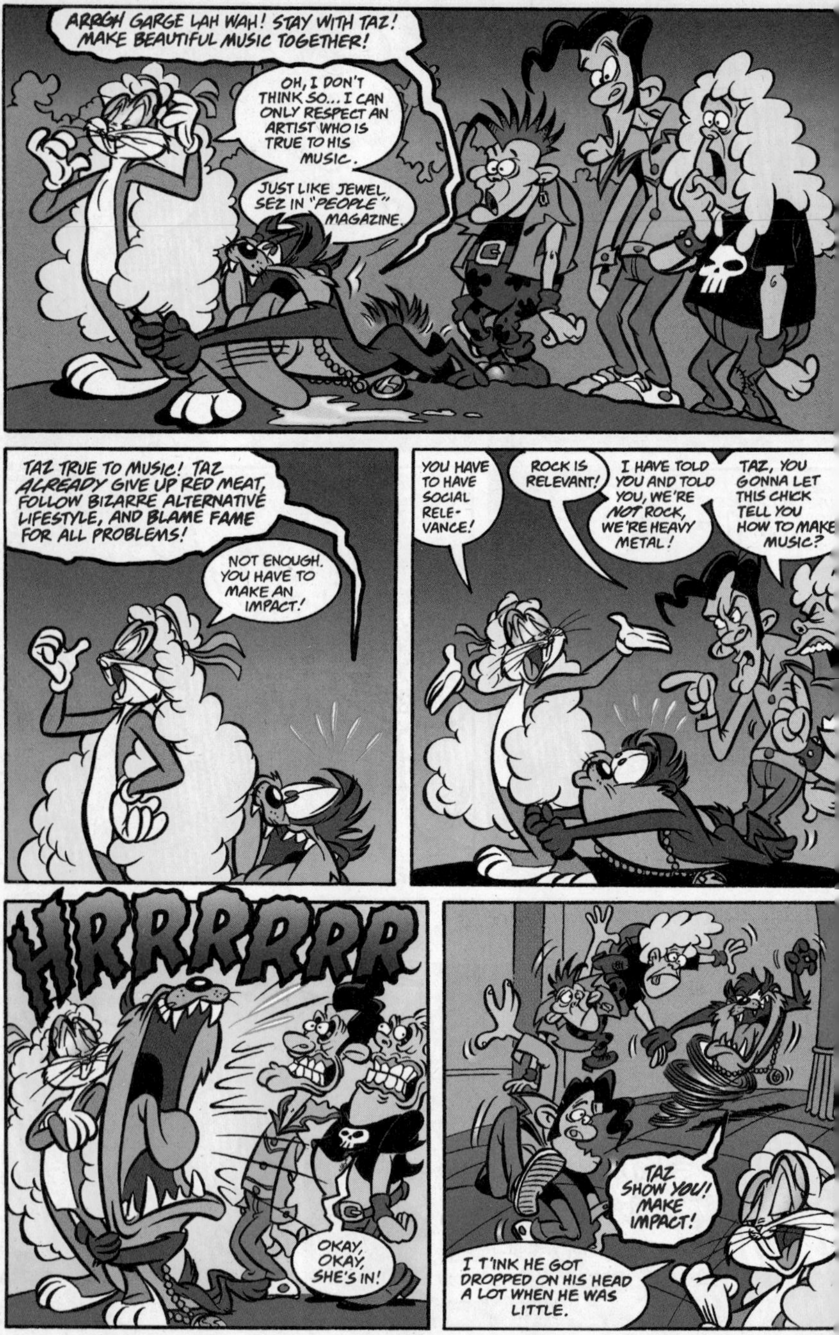
ARRGH GARGE LAH WAH! STAY WITH TAZ! MAKE BEAUTIFUL MUSIC TOGETHER!
OH, I DON'T THINK SO... I CAN ONLY RESPECT AN ARTIST WHO IS TRUE TO HIS MUSIC.
JUST LIKE JEWEL SEZ IN "PEOPLE" MAGAZINE.
TAZ TRUE TO MUSIC! TAZ ALREADY GIVE UP RED MEAT, FOLLOW BIZARRE ALTERNATIVE LIFESTYLE, AND BLAME FAME FOR ALL PROBLEMS!
NOT ENOUGH. YOU HAVE TO MAKE AN IMPACT!
YOU HAVE TO HAVE SOCIAL RELE-VANCE!
ROCK IS RELEVANT!
I HAVE TOLD YOU AND TOLD YOU, WE'RE NOT ROCK, WE'RE HEAVY METAL!
TAZ, YOU GONNA LET THIS CHICK TELL YOU HOW TO MAKE MUSIC?
HRRRRRR
OKAY, OKAY, SHE'S IN!
TAZ SHOW YOU! MAKE IMPACT!
I T'INK HE GOT DROPPED ON HIS HEAD A LOT WHEN HE WAS LITTLE.

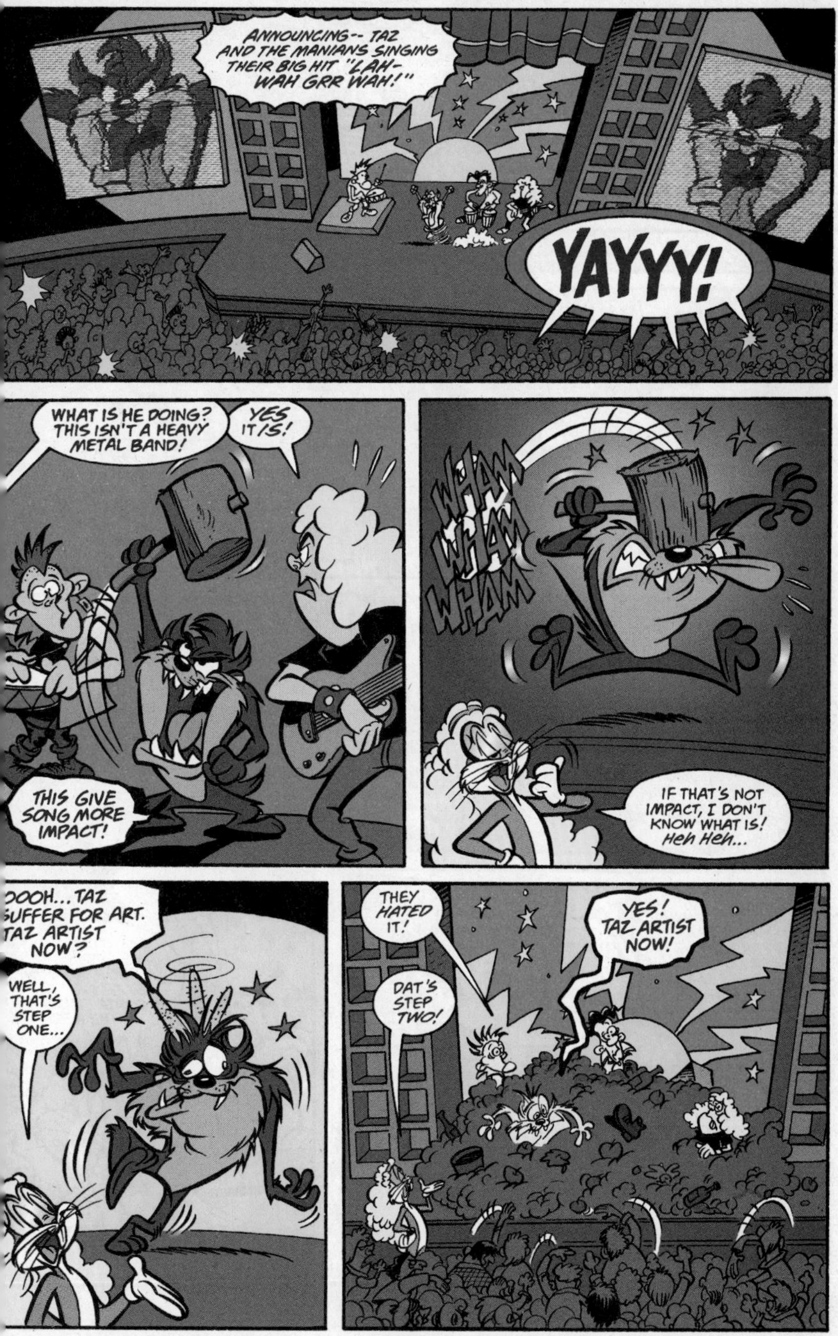

ANNOUNCING-- TAZ AND THE MANIANS SINGING THEIR BIG HIT "LAH-WAH GRR WAH!"
YAYYY!
WHAT IS HE DOING? THIS ISN'T A HEAVY METAL BAND!
YES IT IS!
THIS GIVE SONG MORE IMPACT!
WHAM WHAM WHAM
IF THAT'S NOT IMPACT, I DON'T KNOW WHAT IS! Heh Heh...
OOOH... TAZ SUFFER FOR ART. TAZ ARTIST NOW?
WELL, THAT'S STEP ONE...
THEY HATED IT!
DAT'S STEP TWO!
YES! TAZ ARTIST NOW!

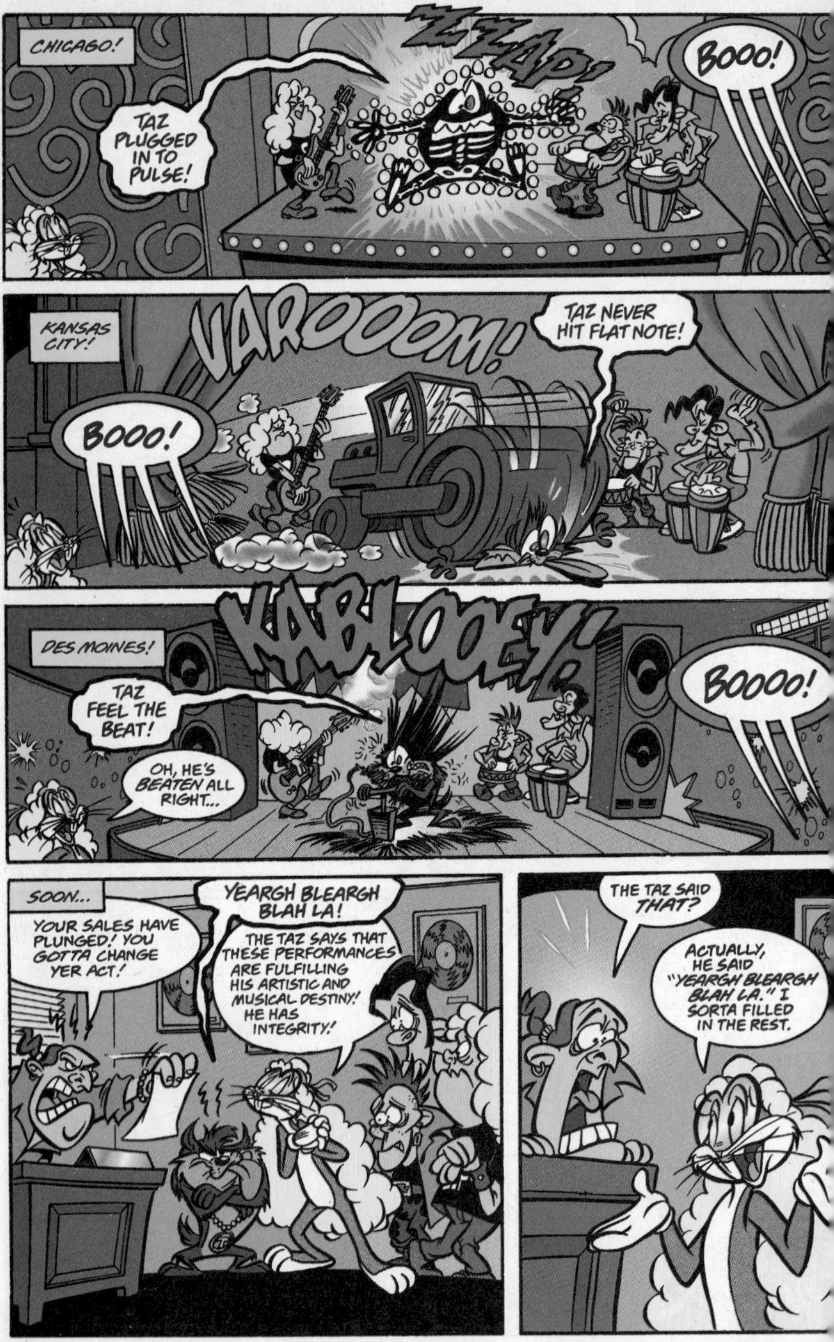
CHICAGO!
TAZ PLUGGED IN TO PULSE!
ZZZAP!
BOOO!
KANSAS CITY!
VAROOOM!
TAZ NEVER HIT FLAT NOTE!
BOOO!
DES MOINES!
KABLOOEY!
TAZ FEEL THE BEAT!
OH, HE'S BEATEN ALL RIGHT...
BOOOO!
SOON...
YOUR SALES HAVE PLUNGED! YOU GOTTA CHANGE YER ACT!
YEARGH BLEARGH BLAH LA!
THE TAZ SAYS THAT THESE PERFORMANCES ARE FULFILLING HIS ARTISTIC AND MUSICAL DESTINY! HE HAS INTEGRITY!
THE TAZ SAID THAT?
ACTUALLY, HE SAID "YEARGH BLEARGH BLAH LA." I SORTA FILLED IN THE REST.

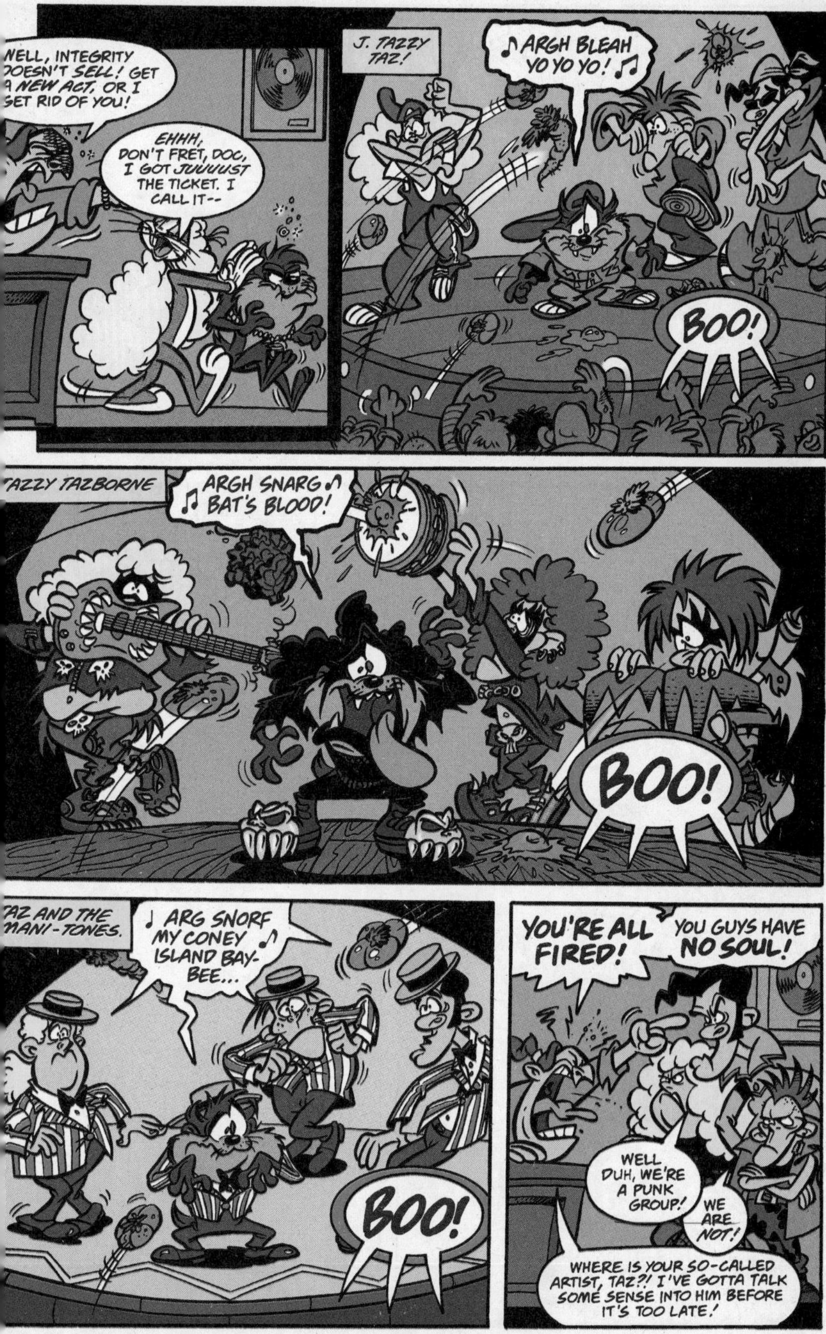
WELL, INTEGRITY DOESN'T SELL! GET A NEW ACT, OR I GET RID OF YOU!
EHHH, DON'T FRET, DOC, I GOT JUUUUST THE TICKET. I CALL IT--
J. TAZZY TAZ!
♪ ARGH BLEAH YO YO YO! ♫
BOO!
TAZZY TAZBORNE
♫ ARGH SNARG ♪ BAT'S BLOOD!
BOO!
TAZ AND THE MANI-TONES.
♩ ARG SNORF MY CONEY ISLAND BAY-BEE... ♪
BOO!
YOU'RE ALL FIRED!
YOU GUYS HAVE NO SOUL!
WELL DUH, WE'RE A PUNK GROUP!
WE ARE NOT!
WHERE IS YOUR SO-CALLED ARTIST, TAZ?! I'VE GOTTA TALK SOME SENSE INTO HIM BEFORE IT'S TOO LATE!

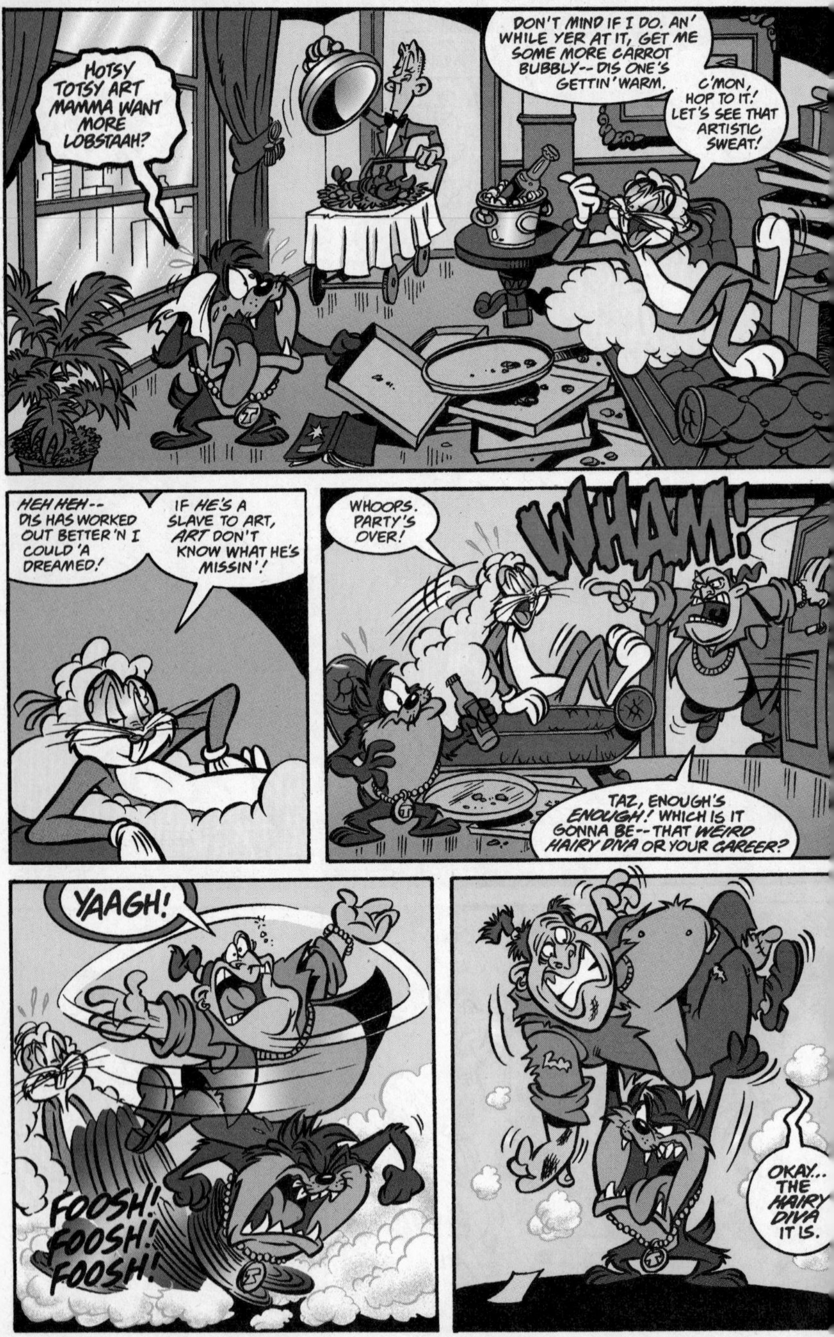
HOTSY TOTSY ART MAMMA WANT MORE LOBSTAAH?
DON'T MIND IF I DO. AN' WHILE YER AT IT, GET ME SOME MORE CARROT BUBBLY-- DIS ONE'S GETTIN' WARM.
C'MON, HOP TO IT! LET'S SEE THAT ARTISTIC SWEAT!
HEH HEH-- DIS HAS WORKED OUT BETTER 'N I COULD 'A DREAMED!
IF HE'S A SLAVE TO ART, ART DON'T KNOW WHAT HE'S MISSIN'!
WHOOPS. PARTY'S OVER!
WHAM!
TAZ, ENOUGH'S ENOUGH! WHICH IS IT GONNA BE-- THAT WEIRD HAIRY DIVA OR YOUR CAREER?
YAAGH!
FOOSH! FOOSH! FOOSH!
OKAY... THE HAIRY DIVA IT IS.

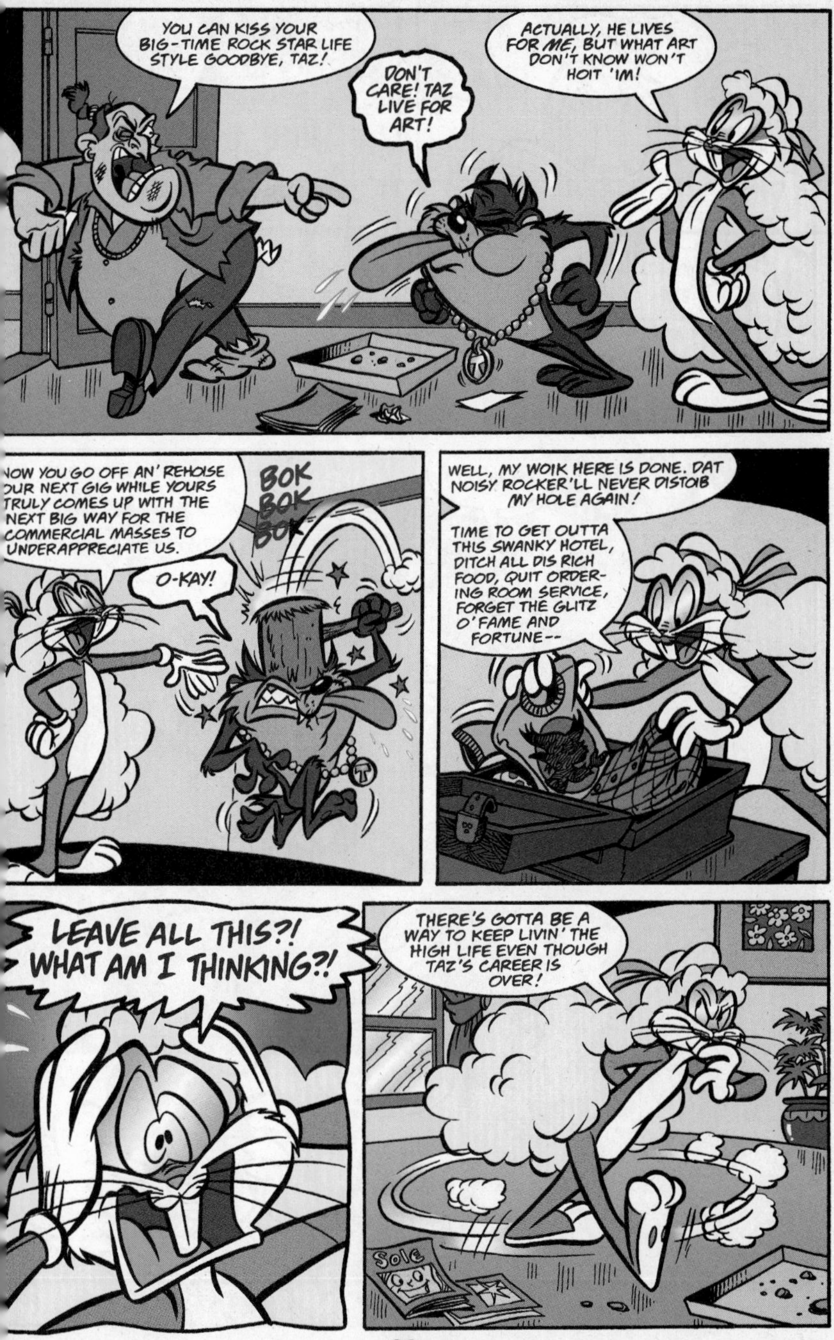
YOU CAN KISS YOUR BIG-TIME ROCK STAR LIFE STYLE GOODBYE, TAZ!
DON'T CARE! TAZ LIVE FOR ART!
ACTUALLY, HE LIVES FOR *ME*, BUT WHAT ART DON'T KNOW WON'T HOIT 'IM!
NOW YOU GO OFF AN' REHOISE OUR NEXT GIG WHILE YOURS TRULY COMES UP WITH THE NEXT BIG WAY FOR THE COMMERCIAL MASSES TO UNDERAPPRECIATE US.
BOK BOK BOK
O-KAY!
WELL, MY WOIK HERE IS DONE. DAT NOISY ROCKER'LL NEVER DISTOIB MY HOLE AGAIN!
TIME TO GET OUTTA THIS SWANKY HOTEL, DITCH ALL DIS RICH FOOD, QUIT ORDERING ROOM SERVICE, FORGET THE GLITZ O' FAME AND FORTUNE--
LEAVE ALL THIS?! WHAT AM I THINKING?!
THERE'S GOTTA BE A WAY TO KEEP LIVIN' THE HIGH LIFE EVEN THOUGH TAZ'S CAREER IS OVER!
SOLE

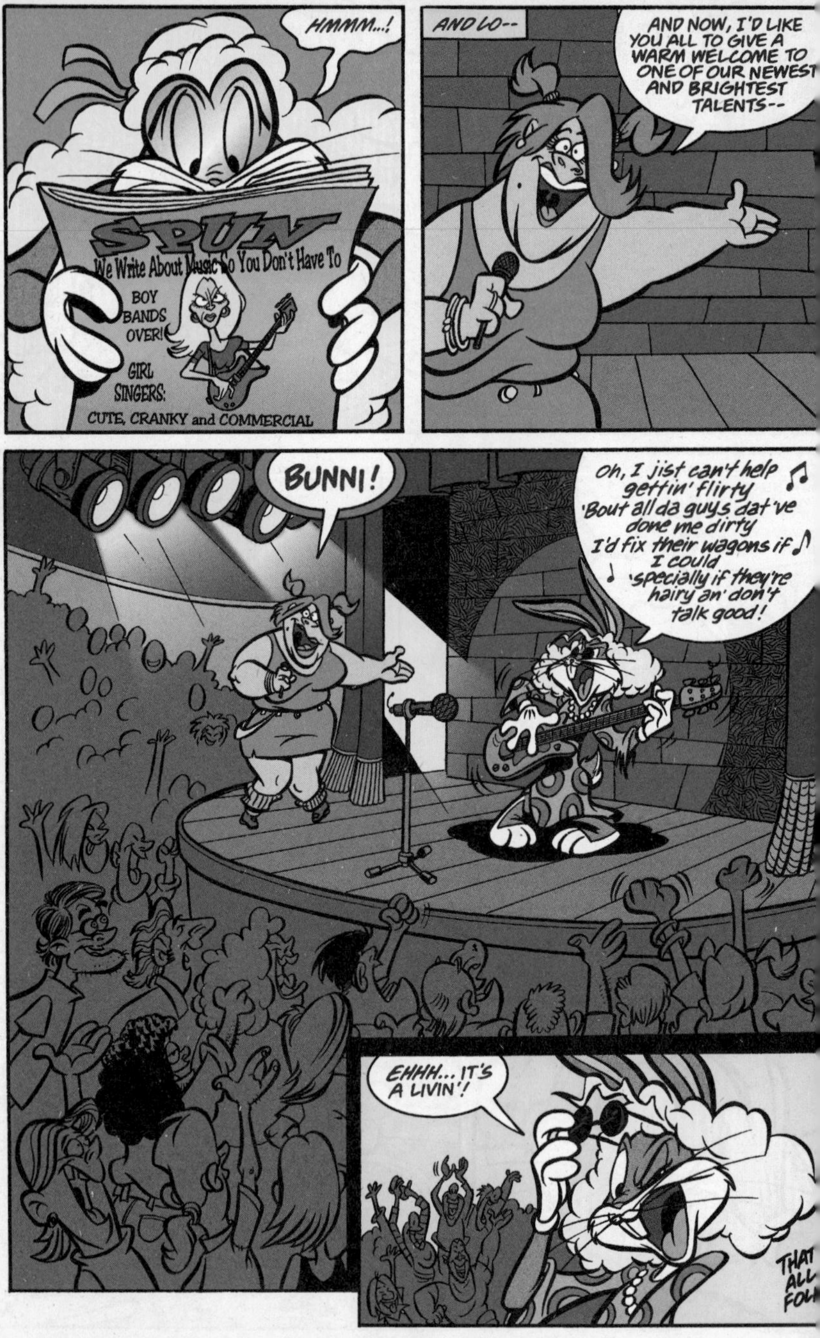
HMMM...!
SPUN
We Write About Music So You Don't Have To
BOY BANDS OVER!
GIRL SINGERS:
CUTE, CRANKY and COMMERCIAL
AND LO--
AND NOW, I'D LIKE YOU ALL TO GIVE A WARM WELCOME TO ONE OF OUR NEWEST AND BRIGHTEST TALENTS--
BUNNI!
Oh, I jist can't help gettin' flirty
'Bout all da guys dat've done me dirty
I'd fix their wagons if I could
'specially if they're hairy an' don't talk good!
EHHH... IT'S A LIVIN'!

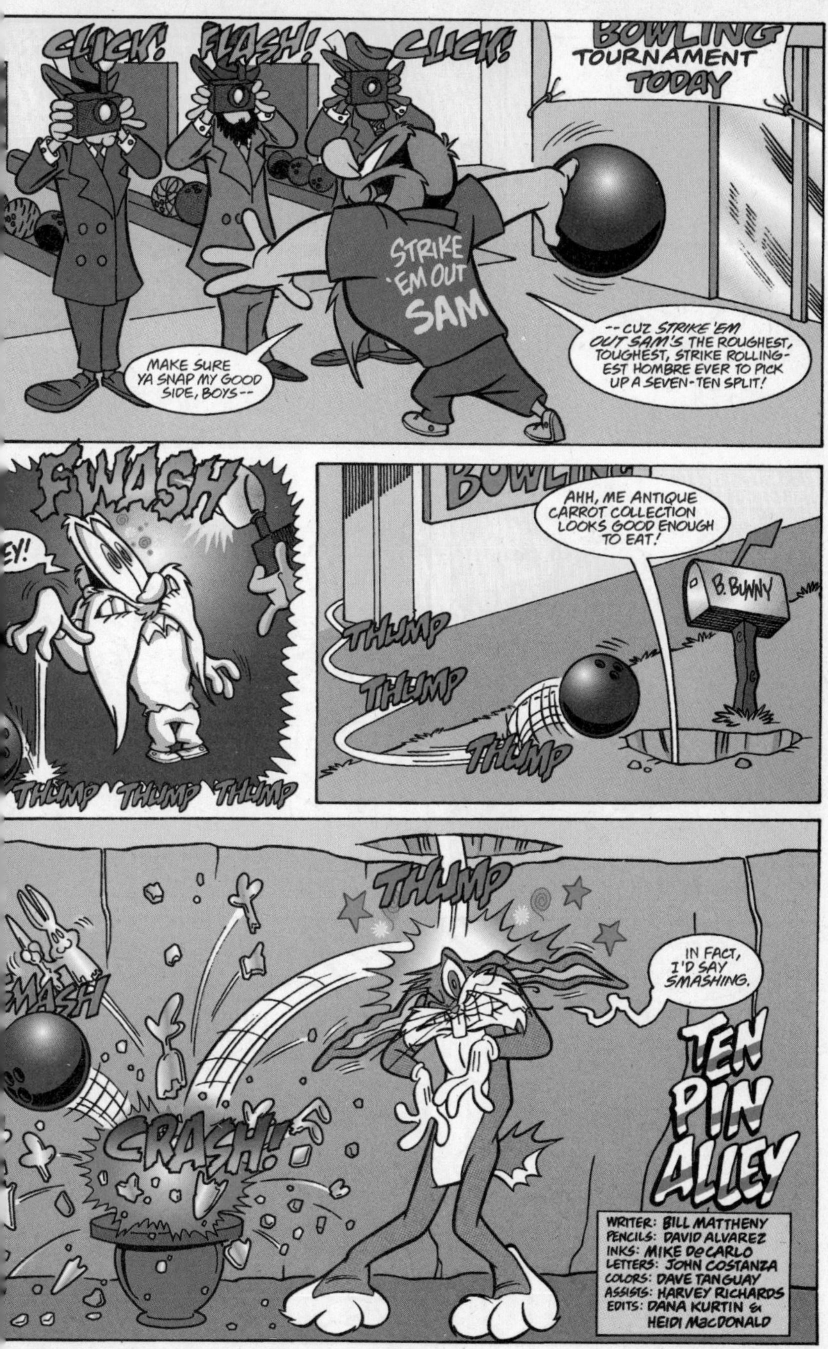
CLICK! FLASH! CLICK!
BOWLING TOURNAMENT TODAY
STRIKE 'EM OUT SAM
MAKE SURE YA SNAP MY GOOD SIDE, BOYS--
--CUZ STRIKE 'EM OUT SAM'S THE ROUGHEST, TOUGHEST, STRIKE ROLLING-EST HOMBRE EVER TO PICK UP A SEVEN-TEN SPLIT!
FWASH
THUMP THUMP THUMP
BOWLING
AHH, ME ANTIQUE CARROT COLLECTION LOOKS GOOD ENOUGH TO EAT!
B. BUNNY
THUMP
THUMP
THUMP
THUMP
IN FACT, I'D SAY SMASHING.
CRASH!
TEN PIN ALLEY
WRITER: BILL MATTHENY
PENCILS: DAVID ALVAREZ
INKS: MIKE DeCARLO
LETTERS: JOHN COSTANZA
COLORS: DAVE TANGUAY
ASSISTS: HARVEY RICHARDS
EDITS: DANA KURTIN & HEIDI MacDONALD

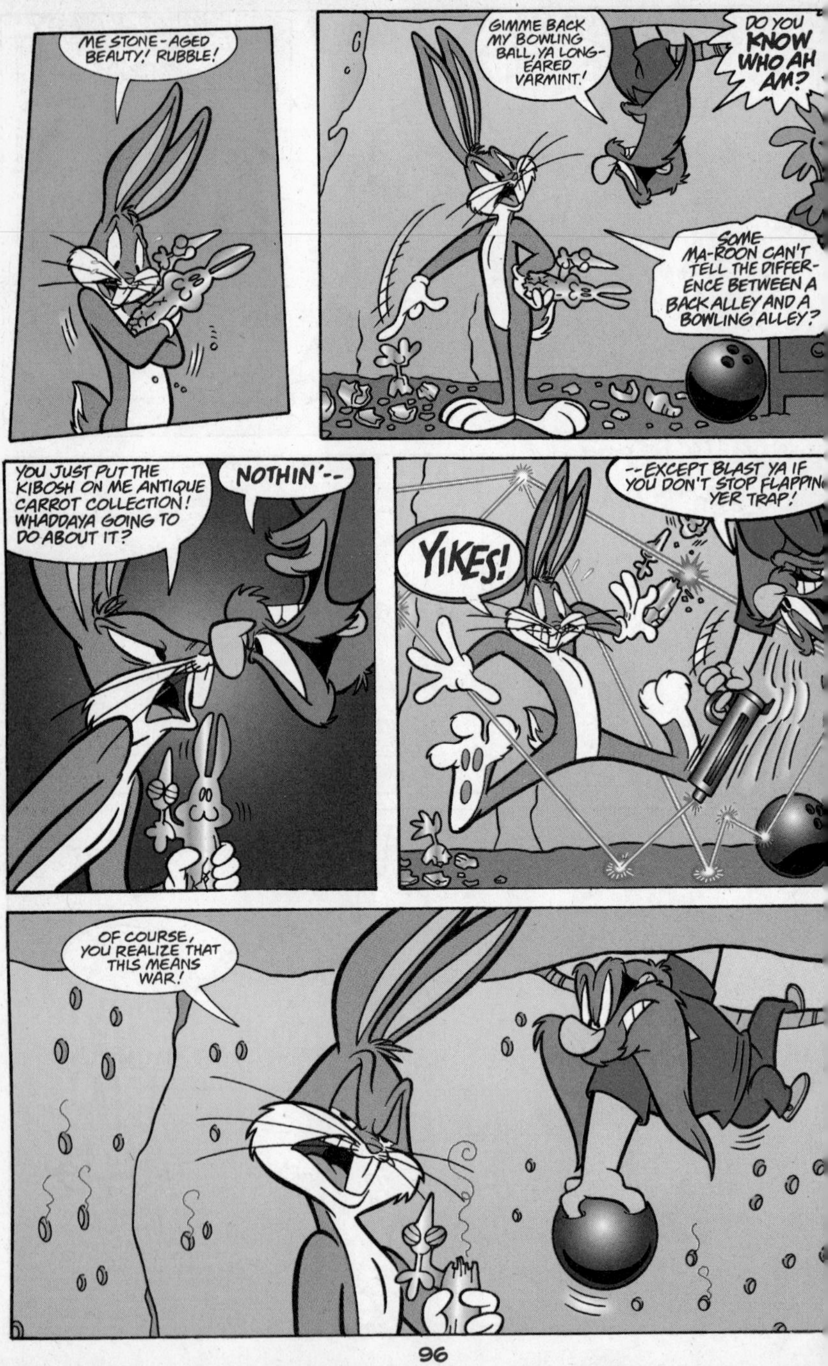

ME STONE-AGED BEAUTY! RUBBLE!
GIMME BACK MY BOWLING BALL, YA LONG-EARED VARMINT!
DO YOU KNOW WHO AH AM?
SOME MA-ROON CAN'T TELL THE DIFFERENCE BETWEEN A BACK ALLEY AND A BOWLING ALLEY?
YOU JUST PUT THE KIBOSH ON ME ANTIQUE CARROT COLLECTION! WHADDAYA GOING TO DO ABOUT IT?
NOTHIN'--
--EXCEPT BLAST YA IF YOU DON'T STOP FLAPPIN YER TRAP!
YIKES!
OF COURSE, YOU REALIZE THAT THIS MEANS WAR!

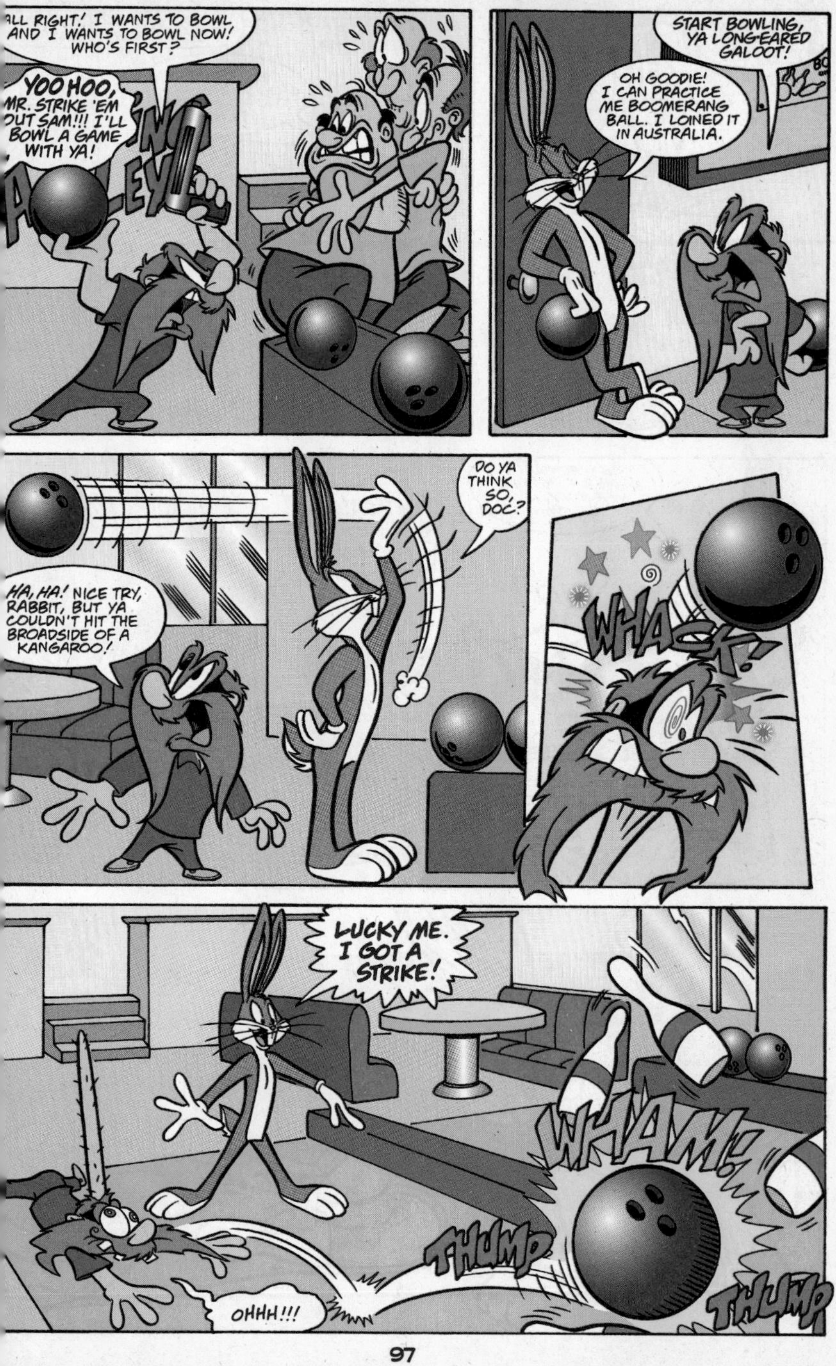
ALL RIGHT! I WANTS TO BOWL AND I WANTS TO BOWL NOW! WHO'S FIRST?
YOO HOO, MR. STRIKE 'EM OUT SAM!!! I'LL BOWL A GAME WITH YA!
START BOWLING, YA LONG-EARED GALOOT!
OH GOODIE! I CAN PRACTICE ME BOOMERANG BALL. I LOINED IT IN AUSTRALIA.
DO YA THINK SO, DOC?
HA, HA! NICE TRY, RABBIT, BUT YA COULDN'T HIT THE BROADSIDE OF A KANGAROO!
WHACK!
LUCKY ME. I GOT A STRIKE!
WHAM!
THUMP
THUMP
OHHH!!!

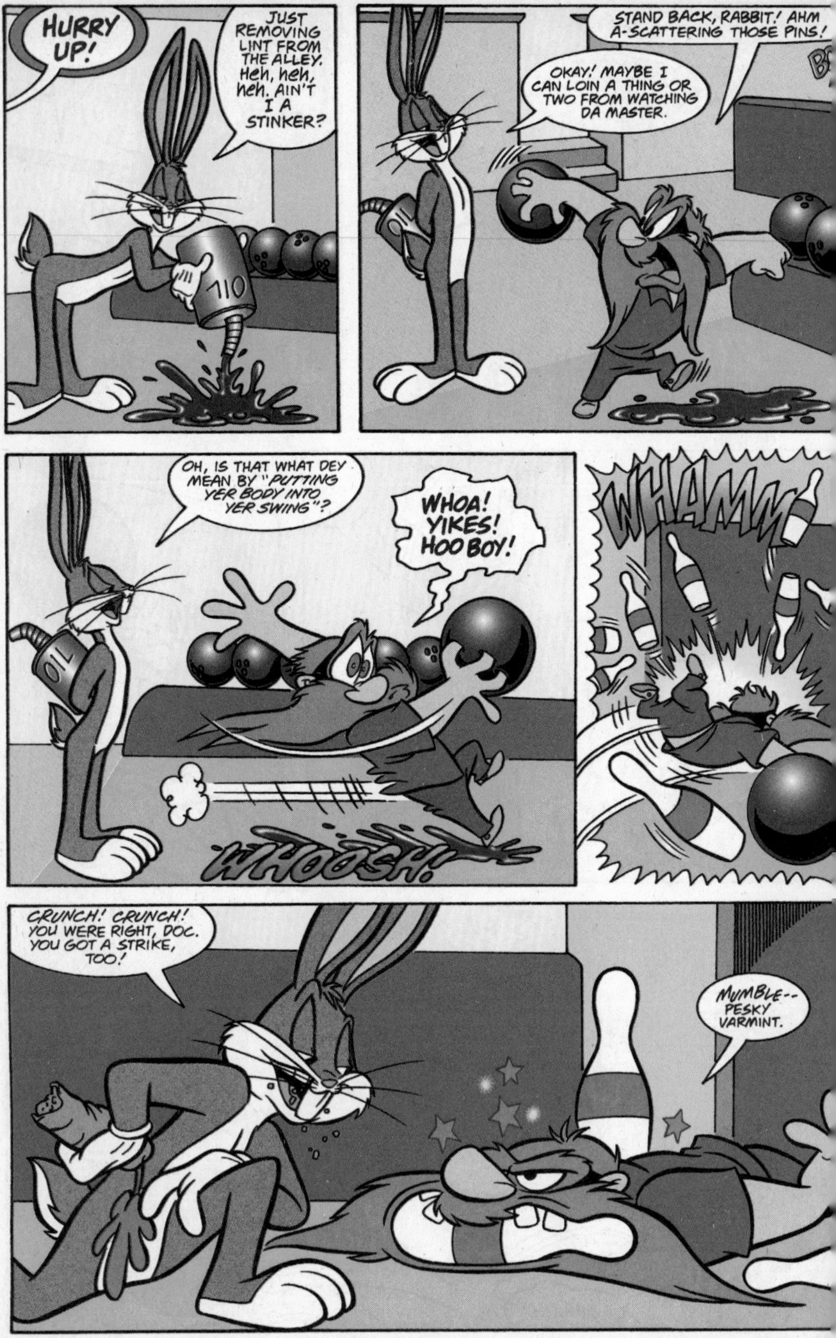
HURRY UP!
JUST REMOVING LINT FROM THE ALLEY. Heh, heh, heh. AIN'T I A STINKER?
OIL
STAND BACK, RABBIT! AHM A-SCATTERING THOSE PINS!
OKAY! MAYBE I CAN LOIN A THING OR TWO FROM WATCHING DA MASTER.
OH, IS THAT WHAT DEY MEAN BY "PUTTING YER BODY INTO YER SWING"?
WHOA! YIKES! HOO BOY!
WHOOSH!
WHAMM!
CRUNCH! CRUNCH! YOU WERE RIGHT, DOC. YOU GOT A STRIKE, TOO!
MUMBLE-- PESKY VARMINT.

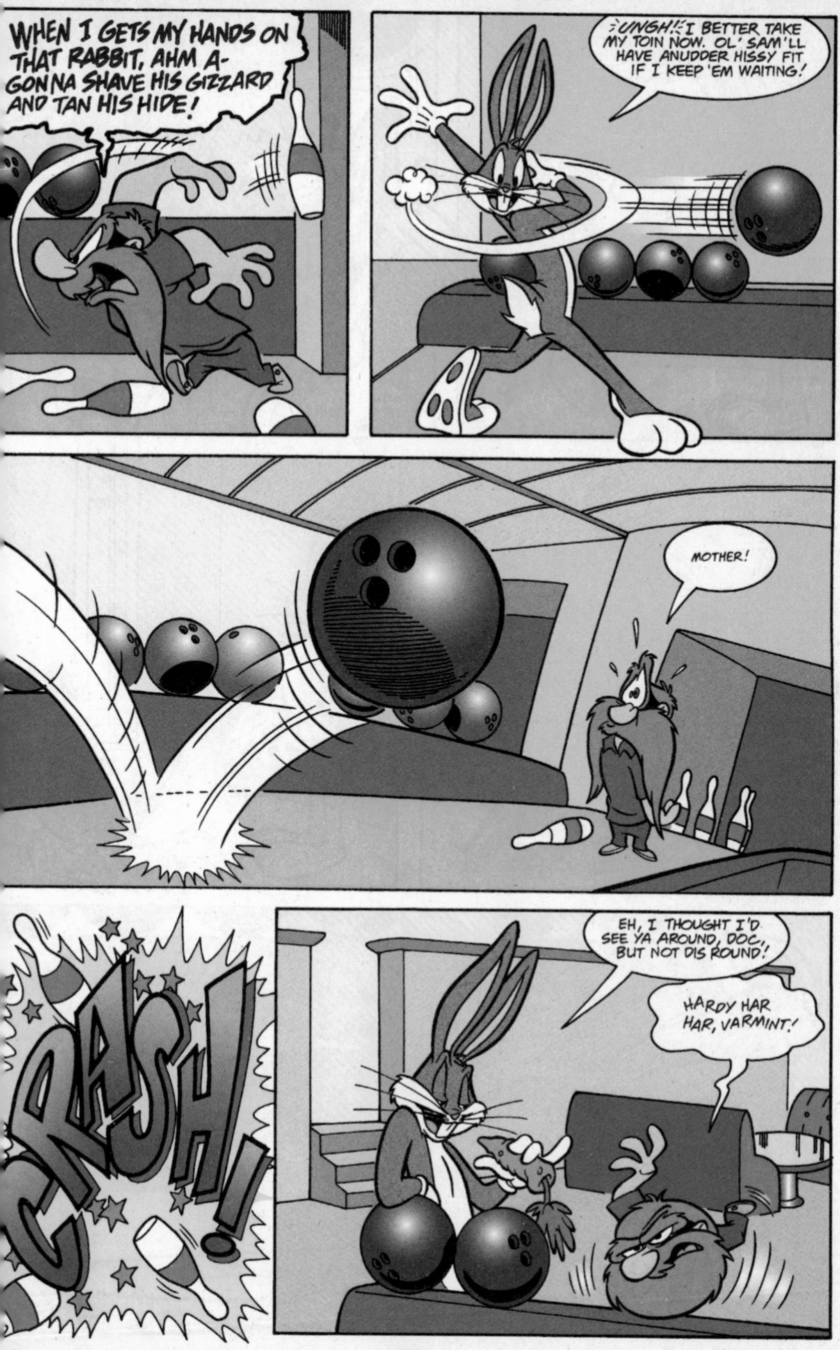
WHEN I GETS MY HANDS ON THAT RABBIT, AHM A-GONNA SHAVE HIS GIZZARD AND TAN HIS HIDE!
UNGH! I BETTER TAKE MY TOIN NOW. OL' SAM'LL HAVE ANUDDER HISSY FIT IF I KEEP 'EM WAITING!
MOTHER!
CRASH!
EH, I THOUGHT I'D SEE YA AROUND, DOC, BUT NOT DIS ROUND!
HARDY HAR HAR, VARMINT!

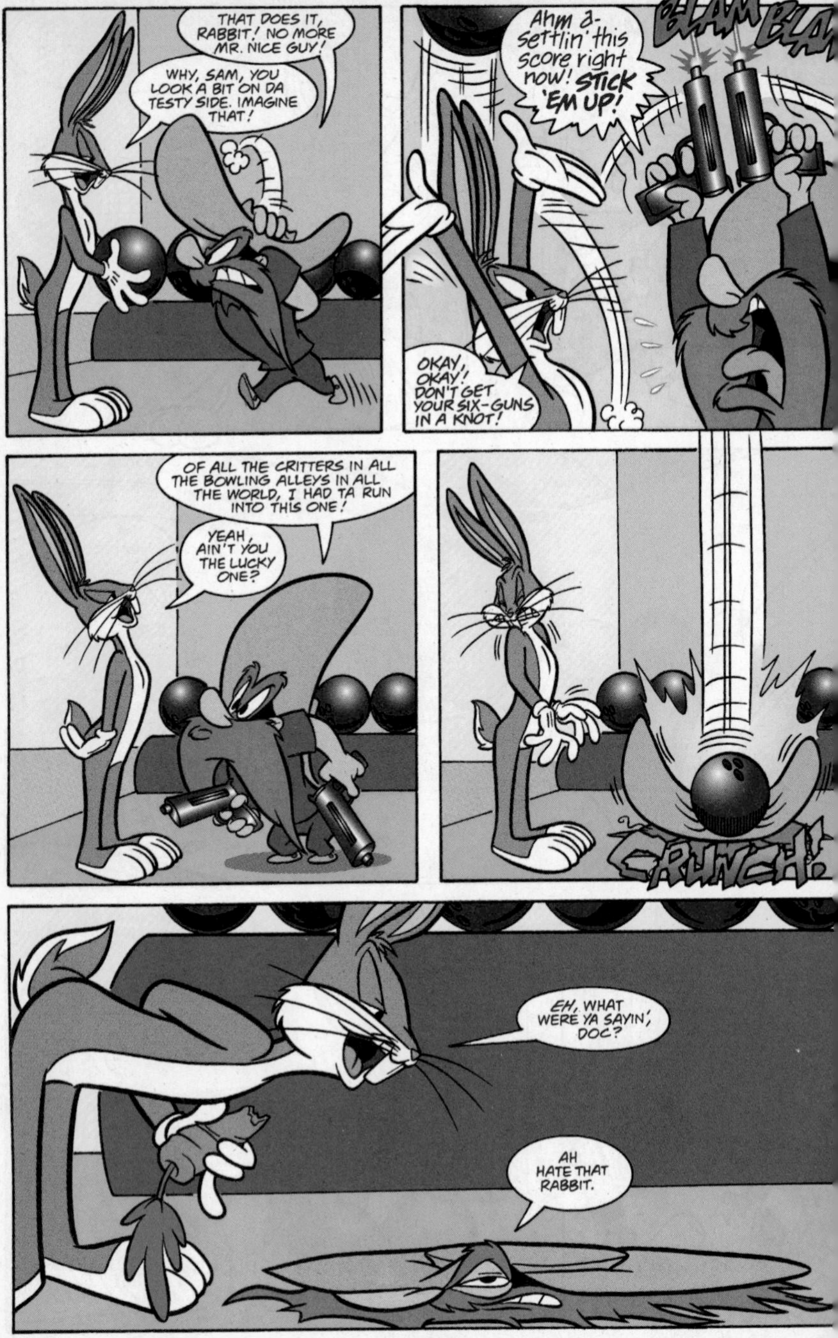
THAT DOES IT, RABBIT! NO MORE MR. NICE GUY!
WHY, SAM, YOU LOOK A BIT ON DA TESTY SIDE. IMAGINE THAT!
Ahm a-settlin' this score right now! STICK 'EM UP!
BLAM BLAM
OKAY, OKAY! DON'T GET YOUR SIX-GUNS IN A KNOT!
OF ALL THE CRITTERS IN ALL THE BOWLING ALLEYS IN ALL THE WORLD, I HAD TA RUN INTO THIS ONE!
YEAH, AIN'T YOU THE LUCKY ONE?
CRUNCH!
EH, WHAT WERE YA SAYIN', DOC?
AH HATE THAT RABBIT.

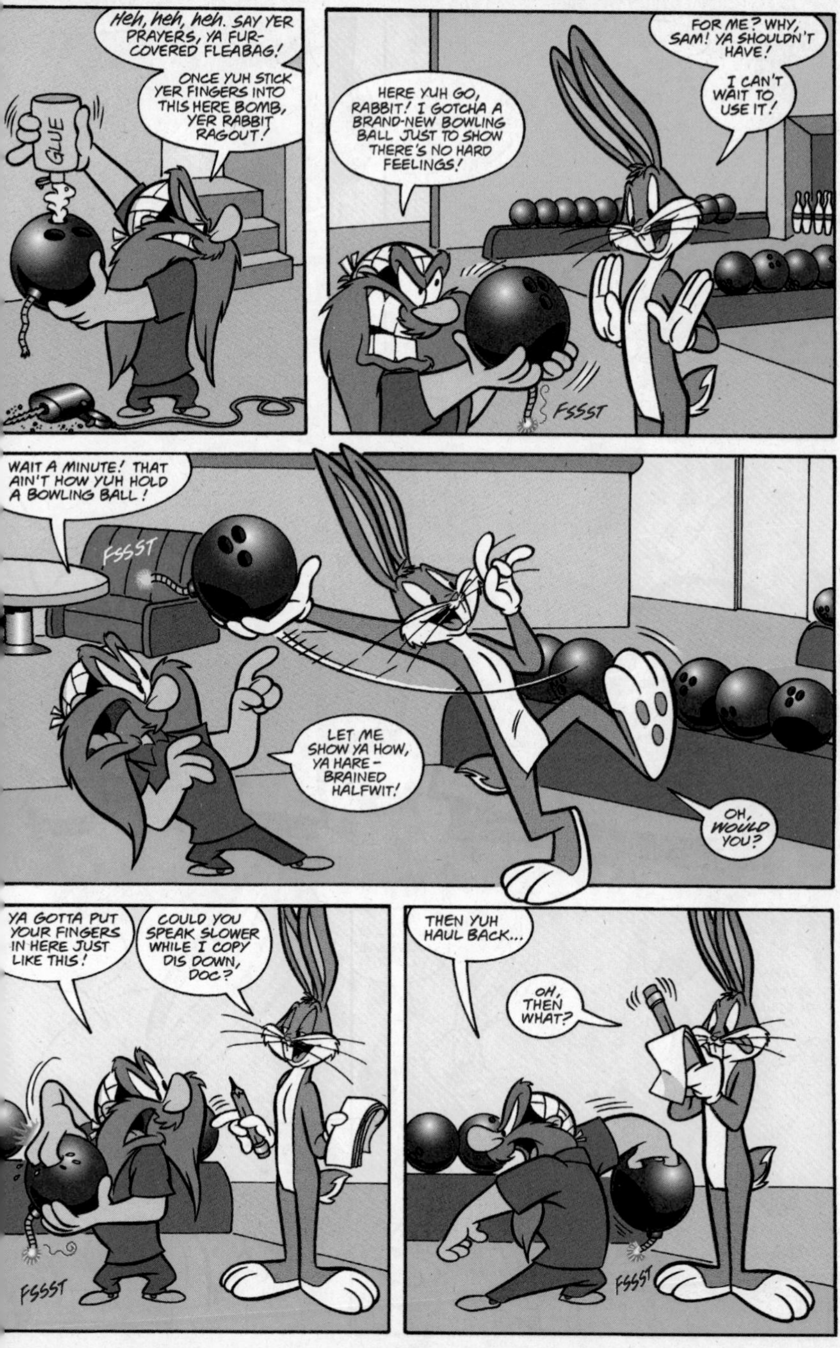
HEH, HEH, HEH. SAY YER PRAYERS, YA FUR-COVERED FLEABAG!
ONCE YUH STICK YER FINGERS INTO THIS HERE BOMB, YER RABBIT RAGOUT!
GLUE
HERE YUH GO, RABBIT! I GOTCHA A BRAND-NEW BOWLING BALL JUST TO SHOW THERE'S NO HARD FEELINGS!
FOR ME? WHY, SAM! YA SHOULDN'T HAVE!
I CAN'T WAIT TO USE IT!
FSSST
WAIT A MINUTE! THAT AIN'T HOW YUH HOLD A BOWLING BALL!
FSSST
LET ME SHOW YA HOW, YA HARE-BRAINED HALFWIT!
OH, WOULD YOU?
YA GOTTA PUT YOUR FINGERS IN HERE JUST LIKE THIS!
COULD YOU SPEAK SLOWER WHILE I COPY DIS DOWN, DOC?
FSSST
THEN YUH HAUL BACK...
OH, THEN WHAT?
FSSST

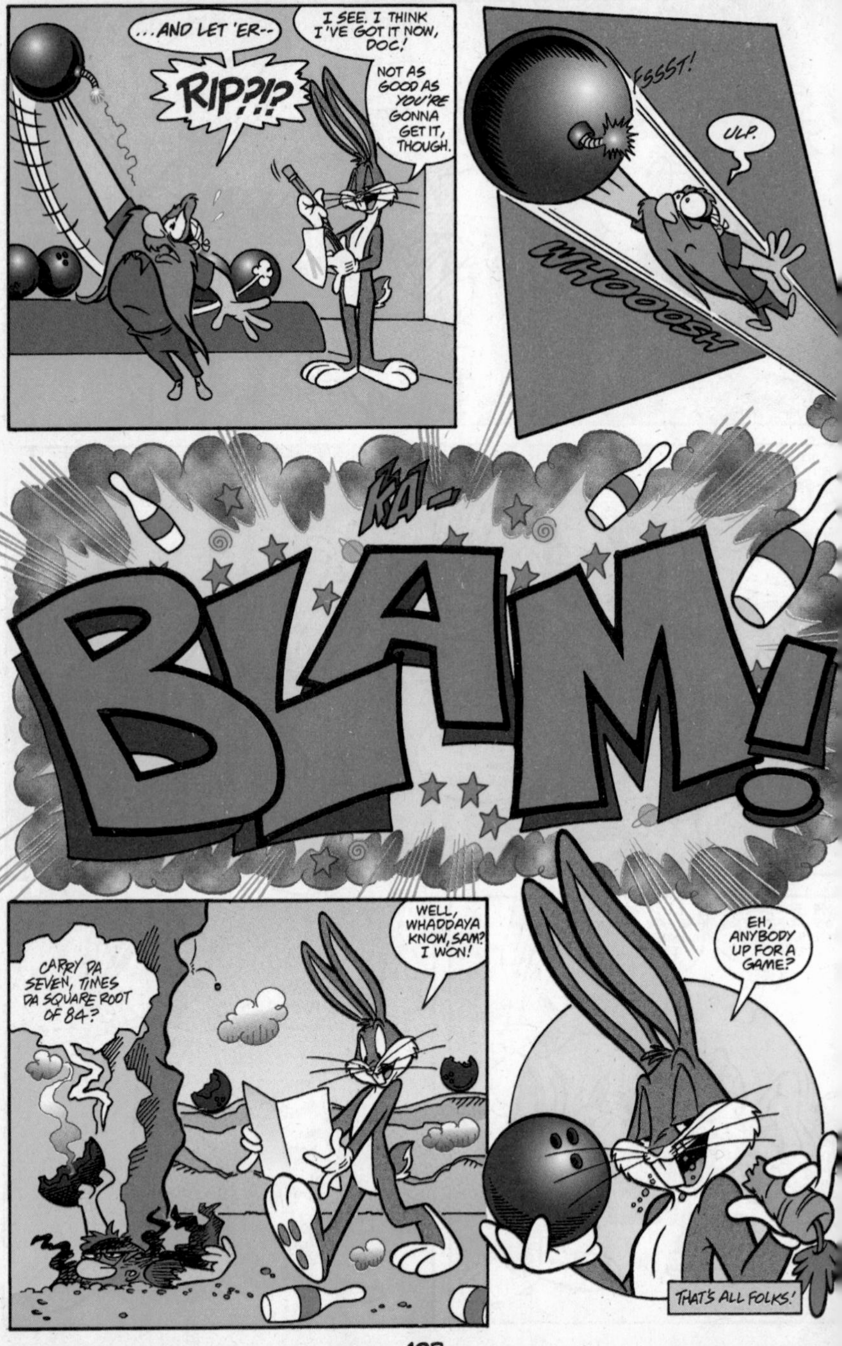
...AND LET 'ER--
RIP?!?
I SEE. I THINK I'VE GOT IT NOW, DOC!
NOT AS GOOD AS YOU'RE GONNA GET IT, THOUGH.
FSSST!
ULP.
WHOOOSH
KA-
BLAM!
CARRY DA SEVEN, TIMES DA SQUARE ROOT OF 84?
WELL, WHADDAYA KNOW, SAM? I WON!
EH, ANYBODY UP FOR A GAME?
THAT'S ALL FOLKS!

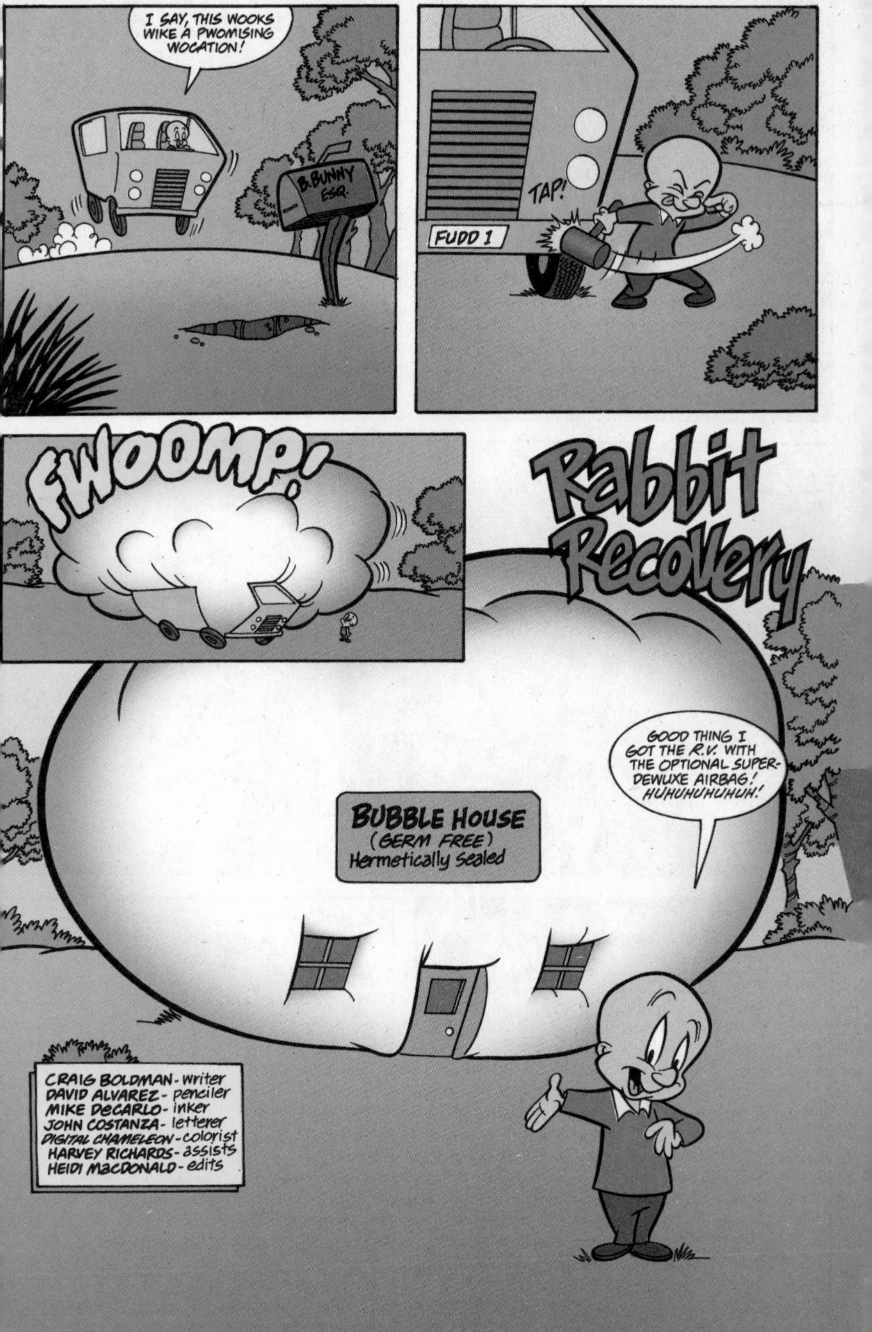
I SAY, THIS WOOKS WIKE A PWOMISING WOCATION!
B. BUNNY ESQ.
TAP!
FUDD 1
FWOOMP!
Rabbit Recovery
GOOD THING I GOT THE R.V. WITH THE OPTIONAL SUPER-DEWUXE AIRBAG! HUHUHUHUHUH!
BUBBLE HOUSE
(GERM FREE)
Hermetically Sealed
CRAIG BOLDMAN - writer
DAVID ALVAREZ - penciler
MIKE DeCARLO - inker
JOHN COSTANZA - letterer
DIGITAL CHAMELEON - colorist
HARVEY RICHARDS - assists
HEIDI MacDONALD - edits

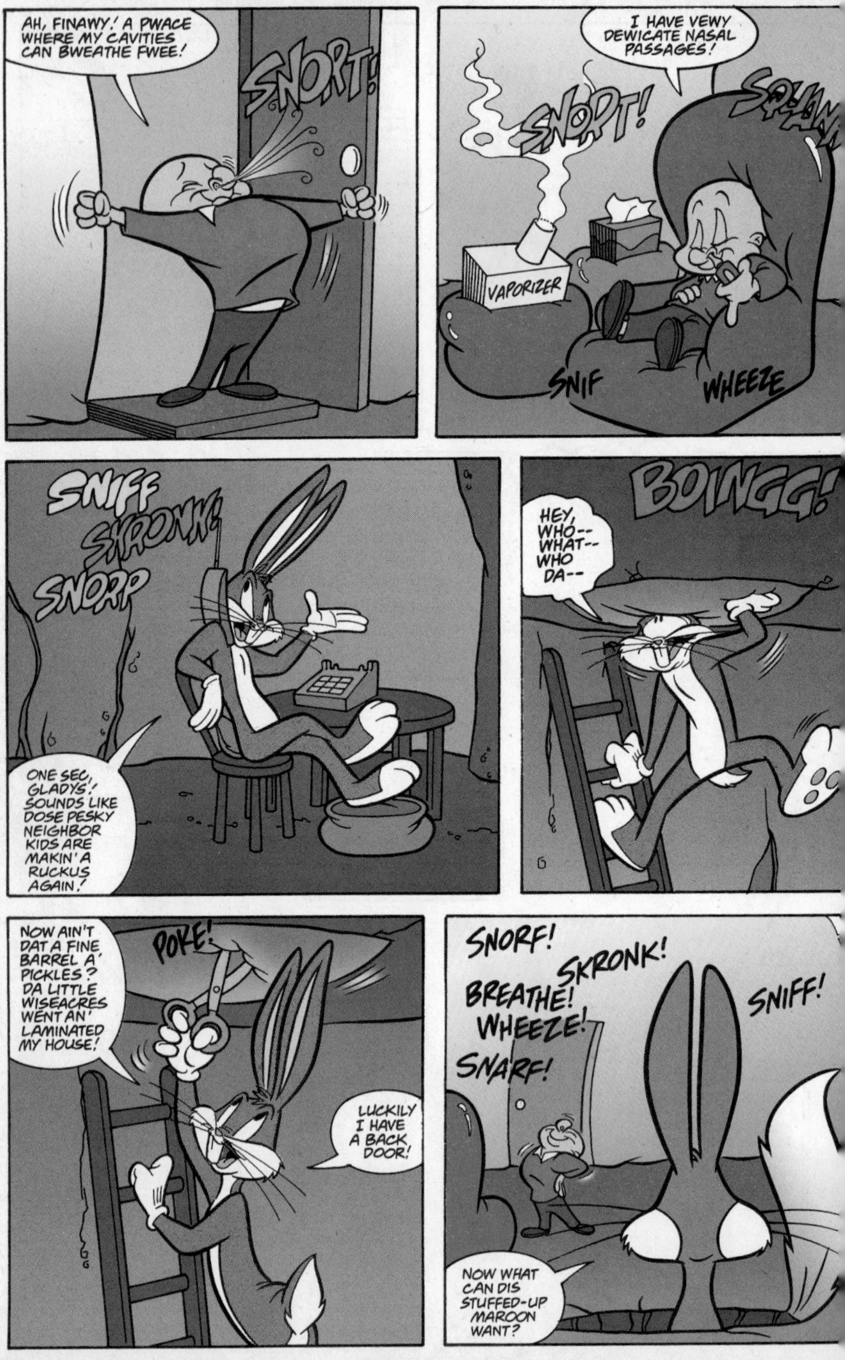
AH, FINAWY! A PWACE WHERE MY CAVITIES CAN BWEATHE FWEE!
SNORT!
I HAVE VEWY DEWICATE NASAL PASSAGES!
SNORT!
VAPORIZER
SNIF
WHEEZE
SNIFF
SKRONK!
SNORP
ONE SEC, GLADYS! SOUNDS LIKE DOSE PESKY NEIGHBOR KIDS ARE MAKIN' A RUCKUS AGAIN!
BOINGG!
HEY, WHO-- WHAT-- WHO DA--
NOW AIN'T DAT A FINE BARREL A' PICKLES? DA LITTLE WISEACRES WENT AN' LAMINATED MY HOUSE!
POKE!
LUCKILY I HAVE A BACK DOOR!
SNORF!
SKRONK!
BREATHE!
WHEEZE!
SNIFF!
SNARF!
NOW WHAT CAN DIS STUFFED-UP MAROON WANT?

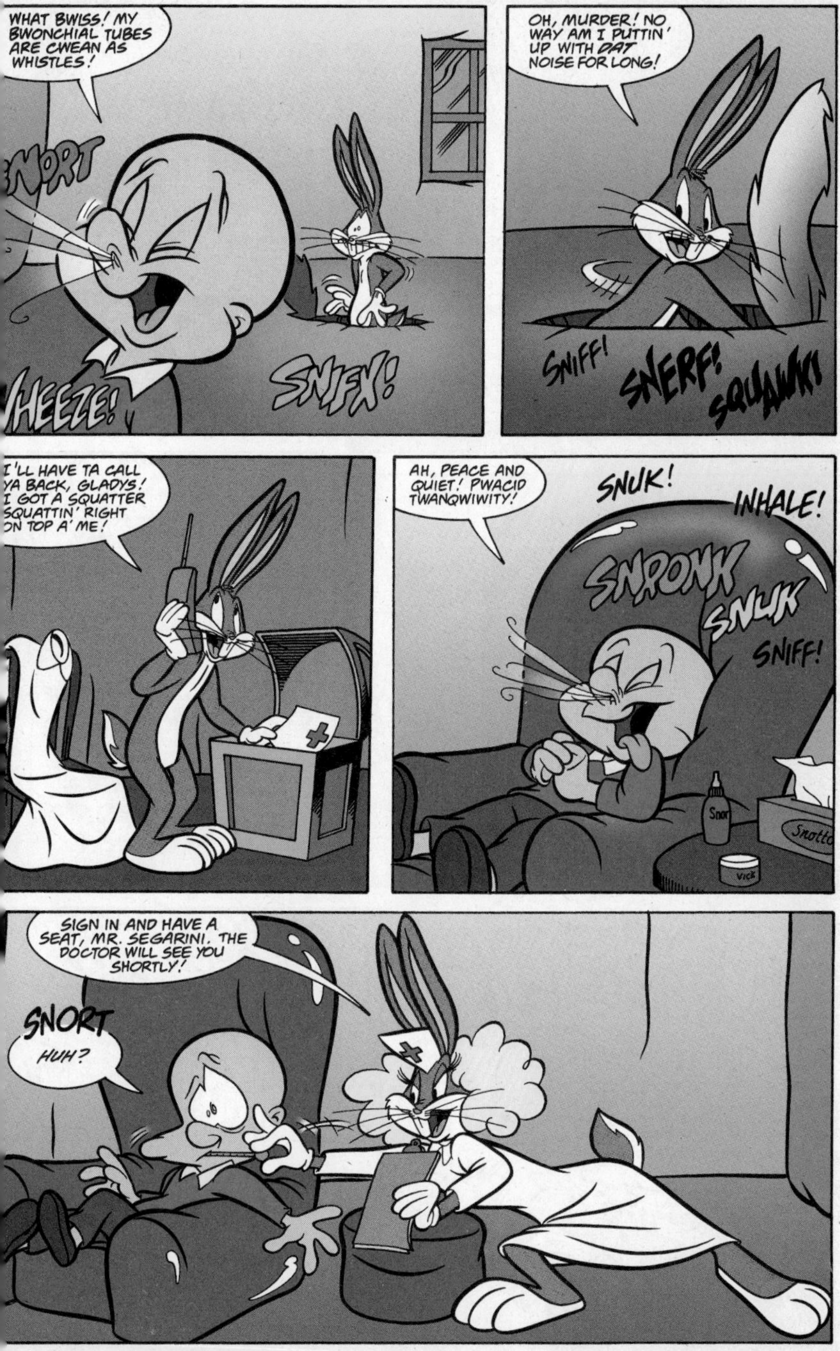
WHAT BWISS! MY BWONCHIAL TUBES ARE CWEAN AS WHISTLES!
SNORT
WHEEZE!
SNIFX!
OH, MURDER! NO WAY AM I PUTTIN' UP WITH DAT NOISE FOR LONG!
SNIFF!
SNERF!
SQUAWK!
I'LL HAVE TA CALL YA BACK, GLADYS! I GOT A SQUATTER SQUATTIN' RIGHT ON TOP A' ME!
AH, PEACE AND QUIET! PWACID TWANQWIWITY!
SNUK!
INHALE!
SNRONK
SNUK
SNIFF!
Snotto
VICK
SIGN IN AND HAVE A SEAT, MR. SEGARINI. THE DOCTOR WILL SEE YOU SHORTLY!
SNORT
HUH?

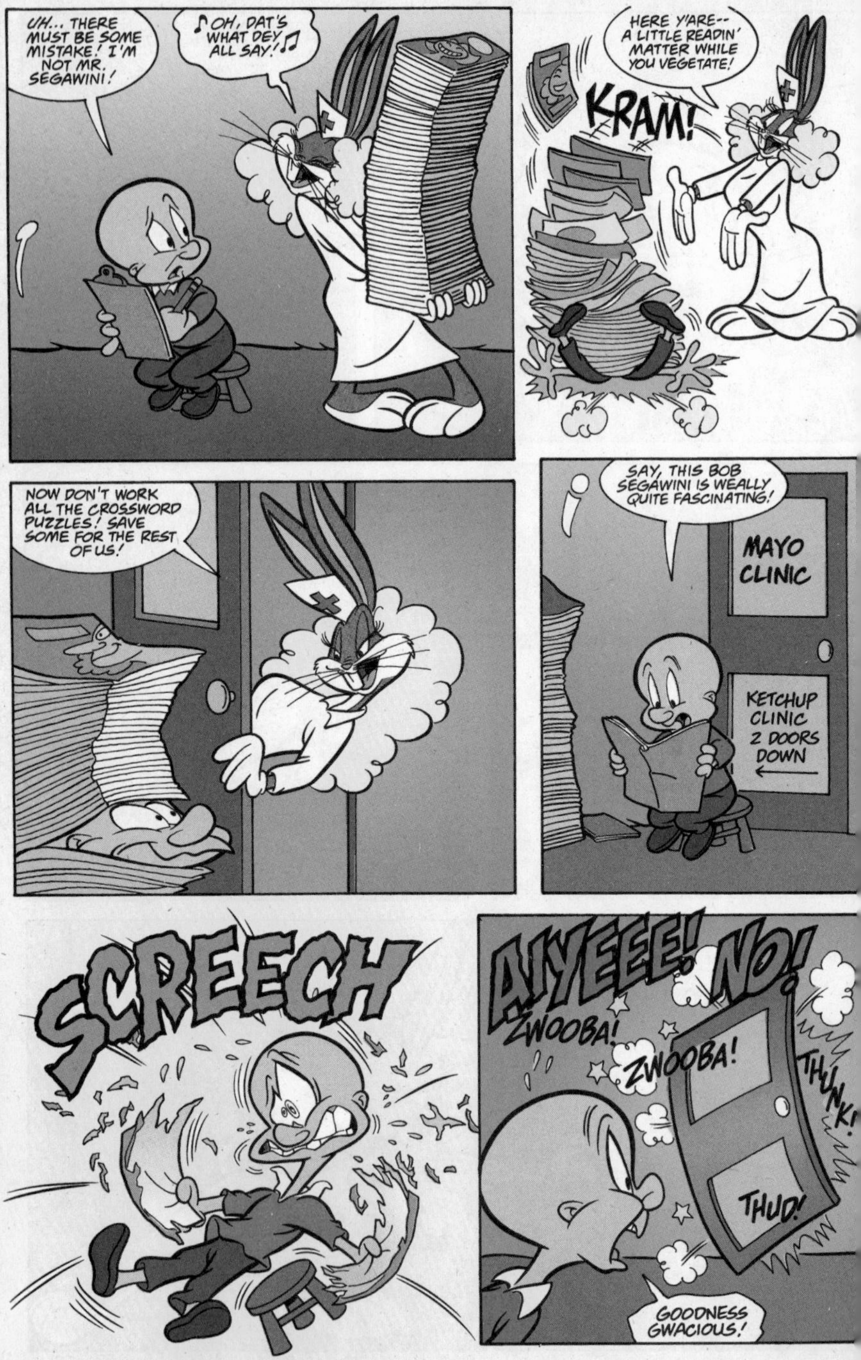
UH... THERE MUST BE SOME MISTAKE! I'M NOT MR. SEGAWINI!
♪OH, DAT'S WHAT DEY ALL SAY!♫
HERE Y'ARE-- A LITTLE READIN' MATTER WHILE YOU VEGETATE!
KRAM!
NOW DON'T WORK ALL THE CROSSWORD PUZZLES! SAVE SOME FOR THE REST OF US!
SAY, THIS BOB SEGAWINI IS WEALLY QUITE FASCINATING!
MAYO CLINIC
KETCHUP CLINIC 2 DOORS DOWN
SCREECH
AIYEEE! NO!
ZWOOBA!
ZWOOBA!
THUNK!
THUD!
GOODNESS GWACIOUS!

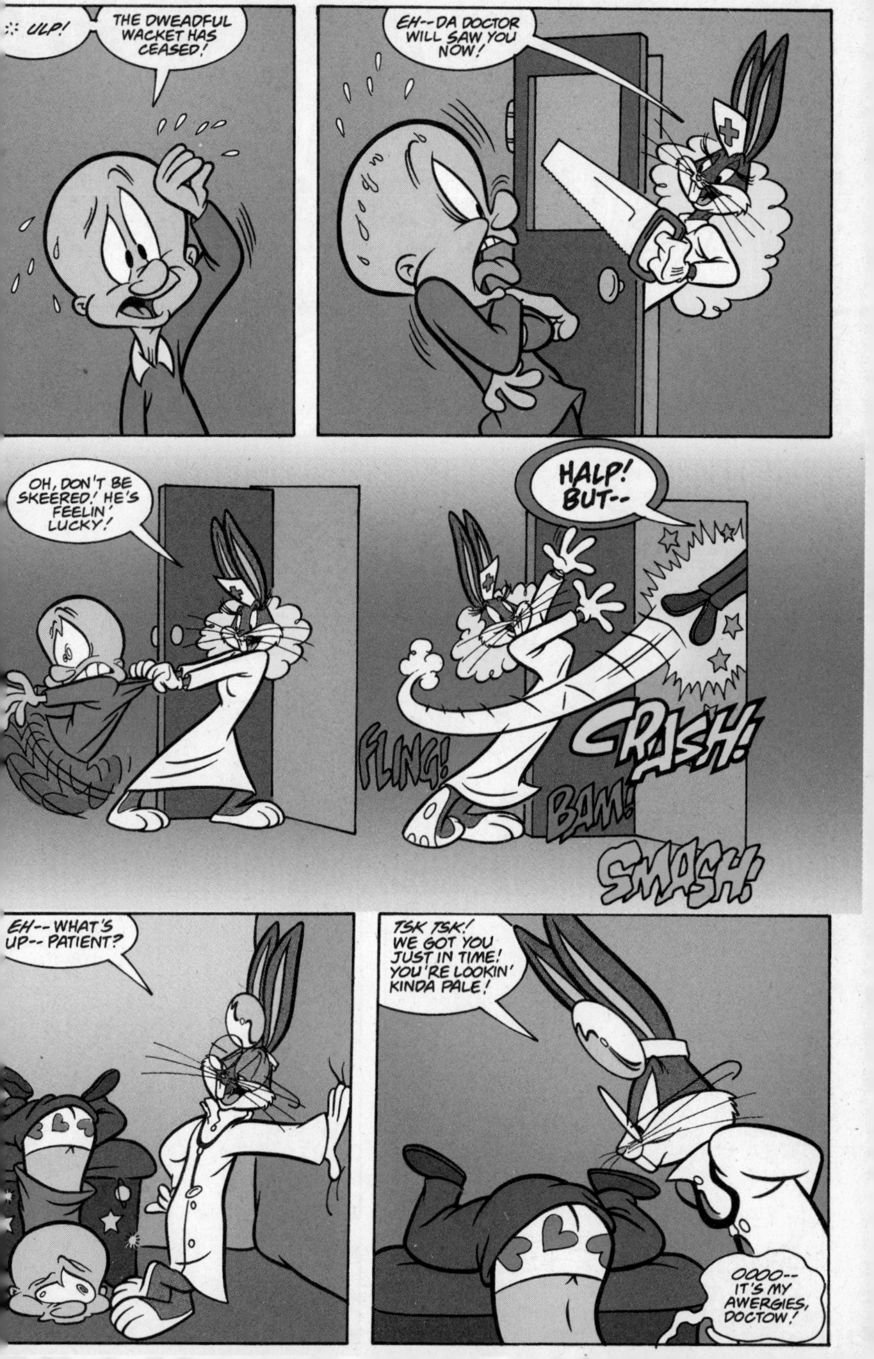
ULP!
THE DWEADFUL WACKET HAS CEASED!
EH--DA DOCTOR WILL SAW YOU NOW!
OH, DON'T BE SKEERED! HE'S FEELIN' LUCKY!
HALP! BUT--
FLING!
CRASH!
BAM!
SMASH!
EH-- WHAT'S UP-- PATIENT?
TSK TSK! WE GOT YOU JUST IN TIME! YOU'RE LOOKIN' KINDA PALE!
OOOO-- IT'S MY AWERGIES, DOCTOW!

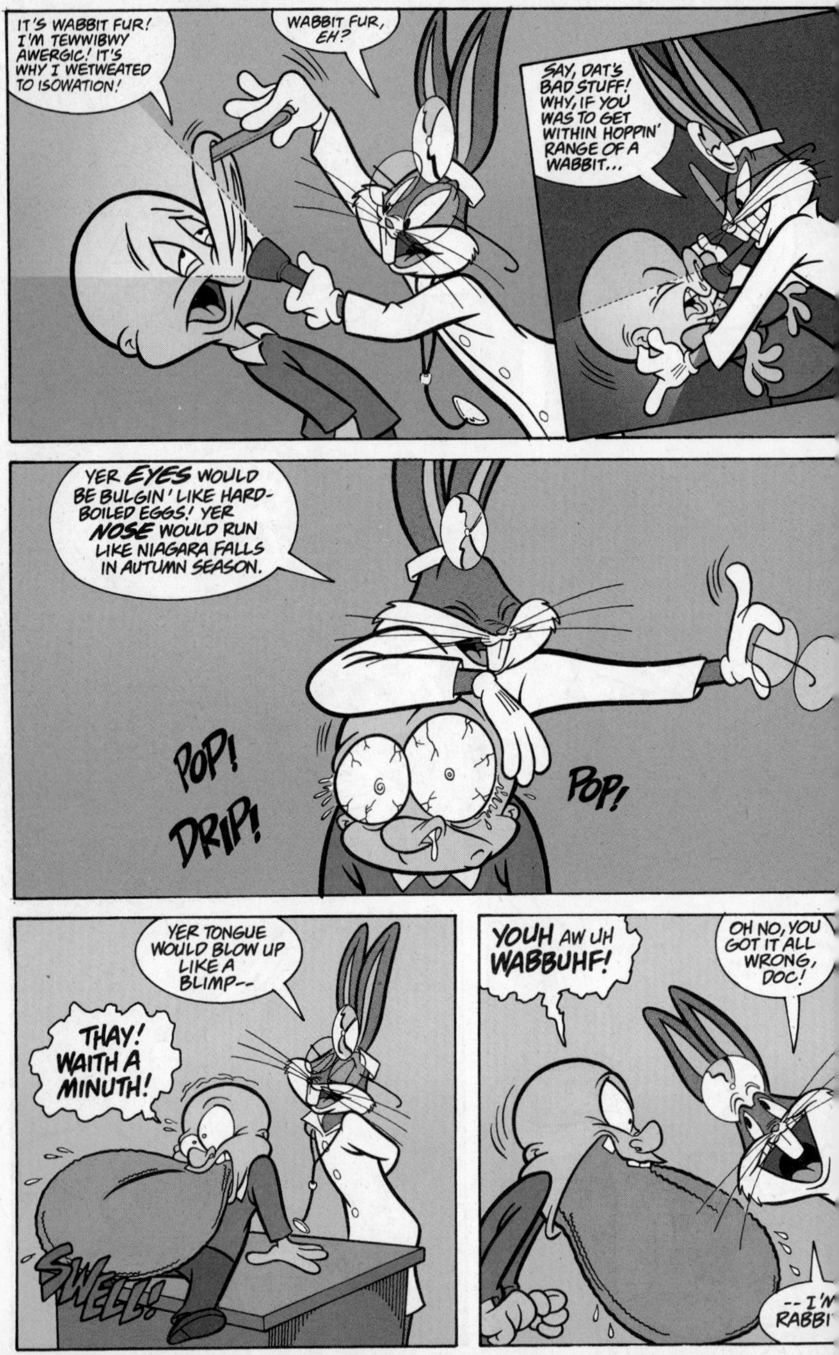
IT'S WABBIT FUR! I'M TEWWIBWY AWERGIC! IT'S WHY I WETWEATED TO ISOWATION!
WABBIT FUR, EH?
SAY, DAT'S BAD STUFF! WHY, IF YOU WAS TO GET WITHIN HOPPIN' RANGE OF A WABBIT...
YER EYES WOULD BE BULGIN' LIKE HARD-BOILED EGGS! YER NOSE WOULD RUN LIKE NIAGARA FALLS IN AUTUMN SEASON.
POP!
DRIP!
POP!
YER TONGUE WOULD BLOW UP LIKE A BLIMP--
THAY! WAITH A MINUTH!
SWELL!
YOUH AW UH WABBUHF!
OH NO, YOU GOT IT ALL WRONG, DOC!
--I'M RABBI

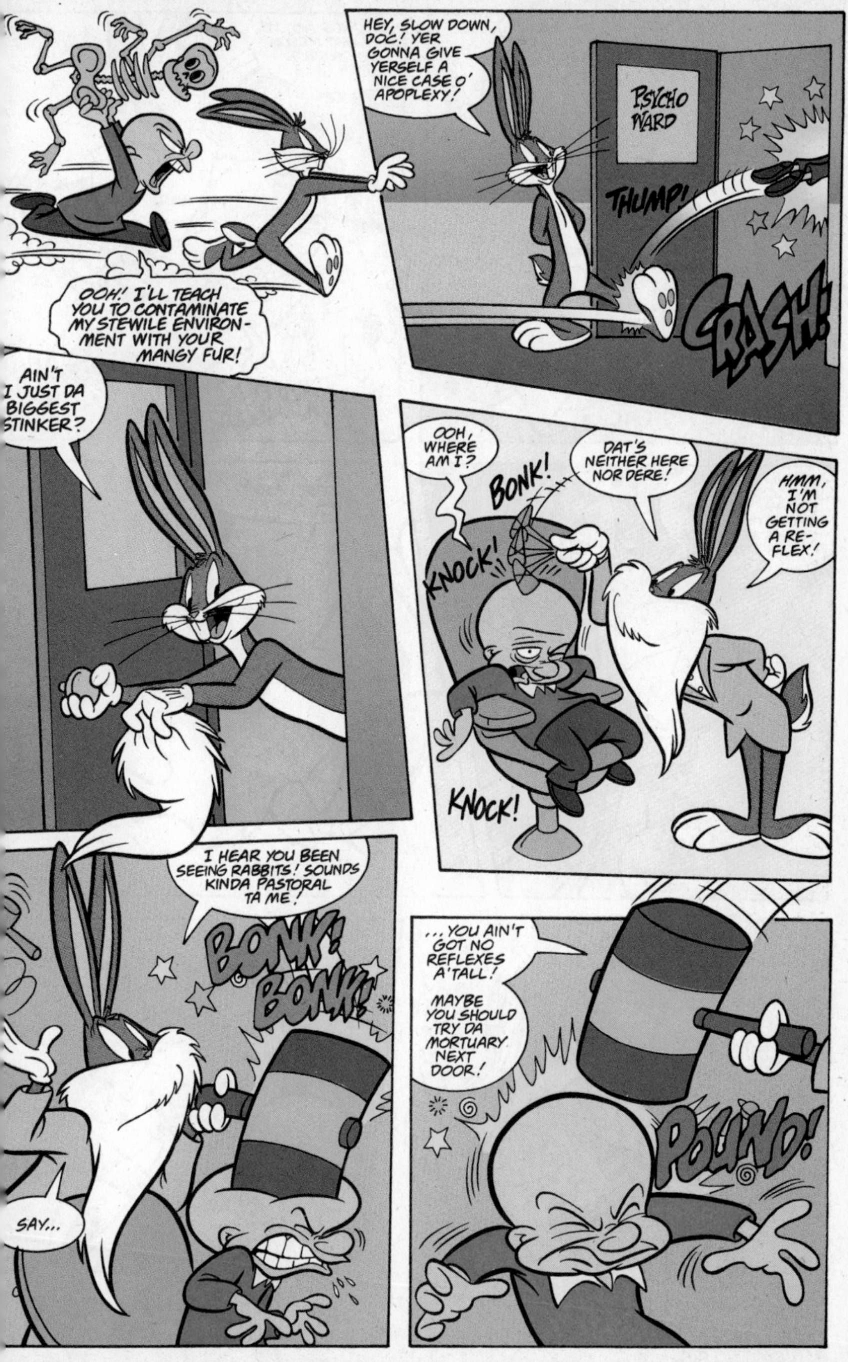
OOH! I'LL TEACH YOU TO CONTAMINATE MY STEWILE ENVIRONMENT WITH YOUR MANGY FUR!
HEY, SLOW DOWN, DOC! YER GONNA GIVE YERSELF A NICE CASE O' APOPLEXY!
PSYCHO WARD
THUMP!
CRASH!
AIN'T I JUST DA BIGGEST STINKER?
OOH, WHERE AM I?
BONK!
DAT'S NEITHER HERE NOR DERE!
HMM, I'M NOT GETTING A RE-FLEX!
KNOCK!
KNOCK!
I HEAR YOU BEEN SEEING RABBITS! SOUNDS KINDA PASTORAL TA ME!
BONK!
BONK!
SAY...
...YOU AIN'T GOT NO REFLEXES A'TALL!
MAYBE YOU SHOULD TRY DA MORTUARY NEXT DOOR!
POUND!

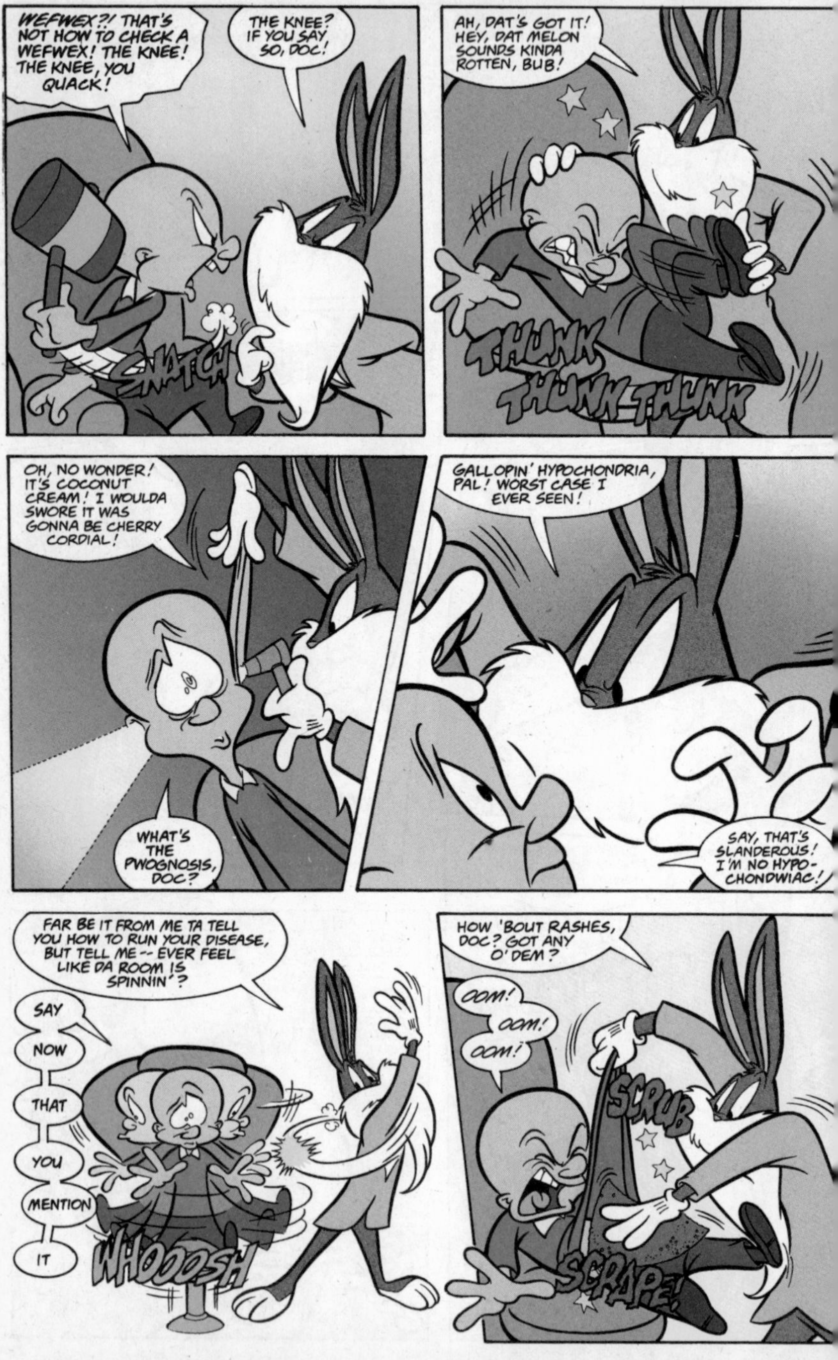
WEFWEX?! THAT'S NOT HOW TO CHECK A WEFWEX! THE KNEE! THE KNEE, YOU QUACK!
THE KNEE? IF YOU SAY SO, DOC!
SNATCH
AH, DAT'S GOT IT! HEY, DAT MELON SOUNDS KINDA ROTTEN, BUB!
THUNK THUNK THUNK THUNK
OH, NO WONDER! IT'S COCONUT CREAM! I WOULDA SWORE IT WAS GONNA BE CHERRY CORDIAL!
WHAT'S THE PWOGNOSIS, DOC?
GALLOPIN' HYPOCHONDRIA, PAL! WORST CASE I EVER SEEN!
SAY, THAT'S SLANDEROUS! I'M NO HYPO-CHONDWIAC!
FAR BE IT FROM ME TA TELL YOU HOW TO RUN YOUR DISEASE, BUT TELL ME -- EVER FEEL LIKE DA ROOM IS SPINNIN'?
SAY
NOW
THAT
YOU
MENTION
IT
WHOOOOSH
HOW 'BOUT RASHES, DOC? GOT ANY O' DEM?
OOM!
OOM!
OOM!
SCRUB
SCRAPE!

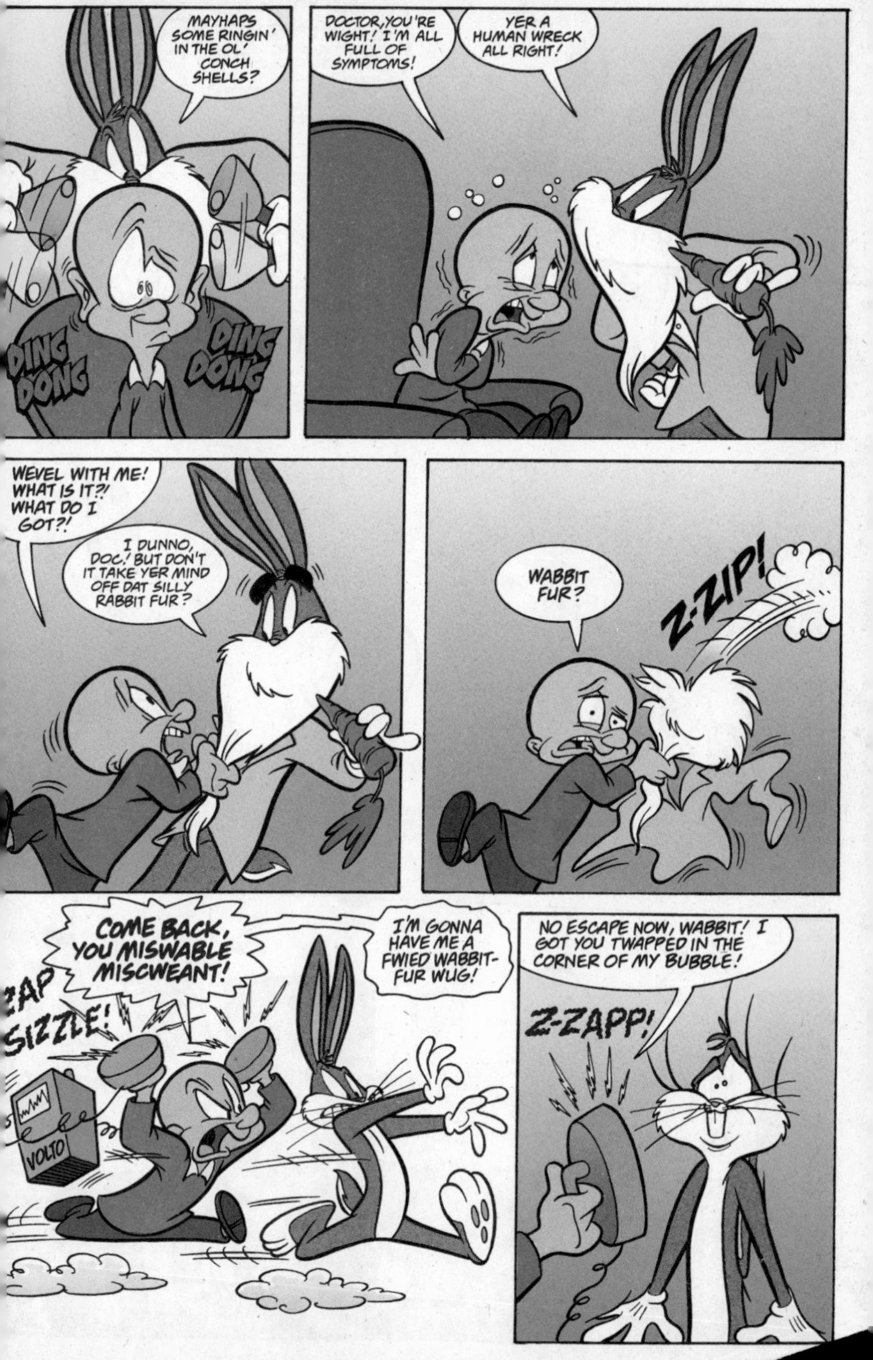
MAYHAPS SOME RINGIN' IN THE OL' CONCH SHELLS?
DING DONG
DING DONG
DOCTOR, YOU'RE WIGHT! I'M ALL FULL OF SYMPTOMS!
YER A HUMAN WRECK ALL RIGHT!
WEVEL WITH ME! WHAT IS IT?! WHAT DO I GOT?!
I DUNNO, DOC! BUT DON'T IT TAKE YER MIND OFF DAT SILLY RABBIT FUR?
WABBIT FUR?
Z-ZIP!
COME BACK, YOU MISWABLE MISCWEANT!
I'M GONNA HAVE ME A FWIED WABBIT-FUR WUG!
SIZZLE!
VOLTO
NO ESCAPE NOW, WABBIT! I GOT YOU TWAPPED IN THE CORNER OF MY BUBBLE!
Z-ZAPP!

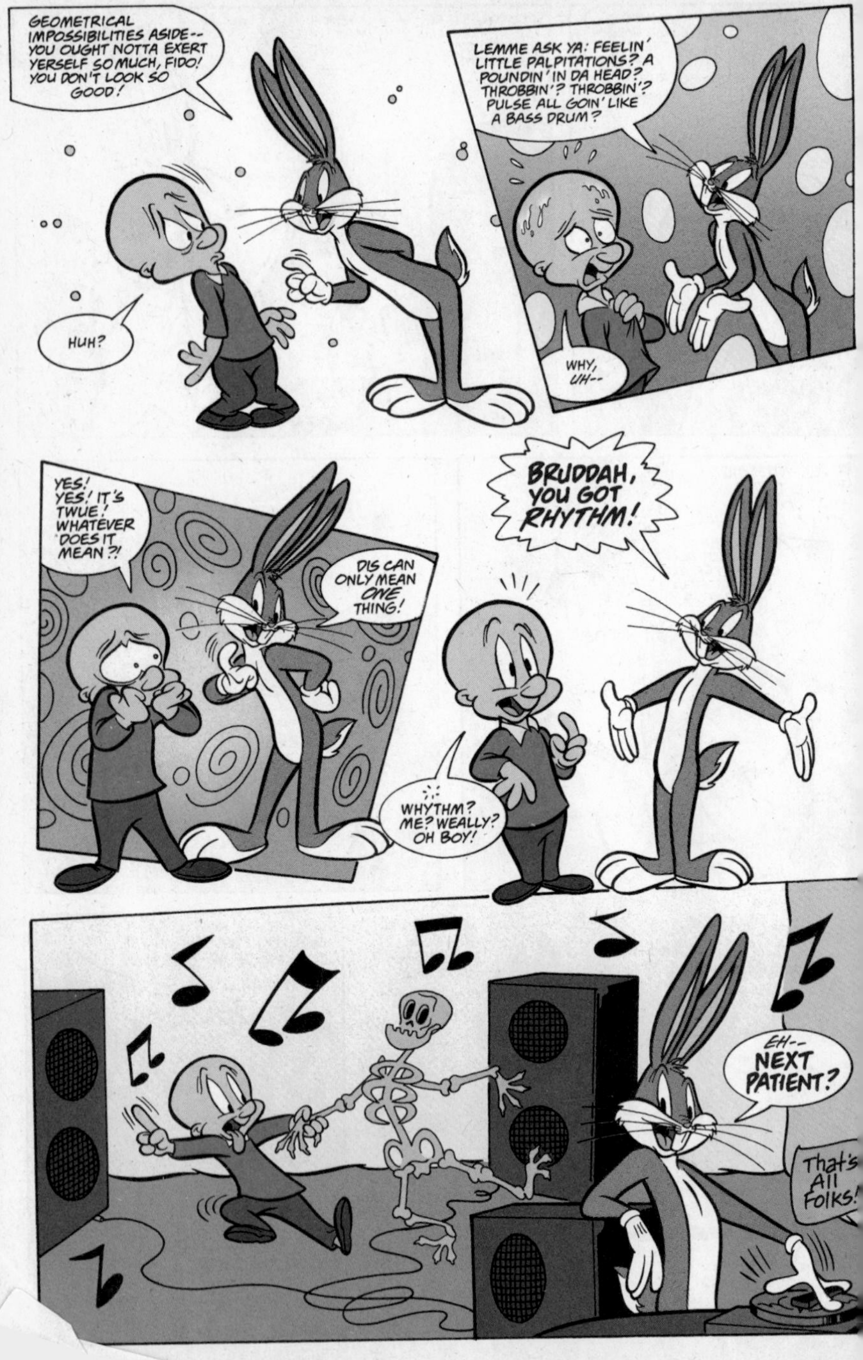
GEOMETRICAL IMPOSSIBILITIES ASIDE-- YOU OUGHT NOTTA EXERT YERSELF SO MUCH, FIDO! YOU DON'T LOOK SO GOOD!
HUH?
LEMME ASK YA: FEELIN' LITTLE PALPITATIONS? A POUNDIN' IN DA HEAD? THROBBIN'? THROBBIN'? PULSE ALL GOIN' LIKE A BASS DRUM?
WHY, UH--
YES! YES! IT'S TWUE! WHATEVER DOES IT MEAN?!
DIS CAN ONLY MEAN ONE THING!
BRUDDAH, YOU GOT RHYTHM!
WHYTHM? ME? WEALLY? OH BOY!
EH-- NEXT PATIENT?
That's All Folks!